THE TOWN BARN
ISN'T THERE ANYMORE

To Joan

Best wishes

guy carey Jr.

Larry Carey

(former neighbors)
cathy + Larry

D0869171

PublishAmerica

Baltimore

First printing

ISBN: 1-4137-3551-7
PUBLISHED BY PUBLISHAMERICA, LLLP
www.publishamerica.com
Baltimore

Printed in the United States of America

This book is dedicated to Violet Hunt, my wife's aunt, who urged me on in all my writings, and to my wife, Cathy, and my children, Michael, Cherie and Colleen, for their understanding and encouragement.

My sincere appreciation goes to my granddaughter Jessie McComb, and my good friend Gloria Varno, who have spent many hours checking and rechecking this manuscript. Without them this book would probably never been in readable English.

Chapter 1

At last my long traverse was over. Standing at the base of Mountain Road looking up at Mt. Fay, I felt the years drifting from my mind and body. Finally it was before me, the hometown where I journeyed toward manhood, the neighborhood of my quashed innocence, the courtroom for my trial of puberty, the harbor of squandered virginity. Sterling, not just my home schooling grounds but also the home of Josh, Eunice, Hester, Emma, Homer, Jason, Francis and Nellie, my brothers and sisters. It saddened me that the town barn wasn't there anymore, but Mountain Road was still the dirt road that I remembered and Mt. Fay hadn't changed. What was it that Josh had written?

Born I was beneath her slopes,
Her woods echoing back, my lives searching cry,
My grave will lie within her view,
When I say my last good-bye.

Poor Josh, I wonder if he ever knew how much his philosophy and writing influenced us; not just the family, but everyone who had known him. The family received letters from his World War II army buddies for years after his death, blessing having known him. Though it's true I never became the writer he was, I well understood his verse standing there staring up at the mountain, allowing the shackles of adulthood to be cast from my shoulders. How did he end that poem?

She hasn't the grandeur of the Alps,
That others have gone to see,
But she looms much larger than that in my mind,
For Mount Fay is my mountain to me.

I wish Josh was able to share this moment of rapture with me. No longer was returning here just a haunting, crazy dream. I was really home.

They say you can't go back and relive your youth, because nothing is ever the same, but I feel now that I have made the right decision to come back here to stay and document the memories of my youth in Sterling. Standing here makes all the years of planning and waiting worthwhile.

When I called the local realtor and asked about property in Sterling, she named several parcels. I asked about the land behind the town barn, and she seemed confused, saying, "The town owns all the land in that area." That saddened me. I asked if that meant the town owned all the way back to the mountain. She said, "No, they own on the other side of the road, on the road going to New Hampshire." I heard a familiar voice in the background say, "He's talking about the old Carney lot on Mountain Road and I think it can be bought, but tell him that the town barn isn't there anymore."

My first thought after closing a deal on that land was to move in a trailer, but the realtor told me that mobile homes were no longer allowed in Sterling. I decided if I was going to build, I would build a replica of the house I was born and raised in. I asked one of our architects to design a house from a picture and my description of what the interior was like. He laughed when he saw the picture and read my interior descriptions but said that it would be fun. The plans became a sense of amusement around the office and many were the crude jokes about my going back to a three-holer. I was used to this kind of ribbing. I never felt like I fit in, despite my years there and the awards I had won contributing to their advertising campaigns. I was so used to their ribbing that I wasn't annoyed, it was kind of prophetic that my last few weeks before retirement would be so mindful of the reason I wanted to leave.

The architect's finished plans were rejected by a Sterling builder, who sent them back saying they wouldn't meet code with a barn and chicken coop connected to the house. He also said that outhouses weren't allowed, even if they were three-holers. The architect laughed at that and said he would modernize the plans for me. But then there were perk test problems and expensive septic designs, so I decided to put the building project on hold.

I had a storage shed with an extra room that would be suitable for writing built on the property while my realtor located a small apartment for me in an old farmhouse owned by an elderly couple. There wasn't much left the way I remembered it on the property. The new storage shed looked out of place among the remembered scraggly apple trees, and where the house had once stood there was little except the half-buried stone foundation and a few charred timbers. I checked the things I had sent to be stored and moved my reclining chair to a position between the two windows, one looking west to the mountain, the other east to town. Settling there gazing at the mountain, I felt like a boy again as I remembered the joy of past escapades in her heights. A car pulling into the yard reminded me that I had an appointment to see my new apartment with the realtor and that dreaming and writing would have to wait until tomorrow.

I followed the realtor, Mrs. Vickers, to the Norwards'. They owned what used to be the Wilsons' home back when I was growing up here. The house had been divided into two apartments, and the one Mrs. Vickers showed me was more than adequate for my needs. Mrs. Vickers told me that her father-in-law, Martin Vickers, lived with them and had filled them in on some of the Carney history. I said, "I remember Marty, he used to chase after my oldest sister, Eunice."

"Oh!" she exclaimed. "Well, we all know the story of your sister running off with some Indian and breaking his heart. He claimed that's why he joined the Army."

I told her I was pleased with the apartment. I asked her to say hello to Marty for me and to tell him that we would have to get together sometime after I get settled. As pleased as I was to know there were still people left from the old days, I was eager to get back to my easy chair at the foot of the mountain and start writing. So the next morning found me settled in my chair at the foot of the mountain.

I couldn't, of course, really remember my first few years here, but being the middle child, I pictured my birth by the experience of being there when my younger brothers and sisters were born. A new baby being born into the family meant a big change in the way things were run around our house. Grandma Taylor always came to stay with us a few weeks before the baby was born, and was she a taskmaster. The older girls, Eunice and Hester, had to do all the heavy cleaning and washing, and when Mother was resting everybody was expected to talk in whispers and walk around on tiptoes.

Once when I complained to Mother, she told me that if it weren't for Grandma I wouldn't even have been here. The story goes that when I was born I weighed almost twelve pounds and had a cord around my neck. The doctor slapped me around some, but he couldn't get me to breathe. With my mother being in such a bad way he gave up on me and tended my mother. But Grandma wouldn't give up, she kept blowing into my mouth while slapping me on the back until I cried. Older now, I appreciate how important she was to all of us when we were born.

My dad worked in the woods logging and like most families back then farmed on the acres they owned or leased. Most jobs available then didn't pay enough to sustain a family of eleven like ours.

My mother also came from a family of woodsmen. Lumbering was the predominate industry in the area where we lived. Mother was the sort of woman who could make the most mundane tasks interesting with stories of how these tasks had been approached at other times by other people. Mother cooking doughnuts on a stormy day was the delight of the neighborhood children, and she had them queuing up in our yard every time it looked like it might storm.

From Dad we learned, and sometimes the hard way, that if we were ever going to achieve anything in life we would have to learn to work, work and work. From Mother we learned that the world was not ours alone and that we should always have consideration for others in all we do.

The description of some of our escapades will seem to contradict the belief I had in my parents, but then, like today, children stretch all boundaries as they traverse their route to adulthood. As the memory of my birth depends on the memories of my family, so will the tales of my first few years depend on my brothers' and sisters' stories.

The first years of my life, if you believe my older sisters, I was a trial in that my initial development was slow and they were changing my diapers long after any girl would have been trained. Being well versed in older sisters, since I still have three, it is my opinion that it was their inability at training, rather than my being a boy, that was at fault. Since we were blessed with very fertile parents, I did not have to suffer the indignities of older sisters alone. My mother had five boys, one older and three younger than me.

Thinking back, I wondered at my parents' choice of names, though I know now that some of them came down through the family. The family names from the oldest down were Eunice, Hester, Josh, Emma, Caleb—me, Homer, Jason, Francis, and Nellie, the youngest. I don't remember Homer being born because we were less than two years apart in age. I vividly remember the births of the last members of my family, as there was almost nine years between Nellie and me. Of course, having Grandma Taylor there every time there was a birth wasn't something you'd forget either.

My early memories are of tagging along with my older brother and sisters, learning about tending gardens, milking the cow, and how important it was to get certain things done each season. A time to plant, a time to weed and cultivate what had been planted, a time to harvest and a time to preserve what had been harvested. I learned how wood had to be cut and stacked for the winter heat and for the cooking fires in the kitchen stove. The cow was a constant learning experience; she had to be led to water at least twice a day and staked to new grass each time. Her stable needed to be cleaned and bedded every day, and she had to be hayed and grained during the winter months. There was the proper time for her breeding to replenish her milk supply, and the hard lesson that most of her calves had to be butchered and

10

sold for veal. Dad explained that the money was necessary for us to keep a milking cow. I understand now how important it was to have a milk cow for a family of eleven in the twenties and thirties. How else could we have had the milk, butter and cheese that were so important to our growth? We also learned that the cute little suckling pigs that Dad bought each spring for us, that we taught how to eat and drink, became the ham, bacon, pork chops and wonderful sausage that we ate in the winter.

I remember the terror the first time I was old enough to help in the butchering. The squealing of the pigs as they were forced into the shed where we kept the ropes and pulleys, the shots that put them down, the hot water and rosin and candle sticks we used to scrape their hair off. I remember getting so sick the first time I saw them gut one of the pigs I had to leave. Dad talked to me, stressing the importance of being able to accomplish what was a necessary job. He made me come back until butchering eventually became just another farm job that needed doing.

Mother instructed how to can, salt and preserve the food that Dad taught us how to seed, raise and grow. Mother, being a more outgoing person than Dad, had at least one and sometimes several of the neighbors involved when she was canning, salting and preserving. She made these sessions so enjoyable that even though a learning process of this type was supposed to be for girls, I found some way to be included. My brothers used to tease me about being interested in girlish things, but the teasing never stopped me from being there when my mother would say, "Girls, tomorrow we are going to have a party."

Before I started school, most of my early childhood memories revolved around my family. When I started school it turned out to be a drag. Learning about nature and life from Mom and Dad had never been a problem for me, but learning the three R's seemed to me an impossible task. If it had not been for the dedication of three of my teachers (though at the time I didn't see it that way), I probably would have spent many more years in the first grade. I realize today, it was their genius that kept me at least abreast of my studies. I was able to move along with my class, even though my brassy older sisters tried to take credit every time I advanced a grade.

My sisters were always at the head of their class, and even Josh was considered a good student. My sisters were always saying that the teachers babied me because they had all been good students. That wasn't true. It was the teachers and my father who showed me the way through my dilemma of the books. The teachers did it because it was their profession, and my father did it because he had a way of showing me a hammering that was worse to take than pounding the books. I learned that lesson the hard way the first time

11

I brought home a report card that said my bad marks were the result of my conduct and lack of attention.

My sister Hester felt sorry for me when I had one of these sessions with Dad and would try to help me. She would say, "Caleb, this is so easy, if you would only put your mind to it."

"Sure," I'd tell her, "this is easy for you maybe, you come with me, Hester, and we'll see how easy it is for you to milk the cow, then we'll see who finds it the easiest to get by that mean old rooster to gather the eggs." I'd tell her, "Hester, I bet you can't do it alone, you always have to have that smart aleck Leonard Cross, who lives next door, help you, or is that just an excuse to be with him?" She would get uppity and slap me one, and that would be the extent of her help. She made me smart all right, just the way Dad made me smart, but those kinds of smarts didn't help your brain develop, at least not in book learning.

My first four years of school, even with my problem of grasping things, didn't seem to carry as much dread for me as the thought of facing the next four years. Our school, like our town, wasn't very big, so the first four grades, one through four, were in one room with one teacher; while the fifth through eighth grades were in the other room with another teacher. The stories that my older sisters Hester and Eunice told about Old Hanna, the teacher that taught the last four grades, were enough to scare anybody. Her name was Hanna Cullings, but Old Hanna is what just about everyone in town called her.

The story was that she was teaching in town even before the town had a school. Well, Old Hanna, according to my sisters and Josh, who by that time were in her classes, was surely something to fear. There was a story about the Cross family reporting Hanna to the school board for her harsh discipline. At the next school board meeting she was confronted with the accusations. It was quite a meeting. The public had been invited to hear her reply, and a goodly number showed up. Something like this in a little town like Sterling in those days was an exciting evening out.

Old Hanna stood to answer, drawing herself to the extreme height and bearing her spinster years would allow. She said, "Mr. Chairman, members of the board, and ladies and gentlemen of the audience, I have not come here tonight to reply to any asinine charges against me. I have only come to remind you of the reason I was hired. I am your children's teacher, and as their teacher I am proud of my ability to teach, I stand on my record. I do not see my role as a parent; if I did I would not be a single woman today. I have been called here because of my way of disciplining. If the parents of Sterling's children can stand on their records as parents as well as I believe

I can as a teacher, then there would not be discipline problems. This is my only statement, thank you and good night." The furor after she left had Mr. Moore, who was chairman of the school committee, pounding on the table trying to restore order while the Cross family and Mrs. Cross's brother Ernest Sledge were trying to arrange a tar and feather party. Mr. Moore, having a healthy respect for Old Hanna's teaching ability, was thinking while he hammered for order. He spotted Mr. and Mrs. Lauren in the audience. The Laurens had a reputation of raising five well-behaved children, and as soon as he had the uproar quieted down he called on Mrs. Lauren for her opinion of Old Hanna's speech. Mrs. Lauren, who was never one for lacking words when a chance like this arose, said, "Mr. Chairman, members of the board, and fellow citizens, I believe in order for a teacher to be a good teacher she has to be proud of her ability, and if there is doubt of her ability then the record of her students is her proof. As for parents, to be a good parent they should be proud of their ability, if they have no doubt of their ability then they can stand on their record, which is, of course, the behavior of their children."

It seemed to Mr. Moore that you could hear a pin drop in the old meeting hall, so he grabbed the initiative and started polling the parents. "Mr. and Mrs. Wilson, how do you feel about this discussion about the role that parents and teachers play?" Mrs. Wilson blurted out, "You're damned right! Parents are responsible for the upbringing of their kids, and a teacher needs discipline to teach and Old Hanna has always known how to keep it. She has my support."

After Mr. Moore had polled carefully selected families that affirmed his belief in Old Hanna, he called on Mr. and Mrs. Cross, asking, "What is your belief? As I recall it was not a question of whether the child was right and being punished but had done wrong." Neither of the Crosses or the Sledges had anything to say. So Mr. Moore called for a vote by the committee members on what action should be taken. A motion was made and seconded that the charge be erased from the records, and the "ayes" easily had it. And so Old Hanna's reign continued on and the stories about her prowess grew and grew.

Josh told me that often the boys in Hanna's classes ended up with red knuckles from what they called the fastest ruler in town. He told about John Muldon. John was a big, fat boy in the eighth grade; he looked like he weighed three hundred pounds. His father and uncles, Don and Joe Muldon, ran the Muldon dairy farm, which was not only the biggest business in town but it was practically the only one, outside of a few small logging outfits, that did most of their business in other towns. John Muldon was always trying to get away with something that no one else would ever try. After all, wasn't John's father one of the most important men in town and shouldn't that give him more power than the rest of us? Most of his life he had succeeded in getting away with his antics, but not with Old Hanna. She would beat him at every turn. Some of the older boys who were big enough used to tease John about this and he would get so angry.

One of Hanna's punishments after she had first used her ruler on your knuckles was to make you stand ramrod straight in the corner of the hall where she could see you from her desk. Every time she caught you slouching she would say, "Straighter or I'll be out there with the yardstick and straighten you."

John had a plan, this was his last year there and he couldn't leave the school without winning at least one battle with Old Hanna. He wrote a note that said, *Our teacher is an old spinster because she was afraid she would scare a man to death if she ever got into bed with one.* He made the note into an airplane and sailed it across the room when Hanna wasn't looking. My brother Josh caught it, but not before Hanna saw it sailing through the air. Josh tried valiantly, at least in his version of the tale, to keep Hanna from getting the note. Her persuasion with the ruler was too much for Josh; Hanna unfolded the plane and read the note. Josh recalled he had never seen anyone ever get so red in his life, her eyes bulged and the veins stood out in her neck so big that he thought for a moment she was going to explode. Hanna marched back to the front of the room and took a few deep breaths while facing the blackboard.

Turning to the class, she said, "I will give you children five minutes to decide, and if at the end of that time I do not know who wrote that foul note, you will all stay after school until I find out." Hanna had not seen the note thrown, but many of John's classmates had seen him do it. The silence and the staring eyes for the next four and a half minutes became more than John could endure, so as the last seconds ticked off he raised his hand and asked, "Teacher, may I please have my note back?" The sheer bravado of this caused a subdued wonder to run through the class, but when they saw the fury of Hanna reaching for her yardstick the wonder turned cold. Striding to John's desk, she said, "Stand up, young man, and come out into the hall."

John, gripping his seat, said, "No way, ma'am."

Hanna said, "Don't make it any harder on yourself by defying me any further," as she whacked him with the yardstick. Maybe it was her fury that destroyed her expertise or maybe it was just John's determination to win just once. We never knew how, but John got the yardstick away from her and broke it into little pieces. Hanna ran back to her desk and grabbed the last

14

two that she had, shouting, "Out in the hall, out in the hall."

John was shouting, "I will not, I will not."

She came back beating him with both yardsticks. John took some really good wallops. Josh said John finally got both hands around the yardsticks, threw himself on the floor, with his weight tearing the sticks from her hands, and quickly he rolled over on them. She grabbed him by the collar of his shirt and tried to drag him out into the hall, but all she managed to do was tear his shirt's collar off. When John's shirt tore, Hanna lost her balance and slammed against the wall. She stood there for a few minutes looking at him, looking like she was going to explode. Then she got a glint in her eye and walked through the hall and right out the door.

There were a few minutes of shocked silence, then the "atta boys" to John started. They were a little too quick to sell Old Hanna short, because in those days we heated with wood, and Hanna had run out to the woodpile. She picked herself out a one- and one-half-inch-thick piece of rock maple that was four feet long, returned again to John and said, "Now, young man out in the hall." John was still lying on the floor. Josh said he didn't know if he was laughing or crying from the beating he was taking, but he shouted, "I will not."

This time though Hanna had a better tool, and she sure changed his mind about that. John ended up in the corner in the hall, though they say he wasn't able to stay ramrod straight. After composing herself in the teacher's room, Hanna returned to the class and, leaning her newfound tool menacingly in the corner, asked, "Do we have any other note writers today?"

So you can see with school not being much fun for me anyway, I wasn't really looking forward to my next year when I moved into Old Hanna's room.

Chapter 2

My fourth year in school was over, and even the thought of returning for my fifth year in Old Hanna's room wasn't going to destroy the happiness of a boy getting out of school for the summer in his tenth year. That year the Hart family moved into town. There were five in the family, Mr. and Mrs. Hart and three children—Jean, the oldest girl; Karl; and Betty, the youngest girl. Their boy, Karl, was almost two years older than I was, but we seemed to like the same things, so we became very good friends and spent most of our free time together that summer.

I got a job stripping the milk cows at the Muldon farm that year. Even though the Muldons had installed automatic milkers a few years back, each cow still had to be stripped of their last milk by hand. I had always talked myself up as being a good milker, so when Dad heard they were looking for someone to help with the stripping he sent me over.

Old Joe Muldon looked me over and said, "Are you sure that anyone as small as you can milk well enough to do his share?"

I told him, "I am the best milker in town."

He kind of smiled and said, "O.K. If you can hold up your end that well, then the job is yours. Mind you now, you have to be here at six every morning and again at five thirty every night, the pay is fifty cents a day seven days a week, that comes to three dollars fifty cents a week. Now if the other boys complain that you're not doing your share, then I will have to let you go. You be here tonight at five thirty and we will show you our routine."

I went running home all excited, imagining three fifty a week for me. The only money I ever saw was a couple of pennies if my Dad had any left over on payday. All that day I could hardly wait to get started. I thought five thirty would never come. When I think back today it's hard to believe how excited I became then over a three fifty a week pay.

Five thirty finally came, and when Mother gave me a kiss on the cheek I noticed tears in her eyes. I ran the half-mile from our house to Muldon's barn, wanting to be on time and make a good impression. When I walked in, Big John, Larry and Reilly Muldon were already there. They immediately started picking on me, not so much Reilly, who was the oldest, but big John and Larry. Larry was only a few years older than me.

Big John said, "Hey, Larry, look who thinks he's a big stripper! Take your clothes off, stripper, take them off, take them off! Come on, Larry, let's help our new stripper learn how to strip."

I was getting pretty scared, and if it hadn't been for the thought of the three fifty a week, I think I would have run out crying. I didn't though. I couldn't let that big man who had just left home on his first paying job come running home like a crybaby, so I stayed and took it. Larry and Big John came after me and though I ran a little, I knew I couldn't escape or beat them in a fight, so I just had to take what was coming. After catching me they began pulling at my clothes. They had managed to pull my pants down and get my shirt pulled over my head when Reilly yelled, "Knock it off! Here comes Uncle Leon."

Leon Muldon came into the barn, looked at me struggling to get back into my clothes and said, "So you're our new stripper. I see some of the boys have been initiating you, which one of them did it?"

At first I was going to tell him, but I knew I was going to be here alone with John and Larry and they would think of something worse if I got them into trouble. So I stammered out, "No-no-nobody, sir, I am just having a little trouble with my clothes."

Leon smiled and said, "O.K., boy, come along and I will show you your section. We keep a hundred milkers in these barns and we have them broke into sections of twenty-five, that gives each stripper one section of twenty-five cows to strip. John and Reilly take care of the milking machines, Larry has one of the stripping sections, the Cross boy and one of the Sledge boys have the others. By the way, John, where the hell are those boys anyway?"

"Don't worry, Uncle Leon, they were here, but Arthur forgot something and Leonard went back with him to get it," John replied.

"Well, you tell them that spunky little Carney boy here has some brothers to replace them if they don't want to be here on time, you hear me, John?"

"Yes, Uncle, I hear you," John shouted.

It made me feel good to be standing there and hearing him call me a spunky kid and all. I thought, *I'm sure going to need a brother or two to survive here,* because I was afraid he had just made two more foes for me and I sure did not need that.

After Leonard and Arthur showed up, Leon said, "All right, boys, we are already ten minutes late. Get busy and make it up. I'll be back in an hour."

Big John ran the milk machines in my section, and though he didn't thank me for not squealing on him, he seemed impressed with my work.

Larry, of course, had to tease Leonard and Arthur about how they were going to be replaced by a little Carney boy. So I turned up being the butt of every joke they could think of.

John's uncle came back in an hour and seemed pleased at what was being accomplished. He came over and watched me strip a couple of cows and nodded his head approvingly, saying, "I think you might do after all, boy."

I guess that he must have only given me this chance because my father and his brother, Joe, were friends. He had had serious doubts about me, being so small and all. Leon went over and talked to John about something that John had done and they were involved in a pretty heated discussion, but I wasn't able to hear from where I was.

Larry's section of twenty-five cows was next to mine. John operated the milking machines in that section too. I had finished stripping my twenty-five cows before Larry and thought that would make Larry mad but it didn't. He just said, "Hey, Caleb! I have something to do, will you finish the last four for me?"

I didn't really want to, my hands were tired. This was the first time I had ever milked this long, and one of those big Holsteins was standing on my toe and wouldn't get off. The boys were standing there laughing while I tried to push that Holstein off. I finally got smart and smacked her one with my milk stool. I really wanted to get out of there and go home, but I couldn't allow them to think that I was a baby so I said, "O.K., Larry, I can do that for you."

They had all finished with their milking and carried their milk machines and pails into the milk house to be sterilized. I finished Larry's four cows and went to the milk house to dump the milk and leave my pail.

John was arranging things in the sterilizer. He said, "Hey, Caleb, before you go, there is one more thing out in the barn you have to do."

I went back to the barn with him, and there sat Reilly and Larry with two quart bottles of home brew. I realized then what it was that Arthur forgot and he and Leonard had gone back after. It was home brew that he had probably stolen out of his father's cellar. They were laughing and giggling while passing the bottle around.

Larry said, "Your turn, stripper, or would you rather go home bare like you almost started out?"

I knew if I went home with beer on my breath and got caught I would never be able to come back, but neither would I be allowed to if I came home nude. I guessed that with the beer in them they probably would strip me again. So I figured I would have to chance the brew; besides, that three fifty a week still looked awfully big to me. I took a big slug out of the bottle, then wiped my mouth with the back of my hand like I had seen my father do and said, "That's not bad, not bad at all, but it's not near as good as my father makes."

Mentioning my father's home brew was a dumb thing to do because Arthur said, "If your old man's beer is so good we will just have to have some of it, won't we, boys?"

They all agreed and started chanting, "Tomorrow night is Caleb's turn, tomorrow night is Caleb's turn," as they passed the bottle around. After we had drunk all the beer, Reilly said, "We'd better let him go home, boys, it must be past his bedtime. If he makes his mother mad we probably won't never get to taste his father's beer."

With chants of, "Don't forget the beer tomorrow. Don't forget the beer, little stripper," echoing behind me, I staggered out of the barn. Now I was really in trouble, my stomach was upset, I was feeling dizzy, and somehow I had to get home right away. I was supposed to be home before eight, and it was already getting dark. I took a towel from the milk house and started to run to the horse trough that was in the center of town. I found that running sure wasn't for me, I fell and tore the knee of my pants, and I thought for sure I was going to throw up before I ever got to the horse trough. When I got there I stuck my whole head under the water and held it there as long as I could. When I came up it seemed to have helped the dizziness, so I did it again and again. Then I heard Josh and Emma shouting, "Caleb, Caleb! What do you think you're doing? Have you gone nuts or what?"

I tried to think of some good story to tell them, but as I stood there dripping wet and stammering, they both smelled the beer on me. "Oh my God, Caleb!" Emma said. "Dad is going to kill you. How could you do such an awful thing, a little kid like you getting drunk?"

If I hadn't been so sick we would have had one of our usual fights. I hated it when she called me a little kid. She was the older sister next in age and liked lording it over me.

Josh said, "Stop it, Emma, this is no time to be picking on him, we have to help him. If I know those boys over at the barn this thing is a put-up job to get Caleb out of there."

Josh knew what the boys at the barn were like even though he never mingled much with the boys in town. They used to call him sissy, softy and some other names but never where he could hear them, because they already found out he was no softy when he got mad. They would tease me about my "sister" Josh. I took a lot of beatings because of this until Josh taught me to ignore them.

"Well!" Emma said. "Put-up job or not, I am not going to get involved with this and get myself into trouble too."

"Come on, Emma!" Josh pleaded. "Help me get him home into the house so he won't get caught."

"No, Josh, not this time. You're not going to sweet-talk me into getting into this mess. I'm getting out of here," she said as she was leaving.

Josh hollered, "Please, Emma, at least promise me you won't say anything."

"O.K., Josh, O.K. And Josh, lots of luck, you are going to need it," she said as she slipped away in the darkness.

"Come on, Caleb," Josh said, "let's get away from the horse trough before someone else comes along. We'll go out behind the library until I can figure out what to do." We made our way through the hedge in front of the library and went behind the building. I was feeling sicker and sicker. Josh asked me how much I had drunk and I told him the best I could.

He said, "Caleb, you are probably going to be sick and we can't let that happen after you get home, so stick your finger down your throat and think of the most sickening thing that you can think of." I didn't want to do it. Josh got mad and said, "Damn it, Caleb! Do you want me to help you or not?" That kind of scared me, because I couldn't remember hearing Josh sound so mad before. I thought about how when our last calf had been born our cow couldn't pass the afterbirth and Dad had let me watch him take it. I felt pretty icky then. Thinking about that and sticking my finger down my throat sure caused a mess to come up. Josh kept hollering, "Bend your head down, Caleb, bend your head down." After Josh had made me do that two or three times more to make sure it didn't happen at home, we snuck back to the horse trough and he helped me clean up, making me rinse my mouth out and gargle repeatedly. He told me if I started to feel sick again to take deep, long breaths until it passed, then he gave me some pieces of wild mint to chew on that he had found in back of the library. I was feeling better and a lot safer now. What a brother that Josh was, he knew everything!

"You are looking pretty good now, Caleb," Josh said, "so let's walk home while I try to think of a way to get you upstairs to your bedroom without Mom or Dad seeing you."

We walked a little way and even though I knew I wasn't normal, I felt much safer than I did before Josh took over. I told him how glad I was that he had found me before I got home and that I really was glad he was my brother. I couldn't imagine having three older sisters to live with without Josh to help me through life. I often have wondered now what life would have been like for me if Josh had lived.

Josh just said, "Hush up, Caleb, can't you see that I am thinking? I have part of it planned. I'll get you in by the front door, you go right upstairs, and we will have to hope Uncle Louis isn't in his room, and if Homer is still awake promise him anything you have to keep him quiet. I'll take care of it tomorrow. Do you have that much straight, Caleb?"

"I hear you, Josh," I said. "But what if Uncle Louis is there and I can't talk Homer into being quiet? I'm not as good as you at convincing people."

"Oh, come on, Caleb!" Josh replied. "Let's stop the buts. Sure there is the chance that we will run into trouble. Now that we have a plan to work with we can deal with anything else that comes up when it does. The main thing is that we have a plan. I can handle Uncle Louis. You just worry about Homer. With his sweet tooth, all you have to do is promise him that with your first week's pay, you will buy him the biggest candy bar he has ever seen. You still are going back to your milking job tomorrow morning, aren't you, Caleb?"

The thought of not going back was very much on my mind at the time, but the tone of Josh's voice let me see that if I didn't get my back up enough to do it, even Josh was going to be disappointed with me.

Well, like Josh said, first we had to get by Uncle Louis. Uncle Louis was my mother's brother and had moved in with us in the early spring of that year. He was a divorced man in his late forties and had fought in the front lines in France during World War I. I never really knew what happened to his marriage, whether his wife didn't wait for him while he was gone or maybe he couldn't adjust to married life after France and the war. He kept his past a mystery, all the years I knew him. We knew Uncle Louis long before he came to live with us as our rich uncle from Maine. He used to visit a couple times a year for a few days at a time. He gave us children each a whole quarter every time he came and he always used to leave Mother some money in a card when he left. Mother told us not to expect that kind of treatment from him now that he had come to live with us. Now that I'm older and have seen the suffering in some bad marriages, divorce is easier to understand.

We really didn't have any bedrooms to spare when Uncle Louis came, so Mother and Dad converted the big hallway at the foot of the stairs into a makeshift bedroom. They closed off one of the three doors and put a half-size bed there to make a room for him. So you can see that getting by Uncle Louis if he was in his room by going in the front door was pretty far fetched. We just hoped he wasn't there.

Mother and Dad's room was off the living room downstairs, so with Josh's plan we would not have to worry about them seeing me.

When we came to where we could see the house, Mother was in the kitchen looking out the door. We waited until she turned away from the door and then ran like hell to get on the other side of the house. Josh went quickly up to the front door and opened it. Uncle Louis was sitting there in his shorts getting ready to get into bed. Josh put his fingers to his lips and whispered, "If you don't say anything about this, Uncle Louis, then I won't say anything about Travis."

Uncle Louis looked kind of blank, then a smile crept across his face and he nodded his head. Mother must have heard us, for she called, "Is that the boys, Louis?"

"Its the boys, May, but don't come in. I'm not dressed," he answered. "They're O.K. so you can go to bed now and not worry." May is what Uncle Louis always called my mother, and it seemed to please her. I never did understand it, because her real name was Helena.

Endearing names or not, mothers can be hell-fire when they are worried about their children. She was outside of Louis's door, shouting, "Hurry up and get dressed, Louis, or get into bed. I have to talk to those boys. Imagine Caleb only ten years old and out to these hours. I just knew there was trouble when Emma came in and said Caleb was all right and with Josh. That was all I could get out of her. I have been half out of my mind since with worry."

Josh and I made it upstairs. Uncle Louis was taking his time putting his pants on, while trying to console Mother. By the time he let her in Josh had managed to get back downstairs. Luck had run with us upstairs, Homer and the rest of them were all sound asleep.

Josh stood on the bottom stairs facing Mother and a concerned Uncle Louis. That night, Josh put on what Uncle Louis was to recall as the best acting performance that he had ever seen in his life.

Josh said, "Mother, I am not sure if I am old enough or smart enough to make anyone understand what it is like to be a boy in these times. I want very much to try, so please, Mother, before you go running up to Caleb, will you hear me out first? If not for Caleb's sake, then at least for me, because I need to be heard."

Mother said, "Tell me he's not hurt, Josh, and then I will listen to you first."

"Oh, Mother!" Josh replied. "You know if Caleb truly needed you, your son Josh would be the first to run and tell you, isn't that true, Mother?"

"Yes, Josh!" she answered. "You have always been a good boy who cared about your family and their feelings, so tell your mother what being a boy has to do with tonight."

Uncle Louis recalled that Josh started out with, "You know, Mom, how we all worry about Caleb because he is small for a boy his age? Well, today he started out on what he believes is his road to manhood. You know, his first paying job and his first encounter with the working world. He got that job because Dad and Joe Muldon happen to be friends, right, Mother?"

"Oh! I guess you're right, Josh. I tried to tell your father that Caleb was too small, but he wouldn't listen. He thinks it's time for Caleb to start learning how to make his own way."

"Dad's right!" Josh said. "That's the point, Mother. Caleb might not get to be too big, and if he doesn't, he has to learn to live with his size. Tonight because of his job he had a little trouble getting home because some of the older boys in town thought they should have gotten that job. A bunch of them got together and ganged up on Caleb. Now don't get excited, Mother, he wasn't really hurt. All they wanted to do was keep him from getting home on time so then you would make him quit and one of them would get the job. I'm not sure how I should say this or if you can understand it, but this is probably one of those times in Caleb's life that it would be better that he didn't see his mother."

"But, Josh!" Mother said. "How can I get any sleep tonight if I am not allowed to hold him and console him?"

"Like I said in the beginning, Mother," Josh replied, "I wasn't sure I could explain to an adult about how it feels being a boy growing up. I know how Caleb feels because we talked about it and he agrees that the worst thing that could happen in his struggle to become more adult himself is to have to face his father or mother right now."

It was then that Uncle Louis decided that Josh had done such a beautiful job that he couldn't see him lose, besides he had an interest to protect himself. So he joined in. "May," he said, "I have to agree with the boy. You know I was one myself once, and most of the points he made about children are pretty valid. We have to remember when we were children. There is always tomorrow, May."

The expertise of Uncle Louis and Josh finally convinced Mother, and after being assured again that Caleb was all right she left to go to bed. Josh came upstairs to where I was lying in bed feeling both scared and sick. I had come to the point where I really didn't care what happened, and I was almost wishing that Mother would come and hold me. Thinking of what had happened and how proud I had been when I left to go to work, my emotions got the best of me and I started to sob.

Josh held me and said, "Hang in there, Caleb, I know it's been a tough day, but the worst is over now. Go to sleep and don't worry about tomorrow. Big brother Josh will always be by your side."

I dizzily drifted off to sleep, dreaming that Josh was some kind of a God whose only job was to protect me. The next morning at five o'clock Josh was shaking me awake so he could see if I was clear headed enough to go downstairs and face Mother and her questions.

He said, "I know that you don't feel too good, Caleb, but you have to listen to me." He told me what he had told Mother for a story and said, "Just act ashamed about last night and don't say anything unless you positively have to."

We went down to breakfast, and though Mother was very concerned about me, Josh kept her talking while I tried to eat and act natural. I really didn't feel all that much like eating, but Josh had warned me that if I did not eat or acted sick, we both would be in trouble. For Josh's sake I sat there giving it my all, when all I really wanted to do was to get in my mother's lap and tell her the whole truth so I could cry on her shoulder. The job and being a big man making three fifty a week no longer seemed enough to compensate for my sickness and the fear I felt about going back to the barn and facing the other boys. Josh seemed to realize this and underneath his banter with Mother, he was whispering little goads to me like, "You have to be a big boy to be a stripper, Caleb. Don't you feel good now that you are one of the big boys?"

I sure didn't feel much like a big boy. Yet, as much as I wanted to quit, I sure wasn't going to let Josh down. I finished my breakfast and started off to work, trying to look as happy as I felt last night when I started the job. Josh walked a little way with me, trying to cheer me up. Remembering about Dad's home brew, I told Josh. He said, "Don't worry, Caleb, just tell Arthur that Dad is all out and he will have to wait until Dad makes a new batch in the fall. If that doesn't do the trick, I know where Uncle Louis has some homemade wine, but for God's sake, Caleb don't mention it unless you are really up a tree about something."

Josh left and I went to the barn. I was the first one there except for Joe Muldon. He said, "Golly Moses, boy, you sure look like something the cat dragged in. I suppose that you had a hard time getting any sleep last night with the excitement of having a new job and all."

"By the way," Leon said, walking in, "you looked pretty good last night. Give us a couple of more days like that and I will have good news for your pa." I was very glad to hear that.

Big John and Leonard showed up, I took my milk pail and went out to the barn. I saw Reilly coming to the milk house.

"How's your day, little stripper?" he chuckled.

I held my head up like Josh had told me and laughed back at him. "I think I will live, but I'm not sure I want to."

Big John was in an ugly mood and batted the cows around a lot, but he didn't bother me any. I sure was thankful for that, because I had all I could handle just doing my milking. Leonard was pretty quiet that morning. He was usually always talking or playing jokes

When Arthur came in, he was a mess. He had a big welt on the side of his face and one of his eyes was black. Boy, he looked terrible!

Reilly said, "For God's sake, Arthur, what the hell happened to you this time? Did you get run over by a horse or something?"

"Shut your filthy face, you know damn well what happened! My father found out about the home brew again." He grabbed his stool and pail and started for his section. The first cow that he picked must have been into some new grass the day before, because just as he sat down she decided to do a real smelly, messy job. Arthur jumped up and ran for the backdoor, heaving all the way. It was then that I realized that what was bothering the rest of them. They all got sick too. I don't know why I did it; maybe I want to be a little like Josh. I went out back and asked Arthur if there was anything I could do to help. He said, "Get the hell out of here, Caleb, and leave me alone." I went back to my milking. Arthur eventually came back to milk and he just seemed to get sicker.

Larry, who had been very quiet all morning, started swearing, "I hope that son of a bitch doesn't think I am going to help do his milking."

"For cripes sake, don't you have any heart at all?" asked Leonard.

"Well! That bastard's your cousin Leonard, why don't you do his work if you care so much about him?" Larry retorted.

"Knock it off, you bunch of little kids, before you have my father in here," called John.

"You are right, John," Reilly said. "Everybody, cut out the damned yelling. If we have to, we will all help Arthur. Now dig in and let's get this damn morning over with."

Just then the door opened and in came Josh. Everybody was kind of relieved to see it was him because we all thought for sure that it was going to be Leon or old Golly Moses Muldon. They all kind of eyeballed Josh, I supposed they thought he had come to pick a fight because of what had happened last night, but he just hollered over to John, "How's your new stripper making out, John?"

"Oh! I guess he's going to make it," John mumbled with a relieved reply.

"Hey, Larry!" Josh said. "I think I should be getting his first week's pay, don't you? After all, I was his milking instructor."

"I would get it every other week if that little twit was my brother," Larry laughingly replied. When Josh heard how badly off Arthur was, he went over to see him. Arthur cussed him out some, but that didn't seem to bother Josh. He just took his milk stool and pail and told him to go out and get some fresh air while he finished his section for him. I came away from the barn that morning feeling much more adult, thinking that I certainly had learned a lot about life in the last twenty-four hours. Wasn't Josh something, coming over to the barn just to let those boys know I had a big brother? It always seemed clever the way he did things.

That afternoon Karl and I were supposed to hike to the upper part of Muldon Meadows and go fishing in Craggy River. I knew a spot where you could always get a good catch of native trout. That morning Mother had insisted that I was going to have to take a nap because I had been so late last night. I had to tell Karl why I couldn't go. I made him swear on his sacred oath that he wouldn't tell anyone. Imagine, a ten-year-old boy having to take a nap because his mother said so. Josh told me that I had better darn well swallow my pride and do as Mother said. He said that it wasn't much punishment when you thought about what could have happened.

Karl promised he wouldn't say anything and suggested that we could fish in the river below the meadow later. He said Roy Cross had caught a couple of large trout there the other day that looked like the stock trout from the Sportsmen's Pond in Lange.

Chapter 3

The next day when I got home from my morning milking, Hester was just finishing milking our cow. Josh was supposed to do that, but he was always conning the girls into helping him with his chores. "I hear you had a little trouble last night, Caleb," she teased. "Pretty rough this getting to be a big boy. Think you are going to be able to take it when Mom and Dad find out? What would you have done without Josh, little man?"

I really lost my temper. It seems my sisters made it their life's work to pick on me. I yelled, "Hester! Mom and Dad'd better never find out from you or anyone else. Don't forget I saw you and Leonard coming out of the corncrib last fall. I know what goes on in there. If I was to tell that I saw you and Leonard at the corncrib and that the kids go there to play doctor and stuff, taking all their clothes off, boy, wouldn't you be in a mess?" Hester turned nearly as white as the milk that spilled from the pail she dropped.

"Caleb! Caleb! For God's sake, Caleb," she stammered, "you know nobody ever, ever talks about the corncrib. If Mom or Dad heard talk like that, half the kids in town would get killed and you would be the first. You know that we all took an oath never to mention the corncrib ever. Besides, I never go there anymore, I'm getting too old for that, and besides, it got too dangerous for me."

I couldn't see the reason it might be more dangerous for her than anyone else, but I had heard that most of the girls stopped going there when they got a little older. Age didn't seem to stop the boys, most of them kept going back. And there were only a couple of the girls who stayed there though when the older boys were around. I didn't understand what this was all about, but I knew I had Hester up a tree. I made her promise over and over that she would never tease me again.

She still seemed shaky when she said, "Caleb, I'm sorry about my teasing. I didn't know that it bothered you so much. I will never, never do it again, but Caleb, you have to promise me that you will never again mention anything about me and the corncrib."

"O.K., Hester, I have to go see Mom now. Don't worry, I won't say anything about you or the corncrib." I went off to see Mom and take my nap, thinking I would never have said anything anyway. I didn't know why it had scared Hester so much, but I finally had the upper hand on one of my older sisters, and I sure wasn't about to forget that.

When I went to the house, Mom and Mrs. Baker were making jelly out of some berries that she and Homer had picked the day before. Mrs. Baker was Clem Baker's wife, and they had only been married a few months. Clem was one of the older boys who used to stay at the Muldon farm and work for them full time. He had a job at the foundry in Lange now and had bought a house in Sterling next to our property at the foot of the mountain. It wasn't much, but Clem was always talking about how he was going to fix it when he got enough money. I liked Mrs. Baker, she was a small and pretty woman and everybody called her Ellie, but my mother wouldn't let me. I talked to them for a while. Mom gave me a piece of bread she had toasted on the stove with some of the jelly on it and a glass of cold milk. It sure tasted good. Even today while writing about Mother's kitchen my mouth waters remembering of how good Mother's cooking was.

Mom said, "Caleb, don't forget what you are supposed to do today."

I said, "O.K., Mom, is it all right for me to go fishing with Karl afterwards?"

"Yes, Caleb," she said, "but don't forget to be home in time to eat. You have to be back at the barn by five thirty tonight."

I went upstairs for my nap. I sure must have needed it, because the next thing I knew Jason was jumping on top of me, saying, "Mom says to wake up, Caleb, and eat your lunch if you want to have time to go fishing with Karl. Can I go with you, Caleb, can I please, can I?"

I felt pretty guilty having to tell him no. I said, "Not his time, Jason, it's too rough for someone only six years old where we are going." The truth was that I wanted to be alone with Karl. He was my best friend and I understood things better just by talking them over with him.

We went to the bend in the river where Roy had told Karl he had caught those big trout. Karl caught one big trout; it measured almost twenty-three inches. That was the only hit we got all afternoon as we sat there watching our bobbers while I unburdened my soul. I realize now that Karl's talent wasn't so much that he had answers, rather it was his ability to listen. Though we didn't often come to any resolutions, I always felt better after talking to him.

We started back to town early so Karl could show his big fish around while it still looked alive and shiny. We carried that big old trout around town teasing both man and boy when we had a chance. We were just splitting up to go home when we ran into Uncle Louis and Josh. Uncle Louis got pretty excited when he saw Karl's fish. Karl was feeling like quite a man by the time Uncle Louis had dragged every intimate detail about catching it out of him. When we reached the horse trough Karl rushed his good-byes and ran home to show his family his enviable catch. The three of us started home when Josh said, "Hey, Uncle Louis, would catching a fish like that be as exciting as going to Travis's, would it, Uncle Louis, would it?"

Uncle Louis said, "Don't overuse your weapons, Josh, some day you might want to go to Travis's."

Josh started laughing and said, "Is my weapon powerful enough to get you to take me there?"

Uncle Louis stopped and took off his hat thoughtfully scratched his head and said, "Josh, are you threatening or asking?"

Josh really broke up about this. He laughed so hard that he could hardly talk. He finally stammered out, "Oh, Uncle Louis, you know I love you and I wouldn't do or say anything to get you in trouble."

We walked on to the house while Josh chuckled to himself. Uncle Louis looked real serious, while I was enviously wishing that it had been me that caught that fish.

We were almost home when Uncle Louis said, "I think you're going to be my kind of man, Josh. When the time comes that you have need for what Travis's has to offer, then you come to me and I'll decide if you are really ready for anything like that."

Most of the summer went like that, the family, fishing with Karl and every morning and evening the cows, the stripping, the barn and the boys with their teasing and jokes. Since I had adapted to their crude ways and proved I was capable of holding my own, I no longer feared going to work.

Then one night while sitting at the supper table, I asked, "Mom, how old do I have to be before I can go to Travis's?"

There was the most complete silence that I can ever remember happening with my family. Dad's fork was frozen in midair and everyone, with the exception of the small children, looked shocked. Mother grew all red in the face and said, "Caleb, what on earth do you think you are you talking about?"

I should have known from the tone of her voice that I was on thin ice, but I didn't and said, "Uncle Louis said he was going to take Josh there when he was old enough. I was just wondering how old that was." I looked at Josh. He looked like he was going to choke to death on what he was trying to swallow. I saw the same kind of look on his face that I had seen when he got fighting mad. Uncle Louis looked so pathetic he reminded me of the story about the man who tried to hide behind his own shadow. Dad sat there, still transfixed with his food in midair, looking at Mother like he expected the world to end. And for once Josh seemed speechless.

Mother wasn't through, and she angrily demanded of me, "Caleb, do you know what happens at Travis's? Wait a minute, even if you do, don't answer me in front of your younger brothers and sisters?"

I knew by now that I was in trouble. I was scared, so I said, "Mom, it's nothing bad, Travis's is just a place where Uncle Louis is going to take Josh when he is old enough. I just wanted to know how old we had to be."

Mother grew positively purple. She jumped out of her chair, shouting, "Thomas, get that man that used to be my brother packed and out of my house before I destroy him."

Uncle Louis said, "You don't have to say anything, Tom. I'll just pack and leave."

Dad shocked me when he shouted, "Sit! Everybody just sit. I don't want to hear any discussions from any of you about this. For you younger ones who don't understand what is happening, I offer a prayer of thanks. To the rest of you who are not so innocent, I say to you: Caleb did not speak those words and you did not hear them, heed what I say, because the law of this house has spoken. Eunice, you clean up the dishes and watch the little ones. I have to go speak to your mother."

It was time for me to be at work so I rushed off thankfully, foolishly wondering what there was about Travis's that could cause so much trouble. While I was milking I asked Big John what was so special about Travis's.

He looked at me in a funny way and said, "Caleb, you dumb little twit, you really don't know, do you?" He hollered to Leonard, "Hey, Leonard, I think we are going to have to get a new stripper, this one is so dumb he doesn't even know what Travis's is."

The rest of the night was pure hell. Larry, Reilly and Arthur joined in on the teasing, calling me mamma's little boy and dumb cluck. I left the barn as soon as I could, still wondering what went on at Travis's. *I am sure my stupidity about Travis's will make me the butt of many jokes at the barn for weeks to come.*

The answer met me at the horse trough. Hester was there waiting. She said, "Caleb, Josh sent me to tell you that he is trying hard not to be mad at you. But damn it, Caleb, didn't you know that Travis's is a whorehouse?"

"A whorehouse! Oh my God, here in our town, a place where they sell women? Oh Josh, Uncle Louis, what have I done?" I felt almost as dizzy as I did the night I drank the home brew. I reeled to the horse trough and splashed water on my face.

I turned to Hester and said, "Please, Hester, don't make fun of me, but I need to know, why do Josh and Uncle Louis need to buy women? And after they buy them, where do they keep them?"

Hester didn't tease me, or laugh at me. She said, "Caleb, oh Caleb, why does it always have to be me? They don't buy the girls like slaves, they just buy the use of their bodies."

Hester had become very gentle with me and I felt good about her acting so kind, but it seemed to me that things were getting more confusing. I said to Hester, "Use their bodies, Hester? Josh and Uncle Louis wouldn't kill anyone."

Hester started getting upset with her inability to get me to understand. "You're so immature, Caleb. How can anyone tell you anything? Wait a minute. I know that you have been up to Muldon's other barn and watched when they took the cows to the bullpen, haven't you?"

Since this was one of the sneaky things that the kids in Sterling did, I had gone, but my mind was not ready to accept that Josh or Uncle Louis would pay money to do what that bull did to a cow. I could see that Hester was really upset, so I said, "Now I understand, Hester. Thank you for helping me. I guess I'd better go home and talk to Josh."

When I reached home Josh told me that Dad had called Uncle Louis and him in for a talk with Mom after Dad had cooled her down some. She agreed to allow Uncle Louis to stay, but she said that if she ever heard the name of that place in her house again, she wouldn't be responsible for what happened. "You know, Caleb," Josh said, "I don't believe you even understand why what you said caused all this trouble."

"Oh Josh, I have been so confused and scared. Hester tried to explain it to me, but I still don't know what taking the cows up to the Coors barn to see the bull has to do with you and Uncle Louis going to Travis's."

Josh laughed and said, "Hester, yes, I guess that would be her way of trying to explain. Caleb, I am not sure that it is safe to try to talk to you or not. First you have to understand that I have never been to Travis's. I was only teasing Uncle Louis because I heard that he goes there. Now, about why he goes, this will be a little bit hard for you to comprehend right now, but in a few years it will make more sense to you. When boys become my age their bodies begin to change and you see girls in a different way and you want to do this thing with them called sex. I guess it is sort of like the bull and the cow, except it's a boy and a girl. You are never ever supposed to do this unless you are married and then it is all right. Now someone like Uncle Louis, who has been married and really got to like this sex thing, goes to a place like Travis's to do it."

I trusted Josh, and though my head wasn't all that straight about this sex thing, I felt much better, but I wasn't looking forward to when that happened to me.

Things stayed pretty cool between Mother and Uncle Louis. Mother mostly just ignored him when the kids were around, but occasionally I would hear Uncle Louis say, "Come on, May, the Lord loves a forgiving person."

She would snap back, "Maybe, but He doesn't love an adulterer." Then she would bend to her work of making and mending our clothes, getting them ready for us to go back to school, which opened right after the coming Labor Day weekend. This bought an end to a memorial summer, my tenth.

Chapter 4

After Labor Day it was back to school in fifth grade with Old Hanna. It didn't take her long to erase any doubt we might have entertained about the stories that we'd heard from the older children. She quickly singled out George Phelps as the biggest troublemaker in the new kids in fifth grade. George lived northeast of Sterling near the state line. Just about the only time I saw him was when we were in school. I always thought of him as being a tough kid, but by the end of the day we realized that neither George nor anyone else in our class was dumb enough to think they were tough enough to challenge Old Hanna. She got her chance to whack us occasionally, but it was more from our lapses of memory than a challenge.

The first few weeks of school slipped by quickly for me, but it was hard going to classes and keeping my job as a stripper. Mother didn't want me to, but I stayed on at Muldon's doing the stripping after school started. Rushing home to get cleaned up after the six o'clock morning shift was always a close call. What upset me was that I had so little time of my own after school. It was such a short time between three and five thirty with the evening meal and all. Mother always insisted that I go to bed as soon as I came in, because I had to get up so early. I found this life tough, but I got to keep seventy-five cents of the three fifty I made each week for myself. I didn't want to give that up, seventy-five cents was really being rich for a kid like me. Even after Mother made me put some of it in my piggy bank, I still had fifty cents to do what I wanted with. It made me feel important when I shared it with other kids. With fifty cents I could buy candy at the store every day and not be broke at the next payday.

Sometimes I would buy a pint of strawberry ice cream and sneak behind the library with Joan Walden and just the two of us would eat it all. I made her promise that she wouldn't tell anyone because it cost twenty-four cents and I didn't have enough money to do this for every girl in town. But I guess the truth was that that Joan was special to me because I always bought the strawberry she liked when I wanted chocolate.

One night when I came home, Josh called me upstairs and said, "Caleb,

35

I want you to hear a poem that I found today. You'll really appreciate this one. It's called 'Dad's Home Brew,' it goes like this."

I recall one time when the kids of our town
were swiping Dad's home brew, and drinking it down.
First it was a quart, then a gallon or two.
If you don't know what happened, you never drank home brew.
My head started reeling and nothing would stay down.
All I had eaten in a month I saw lying on the ground.
When I reached the house and at every step I fell,
Mother started for the doctor, so he could make me well.
But Dad was suspicious, saying hold on a minute or two
While I go down to the cellar and count my home brew
Dad, he started swearing, I started to cry
For even if I got better, I was sure I was going to die.
Dad looked at me sadly, saying suffering was my fate
But he was glad that he had caught us before it was too late.
We are all grown men now and still quaff a few
But you will never ever catch us drinking Dad's home brew.

Josh laughed, saying, "Isn't that appropriate, Caleb, aren't you glad I ran across that poem?"

"That's really good, Josh," I told him, but I knew he probably had written the poem himself. I had found many things he had written hidden in the closet. Some of them were pretty mushy too, about girls and love and all that crazy stuff. I never said anything because this was the side of Josh that the other boys picked on him about when they called him sissy and things. I didn't want him to know I knew about his poetry even though I thought that the boys would probably like this one.

"You really like poetry, don't you, Josh?" I asked.

"Oh Caleb, I hope someday I can explain to you how wonderful it makes me feel when I am able to read and understand the tremendous emotions that are involved in the construction of a good poem. I know that poems are supposed to be sissy stuff, but Caleb, I like poetry so much I have to believe that it's important," he replied.

"That's all right, Josh," I said. "I know how much you like poetry and I do like it when you read it to me. It's hard for me to read it by myself, but it sure sounds good when you read it." I drifted off to sleep that night thinking that the least I could do for Josh was to be someone he could talk to about poetry.

The next day at school George Phelps got Karl and me all excited about the fish he was catching in a small brook that ran through the northern part of Muldon's wood lot. It had been a very dry fall so far this year and the brooks and ponds were very low, forcing the fish to gather in the deepest holes in the streams. The ones close to town were fished out. With George living so far out of town and having no kids to play with except family, he did a lot of exploring in the woods around his property. That was how he discovered the brook with all the fish in it.

"Oh, Caleb!" Karl said." We have to get up there this weekend somehow. There's gotta be a way."

There was a way, but the way with us is walking. I wasn't sure that I wanted to try to squeeze a trip like that in between my milking shifts; besides, I had promised Joan some strawberry ice cream on Saturday. Karl wouldn't give up though and he kept pushing, saying, "Caleb, there's not much fishing left this year. Just think how nice it would be if we came home with our baskets full of nice native trout. Everyone will be jealous of us, like the time we caught that big trout in the river."

I thought, *Sure, Karl,* your *big fish. I didn't even get a hit that day, but maybe if we went, this time I could outdo you.* I could ask Josh to do my morning stripping. If he couldn't, then we could leave after I finished and still get back in time to for the evening milking. After all, it couldn't be much more than five miles up there.

I asked Josh if he could cover for me. He said, "Caleb, it's about time you had a day off. I'll tell you what, I will take the whole day Saturday for you so you and your friends can plan this trip right."

I was so excited that I grabbed Josh and gave him a big hug, saying, "I really, really love you, Josh."

We had finished our planning by Tuesday and I thought Saturday was never going to come. I worried about having to tell Joan, but she said that it was O.K. and suggested we do it after school that day.

I only had sixteen cents left of my pay. I didn't get paid until Friday, that's why I had told her Saturday. I didn't want to tell Joan, so I agreed. I borrowed eight cents from Beverly Stone, who was in the sixth grade. I had to promise to pay her back ten, but I figured this fishing trip was worth the extra pennies.

Saturday finally came, and Karl and I started at the same time as Josh was on his way to do my milking. Karl's grandfather, who had been an avid fisherman, had died a couple of years ago and Karl's grandmother gave Karl all his fishing gear, so he had modern fishing tackle. I didn't have much, just an old bamboo pole with one of Uncle Louis's old reels fixed on it, but I was pretty proud of it. It was sure a lot better than the stick and string I had to use before. The excitement of the trip and the new scenery made the five miles seem quite short.

We saw Mr. Stillisk unloading a bull when we went by his little farm. The bull looked a little crippled. We talked about what he was doing with a bull like that, but we were too excited about fishing to come to any conclusion. The Stillisks were foreign people who didn't speak English well, even though they had been living in Sterling as long as I could remember. There was some talk about her being the wife of some rich, powerful man and running off with Mr. Stillisk and that was why they kept to themselves so much. The only time you ever saw them in town was at the general store or if there was a dance at the town hall.

We met George about a mile above the Stillisk farm, where he led us off into the woods. When we were about a quarter a mile from the road we came to a small stream, we followed that for a little way to where it joined a little bigger stream. George said, "We have to do this just right. The trout spook pretty easy here. Instead of walking close to the bank we have to stay back away from it and each one of us has to find our own hole to fish so we don't tangle our lines." George took the first hole we came to and Karl took the second, and as I was sneaking up on the next one, I saw Karl already putting fish in his basket. I baited my hook and cast into the middle of the small pool. The trout were practically jumping out of the water to get at the bait. They were native brookies, but they were big ones that fought like fury. I had five and had lost four or five more when my line got tangled in the bushes. I had to go up to the water's edge to get it untangled and that ended the fishing in that hole. George and Karl came over to where I was. They had caught about the same amount as me before they stopped biting where they were. Karl was excitedly patting George on the back, saying, "Boy, Caleb, aren't we lucky to have a friend like George? Look, look at these fish. Did you ever see such beautiful brookies in all your life? Let's go find some more holes to fish."

He had a reason to be excited, two of his fish measured over a foot long and that was big for native trout. We went down the brook, taking our holes in the same rotation as before. When I left Karl, it was a long way before I found another hole deep enough to hold any fish. I was way out of his sight when I finally found one that looked promising. I was feeling rather sad, not much chance of me outdoing Karl, not with the fish he had caught at his first hole. I wanted so much just one time to beat him when we went fishing, but I guessed that was never going to happen.

While sneaking up on my new hole I saw the biggest trout I had ever seen in my life. He was almost too big for the hole that he was in. I got so excited that I dropped my worm can. It hit a rock and splashed right into my hole. Boy! Did the fish in the hole ever have a feast, but not old biggy! He just lay there wriggling like a weed being moved by the current. I had a little worm on my hook but he wouldn't even look at it. I tried to hook him and managed to roll him a couple of times but I couldn't catch him. I wanted that fish so much I was almost crying. I thought about calling George and Karl but then it wouldn't be just my fish anymore. Even though I knew it was wrong I took off my shoes rolled up my pants, got a stick and went into the brook after him. There wasn't enough water running in the brook for him to be able to escape from the hole. I finally stunned him with the stick just enough to get a hold on him and pull him up the bank. What a fish! He sure was heavy. I put my shoes and socks back on and hooked my hook into fish's mouth and started hollering for George and Karl. They came running, thinking I must have gotten hurt. You should have seen their faces when they saw that fish. George couldn't even talk, he just stood there with his mouth wide open, and Karl sounded almost as if he was going to cry.

Finally he said, "Caleb, I have never seen a trout like that. It's so big and beautiful I wish this had been my hole and I caught a fish like that."

I wish that I had too, I thought. But no one was ever going to know that I didn't. Not now when I had in hand the fish of every fisherman's dream.

I wanted to start back to town right after I caught that fish, but of course Karl and George thought that wasn't fair, so we fished on down the brook. I hoped and prayed that Karl wouldn't find a bigger fish than mine. By the time we had caught all the fish we wanted and came back to the road, we were all the way down by the Stillisk farm. Old man Stillisk was out in the field trying to catch that bull we had seen him with in the morning. He wasn't doing very well; even though the bull was lame, it still was fast and mean.

When he saw us boys he hollered, "You kids want to earn a dime helping me catch this damn bull? I bought him yesterday. They raised him for breeding but he was so damned mean he banged himself all up when they put him in the bullpen. Everybody was afraid of him so I bought him cheap. I was going to castrate him and fatten him up to butcher this fall. I had him tied to the hitching post, but before I could rope him down he got away."

I told Karl and George that we had an easy dime to make, but it sure didn't end up being easy! That bull gave us a helluva hassle before we finally had him hitched to the post.

Old Stillisk brought a big coil of rope from the barn and said, "Let's make sure he doesn't get away again." Laying the coil on the ground, he wrapped the rope a couple of times around the hitching post then around the bull's horns, pulling his head almost all the way down to the ground and tight to the post. He went into the barn, muttering, "Now I'll show that damn bull."

I had seen little pigs castrated, but what happened next I still find unbelievable. Stillisk came out of the barn carrying a tool that had two long handles hinged together at one end and there were cups with spikes inside placed on each of the handles where they were hinged. He went behind the bull and placed the cups on each side of the bull's testicles and squeezed the handles together with all his strength. My God, the noise and reaction was something to see and hear. The bull bucked and reared and blood was flying everywhere. Old Stillisk was thrown back against the barn and slid down looking dazed. The bull, roaring like a dozen lions, hunched down and broke the post right off at the ground. With what was left of the post was still tied to his head, he started running and bucking out of the yard.

Karl, glancing over at George, hollered, "Don't do—" He was too late, as George dove for the coil of rope. Instead of him grabbing the rope he got caught in the coil and was dragged out of the yard trailing close to the bull. The bull was bucking and rolling all over the field, and George was being dragged, kicked and rolled on. He was screaming with pain. Karl and I went running after him, yelling, "Let go, George, let go!" We knew that George wasn't holding on to that rope taking all that punishment. We knew he was tangled, we just didn't know what else to do. When the bull started to run into the woods the hitching post got caught between two trees and the bull did a complete somersault, the rope broke and George was free. We ran over to him, he was covered with blood, one of his ears was almost torn off, and you could see a bone sticking through his pant's leg. I knelt down by his side and he said, "Oh my God, Caleb, I hurt so much. I want my mother. Hold me, Caleb, please hold me." I took his head and shoulders in my lap the way my mother used to do when I got hurt and rocked him gently.

He said, "Thank you, Caleb, thank you." Then he just sighed, stopped talking and became limp and very quiet.

I sat there holding him on my lap with my tears running onto his battered face, shouting over and over, "Don't die, George. Oh God, don't let him die."

Karl whispered, "Stay with him, Caleb, I'll go get some help."

By this time Mr. Stillisk was coming with his wife running across field towards us. Karl told her how bad it was and she ran back to the house to get some blankets and something for bandages, yelling to her husband to get the pickup and drive it over by the woods. When Mrs. Stillisk got to George, she held his wrist and felt the side of his neck and said, "Easy, boys, he still has a chance if we hurry and all work together. You boys find a straight stick about as long as your leg. I'll see what I can do about the bleeding."

Karl and I ran into the woods and made sure we brought back three sticks, when we got back she had George's head and ear all bandaged, he was wrapped in a blanket and old Stillisk was there with the pickup. She was giving him one helluva a barrage of words but she wasn't speaking English. I didn't know what she was saying, but it sounded real angry. She picked out one of the sticks, and when she pulled back the blanket I could see she had straightened George's leg some and had it bandaged. She put the stick besides his leg and gently but firmly tied it there with some torn sheets.

"We'll take him to the nearest hospital. There's one up across the state line," Old Stillisk said. "We'll get him there, boys. When we know how he's going to be and have talked to his parents, I'll come into town and let you know."

Mrs. Stillisk sat in the truck, and as gently as we could we got George into her lap. He was unconscious, but we knew he was still alive because he cuddled up close to her and moaned, he must have thought that she was his mother.

They left for the hospital. Karl and I just sat there stunned, my mind didn't want to accept what had happened, but the roaring of the bull down in the woods kept me from thinking it was a dream. After we had sat silent for a while, Karl said, "Come on, Caleb, we have to think about getting home. We can take George's fish and put them in the springhouse and leave the Stillisks a note."

"O.K., Karl," I said. "Let's get our stuff and head back to town." It was then that I remembered my fish, my big, beautiful fish. Oh, the glory of bringing home a fish like that was something to live for. Here I was thinking about my life, with George dying or maybe already dead. I felt confused and angry over what had happened, and hurt because it would take away from my glory and guilty about feeling this way as well. I blurted out, "Damn it, Karl, why does it always have to be me?"

"Take it easy, little Caleb," Karl answered, "I know how you feel, but we have to think of George now. Let's take his fish up to the springhouse, you can wash his blood off you up there, and maybe it will help us feel a little better."

We went to the springhouse with George's fish, drew a pail of water and washed up. I couldn't get all the blood off my clothes. Karl tried to help but said, "I guess that's the best we can do for now. Caleb, maybe it would help if we said a prayer out loud." I don't know what made him think like that, maybe because the well house was shaped a little like a chapel. I asked him if he knew one.

He said, "We will just talk to God about how we feel and ask him to help George."

41

We knelt down right there at the springhouse and Karl started, "God, we are just little boys but they tell us that Jesus said You cared about little children. God, one of Your little children, George, needs You bad. We don't know what to do, Lord, or really how to ask. Today I think we learned to love George like Jesus taught. Caleb even cried for him. We need Your magic, God, please won't You use it to help him?"

Karl was quiet for a few minutes and then he said, "Do you want to say anything, Caleb?"

I wanted to try, so I started, "Oh God, I think that I would do anything to be better if You help George. I would even like to wish that George had caught that big fish. I'm sorry, God, about the way I did it. My brother Josh says that when things get real bad, God is always there. Things are real bad today, God, so won't You please come down and help George? Amen."

Karl thought that we should say the "Our Father" prayer too, so we said it together and started our trip home. We didn't talk much on the way back, our hearts and minds were too full, but I sure thought a lot about all that had happened. One thing I learned for sure was that even if you didn't think God answered all your prayers, it was a big help to talk to Him.

We were almost a mile from town when Josh, Emma and Bob Woods met us. Frank Butler, who was one of the lumbermen in town, had been at the Phelps' talking to them about buying some timber on their land when the Stillisks were going by and stopped to tell them what happened. In the rush and terror that followed, Frank never did understand who it was that got hurt. By the time he had gotten back to town and had a few drinks from his emergency kit, the story that he brought back was that a bull had killed one of the three kids that had been fishing up by the Stillisks' farm.

Emma and Bob Woods had been with Josh when they heard the story. Bob lived east of town, his father worked for the state, which owned many acres in Sterling, and many of the families in town owed their livelihood to that. He told us that Josh had been so upset thinking that I might be the one Frank Butler was talking about that he and Emma had a hard time keeping up with him that mile. We hadn't seen Frank's truck go by us, so I guess we must have been at the springhouse praying when he went by Stillisk's farm.

Karl and I told them what had happened.

Josh said, "Caleb, we were so worried when we heard the story that Frank was spreading around that we hurried right out here without going home. We had better hurry home before Mother hears about it. You know how worried she was about you going way up here."

We wanted to hurry, but Karl and I were carrying quite a load. I told Josh and he said, "Bob, let's take their fish for them. They're probably pretty tired after all they've been through."

Bob took Karl's basket and Josh took mine, saying, "Hey, this feels like it really has some fish in it. Let's see what you have in here, Caleb."

He opened the basket and you should have seen his face when he saw my fish. I started swelling with pride and then I remembered George and started feeling guilty inside again.

"Caleb, Caleb," Josh said, "tell me where and how you ever caught a fish like that."

"Please, Josh," I pleaded, "I don't want to talk about it right now. Every time I think about that fish and George and the bull I get all upset. I don't think I can stand much more right now, Josh."

He said, "O.K., Caleb," putting his free arm around me, "I understand."

"I'll tell you, Josh," Karl piped in. He told them about the holes and how we had fished them. He told them about when he and George had heard me hollering and they ran down to see what was up and how they found me there all worn out from catching that fish. I guess Karl didn't hear what I said when I was telling God about being sorry for the way I caught that fish.

We arrived home before Mother had heard about what happened. It was good that we did, because Frank had gone to the Sterling Inn and the more he drank, the wilder the story became. Mr. Banner, who was the owner of the Inn, decided he should find the truth of the matter before Frank raised a lynching party to hang old Stillisk for causing the death of one of the town boys. There were a number of men at the bar and more drifting in, as usual at the end of the workweek. The talk at the bar was getting loud and ugly, so Mr. Banner had his wife take his place behind the bar. He got his Packard from the garage and started driving towards Stillisk's. He met us just out of town and we told him the story about the bull and George while he drove us home.

After we told Mother, Eunice and Hester, Mr. Banner asked, "Helene, would you allow me to take Josh back to the Inn? There are some pretty strong feelings because of Butler's talk. I would like to have Josh help set the story straight. These men are so used to having me pacify them that they are not going to believe me without proof. I heard that Josh was quite a talker. I'd like to take Caleb, but I think at his age he's had enough for one day."

It took a little more convincing, but when Mr. Banner said that he couldn't see Mr. Stillisk hurt by a group of drunks because of some dumb mistake, Mother gave in.

Later that night when Josh came home from the milking, he told me what had happened at the Inn. Josh and Mr. Banner arrived at the same time as Uncle Louis, who was coming in from fishing. Mr. Banner wasn't able to

43

quiet the men down to hear what Josh had to say, so Uncle Louis offered his help.

Mr. Banner agreed, saying, "Please, Louis, we have to do something before this goes too much further."

Uncle Louis, being no slouch as a drinking man, probably understood these men better than Mr. Banner, who never touched the stuff except to sell it. Uncle Louis went behind the bar, taking a bottle and rapping it on the bar loudly and shouting, "Boys, hear this, for the first time in the history of this establishment it has been decided to set up the house."

Josh said that he had never seen such a change. The whole argumentative, boisterous bunch at the bar quieted to a murmur, just for a free drink.

"Now," Uncle Louis continued, "all that we are asking, me as your personal friend and Lester as the proprietor, is that you spend five minutes listening to what my nephew has to say."

Mr. Banner went behind the bar with Uncle Louis and said, "I'll mix the drinks as soon as Josh is done talking if everyone listens quietly. Josh has the truth of what happened straight from his brother Caleb and Karl Hart, who were with the Phelps boy fishing. Everyone, listen closely to what really happened before making any wild decisions."

I could just picture Josh walking up to the bar as he told me what happened. He had a way with words and loved to use them. Josh reenacted the whole scene for me, saying, "Gentlemen, I have been standing listening to the stories passing around the bar and I understand how these wild emotions can be aroused when you are only dealing with half truths. I was asked to tell exactly what did transpire. What I have to tell came straight from the mouths of the participants in this tragic happening, not more than an hour and a half after it happened."

Uncle Louis said later that Josh held the men so spell bound while telling our story that most of them didn't even lift their glasses while he was talking.

When he finished the story, Josh told me he said, "I heard a lot of talk about foreigners when I first came in. A thought occurred to me as I listened and I'd like to share it with you. This country at one time belonged to the Indians. I know there are probably men at the bar that have some Indian blood in their veins, but I don't believe that anyone here is going to stand up and say he is an Indian, so who are the foreigners here?"

With that, Josh left. Uncle Louis recalled that there was a little talk about smart aleck kids but that soon got shouted down. Most of the men believed Josh and, whether they liked it or not, knew he was right about who was a foreigner.

Uncle Louis came home soon after Josh left to see how I was. I showed him my fish, and boy did he get excited. He said, "Caleb let me take it back to the Inn. It will sure take their minds off blaming Old Stillisk."

Back when I had caught that big fish I had planned how I was going to show it all over town. There were some people I especially wanted to show that little Caleb could do something big. I still wanted to do it, but every time I thought of it and how good it would make me feel, I pictured George in my mind, lying there all bloodied with his ear most torn off and that bone sticking out of his leg. I felt so guilty that it would make me almost as sick as I had been from drinking home brew. So I told Uncle Louis, "O.K., take the fish."

After all, I thought people would know it was me that caught the fish and it wouldn't be as if I was being callous if Uncle Louis was showing it around. I waited impatiently with my emotions running wild for Uncle Louis to come back after taking my fish to the Inn. When he finally arrived home he told us all that happened. We knew the fish measured twenty-seven and a half inches long since Uncle Louis had stopped at the general store to have it weighed and measured. It weighed almost twelve pounds on the meat scale. The men at the bar got so excited when they saw the fish that most of the talk about Stillisk died down.

When Mr. Banner saw the fish he said, "Louis, did you catch a fish like that in Sterling?"

"It was caught in Sterling, Lester, but Caleb caught it, not me," Louis replied.

"Louis," Mr. Banner asked, "do you think Caleb would be interested in letting me have it mounted and hung behind the bar? I would have a plaque made with Caleb's name and where and when he caught it. I have seen bigger trout than that, but to have one as beautiful as that caught in Sterling hanging behind the bar would really be something."

"I don't know, Lester," Uncle Louis answered. "I will talk to him. I think that it is a good idea, that way he will have it the rest of his life."

Just then Old Stillisk's pickup pulled up outside and he came into the Inn. A subdued murmur went through the bar as he walked over to Mr. Banner, saying, "I have the doctor's report on George Phelps. I can see by my reception the story has already reached town. First, Mr. Banner, pour me a double shot of rye."

"Stillisk, how could you be so dumb," Frank Butler shouted drunkenly from the corner.

Uncle Louis said, "All right, Frank, that's enough of that. Don't get that started again, we want to hear about the boy's condition."

An approving murmur went through the men at the bar as Stillisk said,

"George is going to live. The doctor said even though he was badly smashed up there were no signs of damage to his vital organs. George's youth and good health and getting him to a hospital right away kept him from going into a coma. They said that they were able to sew him up, so he probably won't have too many bad scars to show for his day with the bull. George has to stay in the hospital for at least a month or maybe longer, but in six months he should be as good as new."

After Stillisk had finished telling about George and the doctors, a murmur started to rise from the men at the bar. It was just then that By Golly Moses Muldon stepped into the bar, saying, "By Golly Moses, Alex, I saw your pickup outside and knew something had to be wrong if you were in town, especially here in the Inn. I know you aren't much of a mixer. Is there any truth to the stories I've been hearing about your bull and the Phelps kid?"

"Yes, Joe," Stillisk said, "there's truth to the stories." He told Joe the story about castrating the bull and how George got caught in the rope, how he and his wife had taken George to the hospital. "I guess I am just stupid like Frank Butler said, Joe."

"By Golly Moses, Alex, it's true that that isn't the brightest thing I ever heard of being done. Why didn't you come and see me if you wanted your bull castrated? We have much better ways today. You know I would have helped you."

"I wish now that I did," said Stillisk. "But you know how I don't want to bother the townspeople, they all think I am dumb enough now."

Golly Moses banged on the bar and said, "Lester, pour me a big shot of your best bourbon over ice." The men in the bar gawked in surprise. They had heard that Golly Moses had a nightcap every night at the end of his day, but no one had ever seen him drink in public. He stood at the bar silently sipping his drink, seemingly in ponderous thought. The men sat silently watching him. After he finished his whiskey he banged his glass on the bar saying, "By Golly Moses, dumb thing or not, the talk of this town should not punish this man any further. He is punishing himself enough. I don't want to hear any more vicious talk in this town about him. The Muldons have spoken." Turning to Alex, he said, "Come on, Alex, it's time for us to get back to farming." And they walked out the door.

After Joe and Alex left, Frank staggered up to the bar from his booth shouting, "Who the hell does he think he is, telling us what to think? Give me another drink and I will tell you what we're going to do."

Mr. Banner said, "I'll tell you what I'm not going to do, Butler, that is give you another drink. You've had more than enough. If I were you I would go home and sober up and keep my mouth shut. I'll tell you who Joe Muldon

46

is. He is a very good man, but he can and will make it almost impossible for you to buy timber for miles around if you are dumb enough or drunk enough to cause trouble for the Stillisk family."

There were murmurs from the men at the bar of, "He's right, Frank, he's right."

Frank gave in, shouting, "All right, all right, if that's the way you all feel. I am getting the hell out of here"

Uncle Louis walked Frank out the door and persuaded Frank to let him drive him to his house. Then he hurried home to tell us what had happened at the hospital and to ask me if I wanted to have Mr. Banner mount my fish behind the bar.

At first I was very excited about the idea, but I started to get those guilty feelings again, so I told Uncle Louis, "I need to think about it."

He said, "I understand but you have to answer very soon, because the fish might not be in shape to mount for very long, and Lester will have to get it to a taxidermist right away."

Josh came in and Uncle Louis said, "You did a good job at the Inn, Josh. Someday I believe that you will talk your way into being the president of the United States."

Josh laughed, asking, "What's the word on George?"

Uncle Louis told him what had happened at the Inn after he left, about Stillisk's report on George and how old Golly Moses had come in and put the finishing touches on what Josh had started.

As I sat there listening to them talk I thought, *I'll talk to Josh. He will understand how I feel about the fish, and tell me what to do.* When they were done talking, I said, "Josh, can I see you in our room for a minute?" When we got to the room Homer was there working on his paintings. He was always drawing or painting. His pictures were very good for someone only nine years old. He didn't want to leave his painting, but I gave him a nickel to put with the money he was saving to buy paint and he left.

I asked Josh to help me. I told him about Mr. Banner's offer and how every time I thought about the fish it made me feel guilty.

Josh put his hands on my shoulders and said, "Listen, Caleb, what happened to George could have just as well happened even if you weren't there. You didn't do anything to cause George to get hurt. I know you feel bad about it, but you don't have any reason to feel guilty."

I said, "Oh Josh, I have to tell somebody or I am going to die inside. I didn't really catch that fish. He wouldn't bite, so I went into the water and got him with a stick. Josh, I talked to God about it. Karl and I prayed out loud prayers up in the Stillisk's springhouse. While I was asking God to please help George I told him I was sorry about the way I caught that fish. Now they want to mount my fish where everybody can see it. Oh Josh, with George hurt so bad by the bull I don't know what's right, please help me, Josh."

"Take it easy, little Caleb," Josh said. "Let's think this out. First, let's talk about the fish. A fish that size would never survive the winter in that small stream, so it's better that you caught it no matter how. Second the bull; none of that happened because of anything that you planned, Caleb, so you shouldn't feel guilty. About talking to God, I'm sure He understood how you felt and you were honest with Him about the fish while you were asking Him to help George. I believe that He was so pleased with your praying for George that He was the one who put the thought in Mr. Banner's head about mounting the fish. So, Caleb, if you want to have that done, I'm sure that God is on your side."

I gave Josh a great big hug and said, "Josh, I'm the luckiest boy in the world. Just having a brother like you lets me know that God is on my side. Let's go tell Uncle Louis it's O.K. to take the fish to Mr. Banner."

Josh and Uncle Louis left with the fish and I went to sit on the couch with Mother. She pulled me close and said, "You sure had some day, Caleb. Now that we know about the Phelps boy we will have to thank God tonight for watching over him."

Monday, when we went back to school, Karl and I must have been asked about Saturday a hundred times. Old Hanna finally had us stand in front of the classroom and tell them what had happened. It caused quite a bit of an uproar when Karl said balls instead of testicles, but Hanna cut that short. When we were through she said, "Children, I want each of you to ask your parents if you can supply a small gift for a sunshine basket for George. We will make a basket of gifts, each dated for the day they can be opened, so he will have something to look forward to every day he is in the hospital. This will make his stay less isolated, especially when each day he is remembered by one of his classmates."

When I got home that afternoon, Mother and some of our neighbors were already planning a sunshine basket, but they agreed with Hanna that George would be happier if it came from his classmates. So they decided to help with that.

When Dad came home that night he said that he had heard that the Muldons had made a sizable contribution to a fund that had been started to help Phelps pay for the hospital and doctor bills. The logging crew that he was working with didn't have money to spare but had decided to go up to Phelps and help cut the logs that Frank Butler was buying from them.

48

The rest of my year in the fifth grade slid by without anything happening that climaxed that fishing trip. It was just the grind of old Hanna hammering those three R's and milking those cows. Mr. Banner took Karl and me up to see George a couple of times at the hospital. The first time we visited, George said, "Caleb, I sure wish I could see a fish like the one you caught again."

Mr. Banner said, "Maybe you will, George, maybe you will."

The next time Mr. Banner took us to the hospital, he had my fish with him mounted on a board. It had a little brass plaque that said, *Weight 11 pounds, 14 ounces. Length 2 feet, 3 & 1/2 inches. Caught on Sept. 22, 1938, by Caleb Carney in the northwest section of Sterling.* When George saw the fish mounted, he got so excited that the nurses made us take it out.

George came home the middle of December, but it was decided that he shouldn't try to go back to school until next year. Karl and I walked out to see him as often as we could. It seemed that it was taking a long time for him to heal, but we saw improvement every time we went. The winter and the school year slid by, and Karl and I started making plans for our eleventh summer.

Chapter 5

Karl and I had been planning our summer all during the school year. We planned for fishing and hiking trips and even an overnight camp-out on the mountain. Mother seemed against our overnight trip, but Josh told her he thought it would be a good experience for me until she was close to agreeing. As we had planned, we hiked up to the Phelps' often that summer and went fishing with George. The fishing wasn't near as good as it had been in the fall, but it was good to see that George was healing well from the injuries he suffered from his tangle with that bull. Karl and I still wondered if we could have somehow prevented what had happened.

One day when Karl and I had been hiking and were resting at the foot of the mountain, Bob Woods and Kate Curtis came up the mountain trail carrying a picnic basket and a blanket. Karl said, "I heard some stories about those two the other night when my mother didn't know I was around. Let's follow them and do some spying."

Bob lived in a house east of town. Kevin Woods, Bob's father, managed the land the state owned in Sterling. My sister Hester was always saying, "Damn that Bob Woods, he thinks because his father is so important in town he can do anything he wants, but not with me he won't."

Listening to Hester had always made me wonder about Bob, so I said, "Yeah, that should be fun, let's follow Bob and Kate."

There was always talk about the Curtis family in town. Welcome Curtis, Kate's father, had left town once for over a year, and his wife Lillian had to go it alone for a while. Uncle Louis always used to say, "Maybe if she had always gone it alone Welcome might not have left." I never quite knew what he meant by that, but I thought by the way he said it that it was something mysterious. Kate and Bob were juniors in high school but I never heard any bad stories about them. So I asked Karl what he had heard.

"Oh, my mother said she wouldn't be surprised if she ended up pregnant, the way they were carrying on."

"Oh, come on, Karl," I said. "They aren't even married."

"Caleb," Karl replied, "you're so dumb sometimes I wonder how you survive with those boys at Muldon's barn. Come on, if Bob knows this part of the mountain I bet they are headed for that stand of Norwegian pine. The one with the thick bed of needles, that's were I would take a girl on a picnic."

Karl and I knew the mountain well, so it wasn't any trick to follow them. Karl was right; they headed right for that stand of pines. They put down the basket, spread the blanket and Bob and Kate started kissing. We were hiding behind some trees; Karl kept leaning further out on a limb so he could see. Bob unbuttoned Kate's blouse, taking off her bra, baring her breasts. The boys at the barn were always talking about her big boobs. My sister Eunice always said that a girl that behaved like her would develop early. I could hear Karl's breathing getting heavier and heavier, as Bob reached around and took Kate's breast in his hand. The branch that Karl was holding broke and Karl fell to the ground. Luckily they didn't see who we were, but Kate had seen something when Karl fell.

She started screaming, "Bob, there are some kids up there. Get them, get them! Make sure they shut their mouths. Get them, Bob, for God's sake, get up and go get them."

Karl whispered, "Don't talk or mention any names, just start running."

Boy, did we run! A couple of times I thought my heart was going to pound right through my chest. Every time we thought we had lost Bob, he would catch up again.

He kept hollering, "Hey, you kids! Stop, wait, I want to talk to you, who are you anyway?"

Karl and I sure didn't want to hear what he had to say or let him find out who we were, so we just kept running. We didn't dare run down the mountain because we knew that when we came out in the open we could be seen and Bob would figure out who we were. I was following Karl, who was zigzagging across the side of the mountain, keeping trees between Bob and us. When we reached a trail by the ledges, he sped down the trail. I gave it all I had trying to stay with him, but I knew it was near over for me. When we reached the middle of the trail I saw Karl swing out on a tree branch and slide down the ledges. Then I remembered our secret cave, that gave me a boost of energy and I sped after Karl. We crawled into our cave, trying to quiet our beating hearts and gasping breath. Bob went right by on the trail above, yelling, "Kids, hey kids, come back! I only want to talk to you, who are you? Answer me, damn it! I said answer me."

Karl and I lay in the cave for a long while before we were able to speak, and even then my heart was beating like a trip hammer. I had never run that far and fast before, and it was still a worry that Bob might find us.

After a while Karl said, "Boy, Caleb, did you ever seen a pair like that before? They were really something, I would have liked to be in Bob's place."

I didn't answer him, but I thought they were probably bigger than any of my sisters', but what was there to be so excited about? They were only things to feed babies with. Karl's mother and sister were almost as flat chested as boys. Maybe he had never seen a girl's breast, or could it be that sex thing that Josh tried to tell me about?

I didn't want to talk about that with Karl, so I said, "Karl, we're going to have to think of some way to get off the mountain without Bob catching us. He's sure to be waiting in the fields where we were to see if he can find out who we are when we come down."

Karl thought about this for a while and said, "You're right, Caleb. Man, oh man, he probably wants us so bad he will sit there until dark. If we can find a way down over these ledges, then we can circle around and come into town from the east. Nobody would believe we had been on the mountain coming from that way."

It took us a long time to find our way down the ledges and we sure got banged up. Once a piece of ledge broke under my feet, and I almost plunged down a thirty-foot drop. Karl caught my belt and pulled me back just in time. When I arrived home it was almost three o'clock. Mother gave me the devil because I missed lunch and asked what the devil happened to my clothes. I told her I had been climbing with Karl.

She said, "I don't know about you and that Hart boy. Ever since he moved into town you two have lived every free minute together. Well, I guess it is all right. He seems like a good boy and you two have never been in any serious trouble, but if you don't come home when you should I'm going to have a talk with his mother."

What happened today might have been serious, I thought. *Karl and I are going to have to be more careful. I would hate to have anything happen that might separate us.*

That night at the barn Reilly came in and shouted, "Hey John, did you hear about Kate Curtis and Bob Woods. I just heard Uncle Leon tell Dad that Bob took Kate up the mountain for a picnic and tried to rape her."

Leonard, who was about to sit on his milking stool to strip his first cow, missed the stool completely, fell over backwards and laughed like a maniac. "Rape!" he said. "My God, is that funny? Bob Woods raping Kate."

All the boys were laughing when Reilly said, "It may be funny to us, but I can assure you that it isn't to Bob or his family." He told us that Kate's father, Malcolm, went to Constable Parks, and when he wouldn't lock Bob up, he went to the state police. After the state police talked to Kate they took

Bob to the lockup for questioning. Kevin Woods has gone to Oscin to hire a lawyer, so he guessed it is serious.

Leonard said, "How can something like that happen? Ah, come on, not with Kate."

"I know," said Reilly, "I've heard the stories, are they really true, Leonard?"

"They're true, Reilly, believe me, they're true, and that's right from the horse's mouth," Leonard replied with a smirk.

All they talked about the rest of the night was Kate and Bob and that sex thing. Larry said that my sister Emma was the one he would like to rape, and Reilly told him to knock it off. After we had finished the milking and were carrying things to be sterilized I caught Reilly in the milk house alone and asked him what rape was.

He looked at me and laughed, saying, "Caleb, Caleb, Caleb, how do I tell you? Do you know when we take the cows to the bull, and most always the cow is willing to be with him? Well, occasionally we make a mistake and take a cow that isn't ready and the bull tries to do it anyway. That's rape. The boy forces the girl whether she wants to or not."

I left the barn heading home thinking about everything I had heard. It was all so very confusing. The way they all laughed about Kate and felt sorry about Bob. I tried to understand what Reilly had told me. It seemed that every time I asked about this sex thing I ended up hearing a story about the cows and bull. If I understand rape, then nobody had better try forcing anything like that on Emma or Josh and I would beat him within an inch of his life. My mind was going like a whirlwind, thinking about what I would do if anyone tried to force sex on my sisters. Then it dawned on me that Bob wasn't forcing Kate to do anything. She was laughing, holding and kissing him as if she was having a good time. She was even helping him unhitch her bra. If rape was anything like Reilly told me, that wasn't rape. Kate acted as happy as the cows that wanted the bull. She sure wasn't fighting Bob, so how could that be rape?

I was by the horse trough when someone hollered, "Hey Caleb." I knew that it was Karl and I was glad to see him, maybe he had some answers to all my worries.

Excitedly, he said, "I am glad I caught you, I didn't want to have to go to your house so late. I had a hard enough time getting out of mine. My mother was angry about the mess I was in when I came home from hiking with you. Have you heard the story about Bob raping Kate today? News sure travels fast in this town. They say that Bob is in jail over at Oscin."

"Karl, what is rape to you?" I thought because of talking to Reilly I might

54

know something that Karl didn't.

He said, "Caleb, Caleb, sometimes I worry about you. Rape is a boy forcing a girl to have sex with him when she doesn't want sex."

"Listen, Karl," I said. "We should probably do something to help Bob. You and I know that he wasn't using any force and they didn't do any of that sex thing when we saw him with Kate."

"I thought about that, Caleb," Karl said, "but just think a minute, what would have happened if Bob had caught us? He probably would have half killed us to make sure that we were too afraid to tell anyone what we saw. I'm afraid if we try to help him, Kate's father will want to kill us. Besides, they will just say that Kevin Woods had hired us to say Kate was willing. I figure that Kate was afraid we were so dumb we would tell our folks about what we saw and then it would get back to her parents. So she made up the story that Bob was trying to rape her. I think that you and I had better keep quiet and not tell anyone about what we saw. That's why I came to talk to you, so we would agree to do the same thing."

He convinced me he was right about keeping it to ourselves and we swore to it. I had to hurry home, because Mother told me if I kept being late I would have to give up my job and I didn't want that to happen. I walked away thinking that if Mother found out about this, it probably would be the end of Karl and I having so much fun together. I went home, cleaned up and said goodnight to my parents and went upstairs.

As I was going by my sister's room I heard Hester say, "I knew it, I always knew that damn Bob was going to go too far some day, but I never thought it would be with Kate or that the police would be involved. I wonder if they will put him in jail? I hope not, I never thought Bob was that bad."

I guess Eunice must have heard the story and came home and told Hester. I don't think I will ever understand girls. Hester has been damning Bob for years, now she feels sorry for him. She never makes any sense lately when it comes to boys. I went to my room; Jason and Homer both were snoring in their bunks. I pulled the sheet over Jason, thinking how much easier it had been to be seven than it was being twelve years old. I heard Josh and Uncle Louis when they came in. They sat down in the hall on Uncle Louis's bed talking. Josh sounded very upset, so I snuck over to the top of the stairs to hear what was wrong.

Josh said, "What do you think they will do to him, Uncle Louis? I heard that Constable Parks said that he didn't want to take him in for booking because he could get twenty years if they make the charges stick. God, that can't happen to Bob. I know he was capable of getting fresh with the girls, but he is not the kind to rape somebody. Especially here in Sterling, where he could have his pick of the girls at Travis's."

Uncle Louis said, "Take it easy with that kind of talk, Josh. You'll be getting me kicked out of the house. I don't know what is going to happen to Bob, but I wouldn't worry too much about that twenty years if I were you. Kevin Woods is a smart man, I hear he already has hired the best lawyer around. I know there has been some talk about that girl and there are ways a good lawyer can prove that she was willing or was involved with Bob or some other boy before. I don't understand about the state police though, usually with kids that young it is settled between the families. There might be some truth to the stories about Kevin Woods and Lillian Curtis. That would explain Welcome running to the state police without bothering to talk to anyone."

My mind and body had about all it could take for one day, so I left them talking and went to bed thinking, *Wow!* Twenty years was a long time in jail. I don't know what time it was when I woke up but I was covered with sweat and Josh was saying, "Caleb, Caleb, what's wrong, you were thrashing around and hollering so I had to wake you. What upset you so much that you're having nightmares?"

When I had my head together I realized what I had been dreaming. I dreamt that Bob was standing behind bars and there was an angry mob with ropes outside hollering, "Hang the rapist." They were busting down the door and unlocking his cell and dragging Bob out when Josh woke me. I was the only one there who wanted to save him, but I was so scared I couldn't move. As I told Josh about my dream, he said, "Caleb, you have to stop feeling guilty about things that you don't have any control over. I'd like to save Bob too, but I don't know how."

I blurted out, "I could save him if I wasn't so scared, Josh. I was there. Karl and I went spying on them. While we were watching Karl broke a branch and Bob chased us all over the mountain. He never caught us or found out who we were though."

Josh said, "Oh my God, Caleb, you sure get into some pickles, don't you? Now tell me exactly what you saw."

I explained it all to Josh. How Karl and I had been sitting dreaming in the sun, when Bob and Kate started up the mountain. How Karl had heard some talk at his house that made us decide to spy on them. How Bob and Kate had kissed and when Bob unbuttoned her clothes she helped him. How Karl got excited and broke that branch, and then how we had to run as if our life depended on it.

"I know how you feel about not wanting to say anything, Caleb," Josh said, "so let's sleep on it tonight, maybe tomorrow we can see a way to help."

I was glad I told Josh; he was always able to think of the best way to handle these things. I went back to sleep, when I woke again, Josh was gone and it was light outside. I jumped out of bed, afraid I was late for my milking. I pulled on my clothes and ran downstairs, shouting, "Mother, why didn't you call me?"

Eunice was in the kitchen with Mother. Mother said, "Take it easy, Caleb. Josh was up early. He said you had a bad night so he went to Muldon's. Aren't you feeling well? Maybe your days are too long. You get up before five thirty every day, then after work Karl and you play, fish or hike all day, you never seem to stop. It's nine or after every night when you go to bed. I just think that this is too much for a child your age, we're going to have to make other arrangements."

"Oh Mom," I said, "it was only a nightmare, Josh didn't have to make a big thing about it."

"Nevertheless," said Mother, "you are going to have to get more rest during the day if you're going to keep those hours."

"What is it that you two do all the time?" Eunice asked. "You seem like a funny pair. He's a couple of years older than you, isn't he, Caleb? Are you sure that it's just kid stuff that you two are into?"

"Eunice!" Mother shouted. "I know how you and your sister feel about Bob Woods, but what right do you have talking to your brother like that? He is not even twelve and doesn't know about such things."

Eunice said, "I am sorry, Mother; you too, Caleb. I guess I'm just upset about losing my job and with the story about Bob and Kate."

Eunice had been looking rather glum the last few days because she had to quit her job at Daniel's, where she worked the last few years. The Daniels were a rich family that bought the old Wicks' place south of town about ten years ago. They had two children and Eunice had baby-sat and helped with the housework there. This summer, Sophie Daniel's younger brother, Bruno, had come to stay with them. I don't know what he did, but Eunice was pretty upset the few days she worked after he came.

One night when she was talking to Dad and Mom, I heard Dad holler, "I will kill the son-of-a-bitch!" Mother quieted him right down though. I never did find out what it was all about. Eunice quit working there and Thelma Bragg got the job. Thelma was a little younger than Eunice and Eunice always seemed to dislike her, so I guess that made it worse for her.

Josh came in, saying, "O.K. if I have a cup of coffee, Mom?"

Mother said, "O.K., but go wash some of that barn off from you before you sit at my table."

She was always complaining how we smelled when we came home from the barn, even though we had our own cow it wasn't the same as being around a hundred of them for three or four hours every day. She always made me hang my work overalls in the shed and wash up every time I came home from the barn.

I finished my breakfast and left Josh, Eunice and Mother talking at the table. I got the hoe and went to the garden. Dad had told me that the garden could use some of that energy that I was burning running around on the mountain and fishing and that I should see to it before he had to take a hand. I was much too familiar with my father taking a hand to want that to happen. I had a plan that every morning after work I would give the garden an hour. Josh came out and joined me, and between the two of us we had half the garden hoed and weeded before we stopped. I sure was going to be proud when Dad saw it tonight.

Josh brought me a dipper of water, saying, "Caleb, I been thinking about a story Uncle Louis told me when he was a little in his cups. Those years that Malcolm Curtis was out of town, he and Uncle Louis worked at a logging company up north. They were friends and raised hell together. They aren't chummy now because of something that happened between them back then. Besides, most of the wives in town think a divorced man is some kind of danger to them, so men are careful how much they associate with Uncle Louis. My idea in telling you this, if you agree, is that maybe Uncle Louis could have a talk with Malcolm. If he knows that there were witnesses to what happened, then maybe this whole thing could be handled quietly. I know I promised you last night that I would not say anything about what you told me, but this way might work without any mention of you or Karl and your spying. What do you think, Caleb, do you want me to talk to Uncle Louis?"

"I don't know, Josh," I answered. "Karl and I have already sworn not to tell anyone, that's why I made you promise last night. Now I have told you and you want to tell Uncle Louis, then he goes and tells Welcome, I don't see how that's going to keep Karl and me out of trouble."

"The way I see it," Josh answered, "Uncle Louis wouldn't have to tell Welcome who the witnesses were. I believe he knows Welcome well enough to be able to convince him without mentioning you or Karl. He might not want to talk to him at all but, one thing for sure, he would never do anything to get you or Karl in trouble if we tell him."

That night when I came in from milking, Josh and I talked to Uncle Louis. I told him what Karl and I had seen on the mountain. Josh started talking about his plan, but Uncle Louis didn't answer right away.

Finally he said, "You know, Caleb, between you stumbling your way towards manhood and Josh's scheming, you two will probably wind up having the excitement of an uncle who has been hanged. You both know that if that's what really happened then I couldn't refuse you. Let me sleep on it tonight and tomorrow I'll decide what to do."

Well, as usual Josh was right, in a couple of days Bob was out of jail and packing to go to a summer school in Pennsylvania. Yuk, going to school in the summer, I wonder if that was any better than jail. Kate went to live with her aunt someplace near Boston, Massachusetts. There was talk around that Kevin Woods had bought the Curtises off. I knew that wasn't so, but I couldn't say anything. One thing I was sure of, however, was that I really had a "can do" uncle and a smart brother.

The summer sped by after that. Karl and I managed to keep busy with our fishing and hiking. We hiked out to see George occasionally. He was doing very well, and it looked as though he would be as good as new when school started. Karl and I were happy about that. We both admitted that we had dreams where we would see George being dragged by that bull and being covered with all that blood. We talked about it and decided that when George was completely well again the dreams would probably stop.

I thought the boys at the barn had finally accepted me for what I was, or had run out of tricks, because they weren't plaguing me all the time. Although sometimes I would end up doing some of their milking for them, Reilly never let it get too far out of hand.

I really should have become suspicious when for over a week they were so good it was strange. Friday night, when Larry's father Don Muldon stopped in to check on things, Larry said, "Hey, Dad, I'm going to be late tonight. The boys and I have decided that as soon as it gets dark enough, we are going to try to catch that snipe that is raising hell with our pasture before some cow breaks a leg in one of the holes that it is always digging."

Don kind of laughed and said, "O.K., Larry, tonight looks like a good night to snipe hunt with a full moon and everything. Try to get home before ten, you know how your mother frets."

After Don left, Leonard hollered, "Hey, Larry, do you think we will have as much fun as we did the last time we went snipe hunting?"

"I dunno," Larry answered, "from what I can see, I don't think that this snipe is as smart as the last one we caught."

"I'm not sure about that," John said, "when they are smart you can guess what they are thinking. If you get a dumb one it's hard to know what's on its mind, and that makes them harder to catch."

"I'm not worried about this one," Larry said. "It will be as easy as the first time we took Arthur, you remember, Arthur?"

"Don't worry, Larry," Arthur replied, "that's not something anybody is liable to forget. Not his first night snipe hunting."

"Yah," said John, "I used to hear Uncle Joe and Uncle Leon when they told stories about the first time they took Reilly snipe hunting. Sometimes I wish that I hadn't heard so much about it, because the best way to go snipe hunting is to get into a hunt without studying on it. Experiencing the hunt that way, and a man has his own tales he'll remember the rest of his life."

Reilly said, "Hey! How about taking Caleb. Maybe if we rush the milking he can help us a little while before he has to go home."

I have to admit that listening to them while I was milking, I had become interested in the snipe hunt and was trying to think what I could tell Mother if I was late. If I told her about the cows being in danger from the snipe she would understand why we had to catch it. I was already so excited about the hunt I was going to ask them if I could go.

I answered, "Hey, that'd be good, Reilly. Besides, with six of us we would be able to catch the snipe faster and we would all get home earlier."

All the boys yelled, "Atta boy, Caleb." Then they started chanting, "Look out, snipe, your hours are few, you're going to get caught by the Muldon crew."

We hurried the milking as fast as we could then I started out on my first snipe hunt.

Leonard said, "Come on, Caleb, we'll go over to the grain room and get a couple of bags, then I'll show you what you have to do."

We got the grain bags and met the other four boys at the pasture gate. Leonard said, "It isn't completely dark yet, so that will give Caleb and me time to get situated on those snipe runs. They're quite far back in the woods, you know. Now, the rest of you wait here until dark and then circle the area of the snipe trails. Remember that the trick is to be real quiet, because if the snipe hears you all the time it will sneak by you, then Caleb and I won't get a chance to bag him."

I followed Leonard across the pasture into the woods. It was darker in the woods but Leonard seemed to know where he was going. We came to a bushy area; Leonard said that was the most likely place for the snipe to come. He showed me how to hold my bag, saying, "You have to get two heavy stones to hold the bag open on the ground. Place the stones far enough apart so the bottom of the opening of the bag covers the trail, then you hold the top of the bag with your legs straddling it. Sometimes snipe run so quiet that you never hear them, that's why you have to hold the bag in your hand. When the snipe runs in you will feel him when he hits the bottom of the bag. When that happens, close the top real quick and tie it. Then holler like hell and we will all come running."

I said, "Don't worry about me, Leonard, I'm used to being in the woods. I hope the snipe comes my way."

I crawled into the brush until I found a small path. I couldn't find any stones so I took a couple of crotched sticks and pushed them through the burlap to hold the bag open across the trail. I couldn't hear the other boys, but Leonard said he would be just over the hill to my right and I knew that everyone was being super quiet because that was the way you hunted snipe.

I began to wonder what a snipe looked like. I had wanted to ask the boys at the barn, but I knew they would only laugh and call me dumb. I meant to ask Reilly when we were alone but I was so thrilled that they wanted me to go I forgot. *Darn, I don't even know what I might catch in this bag. I hope it doesn't bite or is so big I can't handle it. Boy, if this takes too long, Mother will ground me for sure and I will lose my job. I wish I were home. Why am I here straddling a bag I'm holding with both hands?* I had been so excited about the hunt at first, now that it was getting darker and I was out in the woods all alone bent over a grain sack I was starting to have second thoughts.

It was one thing hearing the stories in the safety of your home or with the boys at the barn, but it was scary out here alone in the dark hunting snipe. *What was it that Josh told me to do when the only thing that was scaring me was what I was thinking? I know! He said try to change your thoughts. Maybe if I think about that rape and sex thing that has been buzzing about my life lately I can make some sense of that.* I thought about Josh telling me how it was going to be fun to reach that age, yet when I thought about Bob and Kate and how that ended up, I wasn't so sure. Seemed like the stories about Bob's father and Kate's mother were about sex, and the way Uncle Louis was able to settle things down with Welcome Curtis might have had something to do with sex when they were working up north. I wondered too if the problem that caused Eunice to lose her job when Bruno showed up had something to do with sex.

I was just getting concentrated on this sex thing when I felt a tug on my bag. Wow, I had a snipe! I yanked the sticks out of the ground and started tying the string, hollering, "I got him, fellows, I got him!"

Suddenly the air around me turned so putrid I could hardly breathe. My eyes started running so bad I wouldn't have been able to see even if it was daylight. I hollered for Leonard, John, and Reilly not to come too near. It wasn't a snipe, it was a skunk. I threw the bag from me and blindly drove through the brush, the brush tore my clothes and some of my skin, but I had to get away from that terrible smell. I had beaten myself up real bad before I realized that the smell was now a part of me. After a couple of bad falls, I

61

stopped running and tried to gather my wits.

I called out to the boys, "Hey, Reilly, John, Leonard! Somebody, answer me! I know that you can't come close, but I need some help. I can't see and I'm almost choking to death. John, Arthur, Larry, please, somebody answer." When nobody answered me I was so scared I wanted to cry, not wanting the boys to see me crying. I settled down and started off slowly in the direction I thought the barn might be. I was stumbling along when I heard Reilly yelling, "Caleb, Caleb, where are you, who the hell upset that skunk? Caleb, can you hear me? Answer me, Caleb."

"I'm over here, Reilly," I shouted. "I caught that damn skunk in my bag. I thought I had caught the snipe so I tried to hold it and it sprayed all over me. I can hardly see or breathe."

Reilly started cursing, "Damn those boys! I told them I didn't think this snipe hunt was a good idea. Now I get stuck with all this trouble. Just wait, I'll get their hides for this. Look, Caleb, I'll come as close as I can, now you do what I tell you. First, take all your clothes off except your shoes, even your stockings if they are wet."

"I can't do that, Reilly! I can't walk through town naked! Please, Reilly," I begged.

"Damn it, Caleb, do you want me to help you or leave you out here alone? Take your clothes off before you choke or faint. I'm not going to have to carry you back to the barn. I'll find something for you to wear through the streets. Come on, do as I say, the longer that skunk piss stays on you the longer it will take to wear off."

I did as Reilly told me and followed his voice. I stumbled across the pasture back to the barn. He told me to get some dry hay and rub my body down with it. Boy, it sure smarted with all the scratches I had, but Reilly made me do it again and again. Then he got some sudsy water and a towel from the milk house and said, "Scrub with this, Caleb, it may help. I used the stuff we sterilize the milk things with, maybe it will help."

I scrubbed and scrubbed. Reilly changed the water and gave me clean towels three times, we finally got enough of it washed off so it didn't choke me but I still smelled so bad that nobody would want to be near me.

Reilly said, "I don't know what else you can do about the smell, Caleb. Maybe your folks will know of something else."

Oh boy! My folks! I had forgotten all about them! It must have been after ten o'clock. It was just then that Josh came running behind the barn. He almost ran into Reilly, saying, "Damn you, Reilly, what happened to Caleb? I had to beat Larry senseless to find out what was going on. Oh God, don't tell me he caught a skunk. Damn you, boys, damn you, damn you, you can't allow even one innocent to survive in your world, can you? Now Mother will probably make him quit his job and he'll be the laughing stock of all the kids in town."

"Take it easy, Josh," Reilly said. "It was only a snipe hunt. Nobody knew about the skunk. Half the kids in town have been on snipe hunts, you know that, Josh, it's part of growing up in the country. Why, some of the boys brag forever how brave they were on their first snipe hunt. I figured an hour was long enough. Those other damn fools were for leaving him all night if he didn't catch on. He caught the skunk before I got back to him, so don't give me hell! Get the other boys if you are that mad. Here, Caleb, here's a shirt I found in the barn. You'll have to wrap a towel around your bottom. I couldn't find any pants. I'll walk with you and Josh to make sure you don't get teased into any fights about how you look or smell. I sure hope someone at your house knows something that can get the smell off you."

We started home with Josh and Reilly walking about fifteen paces ahead of me. Leonard and Arthur were waiting by the store. Leonard hollered, "Did you catch your snipe, Caleb? Hey, Arthur, do you smell what I smell? By God, he caught a skunk! That's why he is wearing those funny clothes."

Leonard broke into a fit of laughter, as if he had just seen the funniest thing. I didn't find it funny and I guessed that Reilly didn't either, because he said, "Knock it off, Leonard, and shut your big mouth, or Josh and I will come back and show you something that you won't find so funny."

When we were close to the house, Mother started hollering, "Is that you, Josh, did you find Caleb?"

Reilly said, "I'll see you, boys, you're on your own from here. I'll go back and have a little talk with those two heroes by the store."

"O.K., Reilly, and thanks. Yes, Mom, we found Caleb, but we have a little trouble. Caleb ran into a skunk out behind the barn. The boys have done everything they could to deskunk him, but he still smells awful. We brought him home to see if you could help."

"Oh Caleb, you poor kid," Mother said. "This is a terrible thing to have happen to you. Take him to the barn, Josh. I'll get the tub and we'll see if we can help him."

Mother came to the barn dragging her big washtub behind her and carrying all kinds of bottles and soap. I sure wasn't in any mood for any more scrubbing, though I had to admit I smelled so bad I couldn't possibly go into the house until I got rid of it somehow. Mother and Josh filled the tub with water and Mother told me to get in. She made the water sudsy and started scrubbing me with a soft brush. The results didn't please her, so she poured in some bleach. Boy! Did that sting on my scratches and other places too!

63

Just then Uncle Louis walked in, saying, "Don't tell me that's the skunk I smell sitting in the tub. What are you using on him, May, is it doing any good? I knew a guy who had this happen to him, he said the only thing he found that helped was tomato juice."

"I don't know, Louis," Mother said, "I wouldn't have enough tomato juice anyway. I do have a couple dozen jars of tomatoes that I canned but I hate to waste them if they don't help."

"I think we'd better give it a try," Uncle Louis replied. "At least we'd better get him out of that bleach before he blisters."

"O.K. Josh, run down to the cellar and get a box of those tomato jars. I'm about ready to try anything. I sure hope it works."

Josh went to get the tomatoes while Uncle and Mother emptied the tub and rinsed it out. When Josh got back they poured the tomatoes in a bucket and mashed them up. First I get covered with skunk piss, rubbed down with hay, washed with sterilizer soap, run half naked through town, bleached, and now I'm having a tomato bath! *Please, God, let me wake up and find this a dream.* I stood there in the middle of the tub while Mother and Uncle Louis scrubbed me with rags covered with tomatoes.

I felt like crying, I needed to be alone with Josh, so I could tell him how brave I was standing out there on the snipe trail and how I used his idea about how to think when I was worried or scared. It really worked and everything would have been all right if that had been a snipe instead of a skunk. *I'll ask Josh to tell me all about snipe so next time I can show them boys what a good snipe hunter I can be. That's if Mother ever lets me out of the house again.*

"Hey," Josh shouted, "I think it's working. Would you believe that, a tomato bath? Boy, Caleb, do you look strange all covered with tomatoes and juice. You look like a warrior staggering home from some great battle."

"Shush, Josh," Mother said, "don't make it any worse than it already is. I don't think we are going to do any better than this, do you, Louis? I still wouldn't want to be in a closed room with him though."

"That's O.K.," Uncle Louis said, "We can put some blankets up in the hay loft for him and I'll stay with him. He should smell better in a couple of days, if we have to we can give him another tomato bath tomorrow."

"Let me stay with him, Uncle Louis," Josh said. "Mother can call me in the morning to go to take care of his milking. He's gonna have to be by himself for a few days."

Mother said, "You are a good brother, Josh. Come in the house and I'll round up some blankets for you both."

Josh came back, threw me an old nightgown and we climbed into the loft to fix the blankets. I told Josh he didn't have to stay with me I would be all right alone. He laughed and said, "Caleb, I don't think I should ever leave you alone again. You just seem to get into one mess after another lately. You're just not safe to be out on your own. I bet you don't even know what happened tonight at all."

"Oh yes, I do, Josh. There was this snipe that was digging holes in the pasture and we set out to catch him, only I caught a skunk instead."

"Caleb, Caleb, my little Caleb. Didn't you ever hear anyone say they got left holding the bag? That was what was supposed to happen to you tonight. There is no snipe. It is only a trick they pull when they can find someone dumb enough to fall for it.

"They take you out in the woods, put you on a make-believe snipe trail, then everyone sneaks home and leaves you out there holding the bag. With your luck though, you had to catch a skunk. If Mother discovers what really happened you will be all done working at Muldon's. She will probably find out too. You know that Larry won't be able to keep his mouth shut, every kid in town will know what happened. Boy, it's going to take some doing for you to live this down, Caleb."

"Oh Josh, I thought they were being good to me by letting me go snipe hunting with them. Now you say it was just another one of their dirty tricks. Josh, you have to help me get even with them."

"No, Caleb, getting even isn't the way," Josh replied. "You have to learn from these things not to be so gullible. Now go to sleep, I have to be at work at five thirty and it's after twelve now."

Josh moved as far away from me as he could in the hayloft and in a few minutes I heard him snoring. It wasn't so easy for me though, there wasn't any way that I could get away from the smell. The longer I lay there not sleeping the meaner my thoughts became. Maybe I was gullible, whatever that meant, but nobody should get away with what those boys pulled on me. They probably put me on a skunk trail on purpose, hoping I would catch one.

I thought about getting Karl, catching each one of them alone and giving them a good beating. After enjoying those thoughts for a while, I began to see the drawbacks. They were all bigger than us and we could get caught alone too. It would only take one of them to beat either Karl or me up. I finally fell asleep and dreamt that I was big and strong and went to the barn and made each of the boys back down from me. It was a strange dream; I didn't fight them. I was so happy that they finally showed me some respect. It was late when I woke up the next morning and the first thing I saw was Homer, Jason, and Francis, my three younger brothers, all sitting on the steps looking up and holding their noses.

At first this made me mad, but they looked so funny sitting there that I started to laugh and said, "What do you think, kids, will the cow ever be able to eat this hay?"

Homer said, "I don't know about her eating the hay, but she was begging to get out early this morning and wants to know if she can stay out tonight."

The boys all started laughing hysterically. As much as my situation bothered me, I could see their point. I know if it had been one of them, I would see the humor in it. Mother came out and hushed the boys, saying, "Caleb, I hope you understand that no matter where you go with that smell it just lingers and lingers. You know we all love you, but until that odor dies down you are going to have to stay out of the house. Josh will stay with you at night and I'll give you your meals on the porch. If there's anything else that you want, we'll try to make it as easy on you as we can."

There was no way I was going to be seen on the porch in this nightgown smelling the way I did, so I said, "Mother, if you don't mind I would rather eat my meals in here." She didn't think that was a good idea, but she was feeling sorry for me so she allowed me to have it my way. After breakfast she insisted that I have another tomato bath. I knew they were helping so I accepted it as a necessary evil.

Homer brought me some comic books and Mother gave me a set of my oldest clothes. I had been reading for a couple of hours when I heard Karl calling, "Caleb, can I come in? I heard what happened and I wanna talk to you."

Karl came into the barn and said, "Wow, Caleb! You still smell pretty strong! Haven't you washed it off yet?"

I told him about the hay and all the baths I had taken. He really laughed when he heard about the tomato baths. I couldn't get mad at him though, Karl was the best friend I ever had and it just got me laughing with him.

"I know, Caleb!" Karl said, "let's go up to the mountain for a while. You probably won't be so hard to take being out in the fresh air, and besides, I think you're going to have to wear that smell off."

"O.K., Karl, I think that might be all right, go ask my mother for me."

Mother thought it was a good idea for me to get out in the air. When I went running across the fields with Karl I could even stand the smell of myself better. Karl brought some apples with him, so we didn't bother to go back for lunch. We ate apples by a small stream running from one of the springs.

We sat there eating Karl's apples and drinking spring water. I told him about the snipe hunt and how Josh had told me it was just a trick.

He laughed and said, "Don't feel so bad, Caleb, I didn't know what a snipe hunt was until just now. I probably would have fallen for it myself."

I told him it wasn't just the snipe hunt, it was all the tricks they kept pulling. They were making me a joke to all the kids in town and I needed to do something dramatic to get even with them. I needed to think up a trick that would make them think twice before they picked on me again.

"I'll help," Karl said. "The two of us should be able to come up with something. Let's go up to the ledges. It's best to stay active when you're thinking. Something might happen that will give us an idea."

We spent the next couple of hours hiking the trails through the ledges. We came to the spot where you could walk out on the ledge and look straight down over a hundred feet. I walked out and looked down. It made me feel almost as dizzy as the night I drank the home brew. I told Karl about it. "That's it, Caleb!" he shouted. "Remember how you were supposed to bring the boys some home brew. What if we doctor up a couple of bottles and they all get very sick or drunk from it?"

"I dunno, Karl, I wouldn't want to do anything to hurt them permanently. Just something to let them know I'm not as dumb as they think I am. How would we fix the home brew anyway?"

"I wouldn't tell anybody else, Caleb, but my dad comes home quite often with a bottle of vodka. I think that if Mother let him, he would drink the whole bottle before he stopped. Mother waits until he is feeling the booze, then she takes a little out of the bottle at a time and puts it into a jar. After the bottle gets near empty she hides the jar. I know where she hid quite a few of them. If we mixed that with the home brew that should fix them real good."

"Are you sure that won't hurt them?" I asked.

"Don't worry, Caleb, they're much older than you, and they won't be any worse off than you were the night that you drank home brew with them."

It took ten days and more tomato baths before I was finally without that skunk smell. Karl and I spent that time working on our "get-even plan," trying to make sure the plan went smoothly.

We planned to have Karl come to the barn the night I brought the home brew and tell me to hurry and finish because there were some girls waiting for me. I wasn't too keen on that story, but Karl was sure they would buy it in a minute, so I agreed.

We decided that we should make a test on how to mix the vodka and home brew. One night after I came home, I went down in the cellar and put a couple of bottles out in the cellar window, then went out and hid them in the stone wall behind the house.

The next day I took one of the bottles and went to Lute Pond to meet Karl. He wasn't there yet, so I started skipping stones. I was just getting warmed up to where I could get ten or twelve skips to a stone, when I saw Karl coming. He wasn't alone. Robby Bolts was with him. Robby was Karl's older sister's boyfriend. He and his family lived in the center of the town. He used to work milking at the Muldons', but he and Larry were always fighting and after he had slapped Larry around one too many times he was fired. I didn't know why he was here, so I ran and hid the home brew.

Karl seemed all excited and hollered, "It's all right, Caleb, Robby is going to help us fix the home brew. He caught me sneaking out with the vodka and was afraid you and I were going to drink it. So I had to tell him the truth, now he wants to get in on it too."

I wasn't too happy about this. I had wanted this to be my own get-even trick. Then I thought, there is more than one of them, so it's only fair that I have a little help. Robby was bigger and stronger than all those boys except Reilly and that might come in handy if they got too mad at me. Karl had a small jar that looked like water.

I got the home brew and using a scout knife, I started to open the bottle. I had just loosened the cap a little when it popped and blew off. The beer was all foaming out of the bottle. I tried to cap it with my hand.

Robby yelled, "Set it on the ground, Caleb!" I set it down and waited for it to stop foaming. By the time it did most half of the bottle was gone.

Robby said, "It's probably too green and won't be any good until it's aged a lot longer."

Karl poured some of the vodka into the bottle and after mixing it gently, taking a swig, he spit it back out, saying, "Wow! That's strong, it would probably do the trick nicely, but I doubt that any one would be dumb enough to drink it."

Robby said, "Let a man try that."

He tipped the bottle up and had two or three good swallows before he put it down. He gasped for breath. Wiping tears from his eyes he said, "Wowee! Not even them dumbbells would take a second drink of something like that. That vodka must be one hundred proof and the home brew is greener than grass. Don't worry though, boys, my dad has a barrel of hard cider at home. I'll take some of Karl's vodka and mix it with that, and as soon as I get it mixed right I'll give a few bottles to Caleb. You boys have a good idea here and it's too good not to go through with it. I'll make sure the mix is strong enough to do the trick."

Three nights later Robby and Karl met me when I was on my way to work and handed me three bottles that Robby had fixed up. Robby said, "The clear bottle is weaker than the other two, so see if you can get them to start on that one first."

When I got to the barn nobody was there, so I hid the bottles outside behind the watering trough by the pasture door. The boys came in. They were in a good mood, laughing and joking about something that had happened between Arthur and Thelma Bragg. They were telling him, "You're dumb, dumb, dumb! Arthur, we wouldn't miss a chance like that."

He didn't seem to mind though, he just laughed and said, "Maybe not, but you're going to miss what I got set up tonight."

They all seemed so happy and full of good fun tonight that I began to feel guilty about our plans. We had almost finished milking when Karl came in hollering for me. I answered and he came over acting all excited. He was loud enough for some of the boys to hear when he said, "Caleb, boy! Do we have a good thing lined up! There are some girls over at the swings who asked me to find you for them. How much longer are you going to be?"

I told him we were almost done milking but I had something planned with the boys after we were through.

"Oh come on, Caleb," Larry cried, "that's just an excuse, Karl. He's probably afraid of the girls. I'll go with you."

"No, look, Larry, it's the truth," I said. "I didn't want to say anything because I wanted it to be a surprise. I brought three bottles of hard cider for tonight after we got done milking."

"Hey," Leonard said, "if that's true, Caleb, you run on to your little girls with Karl and we'll finish your stripping when John gets done milking."

"That's swell of you boys, Karl and I will get it and have a little taste before we leave." We found the clear bottle and each took a little taste, then poured some of it out before we took the bottles to John.

Karl said, "Boy, that is good cider! I think it might be fun to stay here, Caleb, where did you get that stuff?"

"It's something my Uncle Louis made. Maybe you're right, Karl, and we should stay and have some more."

Larry said, "Hey! Why don't you boys bring the girls over here? Maybe they like cider too."

"That's a good idea," Karl replied. "Come on, Caleb, let's see if we can talk them into it, maybe we can find a couple of more girls and come back and have a real party."

We hurried out of the barn feeling very proud of ourselves. Karl wanted to sneak back, I really didn't dare. I knew if they caught us they would make us drink too, and I couldn't afford to let that happen again.

The next morning when I got to the barn, Reilly and his father were there. Reilly sure looked a little on the hangdog side, but he grinned at me.

Then his father said, "By Golly Moses, boy, I'm glad to see that you didn't get mixed up in that tomfoolery that went on here last night. I just don't know what it is with kids these days. In my day we would have never dared to do things like that."

Reilly kind of laughed and said, "You know, Pa, I think there were a couple of kids mixed up in that trick, as you call it, that thought they were gonna die."

"Serves them right," old Joe said. "Serves them right. Say, Caleb, do you think you can get Josh over here? Don and Leon are on their way over, but that's still gonna leave us short handed. The way I hear it, you and Reilly are the only ones of the regulars who are going to show up this morning. It seems like those other damn fools got some hard cider last night and tried to drink themselves to death."

I went home and woke Josh telling him that Golly Moses wanted him at the barn because most of the crew was out sick. I ran back to the barn, not waiting for Josh. I knew he would start asking questions that I didn't want to answer right then. I sure felt good about our plan and how well it had worked. I guess we'd showed them!

The Muldons, Leon, Don and Golly Moses finished the machine milking and left Reilly, Josh and me to take care of the stripping. After they left, Reilly said, "You sure pulled a good one last night, Caleb. What the hell did you put in that cider anyway? That wasn't just some cider that your Uncle Louis had made. You almost got me too, I began to realize along towards the second bottle there was something wrong. There wasn't that much cider considering that there were five of us drinking for us to feel it so quick.

"When I started to feel it soon after we opened the second bottle I quit. I tried to warn the rest of them, but they wouldn't listen. You should have seen the mess we had here. John crawled into the hay and went to sleep. Leonard got sick as a dog. Larry fell into the gutter. Arthur went to help him out, but they both ended up covered with manure. You never saw such a sight, they smelled almost as bad as you did the night you caught the skunk.

"I don't know how, because he was so sick, but Leonard staggered out to go home. Somewhere in the middle of the town Uncle Don saw him and came roaring over to the barn looking for Larry. I heard him coming and hid out by the pasture door. Larry was still unconscious. You know him, he thinks he should have the lion's share of everything. Arthur was staggering around, but all he could say to Uncle Don's questions was, 'Larry can't hold his cider, just can't drink it.'

"I thought, *Bet he won't be so smart tomorrow.* Uncle Don got a burlap bag, wiped some of the manure off from Larry then dragged him out and threw him into the back of his pickup, cursing all the while. He hollered for Arthur to come along, but Arthur kept mumbling, 'Got to stay, help poor

John, can't leave him alone, he might get sick like Lenny, ha ha, was that Leonard sick.'

"Uncle Don came back into the barn madder than a hornet yelling, 'Sledge, get your ass into the pickup before I kick it all the way out there for you.'

"Arthur was trying to get up in the hay where John was, still mumbling, 'Gotta save old John.' Uncle Don went flying after him, by the time he caught him Arthur had gotten to where John was.

"When Don saw John, the air turned blue with his cursing, some of the like that I never heard before. He got Arthur and John loaded in the pickup with Larry and took off swearing. I went home and snuck to my room. I heard Dad come to check on me a little later so I knew he must have heard from Uncle Don, but I pretended that I was asleep, hoping he wouldn't smell the cider on me. What the hell was in those bottles anyway, Caleb?"

Karl and I thought that it might come to this and had decided to play innocent. I knew it was going to be harder with Josh there. He had been giving me strange looks while Reilly was telling the story, but I tried anyway.

"I dunno what happened Reilly. It was just some cider I borrowed off my uncle. Maybe he makes it different than other people. I just wanted to bring something so Leonard and the rest of them would stop bugging me all the time about me owing them a drink. I've been sneaking bottles out and when I had three I figured that would be enough, so last night I brought them over, that's all I know, honest."

"Caleb," Josh said, "I don't believe my ears. You've been stealing off Uncle Louis, as good as he has been to you? After we get done here you and I are going to have a little talk. I'm ashamed of you."

"I'll tell you one thing, Josh," Reilly said, "I don't think that the boys are going to be bugging Caleb about another drink for quite a while. I wished there was some of that drink left so I could figure out what was in it. I still don't believe that Caleb is all that innocent about what happened. I guess he owed us one though."

When we left the barn Josh said, "O.K. Caleb, out with it. I know that Uncle Louis doesn't have any hard cider." I hated to tell him what really had happened, but I didn't see any way not to, so I told him the whole story. I told him about how Karl and Robby had supplied the drink, how we practiced mixing it and how Karl and I had snuck off before they started drinking.

Josh gave me a lecture on how wrong this had been and how it would just escalate. They would try bettering me next time. He said that this was what was wrong with the world, everybody trying to beat the other guy at something and nobody was taking time to be himself or herself. So instead of having a world of brotherhood, we had a world of selfishness and war. I didn't always understand Josh when he talked like that. I only knew that it felt better being on the giving end for a change.

The summer ended and I returned to my sixth year at school with the reputation, though I denied it with a smile, as the hero who had shot the Muldon crew down.

Chapter 6

Returning to school, the sixth grade and Old Hanna was something I had avoided thinking about most of the summer, but Labor Day came, signaling the end of summer, and the start of a new school year. Starting school didn't seem as bad that year. We had the excitement of George returning. Many of the children hadn't seen George since he was injured, so of course the story was told and retold. It sure didn't hurt my pride any to hear George telling about my fish and how I had come and held him just before he passed out. Of course some of the boys were still talking about how the Muldon crew got shot down after they had set me on a skunk trail while on a snipe hunt. When they asked about it, I would just laugh and say it was only some wine that my uncle had made. Karl and I had decided not to let the truth out even though we were sorely tempted. I hadn't had any trouble from Larry or the other boys about what had happened, so we thought it best to keep our secret.

George had been moved to the sixth grade along with the rest of our class. He never told us, but it seems that Old Hanna had been going to his house to tutor him. I understood why George didn't say anything about Hanna being there. She had stayed with the Phelpses off and on during the summer. I was glad it wasn't me though. How awful that must have been for poor George having Old Hanna living right with him.

The girls seemed different somehow that year. Beverly Stone would run up and say, "How about a little interest on those pennies, Caleb," then she would grab me and kiss me and try to hug me, but I usually got away.

Karl would say, "Hey! Beverly, how about me?" When she kissed him he would hold her just as long as he could. She would start giggling and wriggle away from him with her face all red. She would run away laughing and Karl would stand there breathing heavy, saying, "Boy! She's getting quite a build. Do you know that, Caleb?" I didn't know why Beverly excited him so much, because she really scared me. Karl and Beverly were seventh graders, and I guess that's what made them different than me. I did like the way Joan held my hand and the little kisses she gave me when I bought her the ice cream. I wasn't scared of her, because she didn't hold on to me the way Beverly did.

My sister Emma was in the eighth grade. One time when she saw Beverly kiss me she gave me a lecture on the way home from school about fooling around with the wrong kind of girls. I didn't argue with her. There wasn't any use in trying to tell Emma that I considered almost all girls to be the wrong kind, especially sisters that butted into my business. I knew if I got her mad she would talk to Mother and I would catch it. So, I just said, "Don't worry about me, Emma. I'll watch out for Beverly. She scares me anyway." She seemed satisfied with that and ran ahead to catch up with Patsy Wilson.

Patsy and Emma were in the same grade in school and they enjoyed spending their free time together. I don't know why though, Patsy was so different from Emma. She was kind and gentle and reminded me of Josh. I guess they were much alike, because I had seen Patsy and Josh holding hands and taking long walks and reading poetry. They always seemed so peaceful that you hated to disturb them. The Wilson place was north of town on the road that went to George's house. Patsy had one older sister and three younger brothers. The one next to her in age was Jake, who was in my class at school. Jake and I had never hit it off; he was one of those brainy types who always seemed to have the right answer. The teachers of course were always using him for an example of what they expected from the rest of us. That sure didn't help make any friends for Jake. He wasn't very good at sports or roughhousing, so we used to get even with him every time we got a chance out in the field. I have to admit that he took his licking a lot better out there than some of us did in the classroom.

One time when Karl and I were talking about Jake, Karl said, "Maybe we don't want to believe it, but Jake has a bigger heart than most of us, no matter what's going on." This was something that I got a chance to learn firsthand that year. Hanna gave our class an assignment to write a first-person story, on some meaningful experience in our lives. Most of the boys were quite upset about having to write anything. I found it easy to write what I felt, so I wrote a very emotional account of how I felt on the day that George, Karl and I had gone on our fishing trip. I tried to describe my emotions on going from the elation of catching the biggest fish I ever saw to the trauma of holding a battered and bloody friend in my arms as he slowly drifted off into unconsciousness. After I passed my paper in, Old Hanna asked me to stay after school for a few minutes. When Old Hanna asked, that was law, so of course I stayed. After everyone was gone, Hanna said, "Caleb, why don't you come up front so we can talk easier?" I moved up front, to the closest desk to hers and said, "I'm sorry, Miss Cullings, if my paper isn't too good. Maybe I can do it over better."

She smiled and said, "Caleb, your paper is good; in fact, it is better than good, in all my years of teaching I have seldom seen anyone in your age group that possessed the talent of making the written word so feeling. Why I asked you to stay was because you need help with your grammar. I believe that you will eventually learn the proper mechanics of writing, but if you were interested I have a program in mind that will help you advance sooner. What I have in mind is for you to work with Jake Wilson once or twice a week. Jake has great ability in grammar and you have a talent for writing emotionally, I am sure that if you work together you both will benefit."

I wasn't crazy about taking on extra schoolwork, but I didn't dare tell Old Hanna no. Jake was all for it, and I ended up spending more and more time with him. We actually stayed after school sometimes on our own to discuss some things with Hanna. I suppose that was the beginning of what became my career, though at the time I never thought of it that way. Jake used to get so excited about what he called my ability to emotionalize the facts. Jake tried to instill in me the belief that punctuation and proper form were necessary tools to a good writer. Old Hanna kept saying that she saw improvement every time I wrote an article. Over the years though, I have met many an editor who would violently disagree with her. The good thing that developed over this period was my friendship with Jake. I could talk with Jake about things that I couldn't with Karl or George. We even talked about this sex thing. He explained about what he called the age of puberty. I asked him if he had reached that age yet and he said no, and he wasn't too sure he wanted to. I told him what Josh had told me and how at first I thought it was going to be fun, but now, like him, I was rather scared. It seemed to me that it caused problems for the boys who had reached that age. Jake urged me to write a paper on how I felt about sex. He said, "No one will ever have to see it, Caleb. It's just when you write it comes out much better than just talking about it." I tried writing about sex, but Jake never got to see it. When I read it over it sounded more confused than I felt so I tore it up and threw it away. The time spent with Jake and the thrill of having him so excited about our writing helped make school easier than it had ever been. If it was possible to happen to a boy, I think I was starting to like school, at least part of it.

My oldest sister, Eunice, landed an office job at the Stuart Tool Company in Oscin. She was able to ride back and forth to work with Mr. Wilson, Patsy's father, who worked there in the factory. He had a big old Packard car and had three other riders besides my sister. Two of them, Ross Bolts and Stanley Braggs, worked at the Lange Shoe shop. Not everyone in Sterling had cars, most of the ones that did, carried riders, like Mr. Wilson, to help with the expenses.

The tool company in Oscin was in the process of adding a new four-story addition to the factory buildings. The steel workers that were erecting the skeleton of the building were an outfit that had been brought in from Oklahoma, and most of the laborers were Indians. We had never seen a real Indian before, so Karl and I made plans to thumb to Oscin so we could see them. Mother found out about our plan and that was the end of that. One night when I heard my sisters talking about the Indians, I snuck over by their bedroom door and listened.

I heard Hester say, "Oh, Eunice, you mean you actually sat and had lunch with him? Is he an Indian?"

"Not a real Indian," Eunice replied, "but he does have Indian blood and he's built like the rest of them, with the narrow waist and broad shoulders. Every time I see him way up there walking those steel beams, my heart just about bursts. Oh, Hester, I think I am in love with him."

"Oh, Eunice," cried Hester, "don't talk like that, Dad will kill you. You know how he is about boys. You only sat on a bench with him and ate lunch, how can you be in love with him? You don't even know what he's really like or anything at all about him."

"I don't know, Hester. I only know how I feel when I see him and am with him. I felt so alive and wonderful just talking to him. He made me really feel like, like a woman. Oh, Harry Jackstone, I do love you. I can hardly wait until lunch tomorrow. Oh Hester, Hester, don't look so worried, be happy for me."

"How can I be happy, Eunice? I've never seen you this way. You were never crazy like this before about a boy. I am scared, Eunice. I'm scared you will do something stupid with this Harry that you will always regret. You have to remember that he's a total stranger who will probably be gone out of your life before you even get to really know him."

"I know, Hester, I know, that's why I have to rush things. I'm going to get him to ask me out Saturday night when we have lunch tomorrow. Then maybe next week I'll bring him to the house for supper if Mom will let me."

Hester said, "Eunice, you really have it bad, don't you? I can't believe what you're planning, please don't tell me any more. I already feel that it's my duty to tell Mother, but I won't. I'll just say a prayer for you. Good night, Eunice, and God be with you, you sure are going to need His company."

Saturday night came. I kept hoping all week I would have a chance to see Eunice's Indian. When I got home from milking Eunice was gone but nobody said anything about it, so I guessed that her friend didn't show up to take her out. When I saw Hester alone I asked her what had happened to Eunice's Indian. She grabbed me by my shirt and practically dragged me upstairs. Josh came out of our room to see what the commotion was. He said, "Hester, what's going on? What did Caleb do to you?"

"He hasn't done anything to me," Hester replied. "He knows something about Eunice's new friend and I didn't want him blabbing about it where Dad could hear him. You know what will happen to Eunice if Dad finds out she is out with a boy who she didn't even let come to the house to pick her up, don't you?"

"You're right about Dad," Josh said, "but you don't have to drag Caleb around like that; all you have to do is ask him to be quiet about it."

"Maybe it's all right for you to trust Caleb, Josh, but us girls can't. You know he is always pulling tricks that get us in trouble with Mom and Dad. How did he know about Eunice's friend anyway? That was supposed to be a secret that only you and I knew, and here he is running around asking where Eunice's Indian is. Here, you take him and make him understand if you think your way is so much better. But I warn you, Caleb, if you cause Eunice any trouble about this I'll get you for it."

Josh and I went into our room. I asked, "What the heck is the matter with her? I didn't say anything in front of anybody, I waited until she was alone. I don't want to make any trouble for Eunice, I just wanted to see her Indian."

"Now look, Caleb," Josh said. "First of all, Hester is very worried about Eunice, that is why she is so cross. Second, he isn't an Indian, and don't you mention that again. It's going to be bad enough around here with him being a complete stranger from so far away. If Dad ever gets to thinking he's an Indian, God only knows what will happen. You know he has forbidden letting half the boys in town visit with your sisters, imagine how he is going to be about this boy. I think we all should do as much as we can to make it easier for Eunice. I talked to her about Harry and she really has it bad for him and it is going to be a lot better if we can have Harry associated with the family than it is to have her sneaking off to see him alone, like tonight. I want you to be quiet about anything you know. I have talked with Eunice and she promised to bring Harry home and introduce him to the family as soon as she can, so let's all give her a decent chance."

The weekend went by without any big uproar from Dad, so I guessed that Eunice's secret stayed safe. On Tuesday just before I left to go to Muldon's barn, I heard Eunice pleading with Mother.

"Please, Mother, you have to help me I want to do what's right, Dad just has to let me bring my friends home. You know how everyone is always talking about Thelma Bragg and the way she is always meeting her boyfriends away from her house. They're even saying she spent most of the night with Frank Butler. I don't want people talking like that about me, but I need to be with Harry, Mother. I think I'm truly in love with him."

"Watch your mouth, daughter. If your father ever heard you talk like that he would lock you in your room every night for a year. I know that you're right, Eunice. You should be able to bring your men friends home. It's the proper way. Let me have a couple of days to work on Dad and I'll see if I can arrange it so you can invite him to supper on Thursday or Friday night. Dad will come and talk to you about Harry. You'd better be careful what you say, especially about how you feel. Just tell him that you are over twenty years old now and that you want your family's opinion about all your friends and be able to entertain them at your home like a proper young lady. We have a few plump young roosters in the hen house that are going to have to be separated from Big Red pretty soon. Maybe we can use a couple of them for a dinner for your new friend."

Eunice jumped up and threw her arms around Mother in a big hug, saying, "I love you, Mother. I'm so lucky to have a mother so understanding. I hope I can always make you as proud of me as a daughter."

I felt good about what I had heard. Eunice was right, we did have an understanding mother. Who else's mother would stand up for their son and husband the way she always did about Big Red? He was the king tyrant of our hen house. He would not only start fighting with the young roosters as soon as they became big enough to crow, but he would tackle anyone who came into get eggs if they were dumb enough to turn their backs on him. My sisters and brothers had been trying for a long time to get Dad to let Mother make Big Red into chicken stew. My dad always said that every family needed a strong head and Big Red was the head of the hen house so we had better keep him. Mother and I would be the only ones in the family that would agree with Dad. She would always say, "Now, children, your dad's right. Every hen house needs a strong rooster to keep order, so you all will have to learn to cope with Big Red."

I didn't hear much about Harry Jackstone the next few days. Friday night, when I was just finishing my supper (Mother often had supper earlier for me because I had to be at the barn by five thirty), I heard something come roaring down the road making so much noise that I didn't know what it was. I ran out on the porch with Homer and Jason close behind me. That's how Harry Jackstone came roaring into our lives, on a motorcycle. Eunice was sitting behind him, holding on tight with both arms. You could see that he wasn't an Indian. He was dark, but not much darker than most of the town boys in the summer. He was big, standing well over six feet tall, and had the broadest shoulders. He was wearing tight-legged pants, half boots and a real leather jacket that had zippers on the sleeves and pockets. The bottom of the jacket was studded all the way around with silver eagles. I figured Eunice was right about Harry. Boy, that's the way I wanted to look when I grew up. Eunice straightened her hair and clothes while Harry set the motorcycle on its stand, then they came up on the porch.

"Boys!" Eunice said, "I want you to meet Harry Jackstone. Harry, the biggest one here is Caleb. Next is Homer, and the third one is Jason. The one you see peeking out of the barn with the dirty face is Francis."

Harry stuck out his hand and said, "Now, let's see if I got you all straight. It's Caleb, Homer, Jason, and the little one playing peekaboo is Francis. You boys must have some times, the four of you all so close together. I never had any brothers, got me a couple of sisters though. Let me go in and say hi to the rest of your family, and then maybe we can have a game of stick ball or something."

His soft, drawling way of talking made you feel as if we had always been friends. For the first time in a long time I started to feel bad about having to go to work. I hung back until I knew I was going to be late, hoping he would hurry up and come back out. I had just started up the road when Harry came out on the porch. He said, "Come on, boys, let's play your favorite game, hey! Caleb, don't you want to play with us?"

I told him I would like to, but I had to help with the milking at Muldon's and I was already late.

"Hey, that's probably my fault, let me ask your mom if it's O.K. to take you to work on my bike."

I didn't believe Mother would let me, but he came out running to his motorcycle, hollering, "Come on, Caleb, it's O.K." Wow, This was going to be something riding into Muldon's on a motorcycle. I climbed behind him. He showed me where to put my feet and how to hold on to the seat on each side, and with a roar I was off on my first motorcycle ride. The boys at the barn all came running out when they heard the noise. Harry wheeled his bike around in front of the barn and let me off, hollering, "See y'all later, Caleb." He roared out of the barnyard with the front wheel up off the ground.

"Hey, Caleb!" Reilly said. "Who's your new cowboy friend? Is he going to be around long? I sure would like to learn to ride a bike like that."

"How about it, Caleb?" Larry asked. "Do you think you can get him to give us a ride?"

"I might, boys, I just might," I answered. "I have a feeling that Harry and I are going to be good friends."

That night at the barn was one of the best nights I ever had there. Having someone like Harry for a friend really made me somebody with the rest of the boys. Even though they were all older than I was, they probably had never ridden on a motorcycle. This was only the third one I had seen. The only one

I knew about in town was the one over in Leon Muldon's repair shop, where they fixed the farm machinery. It belonged to Frank Butler. Story was that he got drunk the day he bought it; hit a tree with it on his way home and they said the bike was beyond repair. I rushed home after I finished milking, hoping to see Harry again, but he and Eunice had gone for a walk around town. I suppose that Eunice wanted the rest of the girls in town to see her courting with him. I got Josh upstairs so I could ask him what happened when Harry met Dad.

"Dad really put the pressure on him at first," he said. "He asked Harry where he was from, how far he had gone in school; if the job he had now was always going to be his line of work, how much longer he felt he would be on the Oscin job, did he know where he would be working next? Harry talked right up to Dad. He said he had been born in Nebraska and his family moved to Oklahoma when he was seven. That he had gone to school for ten years and had hopes of going back. He said that he took the job he had now because the pay was very good and he liked the traveling that was giving him experiences that he felt would be helpful to him when he decided to settle down and raise his own family. After supper he sat and talked to Dad while the girls were cleaning up and doing dishes. I think he came as close to winning Dad over as any boy will. They had a long talk about motorcycles. Dad was pretty much against them, but he finally agreed to let all the children, except the youngest, have a ride with him. Harry really argued for that. He told Dad that he was a very experienced rider and he was twice as careful when he carried a passenger. Dad said, 'O.K., Harry, now I want you to know the rest of the rules around here. The girls have to make sure we always know where they are and who they're with, and Eunice has to be in no later than eleven thirty unless we have made other arrangements.'

"Harry said, 'Don't worry, Mr. Carney, Eunice and I won't break any rules.' Dad excused himself, saying he had chores to attend to. Harry came out and asked me if I wanted a ride.

"Eunice stopped him with, 'Harry, who did you come to see, the boys or me?'

"Harry laughed and said, 'I guess it will have to be another time, Josh.' Then he and Eunice took off for a walk. So now you have the whole story, Caleb. How was your ride? I can hardly wait to get on that Indian."

"Josh, I thought you told me not to mention the word when I was talking about Harry."

Josh laughed and said, "Not him, Caleb, the motorcycle. That's the brand name. You know, like Mr. Wilson's car is a Packard. Harry's motorcycle is an Indian, built by the Indian Motorcycle Company. That's why they call them Indians. I have some papers to finish for school, Caleb. So I'll see you tomorrow."

The next few weeks Harry was at the house. More and more the whole family, with the exception of my dad, was talking as if Harry was the best thing that ever happened in our family. He not only gave our family rides on his bike, but he took half the kids in town riding. We never had so many friends. He even spent time with Reilly explaining the best way to ride a bike. After a couple of weeks he even allowed Reilly to drive the bike while he rode behind, telling him what to do. He wouldn't allow anyone to ride it without him. He explained that he had too much of himself invested in it to have it damaged by someone else. I know that most of the boys in town understood that. Harry became the idol of nearly every boy in town. We all wanted to grow up and be like Harry. Our conversations always came around to "when I grow up and go to Oklahoma, Nebraska, Wyoming, Texas"—and all the other places Harry talked about. Harry might have been the idol of the boys, but Eunice was the envy of all the girls in town and she sure got some competition. I noticed that some of the girls only got to ride with Harry once no matter how much they teased or flirted. Hester used to say she thought that Harry was more in love with his motorcycle than he was with Eunice. That might have been so, but he sure put Eunice in front of all the other girls that were after him. Eunice always seemed more proud of Harry than jealous of him. One of Harry's problems was my sister Emma. She was what the boys called well developed, and she was constantly after Harry. She managed to get more rides than anyone else in the family. I don't blame Harry, it was the only way he could get her to stop bugging him. Emma was always a terror until she got her own way.

One night when I got home from the barn I heard Eunice in her room sobbing her heart out. I knocked and asked what was wrong.

Hester said, "Just leave her alone, Caleb, she doesn't want to talk to anyone right now."

About an hour later Josh came in, I asked him, "Why is everyone was so upset?"

"Upset isn't half the word for it," Josh said. "Dad kicked Harry out of the house and told him never to come back again. I have been trying to tell Emma to leave Harry alone but she just laughed and asked me if I was jealous. Well, tonight she finally did it. When Harry got back from taking you to the barn she ran out and jumped on the back of his bike and made him take her for a ride. I was standing on the porch when they got back. While Harry was still putting the bike on its stand Emma jumped up, put her arms

81

around him and started kissing him. The bike fell, taking Harry with it. Emma held on to Harry still kissing him. When Dad came across the field from work, there was Emma lying on top of Harry and his bike. You know Dad hasn't been too happy with the girls all going crazy over Harry and that was the last straw. He was purple with rage. He shouted at Emma, 'Get into your room and stay there.' Emma scooted for her room and Dad said, 'Now, Mr. Blackstone, you take your lousy bike and whatever gear you have around here and leave. I am only going to say this once. There isn't anything for us to talk about, so hear me good. In five minutes I want you out of this yard and never, as long as I live, let me see you here again.'

"Harry tried to talk, but Dad was as mad as I had ever seen him. He shouted so loudly I bet they heard him across town, 'You have just four minutes left and at the end of that time I'll take a club to you and an ax to that damn machine.' Eunice came running out of the house. Dad yelled, 'You go back in the house, young lady.' Eunice sobbed, 'No, no, no, Dad, I won't leave Harry alone in this.'

"Harry said, 'You do as he says, Eunice. He is your father.' Mother came out and took one look at the situation and knew that this was no time to interfere, so she led Eunice, sobbing, back into the house. Harry picked up his bike while trying to talk to Dad. Dad said, 'I said git, boy.'

"Boy, did he go, he fired up that old Indian, and by the time he was out of sight I bet he was doing a hundred. Dad started to the barn. I tried to tell him that Harry hadn't done anything wrong. He glared at me and said, 'I'm Big Red in this house Josh, everyone'd better understand that.' The only thing he has said since was at the supper table when he said, 'I never want to hear that boy's name mentioned in this house again.' Eunice ran up to her room sobbing. I guess she had hoped that she could talk to Dad after we had eaten, but she's been lying in her room crying every since. None of the rest of us felt much like eating, so one by one we excused ourselves from the table, and of course nobody has dared mention Harry again."

I undressed and crawled into bed with my mind a boiling mass of confusion. Harry was no longer to be a part of our life, no more bike rides, no more would I be the envy of all my friends, nor would we be hearing the stories about all the places that Harry had been. *Damn that Emma, she can cause more trouble than all my sisters put together.* I fell asleep feeling that the best part of my world had ended.

The next couple of weeks things returned to normal around the house. Of course we missed Harry, but nobody spoke about it. I noticed after a few days even Eunice didn't seem too upset. The next Saturday morning when everyone usually slept late, except Mother, who had to get me off to work, my father woke me up earlier than usual, he was yelling at the foot of the stairs.

"Hester, get down to the kitchen right now. Do you hear me, girl?"

Hester answered with a weak, "I'm coming, Dad."

I heard Dad stomping back to the kitchen. I knew by the tone of his voice that something terrible must have happened. Quick as I could, I got dressed and ran downstairs. I caught up with Hester in the hallway and followed her into the kitchen. Mother was at the kitchen table trying to stem a flow of tears with her apron. Dad was pacing the floor, his face a mask of fury.

"Where is your sister, Hester? Where is Eunice? Why didn't you tell us what was going on? How could you be a party to a plot against your own mother and father? Answer me, girl, can't you hear me? I'm asking you a question."

I could see how scared Hester was and I didn't blame her. I got a couple of whippings when Dad was mad, but I had never seen him this mad before. Hester was trying to talk, but she couldn't seem to speak and Dad just kept yelling at her.

Mother said, "Take it easy on her, Tom. I don't believe she even knows what you're talking about, give her a chance to answer."

Dad quieted down and Hester said, "Dad, I don't know where Eunice is, she was there when I went to sleep. I heard her get up in the middle of the night. I thought she was just going to the toilet. I fell back to sleep and the next thing I hear is you yelling for me to come to the kitchen."

Dad grabbed a piece of paper off the table and shoved it at Hester, saying, "You mean to tell me that you don't know anything about this?" Hester unfolded the paper and started to read it. As I was standing on the threshold of the other room I was able to read over her shoulder, it was only fair because it was addressed:

Dear Mom, Dad and family.

Though I know what I'm doing will not seem as much proof of it, I love you all very dearly, even you, Dad. I tried to put myself in your place with your background, then I understood that it was your love for your children that made you do what you did. I pray that someday you will be able to understand why I did what I am doing and Harry and I will be welcome in your heart.

I have not disgraced you, Dad, Harry and I were married in a little chapel in Oscin Wednesday afternoon, and we are leaving this morning for Oklahoma. Harry wanted to come and talk to you, Dad, I felt that at this time it would only cause more trouble in the family,

so I persuaded him not to. We only had two weeks left before he had to return to Oklahoma, we both knew we could not live apart, so we decided this would be the best answer. I will miss you all very much and will write when we get settled, please understand and forgive us.
    Your Loving Daughter,
    Eunice.

As Hester put down the note I noticed she was crying. She walked over to Dad, put her arms around him and with her head on his chest, sobbed, "Oh, Dad, I wouldn't have wanted her to go if I had known. I loved her so much I thought we were too close for her to keep something from me. What are we going to do, Dad, what are we going to do?"

The scowl of rage had left Dad's face and he said, "I guess there isn't much we can do. Eunice has chosen her way. We can only ask that God help us and her too." Dad led Hester over to Mom and went out to the shed. The sadness and pain on his face tore at my heart. As I left the kitchen I met Josh. He asked what all the commotion was about.

Mother said, "Read the note on the table, Josh, it's for the whole family. It's the way she wanted it."

As Josh was reading the note I went back upstairs to get my shoes when I went by Uncle Louis. He asked, "What's going on out there, Caleb? Should I go out?"

"Maybe you should, Uncle Louis. Eunice ran off and got married."

Uncle Louis chuckled and said, "Now I know whose suitcase that was under the stairs. You know, boy, I believe she made the right move. I have always felt that Harry was a man who had a lot of get-up-and-go and I think he and Eunice will carve quite a mark for themselves in life. I'll go out and talk to May and your dad and see if I can help. I'm sure your mother will be able to accept this easily enough, and maybe someday your dad can forgive Harry for challenging the Big Red image he sometime uses in his belief in what is right."

I rushed upstairs to get my shoes with Uncle Louis's words about Big Red sticking in my mind. As I came running back down I asked, "Uncle Louis, don't you believe it's right to be the toughest and strongest when you're the head of the flock?"

He looked at me and smiled, saying, "Caleb, I'm not saying that your dad is wrong. It's just that Big Red has only pure instinct to operate with and he's a champion at using his instincts. Man has a reasoning mind and doesn't have to react on instinct alone. For man to become a true champion he has to use all the abilities that God has given him. You can be assured that your father is a champion. It's just hard for some men to accept that there is a need for their children to have a life of their own, even at the cost of breaking family ties. Give your dad a little time and he will hack it."

I went running to Muldon's barn with my head full. As I moved from cow to cow doing my stripping, I tried to put my mind to rest by sorting out what had happened. Mother and Dad had always defended Big Red's way. I fought to keep him because I have always been able to handle him better than anyone else in the family, except Dad. I guess it was my pride in this, rather than the respect for him, that made me defend his position. Dad used anger and force to control situations, but not like Big Red. He had actually killed four young roosters that we had left in with him too long. I wondered what Uncle Louis had meant by Dad's Big Red image. Dad surely wasn't capable of killing someone like Harry, even if he sounded as if he wanted to sometimes. I thought about Eunice and what Uncle Louis had said about the cost of breaking family ties. As much as I liked Harry, I couldn't see her leaving the family even for him. All of a sudden it came to me. It had to be that damn sex thing that was happening to everybody that made Eunice run away with Harry. I needed to talk this over with Josh. *If sex is going to cause this kind of trouble, I hope I never reach that age of puberty that everyone was trying to explain to me. Oh Lord, how can I escape? Josh says that it happens to everybody and Josh is always right.* As I left the barn that night I thought how much more fun it was to fish and run on the mountain with Karl than it was to understand what older people believe. I had just passed the horse trough when I heard Karl.

"Hey, Caleb, wait up. I want to talk to you."

I hadn't seen him because I was walking along with my head down in deep thought, but there he was with Beverly. They both had their skates over their shoulders, walking hand and hand coming back from Lute pond. My folks hadn't allowed us to go skating yet, but some of the kids had been going for over a week now.

Karl was excited about some plans that we had been making to go ice fishing at the cove of the river as soon as the ice was thick enough. We had talked about doing this many times. Karl had ice fishing equipment that his grandfather had left him. Uncle Louis and Dad had taken one of his types for a model and made six for me. I wasn't as excited as Karl about going, because I knew that it would have to get real cold for a while before my mother would let me go on that ice.

Beverly said, "How come you haven't been skating yet, Caleb? The ice is real good and we have been having a good time playing all kinds of games."

"I've been awful busy lately, Beverly," I answered, "but I will be going just as soon as I get a chance."

"How about tomorrow after school?" Beverly asked.

"I won't be able to go for a while, Bev, because there's quite a bit of trouble at our house and I have to be home as much as I can to help. With my job and all I am not going to have much time for skating for a while."

Karl asked, "What's wrong, Caleb?"

"Ah, Karl, it's a family matter and I'm not free to talk about it," I answered.

"That's O.K., Caleb, Karl has to get me home anyway, but remember our date when you get a chance to go skating."

The rest of my sixth year in school went by fairly quietly and after the drama of Eunice leaving home things became routine again. I had long talks with Josh about things that bothered me about growing up. Most of the time Josh had a way of answering that put my mind at ease. Still he seemed to get upset with my questions about this sex thing. By this time I had heard enough foul language and dirty jokes to understand what happened during sex, but damned if I understood why. I didn't like to upset Josh, so I stopped trying to find out from him. I talked to Jake about the why of it, but for all his book learning he never seemed to have a satisfactory answer.

Karl and I did get some ice fishing in during that winter and when we went skating, Beverly managed to get me involved in some of her kissing games. I tried to act like the other boys did around girls, but I still wonder what they would get so excited about.

That winter flew past, spring came and for the first time since I started school I was sorry to see it ending. Old Hanna and Jake had awakened me to the joy of the written word—a joy that I would have believed impossible a year before. The spring planting and plowing had begun at the farm, school was ending, and I was standing on the threshold of my twelfth summer.

Chapter 7

The last few days of the school year all the boys were making plans for their freedom, some of them quite vocally. Karl and I had many plans for summer excursions. The most exciting was the overnight stay on the mountain, now that Mother had finally decided we were responsible enough. We looked forward to this as if it was the rite of passage that Jake had tried to explain. Something he must have read about in one of his books he was always reading. The last week of school Hanna had asked Jake and me if we had time enough to stay after school a couple of days so she could talk with us. It seemed strange that I was interested in staying, when before, staying after school was deemed punishment. Hanna, when she wasn't practicing her role as principal of our school, was a very understanding person. Not the harsh disciplinarian that most of her students envisioned. She had some books that she wanted Jake and me to read and discuss during the summer, showing us certain exercises in writing that she thought we should practice.

Glenn Collard was standing outside the school when we walked out. He yelled, "Hey, Caleb, can I talk to you for a minute?"

Jake said quietly, "What's up, Caleb? I didn't know that you and Glenn were even friendly."

"I dunno, Jake, but don't get too far away before I'm sure."

"O.K., Caleb, but I don't have much time. We have a family gathering at my aunt's tonight and I told Mother I would be home early so she could go over and help set up."

Glenn was standing over by the swings about fifty feet away from the school door. I walked towards him, wondering what he had in mind. The Collards lived in the Southwest part of town about two miles from the center. There had been Collards in town almost from the town's inception. They seemed to have very little contact with the townspeople and preferred it that way. Glenn was a couple of classes ahead in school and a real giant compared to me. Approaching him I became increasingly apprehensive. Trying to keep my voice even, I asked, "What's up, Glenn?"

Much to my surprise, he said, "I have a plan, Caleb, or maybe I should say a secret, and I've been thinking how much fun it would be to share it with someone else. You know where that little brook is on the backside of the mountain? The one that starts at the springs on the mountain and flows towards Stanfield. Well, a few miles further down the Stanfield Road there is another brook that joins that one and way back on a logging road they formed a couple of small ponds. The last few years when school lets out I have been going there with our horse and buggy and catching more fish out of those two little ponds than I catch anywhere else all year long. I was thinking we only have a half-day of school the last day, maybe you would like to go with me. With your luck, maybe we can catch something big enough to hang over Banner's bar like your trout."

Jake hollered, "Hey, Caleb, you coming?"

"Nah, you go ahead, Jake. I'll see you at school tomorrow. Hey, Glenn, can we get back before five thirty? If I go I have to be back here in time to do my stripping at Muldon's."

"Gee, I dunno, Caleb," Glenn replied, "the last time I went I didn't get home until after dark. I would have gotten into a lot of trouble except I brought home enough fish to feed the whole family for a week. I used a hand line and along with the trout and perch I was catching with my pole, I caught some good bullhead along with a couple of eels. I was so busy catching fish I forgot the time. Can't you get Josh to take your place that day?"

"I'm not sure, Glenn, but I am sure going to try. How about asking Karl to go with us? You know how much he likes to fish."

"No, Caleb, I don't want anyone else to find this place, so you have to keep it our secret. Besides, I don't want him with all his smarty pants gear fishing with me anyway."

"O.K., Glenn, I will let you know tomorrow if Josh or someone will take my job for me that day."

Josh agreed to do my milking, and now that I knew that I was able to go, I became excited about what Glenn had told me. I felt sad that Karl wasn't going and a couple of times I had to tell him a tall tale, trying to explain why I wasn't going to hike up the mountain with the rest of the boys, the last day of school. Glenn had made me feel important when he mentioned my fish at Banner's. I guess that if it hadn't been for Hanna pushing Jake and me together to study I wouldn't even have thought about how much effect an accomplishment like that could have in your life. When I caught that fish, Dad had talked to me about not letting my good luck become foolish pride. I sure wish I had been able to talk to him as I did with Josh about what really happened when I caught that fish. One thing for sure though, prestige, false pride or whatever it was, the fish over the bar was the reason Glenn had chosen me to go to his secret fishing spot. I wondered if those ponds were as good as he described. Waiting the next two days brought back memories of all the excitement of when I got that big trout and the hope that we could catch fish like that again.

The last day of school, Glenn drove his horse and buggy to school in the morning, bringing a feedbag so the horse would have something to eat during our trip. We left the school at noon, eating our lunch as we rode. A little after we had passed where the two brooks joined, we turned off onto an old logging trail. When we had gone as far as possible with the horse, Glenn tied him to a tree and put his feedbag on. Though I couldn't see the water from where we were, I could hear it running so I knew we were close. We took our gear out of the buggy and went down a bank towards the water. The ponds weren't really ponds; they were more of an opening in the brook that got dammed up. I don't believe they were much over an acre in size, but the water was deep. We baited our hand lines and, tying them to the branches on the shore, tossed them out. On the first few casts of my pole I think the trout were jumping right out of the water to get my worms. I had three beautiful trout when I noticed the branch my line was tied on bending right into the water. I rushed over to get it. Glenn was hollering, "Didn't I tell you, Caleb? Didn't I tell you?" as he was having a terrific battle with something on his pole line. I grabbed my hand line and started pulling it in. I thought at first I was caught on the bottom, and then slowly, hand over hand, fighting all the way, the line came in. As the fish got close I could see it was an eel, I had caught a few eels at Lute pond but never anything like this, he was a whopper. It was as thick as a milk bottle and over two feet long. I was scared of it, but I didn't want Glenn to know, so I pulled it onto the bank, put my foot on its back, and stretching his head with my line, I cut his spine just in back of his head. He thrashed around some and curled around my foot before finally quieting down. I took a stick and got my hook out of his mouth. If I had been with Karl I would have just cut my line and tied him to a stick, but I didn't want Glenn to think I was a sissy. I never thought of fishing as being work, but after a couple of hours I was baiting my lines slower and slower. I even wished that the bush that I had my hand line tied on would stop shaking so often. Glenn was excited, he rushed back and forth between his two lines like a kid in a candy store, all the time hollering, "What did I tell you, Caleb? What did I tell you? I bet you are having as much fun as the day you caught that fish hanging over Banner's bar. Boy, Caleb, I wish I could catch one big enough to do something like that."

"I dunno, Glenn," I answered, puffed up with pride and acting like a big shot fisherman. "I don't think we'll catch anything like that here. What I have been catching lately are getting smaller and smaller. Most of them I am throwing back because I have so many good ones."

"I noticed that too," said Glenn. "Let's go down to the other pond. I usually get my biggest ones there so I save it for last."

We moved to the next little pond, threw out our hand lines and tied them to the bushes. While I was baiting the hook on my pole Glenn cast into the middle of the pond. If I live to be a thousand I don't think I will ever forget the next ten or fifteen minutes. All hell broke loose on the water. Glenn's line was slicing all over the water, the fish didn't jump, but it would run on the top, swirling the water into a froth, and then dive to the bottom.

Glenn hollered, "Caleb, Caleb, get our hand lines in so I won't get tangled in them." I pulled Glenn's in first because it was closer to him, then I went back to grab mine. At first it wouldn't move, but then something started fighting me and pulled it out of my hands, I would have lost it if it hadn't been tied to the bush. Glenn was hollering, "Hurry up, Caleb, hurry up, will ya?"

"I'm trying, Glenn," I yelled, "but I got one on my line and it is fighting like hell. Don't worry though, it's staying on the bottom and won't bother your line. It's probably just another eel." The line cut my hands, so I wrapped it on a stick and backed up the bank. Coming down, I wound the slack around the stick. I knew I was going to have a very tangled line but I didn't care. I had to get the line out for Glenn's sake. He was having an awful time and he didn't have a reel on his pole. He only had a spool that was attached to the pole near his hand that he wound the line on. He wound and unwound his line, trying to keep the fish from getting enough slack to get loose. Glenn was so frightened he was going to lose that fish, he kept yelling for me to hurry. I finally got my fish on shore—and what a fish it was. It looked like a monster bullhead except it was all white. I thought maybe it was sick or was just white from old age. I didn't have time to study it though. Glenn was yelling, "Damn it, Caleb, get over here and get a stick, a good one so you can scoop the fish up on the bank when I get it close to shore. This might be the one, Caleb, this might be the one." This sure wasn't the quiet, surly Glenn I knew. He was running up and down the bank, trying to keep the slack out of his line without pulling too hard. He sure wanted that fish something awful. I found a branch that I could break off with a crotch in it. I ran back, holding the stick up so Glenn could see.

He shouted, "That's good, Caleb, that's good. I almost got him now. He's getting as tired as I am. You get ready now because just as soon as he touches the shore he'll try to run again. I don't have Karl's fancy reel with the drag and everything, so if he runs it will probably break my line and I'll lose him.

He's coming in now, get on the right side of the line, put your stick in the water. I'll draw him up beyond the stick, then you whop him up on the bank, and for Chrissakes, don't let him flop back in."

I got into position like Glenn said. Little by little the line came in. I saw the fish as it started to bend the line around my stick. Glenn saw what was happening and walked to his left. This brought the fish right in front of my stick. He yelled, "Now, Caleb, now!" I whopped him and he flew up the bank into the bushes. Glenn went diving after him, jumping and yelling, "I got him, I got him, I got him."

Boy, I thought, *he is crazier than Karl is when it comes to fishing. One thing is for sure—if Karl finds out about all these fish he is going to be mad at me.* I ran up to where Glenn was holding his fish. It looked like some kind of bass, but he said it was a white perch. It didn't hold a candle to the one I had at Banner's. It looked like it might weigh over two pounds, but I thought he had caught his fish with a pole, not a club. Glenn kept saying what a beauty it was. He said, "I know, Caleb, this doesn't look big beside your trout, but this is a white perch and everyone knows that a white perch over a pound and a half is a big perch. I bet this one is over two pounds."

I wondered how Glenn knew so much about fish. I liked going fishing, but sometimes I caught fish that I didn't know what kind they were. Then remembering the white bullhead, I went back to where it was still hooked to the line. When I picked my fish up, I realized that it was heavier than Glenn's perch. My first thoughts were I wouldn't show it to him, but not knowing whether to keep it or not I took it over to Glenn.

"Hey! Wow, Caleb, what the hell is that?" Glenn gasped.

"I dunno, Glenn. This is what I was having such a hard time with when I was trying to clear the pool for you and your perch. I think it might be a sick or very old bullhead." Glenn took the fish and looked it over, squeezing the flesh between his thumb and fingers.

"I'm not sure, Caleb. He doesn't seem to be grubby or anything. Why don't you take him home, just keep him separate from the other fish just in case."

We fished a while longer, though we caught a few more good fish I guess that white perch slashing around the water had slowed the fishing down. We decided we had enough fish anyhow and loaded our catches and gear in the buggy. I was sure glad we weren't hiking; we never could have carried all those fish. As it was, we made two trips to the buggy.

As we were riding home Glenn made me promise again that I would never tell a soul where we fished. I told him I wouldn't and asked him how there were so many kinds of fish in what was really a small brook except where those two ponds were dammed off.

"Well, Caleb," he answered, "my father says that years ago, way up in the Stafford hills, there used to be a big pond that held all kinds of fish. One spring during the runoff the dam broke and left nothing except a small pool. There are old stories about some boys hiking there and scooping fish up by the bushel basket full. Some even swore that they ate smoked fish for over a year. Dad liked to go after native brook trout, so at least twice a year he would fish that little stream that comes from Stafford hills. About five years ago, when I was with him, he decided to go down the Stanfield Road and fish beyond where the stream reaches the road, that's when we found those ponds. Dad says that all those different fish got there back when the dam broke at Stafford pond. We made a pact then to keep this a Collard secret. Dad and I used to come here often ever since that time; that is until he lost his arm at the sawmill. Since then he doesn't seem to want to do anything. I told him this spring I wanted to take one good friend over there so I could have someone to fish with besides my little brothers. They're too much trouble to take that far from home. He said he didn't care because he wasn't going to be able to fish again anyhow. I chose you, Caleb, because I felt I could trust you. You can see how important it is that no one else finds this place. I hope someday to get my father interested in fishing again and I wouldn't want this place all fished out when that happens."

Glenn stopped talking and we rode along behind the clip clopping sound of the horse, both deep in our thoughts. I sensed that Glenn had suffered a great loss in his life after his father got hurt and he sure needed a friend, and he had picked me. Boy, he was handing me quite a handful. Trying to keep a secret such as this from Karl, Uncle Louis and the boys would be some trick when they saw all these fish. I began thinking about what I could tell them. I needed a story by the time I got home that I could live with.

"Hey, Glenn! What if we tell everyone that we caught these fish at Haslings pond? We haven't met anyone yet, and if we get by Whately Road before we do, nobody from town could tell whether we were on Stanfield Road or not. What do you think?"

"I dunno, Caleb, nobody has gone fishing there for a long time. It's supposed to be all fished out, and I don't think anyone will believe us."

"That's just it, Glenn. Nobody has fished there in a long time because it is so out of the way. I think it'll work. Remember the old stories about the fish they used to catch there? You've heard the one about Great-grandpa Daniels, the one who built the Daniels place, and about all the crazy looking fish he caught?"

"Ya, I heard that story many times, Caleb, but my dad says that fish was just a calico bass and those old-timers had never seen one before, and if they had, there wouldn't have been all that excitement to build a story like that one."

"I know that's what some people say, but the stories are still talked about around here and I think my plan will work. You know, Glenn, keeping that spot a secret isn't hard for you because it is a family thing, but my brothers, Karl Hart and Uncle Louis are never going to let up on me if they think I am hiding something from them. I have to tell them a story they will accept. Look, Glenn, I promised you, but I am going to have to lie and that's a sin, according to my mother and I'm not sure that I can handle it if I have to face it every time someone asks me about today. I think if we decide on the story of Hasling pond before we meet anyone and rehearse it some, it will be the best way for me. It's probably the only way I can be sure I don't make a slip about where we were today. Besides, one big whopper of a lie is easier to handle than a hundred little ones."

"O.K., Caleb, maybe you're right, if we stick to pretty much what happened today except for what pond it was, maybe it will work. I never thought about the trouble this might cause you."

We got by the junction of Whately and Stanfield Road without meeting anyone, so the first part of our story was safe. When we came into town, Karl, George, Jake and some of the other kids from school were just coming down off the mountain. Glenn said, "Hey, Karl, do you and George want to see what real fishermen can do?" He held up his white perch and a string of trout, saying, "Take a look in the back if you want to see how Caleb's luck is holding out."

The boys gathered around the buggy, checking through the fish. "My God," Karl said, "look at all the different kinds. They even have a white catfish! The only one I've ever seen was in a picture in my grandfather's books. I think it said that they grow bigger than ten pounds, this one must weigh four or five."

"Ya, I know, Karl," Glenn said. "I've caught some bigger than that one before. He weren't no problem for Caleb, though, he caught him on his hand line. Now if you wanted to see a battle you should have seen me bringing in this white perch, that was really something, wasn't it, Caleb?"

Glenn caught me off base with his story on the catfish, but I had to agree that perch had put on some show. So even though I could see the pout building on Karl's face, I said, "You should have been there, boys. I bet that old perch and Glenn must have fought it out for over fifteen minutes. It sure was a fine sight to see."

Karl said, "Come on, George, let's get out of here."

93

I hollered, "See you tomorrow, Karl," but he just walked off without answering. I could tell by the way he held his shoulders that he was mad at me for going fishing without him. I wonder what made Glenn so angry with Karl and how was I going to be his friend and Karl's too. *Seems like every time I have a good time when I go fishing it ends up badly some way.*

Jake and the rest of the boys left us, hollering, "You'll have to take us up to Haslings pond sometime this summer, Glenn."

"Maybe when I can get the horse and buggy someday, I will," Glenn answered.

Glenn drove my fish and me to the house. Everyone was home except Josh. I was glad of that because that was an awful mess of fish to have to clean alone. They were excited, even my father, who didn't fish, said, "What do you think of that, Mother? Looks like our boy Caleb has put some meat on the table for a few days. Do you think you can do as good next time, Caleb?"

"I don't know about him," Uncle Louis said, "but as soon as I can borrow a pickup I'm heading up to Haslings pond. I haven't fished there and from the looks of this catch nobody else has for years, but they sure will when the story of this catch gets around and I want to get there before it is fished out again."

Josh came home late that night. He had been walking with Patsy Wilson after he finished milking. I was sitting out on the porch when he told me the story of Glenn and my catch was all over town and everyone was planning a fishing trip to Haslings pond. I almost told Josh the truth, but when I thought of Glenn and his father I couldn't.

Josh told me that when he and Patsy had been at the store, there was a group of men talking about war and how we would be involved in it sooner or later. Frank Butler said the government had already started planning for a draft and rationing. The way he saw it, there would be gas and meat and many other things you wouldn't be able to buy without those rationing tickets the government was already printing. There was a big argument on how these tickets would be controlled. Arnold Wilson said the way he understood it, each town or district would have two boards made up of the older men in town. One board to decide who could be excused from the draft, the other to allot stamps for food, gas, tires and other things that were rationed according to need. Ross Bolts said it sounded to him that it would be like the old bootlegging days, with only the crooks making out on the things that were scarce. Most of the men thought, if we went to war there wouldn't be much of that going on. People wouldn't put up with someone making a profit on the materials our boys would need to keep them alive while they were fighting. They agreed that the government would probably have some stiff laws against a black market.

The thought of war seemed to upset Josh an awful lot. To me it seemed like a faraway thing. Besides, didn't America always win all our wars? The next few weeks there was a much talk about the war at the barn. The older boys wondered at what age the draft would start. Reilly said, "The draft doesn't matter to me, because if war is ever declared I am going to join the Navy right away."

John said, "I'm not worried, because I heard farm boys won't have to go if they don't want to."

I told them I was too young to have a war bother me. "Maybe you're right, Caleb," Larry said, "but if it lasts very long they will draft Josh if he's not too much of a sissy to shoot a gun."

"Shut your face, Larry," I answered. "Josh will be a better soldier than any one of you if he has to go."

"Caleb's right," Reilly said, "we're all beginning to find out that Josh always comes out on top if he sets his mind to it, so don't ever sell him short."

One day that summer I was at the horse trough being teased by Beverly when I heard someone yelling, "Caleb, Caleb, guess what happened?" It was Glenn. I hadn't seen him since our fishing trip. I think half the town had been to Hasling, fishing. Uncle Louis was the only one that I knew of who had made a decent catch. People were asking questions, as if they were suspicious of our story. I went once with Karl after he got over being mad at me and we didn't do well and I thought he was going to get mad again. On the way home I got him talking about our other plans and he seemed to be all right.

Glenn was up by the store, so I hollered, "I'll be right up, Glenn."

Beverly held on to my arm and said, "Come on, Caleb. Don't tell me that Glenn and his fishing are more interesting than I am. You'll make me cry, Caleb, you wouldn't want to do that, would you?"

"Cut it out, Bev. You and your damn kissing and hugging are sure going to get me in trouble someday."

I walked towards the store, with Beverly whispering, "When is that someday going to be, Caleb?"

Glenn was all excited, shouting, "Look at this picture, Caleb, look at this picture." He had a picture of a fish mounted on an oval board with a little metal plate under it. I couldn't read the writing on the plate, but I knew by Glenn's excitement that it must be a picture of his white perch.

"Hey, Glenn, how did you do this? I didn't know you could mount fish."

"Naw, I didn't do it," he said. "When I got home from that fishing trip there were a couple of guys there from the Lange Sportsman Club visiting with my father. They got all excited when they saw all the fish and asked to take the white perch and have it mounted to hang at the clubhouse. I told them they could if they put a plaque on it saying it was caught by me in Sterling and a picture for me when it was finished. They agreed to that, saying they would put the date and place it was caught too. I hated to tell them it was Hasling pond but I did. Isn't this great, Caleb, now we both have a fish mounted in a public place, I bet you didn't get a picture though, did you?"

"Naw, I didn't get a picture. I was supposed to, but I guess everybody just forgot about it." I was just as glad, I thought to myself, because I still felt guilty when I thought about that day.

"Listen," Glenn said, "I don't have much time; my uncle is getting ready to leave. Let's plan to meet real soon at the junction of Whately and Stanford Road. We'll meet early in the morning before it gets light so no one will see where we go, O.K? I gotta go now. I'll get word to you when I can get the horse and buggy."

"O.K., Glenn," I hollered as he rode off with his uncle. I had been dreading the day that he would ask me to go again, I think everybody in town was watching for us to get together again and go fishing. It bothered me to have to guard such an important secret as this was to Glenn. I remembered how pleased my family had been with all those fish and how proud Dad had made me feel, so I decided to go anyway.

That night when I went to work at the barn Arthur said, "Caleb, I heard that you and Glenn Collard had your heads together up at the store. What are you and Glenn planning, to show the town how to catch fish again? How about taking your working buddies with you for a change? What's the matter, are you too good to associate with us outside the barn?"

"Oh, come on, Arthur, you know better than that. All the excitement up at the store was about a picture he had. You remember hearing about his white perch? The Lange Sportsmen had it mounted and it's hanging in the clubhouse now. They sent him a picture of it and that's what we were talking about. Besides, Karl and I went up to Haslings pond again and it wasn't worth the hike. It's about all fished out. Probably because it tells on the plaque where Glenn caught that perch and everybody is going there fishing now."

"Hey, fellas," Arthur asked, "are we going to buy that story?"

"Knock it off, Arthur," Leonard hollered. "To hell with Caleb and his fish stories. Let me tell you a story that's a lot more fun than fishing. You remember I told you I had met the kid who is staying over at the Daniels place for a couple of weeks? Well, his name is Leroy Fells. He is Sophie Daniels' nephew. Today when I was over there he took me into the barn that goes with the house. What a place. It has a room off the main floor that he called a den, boy, was it nice, better than any room in our house. It had a carpet on the floor, a beautiful couch and chair and lots of other furniture. The walls were covered with some kind of brownish board that I have never seen before. The outside wall had a long window all the way up to the ceiling, the glass was inlaid in diamond shapes of all different colors. Boy, was it pretty in there when the sun hit that window. There was a great big gun hanging on the wall. It had a powder horn and ramrod and everything with it. I guess it must be old, it looked like one of those guns the pilgrims were carrying in the pictures in our history books. You know, the ones that seem to have a bell shape on the end of the barrel. There was a confederate flag and uniform with sword and all, there were so many things that I can't remember them all.

"Leroy found a pistol and said, 'Let's go try this out, Leonard.' He was holding this little bitty pistol. It had two barrels and it broke open like a shotgun, with the barrels over each other instead of side by side. So I said that we should go out in the woods and try it.

"Then Leroy said, 'We don't have to go that far, watch this.' He slipped a couple of shells in the gun, walked out to the main room, pulled that little pistol up and fired two shots into the beam in the roof. At first I was pretty scared, but it didn't make much noise and I don't think anyone could have heard it outside. We tried that a couple of times and Leroy said, 'Hey, Let's take it down in the shed on the other side of the barn. I saw some bottles and cans out there.'

"Boy, did we have a time. We must have shot that pistol fifty times or more. I got so I could hit a can or bottle every time I shot, and those little bullets didn't even go through the planks in the back of the shed."

During the next few days, most of us from the barn went over to Daniels' to see if we could get a chance to use that little pistol. I think all of us got to try it at least once or twice. Leroy—or Roy, as he wanted us to call him—was riding pretty high with the boys in town. I thought that was rather strange, because Josh had talked to him a few times and said he thought Roy was a little afraid of the country, being brought up in a big city. I would have talked to Josh about this, but if he knew what we were doing he would think it was too dangerous to be fun. Then I would be in trouble with the boys at the barn again, so I was afraid to. After I had been over to Roy's with the boys shooting a couple of times I didn't go anymore. I hadn't asked Karl to go with us because I didn't want him around when the barn boys got on my case and treated me like a little kid. He was complaining that we were way behind on our plans for the summer because I was always off with someone else. I felt bad about that, but some of the time it was him, because he had been working part time for a farmer in Lange. Karl's uncle had promised to take us up the river on a canoe trip late in the summer when the water was low. Karl told me that his Uncle Tom said it was a great way for young boys to prepare for life; paddling upstream. When his uncle could get enough time off from his work, the plan was to camp out a couple of nights on the riverbank, then we would enjoy the trip back, riding the current. We hadn't camped overnight on the mountain like we had planned. I think we were a little anxious about being alone on the mountain at night. Even though it had been exciting shooting that gun and being with the bigger boys, Karl was right, we hadn't been doing things the way we had planned.

One morning Old Golly Moses came to the barn just as we finished milking, he walked around checking the cows; calling them by name talking to each one; almost as if they were family. He gave one a talking to because it had gone through the fence and got into somebody's garden and another because it had been cut on the barbwire. He praised those who had just added calves to the herd and consoling the ones that were going dry in preparation for birth, saying, "Don't worry, Bess, you will be back among our best milkers in no time." This was the first time I had ever seen him act this way. The boys were always laughing about his talking to the cows. I thought it was kind of an amazing feeling that he had, it was something like Josh's feeling for poetry. After he had made his way through the whole herd, he said, "Boys, I want to see you all in the milk house when the chores are done."

After he left, Leonard started cursing, "Damn it all to hell, which one of you bastards have got us in trouble now?"

"Calm down, Leonard," Reilly said. "I think he only wants to explain some changes that he and Uncle Leon have been talking about making this week. Nobody's in any trouble, so lay off."

After we had finished we all went into the milk house and put our pails in the sterilizer. Reilly's father said, "Boys, the reason for all this is simple, as long as everybody understands what is going on. Most of you older boys have been taking the cows we asked you to watch to the bullpen when you see that they are bulling. We have an agreement with a big farm over in Pepperell to swap bulls the second week in August this year. The swap is going to be a few days late, but it will be sometime this week. Now most of you know we have to change bulls every few years to keep a good bloodline. The bull that we are getting has produced some great milkers, so that's why we are swapping for him. The story is that he is mean and dangerous, so nobody goes to the bull pen without Leon or me with them, now I mean nobody, do you all understand that?"

Everyone said they did and started leaving. I was outside when I heard Old Moses speak, "Caleb, come back here for a moment. I have a message for you I almost forgot."

I went back in with my heart in my mouth, fearing one of the Muldon boys had gotten me fired. He said, "You know Bill Collard? At least you know some of his boys from school. I stop by to see him if I have time when I go by his house. He's been having a hard time of it the last couple of years. Yesterday when I saw him he asked me to give you a message from his son Glenn. It sounded kind of secret so I thought that you would like to hear it alone. All he said was, 'Last dark Thursday morning at the junction.'" Old Golly Moses smiled, saying, "I can see by your face that it is good news. Don't worry, whatever your secret is, it won't go any farther than it were meant to."

I said, "Thank you, Mr. Muldon. I have been waiting to hear from Glenn. We have a little trip planned."

He laughed and said, "Enjoy your youth, boy. Have a good time with the Collard boy and your little trip." I left the milk house with the excitement of our last fishing trip flowing through my mind. I sure hoped that Josh was going to be able to cover my job for me. He had been working hay fields and cornfields all summer, and I hated to ask him too often. On the way home I met Josh and Jean Hart in the center of the town. I knew with Josh it was better to speak my mind right out, because if you beat around the bush with him it seemed to make him angry. So I said, "Hey, Josh, I need a big favor."

I saw him wink at Jean, and he said, "What is it this time, little brother? You need me to cover for you so you can sneak off on another of your fishing trips that have been making fools out of every fisherman in town?"

I was shocked at what Josh said and I guess I must have shown it because he came over and put his hand on my shoulder, saying, "Don't worry, Caleb, you know I will help you in any way I can. And listen, Caleb, we all keep secrets and as long as they are not harming anyone by keeping them it's all right. It's not really the same as telling a lie, so tell me what you need me for."

I told him that I needed him Thursday morning. He said, "No trouble, little Caleb, and I won't even tell anyone until I get there." I went home thinking that having a big brother like Josh was the best thing anybody could ever have. He always seemed to know how to make you feel good.

I met Glenn Thursday morning and we came back a little after noon.

Though we hadn't caught any trophies we sure came back with a whopping catch. It seemed strange that we hadn't run into anybody on the whole trip. Glenn drove the buggy all the way to the house so I wouldn't have to carry all those fish. We had the back of the buggy piled with wet moss to keep the fish from going bad. It took almost all the rest of the afternoon for Homer and his friend Alan Stone and me to clean the fish. I don't think any of us was too happy about the big catch before we got through. I was really beaten up when the time came to do my milking, but I knew that I had to go anyway. When I got home that night, Uncle Louis said, "Caleb, I have something I want to give you." He handed me a small framed picture of two fishermen sitting beside a pool. Underneath it said,

All fishermen are liars, except you and me,
and sometimes I am not too sure of you.

Uncle Louis laughed and said, "You know, Caleb, a friend of mine gave me that picture years ago, but I think you should have it now." I laughed with him, thinking how much better I felt about having a secret now that Josh had said it was all right.

A few days later Karl came running down to our house, saying, "Uncle Tom is coming this week. He doesn't have much time, so we can only camp out one night on our trip, but at least he is going to make it while we are still on vacation."

When Karl's uncle came we were the envy of every boy in town. He had a seventeen-foot canoe and even though it wasn't made of birch bark it was painted to look like the ones we saw the Indians use in the pictures in our history books. That afternoon Karl's uncle wanted to check out his tent and camping gear. His tent and gear were all rolled up in a small bundle so it would fit in the canoe. The canoe was already down by the riverbank, so he decided to let Karl and me set the tent up there. After we had set it up, Karl's uncle said, "O.K., Karl, now that you know how to set it up I'll show you and Caleb how to fit it all in a small bundle."

"Gee, Uncle Tom," Karl asked, "couldn't we leave it up and camp here tonight? That would give us two nights out camping."

"I can't do that, Karl, I only have a few days off and if I don't spend at least one night with your folks I don't think they will be very happy with me. I'll tell you what though, I'll leave it up for you and Caleb to use tonight if your folks will allow it."

It took some convincing at my house, but after half promising to give up my overnight trip to the mountain my mother gave in. I never did figure out why she was so against me staying on the mountain at night. When I was done milking that night, I went home, changed and got a blanket. Mother gave me a bag of food and said there were a couple of hotdogs in the bag that we should use up tonight. When I arrived at the river Karl had already started a small fire, so we cooked the hotdogs and sat by the river and talked.

Karl said, "Hey, Caleb, what's the story I have been hearing about Roy Fells and a gun?"

I knew I could trust Karl, so I told him all about the den and the gun and how we had been shooting it.

"Darn you, Caleb," Karl shouted. "I'm Karl, remember, I'm supposed to be your best friend. First, you sneak off twice with Glenn and catch all those fish without me. Now I find out that you've been having all that fun with Roy Fells and you didn't even let me know it was going on. How the hell would you have liked it if I had asked Kenny Walden or one of the other boys to go with Uncle Tom and me instead of you? I could have, you know, damn you, now I wish I had."

I told Karl that I didn't go there anymore and how I thought we might get caught and how I was afraid of what the boys might do to me if I said anything. He finally settled down and said, "I'm sorry, Caleb, I didn't mean to blow up. I know that Glenn needs a friend too, it's just that I don't like him. You are probably right about Roy and the gun, but I still would have liked to have been there, that sounded like fun."

I wanted to ask Karl why he didn't like Glenn, he had never mentioned any trouble between them, but I decided against talking about Glenn. I wanted to have a clear mind for the trip tomorrow. We put out the fire and crawled into the tent and rolled up in our blankets. I started to talk about school, but Karl said, "Caleb, let's not spoil the trip by talking about school. I start high school this year and I don't even want to talk about it, O.K.?"

I said, "O.K., Karl," and rolled over and went to sleep. The next thing I knew Karl was shaking me. It was just getting light and Karl's uncle was cooking eggs and bacon over an open fire, it sure did smell good. Karl and I took down the tent and folded it as he told us to. After we had eaten breakfast and washed the pans in the river, we rolled everything up in the tent, packed the canoe and started up the river. Karl and I took turns helping his uncle paddle, at first it was hard ,but after he showed us the proper way to hold the paddles and use our bodies, it was much easier. Karl's uncle was fun to be with. He taught us how to spot where mountain springs join the river and told us that the next big hole below where the spring water came in the river usually held the most fish; because it was cooler there this time of the year. There was a couple of times we had to take the canoe out of the water because of low water and trees that blocked our way. Tom made a sling out of a grapevine so Karl and I could carry one end of the canoe, one on each side. He called this a portage and said this was the way you had to take your canoes around the dams on the big rivers. Once when we were carrying the canoe, Karl's uncle said, "Now don't get jumpy, but look to your right on the river bank."

"Wow, Caleb, do you see it?" Karl asked.

He was on the right side of the canoe and I had to look behind to see what excited him so much. There on the bank was the biggest snake I had ever seen, it was a good four feet up on the bank and still some of it was in the water.

Karl said, "Let's stop and kill it, Uncle Tom."

His uncle said, "O.K., boys, let's put the canoe down a little ways up from here and we'll talk about it."

I was all for going back and killing that big snake. What a tale to tell the boys when we got back in town. We went a way further before we set the canoe down, then Karl's uncle said, "Let's have a talk, boys. Do we really want to kill that snake back there?"

"Of course we do, Uncle Tom," Karl said. "Caleb and I have killed a lot of snakes but never one as big as that."

Karl's Uncle said, "Let's just sit a minute, boys. Now tell me, why do we want to kill snakes? Do we use them for food? Have any of us ever been attacked by a snake? Do they steal our food supplies or take anything we need to live on? Let's all just think on those questions before we decide that snake's fate."

I thought about what he was saying and snakes began to lose their challenge for me. After thinking about it I couldn't remember anyone telling about a snake really hurting anybody, at least not in our section of the country. I knew that there were snakes that were poisonous, but not around here. Karl said, "Uncle Tom, listening to you tell about snakes makes me wonder, yet nearly everyone I know kills snakes whenever they see one, how come we do that?"

"Well, Karl," he replied, "it is a little hard to explain why people want to kill something without a reason. But if you boys are interested in what I think about why we kill snakes, I'll tell you. The poor snake all throughout written history has been described as a thing of evil. We were all brought up on stories about terrible serpents, even the Bible describes the snake as a portrait of evil. Now mind you, I am not disputing what the Bible says, I'm only pointing out that writers have always used the snake or serpent as a terrible, evil thing. When the truth is, in nature, which to me is really God's way, snakes, like most living things, are not dangerous if you understand them. Well, boys, this is your trip, so what do we do, shall we go back and kill that snake?"

I was glad to hear Karl say, "No, Uncle Tom, I think we should leave it be and go on up the river, is that O.K. with you, Caleb?" We continued our portage with my mind awhirl with the thoughts that Tom's talk had invoked. He made me see things in nature almost the same way Josh helped me understand people. Tom made his lessons about nature seem wonderful. Karl was right, it wasn't going to be easy going back to school this year.

After we put the canoe back in the water, Karl's Uncle said, "We'll stop at the next spot that looks like a good campsite."

"How come so early, Uncle Tom?" Karl asked. "It can't be much more than two o'clock now, is it?"

"It is just about two, Karl, but it might be over an hour before we find a good site. I like to have time to hike around my campsites and enjoy the woods as well as the river. You know your old uncle doesn't get out like this too often, and I want to enjoy as much of the country as is available when I go on this kind of trip. If things go as planned, next year I'm taking a long trip down the Connecticut River through all the states. If I have time to teach you boys how to handle a canoe in rough water before then, maybe I can take you with me, but that's next year, let's enjoy today's trip. Tonight, if I can find the right things, I have a very special treat for you boys."

We found a beautiful campsite on a bend in the river that made it seem as if the river was on three sides of us. We pitched the tent and Karl's uncle had us dig a pit for the fire. He said it was necessary for his surprise. He picked mushrooms and wild onions while we were hiking around the campsite. He told us we were never to do that on our own until we learned which ones were safe.

Karl said, "You can show us now, Uncle Tom. Caleb and I spend a lot of time in the woods, and it would be great to be able to find food like this."

"I wish I could, Karl," he answered, "but it would be dangerous to try to teach you in such a short time. I think I have some books on the subject though, I will send them to your dad and let him decide."

Going back to the campsite, Karl said, "Boy, Caleb, camping with Uncle Tom is as good as those stories that we read in your uncle's sport magazines, isn't it?"

"It sure is, Karl. He knows everything, those writers should go on a trip with him, then they'd learn."

Karl's uncle, chuckling, said, "Now, boys, I really don't know everything. It's just being in the woods or on a river brings out the little boy in me, and

I love it so much I never want it to die. I have studied every book I could lay my hands on that had a reference to the woods and nature. It is important to have knowledge about anything you do. Still, with all the words in the dictionary, I don't believe that a writer can capture the essence of the contact man makes with God's world, camping on a river with two of His wonderful children. It's experiences like this that I can carry in my heart and mind, for the times in my life I'm not so content. Now that's enough philosophy, you boys grab some line and cut some poles. I think our supper is in that pool that we passed just downstream. Turn over some rocks and old logs, you'll find plenty of bait. I'll get our fire pit going."

Karl and I had to move down the river a couple of times, but we had twelve nice trout in no time, we could have caught more, but after listening to Karl's uncle we didn't want to catch any that would be wasted. He had a bed of hot coals when we got back and was cooking the mushrooms and onions, did they smell good. He took the trout one by one as we cleaned them, rolled them in cornmeal and flour that had Italian seasoning mixed in. He said it was one of the first things he packed when he went on a fishing trip. After he coated the fish inside and out, he stuffed them with the mushrooms and onions and closed the cavities with small needle-like sticks. He used some rocks to hold a wire screen over the coals and started the fish cooking; it was a good thing that we were alone, because if anyone smelled those fish cooking, I think I would have had to fight them off. He gave Karl and me the small ones that cooked first. I never tasted fish that good before. We ate all twelve, right down to their crispy tails, mushrooms, onions and all.

After we had eaten, Karl's uncle said, "There is a pool upriver, I bet there are a couple of lunkers in it. I guess I'll try to tease them out." He unstrapped a long, narrow box from the canoe, opened it and fitted together four pieces to make a long fishing pole. It had a thin, narrow reel like I had never seen before. He tied on a hook that had feathers and things on it, saying, "Come on, boys, let's see what it can do." I never saw anyone fish like that, he kept casting and casting, unwinding the line as he did, until he got that old fly just dancing in the air above the water. All of a sudden this big old trout came flying out of the water and grabbed it. What a show he put on. First the fish would run, then Tom would reel it in, then it would run again. When the fish grew tired Tom brought it in by the bank. He reached down in the water and unhooked it without bringing it out of the water. He caught a couple of more and released them in the same way, saying, "Well boys, if we come this way again we will know where to find a good meal when we need it."

We went back to the camp, built up the fire and set around making plans for the morning. When morning came we took the tent down while Karl's uncle cooked breakfast. When everything was packed and ready, he said, "We have enough time to go upriver for a ways before we start back, what do you say?"

I looked at Karl. The look on his face told me that he felt much like I did, so I said, "You know, it's not so much whether we go up river or down, it's just leaving here that bothers me. I feel that somehow this is a special place in my life."

Karl's uncle chuckled and said, "Caleb, the day will probably come when you will look back on today as more of a special time in your life rather than a place. Still, if you boys would rather stay here a while and talk, or better yet take a hike, it's O.K. with me."

After we had gone hiking and had our lunch, we canoed back to town. As we helped Uncle Tom tie the canoe and gear on top of his car, I said a silent prayer asking God to make it possible for Karl and me to go with him next summer.

A few days later, Karl and I were on our way up the mountain, we had plans for a picnic at our secret cave. Leonard Cross came out of the Daniels barn and said, "Hey, Caleb, you want to see something? Roy and I and some of the other boys are going to try shooting that old musket hanging in the den."

I said, "Not today, Leonard, Karl and I have plans."

"Come on, Caleb, come on," Karl cried, "I don't want to miss this, it shouldn't take much time, anyway, I wanted to be in on some of this too."

I remembered what Karl had said the first night we slept in the tent so I said, "O.K., Karl, but I smell trouble for sure."

Arthur, John and my brother Homer were inside. They were already loading the musket. Homer was standing on the couch, pouring powder down the barrel, while Arthur was holding the gun with the butt on the floor. Leonard took the ramrod off the gun and jammed some paper wads down the barrel behind the powder. There was a leather pouch hanging on the gun with metal balls in it, but Roy said, "Maybe it would be better if we don't use them in case they are the wrong size or something."

After they got the musket loaded, Leonard took it over and aimed it out the back window. Roy said, "Wait a minute, a couple of you boys look around outside and see if anyone is close by. This might not be as quiet as the Derringer."

Karl and I went out and looked around. We didn't see anybody, so we went back and said, "It's O.K., Roy."

Roy put a little brass cap on the tube under the hammer of the gun and stepped back, saying, "It's all yours, Leonard, let it go." Leonard rather preened himself and leveled the musket out the window and pulled the trigger, there was a big poof of smoke that almost hid Leonard, while a ball of fire floated across the field behind the barn. The smoke streaked Leonard's face with black soot and everyone laughed at the way he looked.

He got mad and said, "You damn fools don't know how to load a gun. Come on, Arthur, we'll show them how to do it right." They took the musket back into the den. Arthur held it while Leonard poured the powder, He jammed the wads in and put in a couple of the metal balls, taking the rod, he pounded them down hard on the wads. He took the gun back to the window, saying, "Now you're going to see what a musket can do." Leonard pulled the trigger and there was such an explosion that it almost blew our ears off. Homer was about half way across the barn behind Leonard. Smoke filled the barn and Leonard was thrown violently across the room, knocking Homer over and scaring the hell out of all of us. Leonard was lying on the floor, his eyes were rolled back and his face was covered with blood. Homer was lying beside him moaning. We heard some of the women in the neighborhood calling excitingly for their children.

Roy shouted, "Caleb, you stay here with me, the rest of you run outside asking everyone you meet what that noise was and where did it come from. They won't look in here if they see you all running out of the barn." Homer seemed to be all right, so we sent him out in case somebody from my family heard the noise and went looking for him.

Roy was real scared about Leonard, but he was coming to, there was a lot of blood, but I knew from a fight that Leonard had at the barn that he was subject to bad nosebleeds. Roy and I put the musket back in its place and after things quieted down, we went with Leonard over to Lute pond so he could get cleaned up. He said, "My eyes burn, but I will be O.K. That is the last musket I'll ever fire."

With all the talk around town about the explosion, I couldn't believe nobody ever found out what really happened that day. With all the theories that the adults had about it, I never heard anyone who was close to the truth. Summer ended. It was after Labor Day, and Roy had left to go back to school in the city, Karl was going to high school in Lange and I started the seventh grade.

Chapter 8

Starting seventh grade with Karl and Emma no longer there made going to school a new experience. This was the first year I attended school without an older brother or sister in the same school. Homer had just entered the fifth grade, Jason was in the third and Francis had just started his first year. My mind lurched between being the big shot brother and being scared because I sometimes felt alone, especially now that Karl was gone. Jake Wilson seemed happy that school had started, it was good to see George, though he was upset with me because I hadn't been out to see him that summer and indignant about my fishing with Glenn. I still hadn't figured out why so many people seemed to have it in for Glenn. I know he was different, but we all were in one way or another, and outside a little coarseness I hadn't found Glenn that hard to take. Jake was hell-fire for us to get back to our writing, but I couldn't seem to work up the eagerness that I felt last year before we left school. Hanna asked Jake and me to stay after school one night and we talked about what we had been assigned to read and practice writing during the summer. Jake had it all down pat, but I had to admit that I hadn't even given it a thought after the first week of vacation. I tried to explain that with my job and all the things that happened during the summer, I didn't have time. Though Hanna seemed disappointed with me, she said, "Caleb, I don't want you to get discouraged and stop writing because of this. Even if you haven't gained in your ability in formulating your writing, you will still have all the wonderful experiences of this summer to write about."

When Jake and I were leaving the school, he said, "You know what, Caleb? I bet if you wrote about your fishing trip with Glenn, the fire would return to your writing. That must have stirred your emotions almost as much as your story about fishing with George did."

"You're right, Jake," I answered. "There was plenty of emotion on that fishing trip. You should have been there. We were pulling in fish so fast that we hardly had time to talk. Glenn just kept whooping and hollering, 'Didn't I tell you, Caleb, didn't I tell you?' I guess that would make a story worth writing, maybe I will start writing again." *Boy!* I thought. *I'm going to have to watch it with Jake, he nearly got me to slip and say where Glenn and I had been.*

Jake said, "That a boy, Caleb, I bet there are many people who would be interested in a story like that. I'm glad you didn't really lose your desire to write."

"Jake," I asked, "do you know why George and Karl seem to dislike Glenn so much?"

"You know, Caleb, it's funny that you asked. Just the other night I heard my folks discussing that. I guess they didn't realize that I could hear them. I know that Mother was talking quiet and being secretive about it. Mother used to be at Collard's, much of the time, after Glenn's father came home from the hospital, after losing his arm. She worked as a nurse's aide before she was married. The doctors wouldn't let him come home unless he had some professional help. Mother knew that money would be a problem when she heard about it, so she volunteered. She and Gertrude Collard, Glenn's mother, became friendly when she was taking care of his father. Mother still goes to see her quite often. From what my mother says, Bill Collard has been terrible about things since he lost his arm. Not many people stop at the Collard house anymore. Mother says Gertrude needs someone to talk to and she isn't going to let Bill chase her away. It seems that one of the things she needed to talk about was an incident that happened at the Phelps place, when George was laid up after being hurt by the bull. Glenn used to go up there often when George first was hurt. Everyone thought it was caring of Glenn to come and keep George company. You know George's sister Louise? She's in the eighth grade and about a year or so older than George. What Mother told was that George's five-year-old brother Donald caught her and Glenn in the barn and they both had their clothes off. Before they could stop Donny, he ran out into the yard yelling, 'Glenn and Louise are bare-ass in the barn.' Louise's mother was in the backyard hanging out clothes, and hearing Donny, she ran for the barn. When she got there Glenn had managed to get one leg in his pants. Then she grabbed a harness strap and started beating him, he came running out of the barn and down the road with his pants only half on, with her after him. He finally had to let go of his pants to get away from her and that strap. He must have hidden out in the woods nude until late that night, because when Mrs. Phelps showed up at his house with his clothes, he wasn't home. That first night the Phelpses wanted to have Glenn drawn and quartered and I think his parents were almost ready to agree with them. That night, after talking to Louise, Mrs. Phelps became a little concerned that it wasn't all Glenn. She asked Donny what he had seen and he said, 'Louise and George were having a bare-ass dance and Louise was having a real good time twirling and twisting and laughing all the time. It looked like fun.' The Collards and the Phelpses got together and decided that the whole thing should be kept quiet. Glenn got another beating from his dad when he finally got home, and Louise got such a beating from her father that her mother had to stop him. I know that even before I heard this story, Mother used to tell me to stay away from Glenn, and though nobody seemed to know why, the word got out that Glenn wasn't somebody that mothers wanted their kids to play with. I think Karl's problem was different and more of a personal nature. He was extremely upset the last day of school when he found out that the big important thing you had to do that day was sneak off with Glenn to go fishing instead of climbing the mountain with us."

"Christ, Jake, please don't tell me that this is what that sex thing is all about, tearing each other's clothes off and dancing bare-ass? I hope to hell that it never happens to me," I blurted.

"No, Caleb," Jake said, "that's not having sex. I don't even think they had sex, it was more like the bulling the cows do before they are bred, but I am now beginning to understand the feeling of wanting to see a girl naked."

I left Jake and went to the store. Today was a day when I had promised Joan Stone that I would buy her ice cream. Joan was waiting by the store. We bought the maple-walnut ice cream and went to our favorite place behind the library. I really like Joan, she was such a sweet girl compared to Beverly, who was always teasing me for kisses and hugs. I wanted to talk with her about this sex thing, but I didn't dare talk with a girl about it. I remembered how my sister Hester was all upset when I tried to talk to her and I didn't think Joan would even know about the bull and the cows that we always wound up with, every time I asked about sex anyway. I studied Joan, she was a very pretty girl with blondish hair and deep blue eyes. She was starting to develop a figure, as the boys called it, and she always dressed neatly. I wondered what Jake had meant about wanting to see girls undressed. I couldn't understand what was important about that, damn this sex thing anyway. My staring at Joan and my thoughts must have frightened her.

She said, "Caleb, what's wrong? You're looking at me like I was some kind of strange animal, are you mad at me for something? You know we have eaten ice cream like this for a few years now and it has always been a joy I have looked forward to. Now that we're not little kids anymore, maybe we should stop meeting alone. My mother has been talking to me about boy and girl relationships and some of it sounds real scary, though Mother says if you're married and old enough it can be beautiful."

"Oh, Joan, let's not let that damn sex thing take this away from us. In the beginning I started this because I thought you were cute and it made me feel like a big shot. Over the years though, I have come to look forward to our time together as something special. I always feel so much better after being with you. It's like after going to Sunday school, you don't always know why, but it leaves me with a good feeling. This approaching puberty thing has upset me plenty. Lately everybody says it's going to happen, but nobody seems to be able to explain it. I promise you one thing, Joan, I will never want to tear your clothes off and dance."

Joan hugged me tight and said, "Lord, Caleb, I hope not. I always believed that you would be a gentleman when you grew up. I don't want to lose our get-togethers either, but to be safe perhaps we should meet in the park instead of behind the library. We started out hiding this way so the kids wouldn't tease us. Now I think we would create more talk if we keep hiding."

Joan gave me another big hug and a sweet kiss and said, "I have to go, Caleb. Mother said she would pick me up at the store, we're going to Oscin to go shopping."

I rushed home, Mother still insisted that I rest at least some afternoons while I was in school if I was going to stay working for Muldons. I hadn't been doing that and she reminded me that morning. I went to my room, lay down, but I couldn't rest. *Damn it, why couldn't things stay the way they were. Now that sex thing is coming between Joan and me. The boys at the barn talk as if it was the most wonderful thing in the world. But how could that be, if it takes something as wonderful as Joan and I have away?*

When I arrived at work that night, Larry hollered, "Hey, Arthur, did you hear about Caleb's rendezvousing with that sweet little Stone girl? The way I hear it, it's been going on for years, him playing the big innocent with us all this time. Maybe he could teach us a thing or two, how about it, Caleb?"

This was just what Joan had been afraid of, it made me ripping mad. How dare they even talk about Joan? I said, "Shut your face, Larry, or I'll shut it for you."

"You and what army, Caleb, or are you going to get your sissy brother to beat me up?" Larry retorted.

I knew I wouldn't stand a chance against him, he was almost twice my size. So I shouted, in what I hoped was a mean voice, "Fighting you isn't the only way to get you. Even if I can't lick you in a fight there are always other ways to get even."

"Tell us about it, Caleb," Arthur said. "What you gonna do, cast some evil spell over us or what? I know I'll be waking up one day only to find you have grown so big and strong that I'm so scared I piss my pants."

"Oh poor us," John chimed in. "A giant Caleb with his pious attitude the law of the land. What to do, what to do?"

110

"Knock it off, you guys," Reilly shouted. "I don't believe that Caleb will ever grow into a giant, but if I was you guys I would give him a little more respect, it might save you a lot of embarrassment someday."

"Oh sure," Leonard said, "maybe we don't treat him with some respect, he will quit and that will save me from being embarrassed every time someone mentions that he is part of this crew."

"We know, Leonard, about your being embarrassed, because little Caleb holds up his end of the work as well as, if not better than you. I would be concerned about his retaliatory powers if you insist on trying to make him a scapegoat for your bone headedess. History is a great teacher, you boys really ought to be studying your recent history, that would be my advice."

"Oh, come on, Reilly," John said. "We're only poking a little fun at Caleb and his ice-cream date, we're so sorry, Caleb, if we hit a nerve."

"All right, boys, but someday you are going to look back on this day and understand. I just hope it isn't with regret," Reilly replied.

I was happy that Reilly had spoken up for me, but a little concerned on where he was headed with that talk. On the way home, Karl was waiting for me at the horse trough. He talked about being in a new school and said that he missed some of the fun we had going through the town school, but that high school had its advantages, especially all the girls. I teased him about Beverly, asking, "How does she feel about these new girls?"

He laughed and said, "Caleb, Caleb, Caleb, will you ever grow up? Beverly always had the hots for you and that's the only reason she ever had anything to do with me."

I told him, "Damn it, Karl, I heard all the horse manure I want for one day about this sex stuff if that is all you can think about. I'm heading home."

"O.K., Caleb," Karl said. "What I really came for was to see if you could arrange with George for us to go back soon and try those little brooks where we fished the day he was hurt."

"I dunno, Karl, George told me that he hasn't been back there since that day. Seems that he still has nightmares about that bull. I was thinking when he told me that maybe what he needed was to go back and kind of relive that day to get it out of his system. I think the three of us should go back and try reenacting that day for his sake."

"What a wonderful idea. I have to go now, but you let me know when we can go, if you convince him." As he was walking away he stopped, and said, laughingly, "Not an exact reenactment though, Caleb, this time I catch the big fish."

It seemed good to be planning things again with Karl. We hadn't been spending as much time together as we used to before he started high school.

Sometimes I felt as if he thought I was too young for him. He didn't seem interested in doing things we used to do and was hanging out more with high school girls. Karl had told me he was past the kid stage and had reached puberty some time ago, though I never was able to get him to talk much about it. *Well, if puberty means you're not a kid anymore I hope I don't catch it until I'm grown up.*

I went home saying goodnight to my folks and went upstairs. I could hear Hester and Emma talking as I was going by their room. Emma said, "I don't care if he is our father, he is wrong, wrong, wrong." I couldn't help listening to figure what this was all about.

I heard Hester telling Emma, "You should talk about being wrong, Emma. If you hadn't been so foolish Eunice would still be with us. Dad can't help being who he is, but you could have kept from throwing yourself at Harry all the time."

Emma said, "Shut your face, Hester. I'm not talking to you anymore."

I waited by the door listening for a few minutes and nobody talked. I figured that there must be something up that I should know about so I knocked on the door, saying, "Hester, I need to talk to you."

Hester came to the door and said, "What's bothering you, Caleb? Make it quick, Dad is in a bad mood."

"That's why I need to talk to you, Hester. I thought Mother and Dad acted like they were mad about something when I came in and I thought I had better find out what's going on before I stick my foot in it again."

"Caleb," Hester said, "Mother received a letter today from Eunice telling us that she and Harry will be coming by this way, in a few weeks, asking if they could spend a couple days here. When she told Dad about it, he said, 'Tear the letter up. We don't have a daughter named Eunice anymore.' Mother pleaded for Dad not to disown her just because he is so set in his ways. Then, Dad yelled, 'Helen, I want to see that letter destroyed right now.' Mother tore the letter and threw it in the stove and went to her room crying. We tried to talk to Dad, but he sent us flying to our rooms. I'm glad you know, Caleb, because you do have a way of wreaking havoc with your questions sometimes."

I crawled in to bed wondering if I would ever see Eunice again or get to ride with Harry on his Indian. I knew that Dad wasn't a mean or angry father, it was just he had these old-fashioned beliefs that he expected us all to live up to. I guess that Eunice figured that enough time had gone by so that Dad would be more forgiving. I would have doubted that, but she wasn't here to know Dad wouldn't even let us speak her name. I was much too tired to handle all these thoughts, so I fell asleep and dreamed that I was riding with

Harry on some long trip.

When we arrived at school the next day, there was a new boy in the eighth grade. Old Hanna introduced him to the class. His name was Charlie Rice and he had just moved here from California. She explained that his family had spent a year working their way across the country. She did this while showing us all the towns that he had been in since he left. It was interesting and at the same time we were getting a lesson in geography. Charlie seemed older than most of the boys in the eighth grade, maybe because he lost a year of school while traveling. He was sure some different than us country boys. He gave Hanna fits. When she finally gave up trying to reason with him and took her yardstick to him and sent him to the hall he just kept right on walking and went home. The next day he returned to school with his parents. Man, if that had been me, I would have been dragged in with my parents telling Hanna she was right. Charlie's parents seemed mad that Hanna had dared to touch their boy. Hanna took them out in the hall and closed the door so we couldn't hear what was being said. It got very loud a couple of times. In the end Charlie and his parents left with Hanna, saying, "Oh don't worry, I'll be there. You can be very sure of that."

We never found out for sure what happened that night except they had all met with the school committee. Charlie said Hanna was put in her place, but I noticed that he was careful not to challenge her too much after that. It was quite evident that he would get away with things we had never dared and you could see that it infuriated Hanna. It was the talk amongst us boys that we would hate to be in his shoes when she finally lost her cool with him. We all remembered the story about her and big John Muldon when he was in the eighth grade.

Charlie joined our school in October and in late November that year we had an unusual warm spell. We took advantage of the weather stretching our recesses and noon hour as long as we could after the first bell. More than once some of us were late and were punished by having to recite for the class. One noontime after the second bell, Charlie, Louise Phelps and Julie Sledge, Arthur's sister, hadn't returned to class. Hanna started classes as usual, but you could tell she was very agitated. Fifteen minutes went by then twenty, it was finally a good thirty minutes after the bell before the three of them came out of the woods. Hanna's face was flushed and the veins were standing out on her neck like Josh talked about. I could see why he had thought she might burst. The three of them came in and took their seats. Hanna said, "Out in the hall, young ladies, if I can still call you that. And you, young man, come up to my desk this minute. I want you to stand in front of this class and tell us what you and those girls were doing out in those woods." Charlie bowed rather arrogantly to Hanna and said, "Why, Miss Hanna? Whatever can you mean? We just went for a little walk and being the poor city boy that I am, we got lost. I apologize for us being late but I assure you that's the truth."

Hanna said, "So that's your story, a poor innocent city boy lost in the woods. I don't believe a word of it."

"Why, Miss Hanna? What in the world did you think? That I had lured those sweet little country girls out into the woods to have sex?"

Hanna stood there kind of teetering back and forth for a minute, it looked like she was going to pass out like George had done. Then she ran to her desk, grabbed her yardstick and started beating Charlie, yelling, "Out, out of this school, you foul-mouthed city brat, before I kill you." Charlie ran for the door, but he sure took some pounding before he got away from her. As she returned to her desk she seemed so distraught that I felt sorry for her. After she had caught her breath it seemed as if she had a thought that pleased her, because she rather smiled and went out in the hall with the Louise and Julie. We all tried to hear what was being said out in the hall, but all we heard was the girls crying and say, "No we did not, our parents would kill us for even thinking like that."

There was no keeping school after all that excitement, and Hanna excused us early, telling the ones that rode the bus or the wagons to stay in the field until the lower classes let out. Charlie had waited outside and I saw him, Louise and Julie with their heads together as if they were making plans. The next day at school Hanna wasn't there. Mr. Moore, the school committee chairman was sitting at Hanna's desk and Mr. and Mrs. Phelps, Mrs. Sledge and several of the committee members and other children's parents were sitting in the back of the room. Charlie, Louise and Julie weren't in school. George told me there had been all hell to pay at his house last night. His father was so upset that his mother wouldn't let him near Louise. He kept shouting, "This is what I have worked so hard to support, a damned harlot. I want her gone from here, I won't have the whole town belittling the Phelps name, take my name from her and ship her off."

George said that his sister cried all night, he snuck in to see her after his folks had gone to bed and asked her how could she do such a crazy thing. She said, "Oh, George, someone has to believe me. Nothing really bad happened we got to playing kissing games and Charlie got a little out of hand. Julie and I ran when he became so lustful, the running seemed to cool him down but by that time we were deeper in the woods and we did get lost coming out. We were all really worried what was going to happen when Hanna got us, but we never dreamed it would be this bad. You have to find some way to help me,

George, don't let Dad throw me out, I would rather die."

I asked George if he had thought of anyway to help. He said, "No, Caleb, I'm just about going crazy trying to think of something that would convince my father that Louise didn't do what he thinks. I am still hoping for a chance to help her. I know she is a little boy crazy, but this time I don't think she deserves what is happening."

Mr. Moore called the class to order and said, "Your regular teacher won't be able to be with you today. With such short notice we didn't have time to replace her so I am going to be her substitute. Now the first thing we are going to do is get to the bottom of what happened yesterday. Many of the people in town have questions, we have arranged them in what we believe will be helpful in getting the answers. First, do any of you children know precisely what questions Hanna asked those girls yesterday?"

Much to my surprise, George answered, "I do, but I'm not sure you want to hear them."

Mr. Moore said, "On the contrary, young Phelps, that is exactly why we are here. I am sure that no teacher would use language that was offensive in the classroom."

George said, "Well, guess that depends on who is being offended. What Miss Hanna asked these girls, as you call them, was if they let Charlie take off their panties and did he take off his pants, or grab their breasts or have sex with them." George stood and waited, the room was so quiet you could hear people kind of gasping for breath. Then he said, "I want everyone in this room to know that none of this happened, my sister and Julie got caught up in one of Charlie's games and while running away from him got lost. The only bad thing that happened was they came back to school late. Now I know that Hanna is, and has been, a good teacher, but I believe that what happened here was because she had it in for Charlie and he was dumb enough to give her this chance to really get him."

The kids started getting uneasy in their seats and an angry hum was coming from the parents in the back. Mr. Moore rapped on the desk for quiet and asked, "Are there other children who heard this blasphemy?" At first no one answered and George looked at me rather pleadingly. I wanted to help but I had grown to like old Hanna and I didn't want to lie. I stood up anyway and said, "I didn't hear all that George heard, but we heard the girls crying and saying, 'No, no we would never do such things, our folks would kill us!'"

Mr. Moore asked, "Is there anyone else except one of the girls' brother and his best friend who will collaborate this nightmare of a story?"

One by one, at first shyly and then in louder and stronger voices, the class answered, "Caleb's right, we heard what he heard." When it came Jake's turn he said, "Caleb is right in all that he said. I have enjoyed studying under Hanna, she is a fine teacher, but it is true she seemed to hate Charlie. She even threatened to kill him right in front of the whole class."

Mr. Moore asked, "How many of you here heard anything like that?"

Almost in unison, the class shouted, "All of us, Mr. Moore, all of us."

Mr. Moore said, "All right, class, I'm going to have a conference with the committee and attending parents. While I am doing that I want all four grades to open up your books and read about Germany. I want to be able to discuss Germany with you when I get back."

Mr. Moore and all the adults gathered in the hall and closed the doors. There was some very loud heated discussion, but it was impossible to catch enough of it to understand where it was leading. After close to two hours, the meeting broke up and Mr. Moore came back into the room and we started discussing Germany. Of course our thoughts were that all Nazis should be killed. Mr. Moore explained, though it was bad that the German people had allowed a despot like Hitler to rule their country, it didn't necessarily mean that every German was bad. He taught that it was because most people do not really study or understand their governments, and when they don't stay knowledgeable about what's happening in their governments bad things like a Hitler coming to power happens, and that usually means war.

Jake asked, "Do you really believe that somebody like Hitler could become a power in America? We are a democracy, that couldn't happen here."

Mr. Moore said, "It is not likely, but if the students of America didn't fully exercise their rights to become voters and be concerned with the politics and politicians in Washington, then it could be possible."

We had Mr. Moore for a couple of more days. It was different having him teach, we discussed a lot and I learned many things about the world and its different people that I had often wondered about. The teacher who took his place didn't look much older than my sister Hester. I heard she just got out of school herself. We never knew where Old Hanna went, all we knew is that she packed up and moved out of town during the night.

George said Mr. and Mrs. Moore came to his house to talk with his mother and father and Louise and though Louise received a good chastening from his father at least she wasn't disowned. George thanked me for speaking up in class and said for a few seconds he thought what he had said was going to make things worse. I asked him where he got the idea that Hanna had asked the girls those questions?

He said, "Caleb, I didn't know what I was going to say when I stood up.

116

I ended up telling what Louise had told me the night before. And then I thought, *Oh sure, they're going to believe her,* but nobody questioned where I heard that after you and the class spoke. I'm glad that you are my friend, Caleb, everybody else was ready to blame Louise and Julie. I was really scared until you started speaking."

Our new teacher's name was Miss Lacy. She was sweet and soft and never stood a chance. I don't believe she had been trained to handle four different grades at once, and she seemed confused most of the time. I am not sure what caused it, maybe it was our escape from Hanna's strict discipline, but the kids began acting like uncaged animals and the schoolroom was an absolute zoo in comparison to Hanna's classes. By Friday, Miss Lacy just sat at her desk and cried. At first this awed the kids enough so they were quiet, but only for a while. Finally we became so noisy that Mrs. Stange, the teacher from the other room, came in to see what was wrong. She shouted us down and said we should be ashamed of ourselves. She tried to console Miss Lacy, but she just kept her head on the desk sobbing. Mrs. Stange called Jake up to the desk and asked him to go to the woodshed and see if the janitor was still there. Jake came back with Mr. Williams, our janitor. Mrs. Stange had returned to her room to maintain order. She met with the janitor in the hall, then he came into our room. He went over and put his hand on Miss Lacy's shoulder and tried to talk to her without success. Walking to the front of the room, he eyed the class menacingly. After eyeing us, he said, "I want each of you children to come forward quietly and write your full names on the blackboard. We'll start with the row nearest the window wall." One by one we went quietly to the board. As each one of us stepped back he would say. "Oh, I know your parents well." Or, "I worked with your dad." It didn't take a genius to figure out what he was telling us. After everyone had written their name, he said, "Now I want each of you to write a little essay to explain today's behavior to your fathers. I was planning on being here until dark tonight and no one in this room is leaving school until they are finished, so get busy."

I hadn't been too involved in the rowdiness, most of the time I had been deep in thought about what had happened to Hanna. I was sad about the way everything had turned out and had my suspicions on Louise's story. I remembered when she, Julie and Charlie had their heads together in the park and wondered if they hadn't worked out that story. I wrote a long, emotional paper on how sorry I was that Hanna had to leave and that my behavior if it had been unruly was because of my disappointment and confusion over losing her as a teacher. I thanked Hanna in my writing for the extra hours that she had given Jake and me. I wrote that I hoped someday she would see my name in print because of her efforts. I was proud of what Jake called my knack for making people feel when I wrote. My hopes were that not only would this paper save me some trouble, but perhaps add to my reputation as a writer. When the final bell rang, Mr. Williams sat in the doorway collecting our papers, repeating to each kid, "Remember the city kid that we had to expel because of the way he acted." Some of the boys, George and Glenn among them, were still poised over their papers looking like they had seen a wildcat springing at them. Glenn asked Mr. Williams if I could help him with some words, he nodded. So I stopped at Glenn's desk. He had scribbled out several things he had written and had absolutely nothing to pass in.

Glenn said, "Help me, Caleb, or I'll be here all night and my father will murder me just for having to stay after school."

"Look, Glenn," I said, "just write 'I'm am extremely sorry that I followed the class in their unruly behavior, it was an unjustifiable slip of my upbringing.'"

Glenn started writing what I said, asking how to spell some words, repeating, "Will this really work, will it, Caleb, will it?"

"I hope so, Glenn," I answered, "but you're in a damned-if-you-do-damned-if-you-don't situation and it's the best I can think of right now." George waved me over and showed me his paper, it was dreadful but I didn't want to tell him, so I said, "I think that will pass in this case, George." Outside school everyone was talking about what was going to happen to our papers. We all knew that there would be hell to pay if our parents knew what was really happening in our school since Hanna left. I went to the store to meet Joan. Today was the day we usually had ice cream. When it was too cold for ice cream, we would buy candy bars on the days that the library was open and go there to be together. It wasn't very private this way, but Joan didn't want us hiding and it was a place to stay warm. Joan seemed upset when I met her. She said, "Caleb, I was glad to see you didn't join in all the foolishness that went on in school. I don't know how those kids could treat Miss Lacy so cruel. It will serve them right if their letters get them all horsewhipped. I felt so sorry for her, she had worked hard to get her teaching certificate, and to have her first job end like this."

I told Joan I felt bad for Miss Lacy too and thought that I should have mentioned that in my paper. I really didn't want to talk school. I missed the talks we used to have about our feelings, it seemed that Joan shied away from these subjects lately. I knew from experience that I would not get one of her kisses if we parted at the library, so I said, "Joan, let's leave early enough so I can walk you home."

She smiled and said, "I'd like that, Caleb, it will give us more of a chance

118

to talk."When we left the library we didn't talk much, just held hands, with Joan occasionally brushing against me as we walked. Joan had changed lately. I had noticed this kind of change in my sisters, and it was like all of a sudden they weren't little kids anymore. With my sisters it was as if most of the boys they knew abruptly became their enemies, or in cases like Emma's, they became boy crazy. With Joan, the change was in not sharing what we thought about things, it was as if she wasn't sure she could trust me with her thoughts anymore. I supposed it was this puberty thing, when I looked the word up at school it was about being physically able to do this sex thing and growing pubic hair. I know that some of the boys at school were excited about what was happening to them, but others were actually frightened by the changes they were experiencing.

We had almost reached Joan's house when she stopped and put her hands on my shoulders, saying, "Caleb, we have been close for so long I can almost hear you thinking. I wish we could be as free as we used to be." With tears in her eyes she hugged me, kissing my cheeks, then after pressing her lips hard to mine she turned and ran home. After the impact of her show of affection had passed, I merrily started home. I felt marvelous, Joan had done what I had wanted to do for some time, and it was like the first time we held hands or when she first started giving me little kisses on the cheek. *Puberty be damned, I think I am truly in love.*

When I got home Josh and Homer were talking upstairs. Homer seemed upset, Josh said, "Hey, Caleb, what's all this about writing a letter to Dad explaining your behavior today? Homer is scared to death about what's going to happen to him."

"I dunno, Josh," I replied, "things were pretty bad at school today and Mr. Williams ended up taking over the class. He had us doing that as punishment for the way the class behaved. He never said he was going to give them to our parents. Lord, there will be hell to pay all over town if he does."

"Homer," Josh said, "let's look at the positive side of this, he may not pass them on. I don't want either one of you blabbing what I say, Mr. Williams is a very talented man but he is illiterate. So I don't believe he is going to put himself in the position of having to discuss those letters with the parents of this town."

Homer jumped up and hugged Josh, saying, "Josh, I was thinking when I wrote the letter, Josh will know what to do. I'm so lucky to have you for a brother."

I wasn't sure if it was because I saw Homer taking my place with Josh, or because I wanted Homer to look up to me. Feeling slighted by this exchange, I scoffed, "He still might pass them in, Homer, you would have been better off behaving, or formulating a letter that would save your butt."

Homer made as if he didn't hear me and ran out. Josh said, "What's come over you, Caleb? Even if those letters do get passed on, that's a better time to deal with it than worrying for days about something that might never happen. You know that I only have one more year of high school and it looks like I might have to join one of the services or be drafted. I hoped that Homer and the rest of the young ones would have you as big brother then."

"I'm sorry, Josh," I answered sheepishly. "I guess hearing you and Homer together made me see another thing I'm losing becoming a man with this puberty bunk and it hurt."

"Oh, Caleb, little Caleb, that's a good example," Josh said. "Here you are worrying and making matters worse, puberty is neither the hell nor the heaven that you hear about from the boys. What it is, is a physical change that happens in your youth that presents you with the joys and challenges that help develop what you are. Your body will test your will and give new meaning to the saying 'mind over matter,' but your morals will meet the test if you have faith."

"Oh, Josh," I exclaimed, "I wish it was as easy for me to accept your wisdom as it was when I was like Homer. All my friends are changing, not only the boys, but Joan too. I sometimes have this awful feeling that I'm about to lose the most precious thing I own."

"Caleb, Caleb, Caleb," Josh replied as he was rubbing his head and twisting his hair. "You aren't going to lose anything, you're going to gain something. We don't lose our childhood to puberty, we build on it; you don't become an adult the way you go from grammar school to high school, you grow into it. There may be a certain age when people think you should act adult, but adulthood doesn't come with just age. It comes with a way of feeling, believing and understanding that is a part of all we've ever been including when we were little children. In my readings some people get there late in life, while others don't ever quite make it. You should relax, Caleb, and relish each day like it was one of your fishing trips, instead of worrying so much."

I knew Josh was right. I wished that I could rush off as happy as Homer had with his explanation, but I couldn't. Maybe it was because of the time I spent at Muldon's barn with the older boys and their smutty stories that made puberty so scary. I didn't see the joy in it that Josh talked about, only the challenges.

Mr. Moore took over teaching at school, while the committee searched for a new teacher. Miss Lacy had left town the same day Mr. Williams had to take over for her. I heard she was still crying when she left. Mr. Moore kept the class under control, but he was more a lecturer than a teacher, he and Jake had some interesting debates about current news. Jake was a pacifist while Mr. Moore believed that America would eventually be involved anyway and the sooner we fought those Nazis, the quicker it would be over. Most of the boys bragged about what they were going to do when they joined the Army, but some were more apprehensive and didn't see it as such a faraway thing. I hadn't really given it much thought before these debates and Josh said it looked as if he would have to go. What little I had thought about it seemed frightening, though I wondered how I would do slogging through the body-filled trenches of France, like Uncle Louis had done. I actually prayed that neither Josh nor I would ever have to find out how heroic we would be.

It was almost a month before the school committee found a replacement, this time it was a man. His name was Alan Vickers. He was a short man, built like a fighter, with muscular arms and a bull neck. We were all anxious the first day he was to teach and were in class and seated before the last bell. Mr. Vickers walked on the balls of his feet as if he was ready to pounce at any moment. At the front of the class, he stopped and said, "Good morning, class, my name is Mr. Vickers. To help me get to know each one of you, I'm going to ask each one of you to come forward when I call your name." As we stepped forward Mr. Vickers shook our hands and gave each one of us a nametag, instructing us to wear it on our left shoulders. After we all had nametags, Mr. Vickers said, "Now children, I'm not given to threats, because I believe that you have to carry them out if you make them. Unfortunately the briefing I received on the behavior in this classroom is abominable and would seem to require harsh methods of control. It is my belief that behavior is taught by parents at home, not by the teachers at school. My method of handling any unruly behavior will to be to ask the student to go home and bring their parents back to school so I might discuss their child's problems with them."

It became very evident at recess time that Mr. Vickers had struck the right nerve. None of the terrors of the classroom deemed it advisable to be in the position of having to bring their parents to school. I know that if that happened to me, it would be scarier than any old war front, because I could well imagine the fury my parents would be in. Things at school settled down for the next few months, and for the first time since Hanna had left we had real lessons with a teacher who had us under control. Mr. Vickers for the most part was amiable, though on a few occasions he had displayed some seemingly unreasonable anger. One day in the last of April, Mr. Vickers was doing playground duty when Glenn's brother, Darren, refused to share the swing he was using. Mr. Vickers tried to talk to him about sharing, but

Darren was adamant. He wasn't going to give up the swing, and when Mr. Vickers attempted to lift him out, Darren held tight to the chains, screaming. Mr. Vickers angrily yanked him from the chains, tearing some flesh off Darren's hands. Darren lay screaming on the ground, holding his bloody hand. Glenn went running to him, took one look at Darren's hand and shouted, "Is this how you do your fighting, Vickers? You 4 F son-of-a-bitch, beating up fourth grade kids."

What happened next was like an explosion. Mr. Vickers hit Glenn two mighty blows that you could hear across the playground. Glenn collapsed beside his brother with blood running from his nose and trickling from his mouth. Mr. Vickers stared at them for a moment and then he strode into the school. Mrs. Stange came running out of the building, saying, "Oh my God, I saw what happened, did he kill him?" By that time I was by Glenn's side and answered, "No, Mrs. Stange, he is breathing, but it's pretty ragged. He needs a doctor."

Mrs. Stange yelled, "Jake Wilson, run down to the Inn and have them call a doctor quick."

Jake must have run like the wind, because it was only a few minutes before Mr. Banner was there with his big Packard. He rushed over to Glenn and checked his pulse and breathing, then looked at Darren's hand. He said, "Mrs. Stange, I don't believe we should wait for a doctor. I'll take them both to the hospital. The older Collard boy's condition worries me. I'll take the Wilson boy to help me, perhaps you should send one of the older boys to find a constable or call the Oscin police. Mr. Vickers has done a terrible thing here, and he should be held accountable."

George, Jake and I helped Mr. Banners carry Glenn over to his car. Jake sat inside holding Glenn's head as they drove off. George said, "Don't this bring back memories, Caleb? What in the hell do you think possessed Mr. Vickers? I knew he had a temper, but this is insane."

"I'm not sure, George," I answered, "whether Darren had already driven him over the edge or it was what Glenn said, but whatever made him snap, he's in a heap of trouble even if Glenn comes out of this all right." Mrs. Stange herded everyone back into class. Mr. Vickers was nowhere to be found, so she sent Homer to find Mr. Williams. Mr. Williams came into the room, saying, "Well what do you know, here I am a teacher again. I believe our first duty is to pause a moment in prayer for the Collard boys. Now that we have done all we can do for them right now, I want everyone to continue with the lessons they were on before lunch hour. If you are already done, redo it, there is always room for improvement. Now if any of you feel like playing games because I'm filling in, remember the letters you wrote for me last time, I kept them all."

Mr. Banner, Jake and Darren returned just before the final bell, Darren's hand was bandaged and in a sling close to his shoulder. Mr. Banner said that Glenn was going to be all right, that he had a slight concussion and the doctors felt it was better he stay at the hospital until they were sure it was nothing more. I spoke to Clem Baker, our constable, and he said that Mr. Vickers was detected acting strangely in Oscin and was being held at their police station. The school committee would meet tonight with the Collard family to decide how he would be charged.

George came home the following day and outside of a couple of shiners he said he felt O.K. The police discovered that Mr. Vickers had a record of violence. He had served time for assault with a deadly weapon because he had been a professional boxer for a while after he graduated from college. He was thrown out of boxing because of his temper and only recently had been using his degree to obtain teaching jobs. His only teaching experience before he came to us was as a temp in other schools. Evidently this was the first time he had lost it as a teacher. Mr. Moore again became our teacher and the war debates began anew. The German army was advancing across Europe and Japan was invading throughout Asia. There was a definite feeling that it was only a matter of time before America became involved. Jake argued that Americans were ill prepared for a war either mentally or physically, while Mr. Moore railed at our politicians as being weak-kneed pansies.

Mr. Moore was only with us for a few days. Our new teacher, Mrs. Putnam, had been out of teaching for almost twenty years. She had chosen to stay home and raise her own children. Her children where grown now and she had been talking about returning to teaching. She lived in Stanfield, the next town west of Sterling, and one of our school committee members who knew her persuaded her to come to our school. Mrs. Putman was not a Hanna, Vickers or Miss Lacy. No big speeches, just a quiet, "Good morning, class, I am your new teacher, Mrs. Putman. Please introduce yourselves when you speak, until I am familiar with your names. I have been hired to finish out the school year. If we develop a good relationship I will consider returning next year." She seemed to anticipate from who or from where, trouble would come from by her third day. She had quietly changed our seating arrangements, placing those who needed help or control at the front of the room. The desk and chairs of our school were bolted to the floor in rows. The row closest to the door was one desk shorter than the other rows, to allow access to the hallway door. The first seat in the second row she left empty. We wondered at this for a few days, until Dennis Bolts, who was in the sixth grade and had developed into one of the school bullies, started giving Mrs. Putman a hard time. She moved Dennis into the empty seat, this placed him close to her desk and seemed to work for a couple of days. Dennis, who seemed to think of himself as a leader, started using his front row seat as a stage, shooting spit balls when the teacher's back was turned; making shuffling noises when she spoke and generally disrupting the class. Mrs. Putman allowed this to continue a couple of days until it became evident to all the class what he was doing. Then she said, "Dennis, I am beginning to believe that you don't like being here with us, is that true?"

"Nobody wants to be cooped up in a stuffy old school listening to dumb teachers," Dennis replied.

I figured that all hell was going to break loose as old Hanna would do, but Mrs. Putman calmly said, "Well, Dennis, I don't seem to be able to keep your attention, so you probably are wasting your time here. Here's what we'll do. You gather up your things and leave, go home and convince your parents that school is a waste of your time and go on with your life. If you are unable to convince them, then have them come to see me and I will explain to them why school is such a waste of your time."

Dennis said, "No, no. I don't want to do that."

"I'm sorry, Dennis," Mrs. Putman said, as she lifted him from his seat and forcefully pushed him out the door. "I believe you haven't left me a choice." Without further mention, Mrs. Putman went back to teaching our lessons.

A few days later Dennis was back in school sitting at his old desk, with that empty front row seat a vivid reminder of what Mrs. Putman was capable of. In the few weeks of school that were left we developed a fondness for Mrs. Putman and her way of teaching, and most of us hoped she would return next year.

School ending was different for me this year, Karl and I weren't together much anymore and we hadn't made any big plans on how we were going to spend our summer. Karl wasn't excited about doing things we used to plan, though there was some hope we could join his Uncle Tom on part of his trip down the Connecticut River. One reason Karl and I didn't get together as much was Lisa Magee, a girl he met in high school. She lived in Lange and Karl was always looking for rides to go see her. I dreaded the way my friends were changing. Karl, George, Glenn, nobody seemed to be excited about the exploring, fishing and mountain climbing that had always been in our summer planning. Even Jake had changed, though he had never been much for anything but reading and writing, the stories he used to talk about were by Jack London and Robert Service and the like. Now he was reading all kinds of mushy stories by authors I had never heard of. I suppose that it was because of this damn puberty that things were different. At least we were still going to climb the mountain on the last day of school. One thing for sure, I wasn't going let puberty dissuade me from enjoying being young during my thirteenth summer.

Chapter 9

The last day of school we all climbed the mountain. Because it had been a very dry spring, the state fire warden was manning the fire tower and we all had a chance to sign his visitor's book. It seemed strange not having Karl with us anymore. Glenn made a point of the fact that this would be the last year he would be doing this kid stuff. I guess that going out of town to school was a part of the passage of growing up. I was glad I had another year for the kid stuff he was mocking. It was scary to me even thinking about changing. I had great plans for the summer. Karl and I were definitely going to spend a night or two camping on the mountain and his uncle's Connecticut River trip was scheduled to start the in middle of July. He was beginning the trip in Colebrook, New Hampshire, and was to call Karl's parents when he would be in Littleton and we would join him there and stay with him until we reached Stanfield, Massachusetts. He planned to continue through Massachusetts and Connecticut after a layover in Sterling, until he reached Saybrook, Connecticut. I had talked to Dad and Mother about using my savings to buy some good fishing and camping gear. I already had the fishing tackle with a new pole and reel, and Mother was talking with Karl's mother about what else I would need. Glenn and I had planned a fishing trip to his secret place the next day. Josh wasn't able to do my milking that morning, so we had to leave a little later after I was through. I met Glenn where Stanfield road joined the road leading to Hasling Pond. It was an exciting day for me, because this would be the first time I got to use my new fishing gear. Glenn was rather sullen when he saw it and didn't talk much as we rode away. About half way there just after we rounded a corner, Glenn stopped the horse to rest. We heard a noise behind us as if something had slid on the sand. I didn't see anything, but Glenn said, "Caleb, we're being followed."

"I didn't see anything, Glenn," I answered, "but I did hear the noise. What do you think it is?"

"I think it's one of your damn friends spying on us," Glenn replied. "My daddy told me this was what would happen if I took you with me. I should have kept it just my secret."

"Come on, Glenn, you know I haven't told anyone. If I had, the whole town would have been over there fishing," I answered angrily. "I admit that it has been damn hard on me to keep such a big secret, but I have. Besides, if I had told anyone, why would they need to be spying?"

"I'm sorry, Caleb," he said as he set rubbing his head, "but your buddy George has been giving me a lot of shit about his sister. I wasn't the one who got her in that trouble at school, yet when I tried to visit him at his house, they practically threw me out on my ear."

I knew that Glenn didn't think anyone but the Phelpses and his family knew about him and Louis's bare ass dance in the barn, but he must be rather thick if he thought he would be welcome there again. I wanted to question him, but instead I asked, "Do you think one of us should sneak back and have a look to see if we are being followed?"

"That's a good idea, Caleb," Glenn said, "I'll go on a little ways with the horse while you sneak back to the corner and have a look."

I snuck back to the corner and hid in the bushes while Glenn drove ahead. I saw Karl come out of the bushes with his bicycle. He rode up to the corner, but when he saw Glenn stop he darted back. I had seen someone else moving in the brush behind him but couldn't make out who it was. I hurried back to the wagon and told Glenn what I had seen, asking, "What do you think? Shall we let them know we are on to them?"

He started the horse up and said, "Let's think about it first, maybe there's a better way. I know what, Caleb, let's go past were we turn off and go down by the Stanfield line and fish the brook where it comes back to the road. It will make quite a ride for them and maybe teach them a lesson."

"I think that's a good idea, Glenn," I answered, "if anybody asks, we can tell them that we had been hearing nobody is catching anything at Hasling Pond so we decided to try a new place."

We drove to the Stanfield line where the brook rejoined the road. We caught a few good trout, but nothing to brag about. We didn't fish long because I had to be back in time to work that night. Karl and his cohort didn't show their face, but there were a group of kids suspiciously waiting when we returned to town to see what our catch was. We took much kidding, but Glenn's secret was still safe.

Karl and I finally got to spend a couple of nights on the mountain, but the excitement of that was overshadowed by our plans to join his uncle on the trip down the Connecticut River. Karl fell in love with my new fishing gear and took pride in showing me how to use my new fishing reel. I practiced every day, thinking someday I would be able to cast like Karl's uncle. The middle of July finally came. We knew that it wouldn't be long before we would be going to Littleton to meet Karl's uncle. As tired as I was some nights, the excitement of the trip sometimes kept me awake.

One morning at breakfast, Mother said, "I swear, Caleb, this trip of yours seems to have taken on a life of its own, it's all that you and Karl have lived and breathed since school let out. I went shopping with Karl's mother yesterday and I have a surprise for you when you come home."

I went to Muldon's barn all excited about my surprise, I needed a sleeping bag, but what Karl and I dreamed about was having a tent of our own. We didn't have enough money between us but hoped our parents would help. We knew these were tough times financially for our families, so we tried not to let it get too important, but still we dreamed and wanted. I was stripping my twentieth cow when Joe Muldon came running in, shouting, "Arthur, you stay here and finish stripping, the rest of you boys come with me, there is a big fire at Caleb's house."

I dropped my pail and ran for home, when I was in sight of the house my heart sank. There was fire coming from the doors and windows, and the few people that were there were trying to get the animals out of the barn. My mother was in the middle of the yard with some of the children screaming. I only could see Homer, Jason and Francis with Mother, I thought, *Oh my God, the rest of the family is still in there.* Rushing to Mother's side, I saw Emma and Nellie sitting in the garden, crying their eyes out. When I reached Mother, I shouted, "Mother, where are Josh and Hester?"

"They're gone, Caleb," she sobbed, "went to work before the fire started." My heart jumped into my throat at her first gasp of "they're gone" and almost choked me before I realized what she was saying. The fire was way beyond anything that could be controlled by the time the men left in town had arrived. It was decided to let it burn itself out rather than risk anyone getting hurt. The women of the neighborhood came and started gathering my brothers and sisters while trying to console my mother. Mother kept sobbing deliriously, "Gone, gone, everything we own gone, my new kitchen, my mother's china, everything, everything, all the money we have saved, Caleb's new tent, all our clothes, everything, everything."

Ellie Baker put her arms around Mother, saying, "Helen, all your children are still here and Dorothy Hart and Dee Laurins are going to take care of them for now. Why don't you come with me away from here?"

Mother cried out, "My home, my home, how can I leave?" She collapsed in Ellie's arms. A couple of the men who had been standing around, feeling helpless, helped Ellie get Mother to her house.

Karl's mother came over to me and said, "Caleb, your sisters are going to Mrs. Laurins's house, I'm taking your brothers to my house and I want you to come too."

I asked her to wait a few minutes so I could talk to them before they left. They were all dressed in their nightclothes except Jason, who had a habit of sleeping naked, all he had was a blanket wrapped around him. For the first time it dawned on me that the only thing we owned was the clothes on our back. I started understanding Mother's pain. I had planned to say something to help the terror that was in their eyes, but I was too choked up to talk, that fear was in me too. I hugged each one and told them not to be afraid, all the time wishing that Josh were here to help. Though I was sobbing now, I thanked Mrs. Hart for taking my brothers and told her I would have to stay there in case Hester or Josh came back. The last of our home was collapsing into the cellar. People began drifting off one by one to return to their work. I sat watching the furious flames devour the last of what had been our home. How could this be? This was the home where I was born, the place where I escaped the outside world, the center of my life's compass, how could it be gone? I threw myself on the grass sobbing, seeing and hearing Mother in my mind. *Gone, gone, everything gone, my new kitchen, Caleb's new tent.* Oh the pain. It hadn't registered when she first said it. A new tent, my fishing gear, gone all gone, sobs wrenched my whole body as I cried out, "Why me, Lord?" As I lay there sobbing Muldon's truck came down the road. It was Josh, he had left early that morning delivering wood in Lange.

Josh sat in the truck for a moment, then got out and came and held me, saying, "Are we all still here, Caleb?"

I told him yes, through my sobs.

He sat there holding me for the longest time, not saying anything. Finally, he asked, "Where are Mother and the rest of the children?" After I told him, he said, "I think we should go and see that they are all right."

"You go, Josh, I need to stay here. I'm not ready to face anyone right now," I sobbed out.

"I understand, Caleb," Josh said, "but I think I should go."

Josh left with the truck and I was alone in my own special pain, picturing my lost tent and fishing gear. As I was lying there sobbing someone was coming across the field, it was Dad. As I watched him come through the field he seemed to grow older before my eyes. The closer he came to the house the more his shoulders slumped. He walked into the yard without speaking. Like Josh he quietly stared at the timbers burning in the cellar hole. After what seemed a long time, he said, "Caleb, is Mother and all your brothers and sisters still with us?"

Oh God! What he must have been thinking. I jumped up and ran to him, saying, "We are all here, Dad, and we're all safe."

The weariness and aging seemed to lift from his shoulders as he put his arm around my shoulder and said, "Thank God for that. We can always find another house."

After tearing my heart out the last few hours with the pain of losing my sleeping bag and fishing gear, my father's words slapped me with shame. He, with the clothes on his back, his only possessions, could see a real reason to thank God when all that he had earned with a lifetime of sweat lay burning in a cellar hole. I had never thought of Dad as a very religious man, but there was a tone of gratitude in his "Thank God for that" which clearly showed a faith that I would always remember. "Come on, Caleb," Dad said, "let's gather up the clan and start putting this family back together."

As we were starting to leave, Mr. Banner pulled into the yard driving his Packard. He got out of the car and came over to Dad. He said, "I'm terribly sorry, Henry, some of the boys at the Inn have started a collection to help your family get a new start. I just bought the Ward place on the Stanfield road and we had given some thought of selling the Inn and my wife wanted a place to stay here in Sterling if we did. Nobody is using it now and I would like you and your family to use it until you find a new place of your own."

Dad said, "That's very generous of you, Leslie. I'm sure that it would be better for the family if we had a place were we could be all together right now. I'll talk to Helen and see how quickly we can get settled there."

When we arrived at the Bakers', Mother had regained her composure. Marian Banner had already been to see her, so she knew about the Ward place. The women of the town were already digging up furniture for the house. Frank Butler was driving around picking it up and delivering it to our new home. Alice Hart was combing the neighborhood trying to find clothes for all of us. She brought back a couple of boxes full of clothes, my size with just about everything I would need in them. At first I was excited to think that I had so many new things, but when I heard Mrs. Hart and Mother talking about poor Mrs. Bennet, I realized where the clothes had come from. Norman Bennet had started the fifth grade that year, and halfway through the school year he had died of some kind of sugar disease and these were his clothes. Luckily I still had my barn clothes on and no one had complained about the smell yet. Dad had gone to help Frank Butler, Josh came back and we started to walk to the Ward place to help set up the furniture. I was glad to be alone with Josh. I felt as if a horse had kicked me. The fire; my fishing and camping gear; seeing Dad's first reactions; and now getting Norman's clothes after he was dead. Tears were rolling down my cheeks.

"It will be all right little, Caleb, it will be all right," Josh said.

"Oh, Josh," I cried, "I can't take any more. How can I tell Mother and

Mrs. Hart that I can't wear Norman's clothes, they seemed so proud that they found them for me."

Josh was quiet for a few minutes, then he said, "Caleb, do you believe in heaven and angels?"

I thought of Dad as he was coming across the field towards his burning home, how he had looked, the fear on his face before he asked about the family. I remembered how the life had pumped back into him when he heard my answer and I said, "Yes, Josh, I believe."

"If you truly believe, Caleb," Josh replied, "then think about it as if it was you who had died and you were an angel looking down on someone in trouble, wouldn't you want to help?"

"Of course I would want to help, Josh," I said. "Isn't that what angels are supposed to do?"

"See, Caleb, Norman sees this as a chance to do good. His mother said Norman would have wanted to do this. If you believe it's not just what he would have wanted when he was here, it's what he wants to do now as God's angel," Josh explained.

I needed to believe that Josh really felt what he was saying if I was going to be able to wear Norman's clothes. So, I said, "Josh, do you truly believe that Norman is really able to see and hear what's happening to us?"

"Caleb, Caleb, little Caleb," Josh replied, "How can I make you understand what I believe? I believe that Jesus was sent to us to teach about God's love and how not to fear Him. He promised that God would be waiting for us, to forgive and accept us as we accepted Him. He promised that God had room for all of us, so I believe for every angel that you hear about, there are thousands more watching and waiting to help when we let them. I believe that Norman is one of those angels now trying to help, and for his sake you need to allow it."

We were nearing the Ward house so I thanked Josh for helping me, hoping that I could believe, so it wouldn't hurt so much wearing Norman's clothes. We were soon involved in setting up furniture. The boys' room was upstairs, kind of an attic affair but roomy. There was only one bedroom downstairs so we converted the living room into a bedroom for the girls. The neighbors brought food as well as furniture and clothing, and by the time I returned from milking that night, the whole family was settled in our new home. For the younger children it was a new place for exploration and excitement, for the rest of the family the weariness and despair were taking their toll. I heard Hester and Emma sobbing in their room and I could hear the fear in my parents' voices as they privately discussed their options. Dad and Mother went to the bank the next day to explore their borrowing capabilities. They returned with more enthusiasm than we had been led to expect. Dad hadn't trusted banks since the twenty-nine crash, which was why all of our savings had gone up in smoke with the house.

A couple of days after we had settled into the Ward house, a Mr. Barr who owned a fifty-acre farm on Stonybrook road, a road off the Stanfield road about a mile and a half out of town, stopped to talk to Dad. Mr. and Mrs. Barr were elderly, and he and his wife had decided to sell the farm and move to their son's home in Haverville. He and Dad had several conversations over the next few days. Then one night Dad asked us all to be together to discuss what we might do. He explained that because the mortgage on the house that burned was almost paid off, there was enough insurance money left to make the down payment on the Barr place. We all cheered, but Dad said, "Before you get too excited, let me finish. If we buy Barr's, then the monthly payments will be much more than what we have been paying, this will mean that we all will have to be a little more frugal. Tomorrow night I meet with Mr. Barr and I have to have a yes or no answer, because he has another buyer. Most of you older children have been earning money and contributing to running the house. If we buy the farm then it might mean that you have to contribute more and I want that understood before I say yes." We all assured Dad that we were with him and thought buying the farm was right, because along with having that big house and all that land we would get to stay in Sterling.

The next morning before I went to work, Mother called me aside and said, "Caleb, your father doesn't know this yet, but I have been putting two dollars a week of your money in the bank since you started milking for the Muldons. Even after I used some of it to buy your camping and fishing gear, there is over four hundred dollars left. I want you to consider if we should add that money to the insurance money for the down payment on the Barr place, which should cut the monthly payments down so we won't have to worry about making them. No, no, Caleb, don't answer me now, think about it for a while and I'll discuss it with you later."

The boys at the barn had been strangely kind to me since the fire and even said some surprisingly encouraging things for them. That morning though I was full of myself. *Four hundred dollars, imagine!* I had four hundred dollars, I was rich. The things I could do roamed my mind like a merry-go-round with each horse getting prettier. The camping gear and fishing gear I could buy with that sure would outshine anything Karl ever had. I could buy my own tent, my own canoe—maybe I could even have a motorcycle like Harry's. I was so puffed up with myself that I hardly remembered what I was doing until John said, "What the hell, Caleb, aren't you awake yet, you could at least wait until I milk them before you start stripping them."

In my daydreaming I had jumped ahead of John and was stripping a cow that he hadn't milked yet. I laughed and said, "Sorry, John, my mind was elsewhere. It looks like we are going to be buying the Barr farm and I am so excited that we're going to be staying in Sterling."

John said, "Hear that, boys, I guess we won't be getting rid of this little twerp after all. We're fated to be stuck with him forever."

"Hell," Reilly said, "I remember, John, when you swore that he would never be able to keep up with you, now he's waiting for you, so what's your beef?"

"That was when he was a little snot-nosed kid," John replied. "That was over four years ago, and even if he hasn't managed to grow much, he has become a first-class milker."

This was going to be great day, first I found out I'm rich, then I was being complimented by John and this afternoon Joan had said she wanted to meet me at the store. Even having to wear Norman's clothes wasn't going to ruin this day for me. Mother had gone to the Barr place with Ellie Baker to plan how the rooms would be used. I went back to the store to meet Joan around noon for ice cream, and then we went to the park in the town common. We talked about the fire and all the things that had happened since. I told her about the four hundred dollars, at first she was as ecstatic as I was, but later, she said, "You're going to give it to your parents for the farm, aren't you, Caleb?"

"I dunno, Joan," I said, "to tell the truth I've been dreaming all day about the things I could buy, not thinking much about what Mother had really asked." I watched my dreams float away as I considered the question. My canoe, tent, fishing gear and motorcycle all sadly drifting from my mind as reality sunk into my brain. It hurt and I must have shown it, for Joan held me close to her, saying, "Poor Caleb, seems like you were born under an unlucky star, but look at the bright side. How many boys your age are able to help their folks that much?" I didn't feel unlucky at that moment, Joan was developing quite a figure and she was holding my head against her breast, and in a strange way I was enjoying it.

Larry and Leonard came driving by in Muldon's wood truck. Larry shouted, "Hey, Caleb, if you two want to make out you better go back behind the library."

Joan jumped up with her face all red and said, "I wish you didn't have to work with those filthy-minded boys, Caleb. It is a wonder that you stay as decent as you are, working with them."

I was more than a little upset with them at the moment, but it was rather dumb to be cuddling up like that right in the middle of the park where everyone could see us. I said, "You know, Joan, it was dumb of us, maybe we should still meet in a more private place."

"Caleb Carney, whatever are you thinking? Maybe you have been working with those boys too long," she said, flipping her hair over her shoulder. "Come on, walk me home before I lose my temper with you."

Walking towards her house, I said, "Joan, you know I was always going to help my parents. Was it really wrong to dream about being rich and wanting all those things?"

We were almost to Joan's house. She put both hands on my shoulders and stared into my eyes, saying, "Caleb, I believe that you're the type that will always try to do the right thing, no matter how hard it is. I know what it is to dream, and the older I get, the more I want to have things I can't or do things that we shouldn't. Oh, Caleb! I wish life was always as simple as it used to be when we met every week behind the library to have ice cream, at least then all we had to fear was other people, not each other."

There were tears rolling down Joan's cheek, she wrapped her arms around me so tight I felt as though she wanted to make us one. Then she kissed me long and hard on the lips before whirling away and running for her house in tears. I just stood there for a few minutes trying to sort through my emotions, but it was like trying to catch a shooting star blazing through my body. The fire, the new home, the farm, the four hundred dollars and now this excitingly confusing new Joan, I felt completely addled. I was going to have to have a talk with Josh about all this as soon as we got settled at the farm.

Mother was back at the Ward place talking to Josh when I got home, she said, "Well, Caleb, have you come to a decision?"

"Yes, Mother," I answered, "there really wasn't any question what I should do. I just needed to fancy being rich for a while."

Josh laughed and said, "Mother told me about your savings, Caleb. I wish I had been that smart, then mine wouldn't have been lost in the fire. Dad might be a little upset about all this, but the end results will make him happy."

That night when I came from work Dad was waiting. He said, "Caleb, we need to talk. I want you to know what a great benefit your savings are going to be for the family. Mr. Barr and I have finally agreed on a price of three thousand dollars, now with your money and the insurance we will have over half of that without borrowing. That means less of a monthly payment, leaving more money for your mother to run the house. I never thought your stripping job would become so important. We have all been proud how you have stuck to it all this time, but I never imagined anything like this. Your mother and I have been talking and we believe that everyone would feel better if you used a little of the money on yourself too. We know how bad you felt when you had to give up your Connecticut river trip, we think it's better that you gain something personal from this money."

I hadn't talked about the river trip since Karl had left. That day the pain was so bad that I had to go off and cry by myself. I really thought staying home was the end of me, then I thought of Dad and his response to the fire and decided that I had to be as brave as he had been and put this behind me. But it still was so painful I couldn't think about it. I had been worried about getting to work from the Barr place. So I said, "You know, Dad, it probably would be a good thing if I had a bicycle to go back and forth to work when we live on the farm, it would save a lot of my time."

Dad said, "That's good thinking, Caleb, Mother thought that we should at least replace your fishing gear. I believe we should do both."

The next day we started our move to the Barr place, the house had four big bedrooms upstairs. One for Josh and Uncle Louis; one for Hester, Emma and Nellie; one for me, Homer, Jason and Francis; and the front one for Mother and Dad. As sad as it had been to lose our old house, it was good to have all this room. It took a week before we had everything settled. We had managed to save our cow and chickens from the fire, and this was a much better place for the cow because she had her own pasture. Big Red and his flock had a big chicken house and the barn was separate from the house. The excitement and planning needed in our new environment soon erased the gloom that had settled on the family. By the middle of August we had made the Barr farm our home.

One of Josh's friends, Lourin Bennet, had joined the Army last fall, his sister Irene told Josh that he had written and asked her to sell his bike, so Josh and I went to look at it. It was a fine-looking red Schwin. Irene was there when we arrived and Josh asked, "Why is he selling the bike, Irene?"

"It's a little hard to explain, Josh," she replied. "He found out that he doesn't like being a soldier, he said the war in Europe scares him and if you read between the lines, it's like he doesn't believe that he's coming back home. My mother wanted to send him the money without selling the bike, but Dad said no, that he was man grown and needed to face things as a man. I believe that Dad thinks that parting with boyhood things would help him do that."

I rode the bike around the yard a couple of times. It was a fine bike that showed the care it had been given. I gave Josh the thumbs up sign and he paid the seven dollars that they were asking for the bike. I rode off with the bike as fast as I could peddle, leaving Josh talking with Irene. I was planning on whizzing into town to show off the bike, but some of the things Irene had said haunted me. I rode back and met Josh and walked beside him pushing the bike, saying, "Josh, do you really think Lourin is going to get killed fighting in Europe?"

Josh walked along without answering for some time before saying, "I dunno about Lourin, but from the looks of things, Americans will be fighting in this war sooner or later and when they are, many of them won't be coming home. There's talk of drafting boys that are only eighteen, most of the high school boys are talking about joining as soon as they graduate so they can pick what service they go in."

"What about you, Josh? Are you going to join next year?" I asked.

"I have to tell you, Caleb, that even thinking about it scares me. Not because I'm afraid for myself so much, I just know I wouldn't be able to shoot anybody. I would make a darn poor soldier. I am hoping when I have to go I can get in a medical corps or some duty where I'm not expected to kill anyone. This is very hard for me because I believe that we owe it to our country to serve in times like these, but I don't believe that any type of training could get me to shoot another man," Josh answered.

I could see that Josh was really concerned about what might happen if he was drafted. I knew this was his soft side, that the boys at the barn were always kidding me about, but I never realized it was this bad. I said, "Oh com'n, Josh, you couldn't possibly be worried about killing one of those Nazis after all the things that they have been doing."

"It's much more complicated than that, Caleb," Josh replied. "I'm not sure I understand it all myself, so don't ask me to explain. It's not something that I like to talk about, so ride off and stop pestering me with questions."

I rode off wondering how I was going to feel when I had to fight in the trenches as Uncle Louis had, but arriving in town and showing off my bike erased all thoughts of war from my mind.

The last of August flew by and before we knew it, we were back in school. Glenn had moved on to high school with Karl and now only George, Jake and I of the old gang were left in Sterling with Mrs. Putman and the eighth grade. Though Mrs. Putman didn't control with the terror that Old Hanna had, she did control and I must say school was more enjoyable now. Without Hanna, Jake and I weren't doing any writing beyond school reports, though Jake was working on a war story and wanted me to help him emotionalize it. I read part of it and told him I couldn't get a feeling for it and probably wouldn't be able to help. George was always worked up about the war. His father listened to all the reports on the radio and read everything he could find about it, all the time lamenting the loss of his arm so he couldn't go and fight. Mrs. Putman said we should be aware of current events, and once a week we had open discussions about what was happening in the world. Some of the stories that the kids told were awfully gory. Mrs. Putman said that we should keep an open mind about some of them, because the governments on both sides of the war were capable of embellishing the facts to make their people angry enough to fight. Jake gave a speech about the Germans using words as a weapon, it was called it propaganda. He said the Germans twisted the truth around to make people believe what they wanted them to believe. He thought that we should do all we could to combat this misinformation, but we still shouldn't send troops over there. He and George would get into some loud discussions about that.

The excitement of the war and our debates made the first months of school really fly. The week before our Thanksgiving Holiday break, I came home from school one afternoon and Harry's Indian was parked in the yard. Eunice, Harry, Mother and Josh were in the kitchen when I went in. After I gave Eunice a big hug and grabbed Harry by the wrist, using the handshake he had shown me, I asked, "Are you going to stay, Eunice? Are you and Harry going to stay for at least a while?"

Eunice came over and put her arm around my shoulder, saying, "We would like to, Josh, but it's up to Dad. We are hoping enough time has passed that he can forgive us."

Mother said, "I wish I could help more, Eunice, but he hasn't allowed us to even use your name when he's around. And as much as I love you I can't confront your father and cause a battle that could destroy the family."

Harry said, "We understand your position, Mrs. Carney, but I believe that if he would only sit and talk with us he would understand. I don't want Eunice to have to keep living with this pain."

"I understand that, Harry," Mother answered, "but if Henry comes in the yard and sees your bike, he will be so angry by the time he gets in the house the only voice going to be heard is his."

"O.K. then, I guess we had better leave," Harry said, his voice rising.

Eunice went and held Mother, tears flowing down her face, saying, "Oh, Mother, I so much want us to be family again, it isn't fair that I have to choose between Harry and Dad."

Josh, who had been quiet until then, said, "Look, Mother, I believe we should have Harry leave and Eunice stay and talk to Dad alone. If there is any chance of his understanding it will come from his love for her."

"No, no," Eunice sobbed, "Harry and I are one now, we have to do this together."

"I think Josh is on the right track, Eunice," Harry said. "I will go back to our room in Oscin and if you need me you can call me there, it will be good for you to spend what time you can with your family."

Harry left. Mother, who was visibly upset, went about getting my supper ready so I could go to work. When Hester and Emma came in, Eunice went up to their room with them. When I returned from work that night Dad was out in the barn doing some chores. Mother was in the kitchen baking, Josh and the girls except for Nellie were gone. Homer, Jason and Francis were in our room. I asked Homer what had happened.

He said, "It was great, Caleb. When Dad got home Eunice stayed up in the girls' room until after supper. When Dad was sitting in his easy chair she went down to him. Jason and I snuck upstairs and watched through the floor register.

"Eunice walked in and said, 'Hello, Dad, I love you and I've missed you so much I just had to talk to you again. Please don't send me away, Dad, until you hear me out.' Dad just sat there with a surprised look on his face while Eunice continued, 'I need to know that you love me, Dad. I know what I did hurt you, but remember how it was when I was your boy until Josh came along, teaching me to milk the cow and hoe the garden?' She picked up his hand and said, 'I used to think these big, callused hands belonged to the wisest person in the world.' She sat in Dad's lap putting her head on his shoulder and said, 'I couldn't help loving Harry any more than you could help loving Mother when you met her, Dad. I need you, Dad, I need you to love me, to accept Harry, and I need you to be grandfather to my children.'

"I swear, Caleb, I believe that Dad had tears in his eyes as he put his arms around her and held her with his hand in her hair. Finally, he said, "Tell me, Eunice, where is this biker of yours? Did he hop on his Indian and leave you?' And then, Eunice said, 'No, Dad, he is in Oscin waiting to have a talk with you. Josh thought it would be wiser for me to see you alone first. I'm glad I did, Dad, no matter what happens I'll always have tonight, but please tell me you'll see him.' Then Dad said, 'You will have to let me up now, Eunice. I have some chores I have to attend to in the barn.'

"Mother came into the room after Dad left and held Eunice for a moment and then sat holding her hand, having a quiet conversation we couldn't hear. When Dad came back in, he said, 'O.K., Eunice, maybe I was too quick with you two before. Have Harry come around tomorrow.'

"Just before you came home, Caleb," Homer finished, "Josh and the girls came in and they decided to take a walk around town, I guess Eunice wanted to see if it changed without her."

This was great news. With Harry back with his Indian, I would be a favorite with all the boys in town. The next morning at work, Reilly said,

"Caleb, I hear that Harry is back in town with his Indian. I'd like to talk to him if it's true. I found a couple of old motorcycles like the one Frank Butler has at the repair shed and he said I could have his old one if I could fix it. I think I can get one of them operating with a little help."

"Well, Reilly, he was in town for a while yesterday and he might be here for a little while. I'll tell him about the bikes though, I'm sure he will be interested," I answered.

All the boys at the barn were excited to hear that Harry might be back. The thought that he might be sure was working in my favor. When I arrived home from school that day there was a pickup truck with a small trailer behind it in the yard. Harry and Eunice were in the house with Mother and Emma. I said, "Gee, Harry, I didn't know you had a pickup too."

Harry gave me a little cuff on the arm, saying, "What did you expect, little Caleb, that I would be riding your sister around in the snow on the Indian, carrying everything we own on our backs?"

Eunice said, "Harry has many tools of his trade back in Oklahoma. He plans to have a construction company of his own in a few more years. The reason we are here now is because he has a job working on renovations at a big office building north of here that will last all winter. We had planned to go south this winter, but the company Harry was working for lost the bid on that job."

"Hey, Eunice," Harry said, "you reminded me of something I thought of when I first met your family. Wouldn't it be wonderful if I trained your brothers in my line, then we could have a family company? Don't you think that Carney Jackstone Construction would make a good name?"

"I would really like that, Harry," Eunice replied, "but that is a few years down the road, isn't it?"

"Sure it is, Eunice, but it will be that long for your brothers to be old enough for that kind of work. If they all work as hard as little Caleb here does," he said, rubbing my head, "then we will be rich men in no time."

I liked being around Harry, he had a way of making everything sound so easy. Imagine the Carney boys in construction. I told him about Reilly and the bikes he had bought, and he said, "Tell you what, Caleb, let's get the old Indian off the trailer after you eat and I'll give you a ride to the barn so I can talk to Reilly about them."

Everyone at the barn was excited about Harry being back. He made an appointment to look at Reilly's bikes the next day; even though he wasn't going to be here long, he was interested.

Harry went back to the house, and after supper he and Dad were out in the barn talking for a long time. That night when I got home Harry and Eunice were still there. I asked Josh how it went with Dad. Josh said, "Everything seems O.K."

When Eunice mentioned they had better head back to their hotel room in Oscin Dad said, "There is no need of family spending good money on a hotel when we have all this room here." Eunice got teary eyed and hugged Dad, while Harry went over and put his arm around Dad's shoulder. Dad, looking a little uncomfortable, said, "Mind you all now, I might have been a little harsh with Eunice, but these two are not an example of how I want things done when it comes time for any of you to leave home."

Eunice and Harry left the day after Thanksgiving. Harry said they would only be a couple of hours' drive away and when he got settled in his new job they may be able to come back for a weekend.

Mrs. Putman had asked us to write an article over the holidays on what we were thankful for. I wrote about Eunice and Harry's homecoming and what a joy it was to be a whole family again. Mrs. Putman gave me an A, writing on the report that I showed great promise.

I had talked Glenn into letting Karl go fishing at our secret spot, after we swore Karl to a blood oath to keep our secret. It was cold the day we went and ice was skimming the water at the ponds, but man, did the fish bite. Karl was ecstatic. We caught so many fish we had to make two trips to get them all to the wagon. I had to go to work right after we got home and Homer, Jason, Josh and Uncle Louis had just finished cleaning the fish when I returned from work.

Uncle Louis said, "You know, Caleb, it is a mean enough trick not to let anyone know where you fish without sticking us with the dirty work."

I could see that nobody was very happy about having to clean my fish. I felt guiltier when Josh said, "Yeah, and now Dad wants me to build a smoke pit tomorrow so we can smoke these fish and Homer and Jason have to dig up dry hickory and applewood to do it with."

I really liked catching all those fish, but living with the secret was getting harder every time I went there. When I was alone with Josh I told him about Glenn's father and how he stopped going fishing with Glenn after he lost his arm and why I had promised Glenn never to tell. Josh said, "I thought it must have been something really drastic when you couldn't tell Uncle Louis, but I believe you are doing the right thing, Caleb."

As always, I felt better after talking to Josh, so I said, "Josh, I been wanting to talk to you about Joan, she's been so different lately. She gives me big hugs and kisses, then she starts crying and runs off. I don't know what to do, she has changed so much."

"Oh, Caleb, little Caleb," Josh answered, "the mysteries of womanhood.

141

I'm not sure there is an answer. You have to understand that girls reach puberty too and sometimes it is emotionally harder for them to accept their body changes. You just have to be good to Joan, because she needs a friend of the opposite sex she can trust right now. I know that this may seem strange to you, but you will understand it better when you change."

That damn puberty thing again, I hadn't said anything to Josh, but I decided I wasn't going to change, if I could help it. Talking about sex, dreaming about it and I am sure lying about it was the main topic at the barn most days, and though I pretended to go along, most of it disgusted me. This was one time that Josh didn't seem to have the answer, at least not one that really helped me understand. The next time Joan and I met it was so cold that we went to the library pretending we were doing homework. She told me that Glenn and my fishing trips were getting to be the talk of the town, and she wondered how I was able to keep it secret. When I walked her home she talked again about secrets and said, "You know, Caleb, as we grow older some things have to be kept secret. I bet you hear a lot of secrets working with Larry and Leonard and the rest at the barn, especially about the girls around town."

"Ah, Joan, you know I hear many stories, but most of it is just bragging. I don't believe half of what they say," I answered.

"Caleb," Joan asked, "if-if you ever did a shameful thing with a girl would you tell about it the way they do?"

"Joan-Joan. Don't, you're scaring me," I replied. "I don't even think about doing the things they talk about, so I wouldn't have anything to tell." Joan hugged me with her whole body while giving me a kiss and then ran for her house laughing. I walked back to the park to get my bike, thinking, *It's as if everybody knows a big secret that I am supposed to know and don't.* I rode home wondering if everyone felt so confused at my age or was I just numb to the reality of life. Maybe I was wrong to want everything to stay the same, but puberty, growing up, having to go away to fight a war, scary things to have to face. It would only be four more years before I would be old enough for the draft that they said was coming. When I got home, Homer and Jason were having a snowball fight, so I joined them and soon forgot my troubles.

The next morning, just as we were finishing our milking, Don Muldon came in and said, "Well, boys, it has happened. Right now while we are standing here the Japanese are bombing Pearl Harbor and destroying our fleet. One thing for sure, everything will be different now, most of you boys will be in the Army in a very short time. John here might be able to get a deferment, but I don't believe we will be able to help any of the rest of you stay home."

Reilly said, "I can't speak for the rest of them, but I'm going tomorrow to join the Navy if there is any left to join. We can't stay here and hope for someone else to do our duty."

"How about the rest of you?" Don asked. "It looks as if the Muldons are going to need to find some more milkers. How about your brothers, Caleb, are any of them near as good as you at milking?"

"My brother Homer has been milking at home for a few years now, but he's too young to be working here"

Don laughed and said, "You couldn't have been more than ten when you started here, Caleb. We all thought it was a joke when we hired you, but you proved us wrong. What is Homer now, about twelve? We are going to be depending on younger boys if we want to keep the farm running."

When I got home Dad was in the barn, Uncle Louis and Mother were in the kitchen. Uncle Louis looked awful. Mother was saying, "Louis, don't you think Josh can get into a medical unit or something like that when he has to go?"

"I hope so, May," Uncle Louis said, "but when I think how screwed up things got when I was in the Army, half the men I fought with claimed they were supposed to have been somewhere else. I wish that Josh wasn't so much of a pacifist. I have seen some of the problems that can cause in a battle. I'm going to talk with the commander at the legion and see if he can help if Josh joins, instead of waiting to be drafted."

Uncle Louis left and Mother looked as though she had been crying, so I said, "Don't worry, Mother, we'll beat those sneaky Japanese and make them wish they had stayed in Japan where they belong."

Mother said, "Oh, Caleb, I know we'll win the war, but it will be at a horrible price and mothers all over the country are crying today because they know it will be their boys who will be paying it. I just hope we win it quick enough so you and Homer don't have to go too."

Dad came in from the barn, asking, "What's with Louis, Helen? He looks like someone pole-axed him."

"It's the war, Henry," Mother replied. "It seemed to bring back horrible memories, and he is getting more and more depressed about it."

Uncle Louis became a changed man. He didn't work for weeks, and every day he would head for the Inn or the Legion in Lange and either stagger or be carried in late at night. I would sometimes hear Josh go help him up the back stairs. Then one night most of us woke to a big crash on the back stairs. Rushing out, we found Uncle Louis lying at the bottom of the stairs unconscious and bleeding. After carrying him to his room, Mother and Dad cleaned him up and checked him out. He came to, enough to say he was O.K.

I heard Mother check him several times through the night. The next day Mother, Dad and Uncle Louis had a long talk, and a few days later he went back to work.

Laurin Bennet, the boy who had sold me the bicycle, must have been a prophet. He had been wounded in the attack on Pearl Harbor and died in an army hospital a month after the attack. They shipped his body home and the whole town turned out for his funeral. I never saw so many uniforms as there were at those services. The legion flag carriers all stood at attention while the gun bearers fired a salute. Some of the kids picked up the empty shell casings to keep as souvenirs, marking them, "Bennet is the first Sterling casualty of this war.' Uncle Louis said, "I hope that they are never able to add to that collection." It didn't seem likely though that Lourin would be our only loss, because most of the unattached young men in town had either joined a service or were being drafted. There was talk of drafting young fathers now and even boys who just got out of high school. At school most of the games were about bayoneting or shooting Japs or Nazis. Mrs. Putman used the battle zones as a combination current event and geography lesson. With the studies at school and the horror we were hearing about on the radio, talk of the war became very prevalent in our lives.

Reilly and Leonard left to serve; Arthur had tried to join but couldn't pass the physical. Homer started working with us, Mother wanted it to be only part of the time, but Don hadn't found enough milkers and kept him full time. Jake only worked one day before quitting. He said he couldn't stand smelling like manure all the time. Arthur's sister Janet came to work with us. Don told us he wasn't going to put up with any of our tomfoolery and we were to watch our language around her. He didn't have to worry though, she could turn the air blue with her cussing and she was always picking on Homer. I had to bail Homer out a few times, but he was tougher with the boys than I had ever dared to be. His big problem seemed to be with not having enough sleep, he kept falling asleep in school. Larry was always cursing at his father and uncle because they managed to get him deferred along with John. He was always saying, "Here I am, still stuck in this cow shit when I could be out seeing the world." I thought there were better ways of seeing the world than fighting a war, but I suppose for some farm boys, this was their only chance.

Winter went by fast, and when the Muldons started their spring planting they asked me if I could work some afternoons. Mother said not during the week while school kept but on weekends if I wanted. One day after school Karl came by with Beverly and another girl from high school that I had seen Karl with a few times before.

Karl said, "Hey, Caleb, do you have a few minutes, can you come up to

Beverly's house and help me out with something?"

I didn't want to get involved in any of Beverly's kissing games, but I hadn't seen Karl for a while and we had always been close friends, so I said, "O.K., Karl, but I'll ride my bike up so I can get home sooner."

Beverly came running over and gave me a hug and said, "I'll ride with you, Caleb, on the handle bars."

She jumped up on the bars and leaned back in my arms. As I was pedaling away I saw Joan coming down the school stairs, she gave me a frosty stare and walked huffingly away. I didn't have time to worry about Joan with Beverly wiggling around on the bike. I was having all I could do to keep from falling. After we had gone a little way, it became too steep for me to pedal, so we walked. Karl and the girl he introduced as Tammy caught up with us. When we got to Beverly's house no one was home and when we went in Tammy and Karl ran upstairs, shouting. "Com'n, Caleb," Beverly practically dragged me up the stairs. Karl and Tammy were climbing into the top bunk in the bedroom. I had never seen Karl so excited. Beverly pulled me into the bottom bed right on top of her, saying, "Got you now, Caleb."

I started to say, "Beverly, what the hell—" but before I could finish, she pulled my head tight against her breast and started unbuckling my pants. By accident or on purpose, I didn't know, she caught my penis in her hand. She seemed kind of shocked, then taking both her hands she held my head tighter to her breast, saying, "Caleb, dear little Caleb, you can't do it yet, can you? Don't say anything, just lie with me and wiggle the bed a little. I won't tell anyone." I tried to leave but Beverly said, "Please don't, Caleb, just wait a few minutes longer, then we will go downstairs." Karl and Tammy were having a hell of a time on the top bunk from the sounds of Tammy's giggling. After what seemed like forever, Beverly said, "O.K., Caleb, let's go." We went downstairs. Beverly held me for a moment just looking at me, then she gave me a big kiss and said, "Maybe next time, Caleb."

I ran to my bike and took off, wondering what the hell was Karl thinking getting me mixed up in this, especially with Beverly. What the hell did she mean she wouldn't tell? *Is everybody supposed to believe we had sex? Damn that Karl, this whole thing was a setup between him and Beverly. Joan saw me leave with her, if she thinks I'm like the rest of the boys at the barn she will never speak to me again.* All the way home I kept thinking of the awful things I could do to Karl. How could he do this to me after I talked Glenn into letting him go fishing with us? Somewhere, somehow, I vowed Karl was going to pay. By the time I arrived home though, I was thinking it hadn't been that unpleasant lying in bed with Beverly. Even if what she did was a little embarrassing, her good-bye kiss and the "Maybe next time" had thrilled me somehow.

When I arrived home, Eunice and Harry were there, they hadn't been able to come down all winter because the job Harry worked on was behind schedule. He had been working twelve-hour shifts six and seven days a week since he left. They were taking a vacation and going to stay with us a couple of weeks before heading back to Oklahoma. Harry said, "Caleb, I'm glad you're home. I haven't had time to ride that old Indian much all winter. What do you say we take it off the trailer and take it for a spin?"

Man, riding behind Harry was just the thing I needed after what I had been through. Harry made sure every boy in town saw us. I saw Joan over by the library and asked Harry to stop.

"Changed your riding partner huh, Caleb? Is this more fun than you had this afternoon?" Joan said haughtily as she walked away.

"Whoa, Caleb," Harry said, "what is it you have you been up to?"

I wished that I could have talked to Harry about what happened, but I didn't think I was even going to be able to tell Josh about this. So I said, "Just a little jealousy I guess, Harry. I gave another girl a ride on my bicycle today and she saw us." Saying that made me think of Karl. If Tammy and Beverly didn't do any blabbing about what happened that was a story I could live by.

The next two weeks I was in seventh heaven. Harry was giving everyone in town rides that wanted them. I noticed that some of the girls only got to ride once. I don't know if that was because of Eunice or not. Harry even went over and looked at the bikes Reilly had been working on before he went in the service. He left Reilly a note encouraging him to keep working on the bikes, saying they were worth it. There were some tearful discussions at home. Harry had been deferred from the draft because that was a war production factory that he had been working on. Now he had signed up for the Sea Bees. He said they were a construction outfit that worked even under fire. Eunice was pregnant and even though the baby wasn't going to be born until next winter, Mother was insisting she stay home with us. Harry said her home was with him until he had to leave and then they would decide where Eunice was going to stay. If she could travel, then she probably would come back. When the time came for them to leave, Dad had a talk with Harry, saying that when her time was due she really should be with her family, if he couldn't be around. Harry assured everyone that was his plan, if everything worked out right. It was a sad day for all of us when Harry and Eunice were leaving. Dad and Josh were working when they left, but Mother and the rest of the family were there to say good-bye. Mother and the girls shed sad tears for losing Eunice again, and the boys and I were filled with sadness about losing Harry and his bike.

The last day of school came and we all climbed to the fire tower on the mountain. George and Jake joked about Glenn telling us last year he wouldn't be a kid anymore, saying this would be our last year as kids too. I hated to think like that, but in my heart I knew things were changing. Instead of a wild summer of hiking, fishing and canoe trips, this year I was looking at more hours in Muldon's fields. Working to buy saving stamps and war bonds. Josh had received his draft notice and would be gone in a couple of weeks, making my fourteenth summer, at least in his words, the summer I had to become a big brother.

Chapter 10

My fourteenth summer, if not the summer I grew up, was definitely a summer of big changes. No longer the crazy, lazy days of fishing and hiking, but a summer that introduced me to the many different aspects of running a big farm. I met Joe Muldon one morning and asked about getting a raise, saying that I needed to help the family finances more now that Josh had to report for the draft in a couple of weeks. We had counted on Josh's pay to help with the farm mortgage. He said, "By Golly Moses boy, I like your spunk but if I gave raises to everyone who works for me who's in trouble, I'd go broke. I'll tell you what though, with so many of the boys going off to war I'm going to be short of help all around the farm, so we can arrange for you to work in the fields for a few hours during the day, that way we both benefit." I left the barn happy that financially I had been successful, but with a sickening feeling that there were many things about growing up, besides puberty, that I was going to find unpleasant. Jake had asked me to meet him that morning so I biked to the school grounds, thinking how things had changed. I hardly saw Karl anymore with his new high school friends and the job he had in Oscin at a clothing store. George had taken a job helping at one of Muldon's wood lots that was by his house. Glenn was working with his father, who had gone back to work in the woods, with a hook replacing his lost arm. Even Joan was working three days a week for an aunt, who grew flowers that she shipped to the cities. Jake talked about how a war made everything advance faster because of the great demands that war put on men and material. I wondered if these were the kind of things that Jake meant. He was always saying that great wars forced man and the world to expand faster than man was able to handle, throwing their destiny out of control. I know seeing summer plans go out the window made me feel as if my life was out of control. I sometimes felt that Jake's talk was just showing off, but the teachers say that readers like Jake will be the future leaders of the world. We teased him about that, imagine, bookworm Jake a leader. He wouldn't fight with his fists, though he was always ready for a debate.

As I was riding by the library Jake came running across the park, shouting, "Caleb! Caleb, wait until you hear the news."

I had never seen Jake so excited. By the time he reached my side he was gasping for breath and I couldn't understand what he was trying to say, so I said, "Jake, take deep breaths and count slowly to ten."

"Caleb, Oh, Caleb, I just got word they are going to let me work at the newspaper as a part-time apprentice. It's like a dream come true. I didn't think I would get a chance like this until late in high school. I took their test when I heard they were losing people to the draft and were hiring younger boys. My score was better than some high school students who applied, so they're giving me a job. Apprenticeships don't pay much, but I would gladly work for nothing to be in a newsroom. Before I got the news, I had planned to meet with you to see if maybe you wanted to go fishing or hiking with me, now that Glenn and Karl aren't around so much, but I guess now I won't have much time either."

I hadn't thought about Jake as a hiker or fisherman, but thinking about some of his writings I should have known he had an interest in them. I wondered if he had been offended because we never thought to ask him if he wanted to go with us. *Funny how you don't see things that are right under your nose sometimes,* I thought. I said, "That's great news, Jake. I'm happy for you. I guess the war brings some good after all, huh, Jake?"

"No, Caleb," Jake replied, "as excited as I am about this opportunity I believe we would all be better off just having our usual idealistic summer."

"I agree with that, Jake," I said as I recalled past summers. "I believe even though I'm going to be working more hours this summer too, we should make it a priority to go fishing and hiking. I would hate to think of a summer vacation that didn't include the thrill of a good fish on the line or the excitement of an overnight camping trip. That's it! Jake, we can camp out on the mountain some nights even if we are working more hours."

"That sounds great, Caleb," Jake said, "we'll get together and do some planning after I know what hours I'll be working. I have to go now, Mother wants me to check with the Harts about getting rides to Oscin when I start work."

I pondered the rapidly changing direction of life as I rode my bike home. The more I found out about growing up, the more I disliked what was happening. *The fire, a new home, different schools that separated friends, the war taking men and boys away from town, summer joy transformed to labor, it's more than a boy can stand. Then there is this damn puberty thing that's generating those crazy dreams that scare me to death. This morning when I woke up it felt as if I had wet the bed. Mother is going to kill me. Damn that Karl and Beverly, they did this to me. I dream all the time about that day in her bunk and it's sometimes different in my dreams, I think I'm beginning to understand Karl's excitement that day. All I hear from my family is how wrong doing things like that are and how God is against it. Karl says if God was so much against it He shouldn't have made us feel this way. I don't know about God, my family, or Karl's feeling, I only know that what I feel is driving me crazy. I'm afraid to be alone with girls anymore, and talking to God is out of the question, for what I feel will send me to hell for sure.*

When I was pulling into the yard, Nellie came screaming out of the hen house with her arm and side of her face all bloody. Big Red was right behind her and chickens were scattering all over the yard. Mother came rushing out of the house. Uncle Louis, who was home for a few days between job changes, came running from the shed to help. When I reached the house, Mother was trying to comfort Nellie while Uncle Louis cleaned her cuts. Nellie was crying hysterically, she had an ugly scratch close to her left eye, the length of her cheek, and several cuts on her left arm. Mother and Louis cleaned and bandaged Nellie's wounds and quieted her. Uncle Louis walked towards the shed, saying, "I say this is the final straw, May."

Mother rushed after him, saying, "Maybe we should wait, Louis." He didn't answer. Grabbing a burlap bag, he cornered Big Red by the fence and wrapped him in the bag; then striding to the chopping block by the woodshed, he took the ax and in one blow whacked off his head. If you never understood the expression "like a chicken with his head cut off" you should have seen that show, blood and Big Red were flying everywhere. After he quieted down, Uncle Louis took him inside, telling Nellie, "You'll never have to be afraid of Big Red again. Your mother is going to make him into a stew." To Mother, he said, "No matter what happens, May, remember it was my decision. I am sure that Henry would have reacted in the same way if he had been here, it's my concern, not yours."

Jason, who was comforting Nellie, said, "I am glad he's dead, Uncle Louis, Francis and I never went in the chicken house alone. We tried to tell Nellie that Big Red could be dangerous, but you know how she believes she can control animals. I hope Dad isn't going to be to mad at you for killing that rooster, he's had it coming for years."

I told Mother about talking to Old Golly Moses about more money. She said, "I don't know, Caleb, you have to get up so early and some nights you don't finish milking until almost eight. I don't think that a growing boy like you should be working such long days. Maybe if you gave up the morning milking so you didn't have to start so early it would be O.K."

I knew because it was so hard getting strippers that would keep those hours, they would never let me leave the barn for fieldwork. I said, "I will only be working in the fields a few days a week, Mother, and only a few hours at a time when they're short of help."

"O.K., Caleb," Mother replied, "but I'll be watching, and if I think you are getting over tired, you'll have to give it up."

Emma came in, saying, "Mother, everyone in town is asking what the date is for Josh's going-away party. They've already started to collect money to buy a watch for him like they have for all the men who have gone. I know that Josh hasn't wanted to talk about it, but in all fairness his friends want to be able to say good-bye and wish him well."

"I know, Emma," Mother sighed, "several of the mothers in town have been working on a party. It became too complicated to know who to invite so we have decided to have an open house, potluck at the town hall. Ellie Baker has asked about using the town hall and we'll have an answer on the date after the selectmen's meeting tonight. Josh will be all right about the party when he sees all of his friends there. It isn't the party that's upsetting Josh, it's he doesn't believe he is capable of being a good soldier. We can only pray he is able to find a niche where he isn't expected to do any killing."

I left while they were discussing the party. I had agreed to meet Arnold Sledge at the foot of the hill around one o'clock. He said he couldn't pump his bike up that hill and wanted to show me something. As I coasted down, Arnold was sitting back in the woods, waiting. I called, "What's up, Arny?"

He unwrapped a blanket that he had tied on his bike, revealing a rifle, saying, "What do you think of this, Caleb? Roy Cross said he found it and didn't dare take it home so he gave it to me. My dad said I was old enough to have a rifle, if I was smart enough to stay out of trouble with it."

Josh had a rifle, but he would never shoot anything except targets. Mother wouldn't let me take it without him, so I hadn't been able to go hunting as some of my friends were doing. I said, "That's neat, Arny, have you done any hunting yet?" I was feeling very envious about the rifle. Arny was two or three years younger than me with a rifle of his own. I thought that mentioning hunting would throw him off, but he answered, "Ya, Caleb, I've been a couple of times, but I haven't shot anything yet, wanna go in these woods with me?"

I knew Mother would object but I couldn't let Arnold know that I wasn't even allowed to use a gun myself, so I said, "I got a couple hours to kill, Arny, I hope you have some bullets for that thing."

"I only have a few bullets, Caleb, but that will be enough unless we run into a pack of wolves or something," Arny joked.

We hiked into the woods, headed for the mountain trail. I knew if we didn't see anything else we would see porcupine to shoot at the foot of the ledges. We had just about reached the trail that led to the foot of the ledges when we heard a screeching, moaning noise that raised the hair on the back of our necks. Arny was all for getting the hell out of there, but between wanting to show how brave I was and needing to know what it was, I said, "Com'n, Arny, you have a gun and we are supposed to be hunters, aren't we?" A little farther up the trail we saw something moving, it seemed to be stuck or something, because it didn't seem to move very far from where we first saw it. As we got closer the screams seemed almost human.

Arny was beside himself, not knowing whether to run towards the sound or run away, when he said, "Damn, Caleb, it's a cat caught in a trap or something."

I saw that it was a bobcat in a steel trap and I said, "Shoot it, Arny, put it out of it's misery."

He was shaking so much that he shot twice and missed and the cat crouched down at the sound of the rifle. I hollered, "For Christ's sake, Arny, walk up to him and finish him before you run out of bullets."

He walked up and put the rifle almost to the cat's head and shot it right between the eyes. We both stood there startled by what had happened. This was a long way from shooting a porcupine or a few squirrels.

Arnold said, "Caleb, what are we going to do with it?"

"Well, Arny," I replied, "we can just leave it for the trapper or make like great hunters and throw it over our shoulders and bring home the quarry."

"I want to take it home," Arny said, "but what do I tell people how I got it, Caleb?"

I thought about my fish on Banner's wall and understood what he was feeling. I said, "Look, Arny, if you want to, take it home. I'll forget that I was ever here and you can tell any kind of a story that you want to." We carried the cat out to Arny's bike. I helped him tie it on.

He said, "I feel very strange about this, Caleb, maybe you should help me with a story."

I knew his feeling well but felt he would be all right once he got musing about a story. I said, "Look, Arny, just pedal slow back to town. By the time you get there I'm sure you'll know what to do." He couldn't pedal his bike with the cat and the rifle both tied to it so he went down the road pushing the bike, what a picture this presented. I imagined the excitement he felt and the stir it was going to cause when he arrived in town. I wondered what his story would be and how it would affect his life. When I arrived at work that night, Janet and the boys were all excited about Arnold's bobcat. It seems that the whole town found it hard to believe that Arny made such a good shot. The story was that Arny got a shot off just as the cat was going to leap at him and hit it right between the eye's. He had brought the cat to the Inn and Mr. Banner was going to have it mounted and displayed there just like my trout. Homer said, "Caleb, weren't you with Arny today?"

"Yup, I met him just before he went hunting at the foot of the hill by the farm, he was showing me his new rifle. I had no idea that he was going to make himself into such a great hunter."

Janet said, "Neither did anyone in our family, Mother was against him even having a gun, but Dad says every boy should know how to handle a gun nowadays and get used to killing. He believes that this war is going to last a long time and boys like Arnold will be fighting in it when they are eighteen. I have to tell you though, coming home with that cat sure made a hero out of Arnold, especially since Mr. Banner is going to have it stuffed and mounted. Didn't something like that happen to you, Caleb?"

"That's right, Janet," I said, "that big trout hanging on the wall at the Inn is mine." We were finishing milking and I was glad to leave, it was uncanny how alike the two events were. Arny with the trap and me getting the fish with a club now were lies that we both would have to live with. I didn't like the feeling of guilt that those memories brought back.

On the way home I saw Karl and Beverly by the horse trough. Karl hollered, "Hey, Caleb, come over here, Beverly wants to talk to you."

Man, I sure didn't want to talk to her, but I couldn't think of a way to get out of it, so I replied, "Sure, Karl. Hi, Beverly, long time no see, what can I do for you?"

"Come on, Caleb, take a walk with me. I have something I need to talk over with you in private."

"Ya, Caleb," Karl said, poking me in the ribs. "She wants to know what to name the baby."

Beverly slapped Karl, saying, "If you know which side your bread is buttered on, Karl Hart, you'd better learn to shut your mouth."

I walked towards the park with Beverly, strangely excited but scared to death. I said, "What's Karl talking about, Bev? Are you really having a baby?"

"Oh my God, Caleb," she said, "when are you going to grow up and stop being so gullible? I only want to tell you our little act worked and Karl and Tammy think we did it. At first I thought you might have blabbed to Karl, but I know he would have been teasing me by now if you had. I wanted you to know that your secret is safe with me." She kissed me and whispered, "I'll always be there for you, Caleb."

I thought I was going to explode. I pulled away from her and said, "Beverly, you have to quit this kissing me all the time. Joan saw us that day

154

you were on my bike and she has been mad at me ever since."

"Oh, so it's Joan, is it! Well, let's see if Joan can do this for you." She held me very tight and kissed me with her tongue running all over my lips and mouth, I thought I was going to burst into flames. I pulled away shaking. Beverly laughed and ran ahead, saying, "Ask Joan to top that, little boy."

Karl walked off with Beverly, shouting back laughingly, "Don't worry, Caleb, I'll take care of things for you."

I jumped on my bike and rode towards home as fast as I could pedal, with every nerve in my body tormenting me. *Damn that Beverly, she makes me want to do the things that will send me to hell for sure. Things I've been dreaming about. I'll have to talk to Josh, maybe I shouldn't do that with him going away. Damn the war, damn puberty, damn this growing up, damn, damn, damn.* The bike ride and the anger cooled my crazy nerves by the time I arrived home. At the house I heard Homer screaming in his room. I rushed in, hardly hearing Hester's warning, "Don't, Caleb." I burst into the room and Homer was squirming on the bed, where Dad and Mother were working on his penis.

Mother yelled, "You, you and those filthy boys you work with are responsible for this."

"For what, Mother," I cried out, "what happened?"

"He has his foreskin stuck back and you know why that happened. Now get out of here before Dad smacks you," she replied.

Hester was waiting when I left the room. She said, "I'm sorry, Caleb, don't be too hard on yourself. Boys will be boys, you know."

I went out to the shed and sat on the steps wondering why everyone thought I had done something wrong. Homer was still crying out in pain, I couldn't imagine what his problem was. Getting your foreskin caught has happened to most of us boys at one time or another, but I never heard anybody say it was that excruciating. Homer must have been a special case though, because after a half-hour of his screaming Dad came out and started the Model-A and he and Mother left with Homer to see a doctor.

The next morning before I went to work, Mother said, "We are sorry, Caleb, about last night, we shouldn't have blamed you like that. Homer had an infection under his foreskin and that was what caused the swelling and all the pain. He had to be circumcised so he won't be working for a few days, so tell the Muldons." I was still confused why anyone would think what had happened was my fault. I certainly hadn't talked to Homer about this sex or this puberty thing—I still was trying to comprehend what the hell it was all about myself.

The next few weeks were haying time and the Muldons asked me every day to work in the fields. By the end of the first week I was so tired that I was falling asleep during the evening milking. The middle of the second week, Mother said, "All right, young man, you either tell the Muldons that you are only able to work in the fields three days a week or I'll have to go and talk with them myself." I certainly couldn't have Mother fighting my battles for me, so I told Golly Moses that my parents needed me at home more, now that we had a farm of our own, and I would have to cut back working in the fields.

"By Golly Moses boy," he said, "I don't know how I'm supposed to get my haying done. It takes longer with you younger boys and most of you can't work enough hours for me to keep up. Arthur's sister Jennie was after me for a job. She says she can milk, her sister Janet worked out, maybe I can have her take your place in the barn so you can spend more time in the fields."

I wasn't too keen on losing my milking job. I was more comfortable there than I was in the fields. Haying was heavy, sweaty work. I said, "O.K., Mr. Muldon, I'll talk to my parents and see if I can work those hours." I figured I could make up a story that would keep me in the barn later. That night, Jennie was at the barn milking with her sister Janet. Larry said, "Guess what, Caleb, Uncle Joe talked to us about Jennie coming here to take your place and Janet asked if she could try it out in the fields for a while. Uncle Joe was skeptical about her being able to hay, but we pointed out that she was bigger than you and probably could work harder so he's going to let her try. Ha, ha, guess you won't be getting away from us after all. I was looking forward to someday having an all-girl milking crew. If they won't let me get away from here in the service then I might as well start building a harem right here to have fun with."

Janet said, "Let me tell all you sons-o-bitches something. If one of you harms Jennie I'll come back and cut your testicles off with a dull knife, you all got that?"

John Muldon said, "Come on, guys, let's not get started with that horse shit. You know what Dad said he would do to us if there was any trouble with the girls working here."

"Sure, like he's going to be able to fire us," Arthur said. "You can't find help enough now."

Homer surprised me by joining in, saying, "You shouldn't get so upset, Janet. Jennie's been around enough boys to know how to take care of herself."

"Oh wow, Caleb," Larry hooted, "looks like one of the Carney boys isn't so all sweet and innocent. Tell us more, Homer, tell us more, what kind of girl is she?"

156

I was ready to jump in and rescue Homer, when he said, "Cut the crap, Larry, I'm only saying that Jennie is a respectable girl who can take care of herself around the jerks that some of the boys have turned into. I've seen my sisters handle those situations, and Jennie ranks right up there with the best."

"O.K., O.K.," Larry said, "I wasn't serious about the harem. Caleb, what's with Homer? Do we have another Josh with big speeches defending the underdog, or is he just sweet on Jennie?"

Jennie laughed and said, "Homer is sweet on every girl in town he's tall enough to kiss. I think he must have caught Beverly Stone's kissing disease, good thing he's not tall enough to kiss her. I hear Caleb is though. He was seen locked up with her in the park a week or so ago. How did you get away, Caleb, or did you?"

"What the hell," I answered. "You don't think I have her in my pocket, do you?"

"Maybe not in your pocket, Caleb," Janet said, "but in your heart or at the very least on your mind, if what I hear goes on is true."

"Not our little Caleb," John jested, "why, I don't believe our pure innocent Caleb even knows what a woman is for, maybe he's merry like Josh." I ran at John, swinging my pail, but Arthur grabbed me from behind as Homer came running to my aid. Arthur said, "Calm down, Caleb, John knows that Josh isn't a homo, he's just yakking. We've always joked about your brother and his feminine beliefs, but we know he is a man."

"That is one sure thing I can vouch for," Janet said.

Jennie said, "Janet, what are you saying, for God's sake, watch your mouth."

"Don't anybody get too excited," Janet said. "I'm only telling you that I have it on good authority that Josh is all man. It's not something I found out for myself, though I might have given the chance."

Golly Moses came in, saying, "I've talked it over with Don and he feels that we will have to be using girls before the war is over so we're going to give Janet a try in the field if Jennie is able to take her place."

John said, "Jennie checks out just fine, Dad. She's like one of the boys already, we were just talking about how well the girls milk and how much better they fit in here than we thought they would."

Later, as Homer and I were biking home, Homer asked me why I was so upset about what John said about Josh. He said, "You know, Caleb, that they've always joked about Josh and his soft ways. I asked Josh about it years ago and he told me not to let it upset me, that we all have to be who we are if we are going to be comfortable in life."

"I know, Homer," I answered, "Josh has talked to me about it and said that talk doesn't make a man, history does. That there was nothing wrong with his libido, I had to look up the word and it has to do with wanting sex. Still, joking or not I still have a hard time holding my temper when those boys get going. Now that he's leaving, it makes me madder, I wish those boys could know Josh as we do."

We had reached the hill to the house and Homer couldn't pedal the bike up the hill so I got off and walked beside him. He said, "You know, Caleb, it's funny how much we all depend on Josh, especially when we get in trouble. Josh says that I'll have you after he's gone, what worries me is who will you have, after all, it's you who always seems to get in trouble. When I got the skin caught back on my prick, Mom and Dad immediately started blaming you. And after the pain stopped I got to thinking I could get away with a lot of things if you were going to be blamed. I guess that would be damn stupid now that you're going to be big brother."

"One thing for sure, Homer," I replied, "I don't need any help in getting into trouble. Mother said she thinks they should have made that my middle name. Speaking of being big brother, what was all that about girls and kissing I heard about at the barn? Jennie seems to know something about you that I wasn't aware of."

"Weren't nothing, Caleb, honest," Homer laughed. "A bunch of us got together playing spin the bottle, I liked kissing the girls and I guess they liked my kissing. Now other girls are teasing me saying, 'Kiss me once, kiss me twice, Homer kisses awful nice.' A couple of the girls seemed serious so I kiss them, now it's got to be like a game."

I remembered what I felt the last time Beverly kissed me and thought when kisses starts affecting Homer like that he will go insane playing those games. When we reached the house, Mother, Hester and Josh were in the kitchen talking about Josh's party. Josh looked down in the dumps. He hadn't been himself since he received his draft notice. Mother said, "Josh, you have to snap out of it. All your friends are working hard to make your send-off something special."

"If they want it to be special for me," Josh replied, "then they should find some way that I can serve without carrying a rifle."

"Josh, what are we to do?" Mother answered. "You wouldn't let the Muldons try to get you a deferment as a farm-hand and you refuse to join the conscientious objectors. The recruiting sergeant said he would try to help even though you had already received your draft notice, but it was mostly out of his hands. Maybe you should have joined the Navy when Reilly did, then you wouldn't have been in combat."

"Oh, Mother, if my own mother doesn't understand, how can I expect the rest of the world to? Even if I didn't see anyone being killed when you fire those big Navy guns, people die and I couldn't live thinking I had anything to do with their death," Josh said, holding his head in his hands. "I'll be all right for the party Friday, Mother, I just need someone who understands me."

Homer and I went to Josh and hugged him, saying, "Josh, we understand. That's what we discussed on the way home, how your soft side made you such a wonderful brother and how scary it was going to be without you here."

Mother and Hester both came to Josh telling him that they had no troubles or doubts about who he was, that they were only concerned about his predicament and wanted to be helpful. Josh said, "I know you are all with me. I didn't mean to make myself a burden on the family, it's just for the first time I'm fearful of what the future holds. I talked to the pastor and he advised me to put my trust in the Lord and to place my troubles in his hands. I have agreed to meet with him again. I believe and like little Caleb, I confess to talking to God when I am troubled, I'm just not sure I hear any answers."

It was painful seeing Josh like this, he had always seemed immortal to me. Homer and I both had nightmares about being without Josh that night. We talked about it on the way to work the next morning. Homer was logical about it, saying, "You know, Caleb, I guess this is what growing up is all about. You know how it was when we were little, we thought Mother and Dad could do anything. Then when we grew older it was so disappointing to find out that it wasn't true. I guess that growing up is understanding these things and being able to go on without losing the strength gained from those times in our lives."

I said, "You know, Homer, you sound more like Josh than I do, perhaps you should play the role of big brother."

Homer laughed and said, "Oh no, Caleb, that's your business. I'm going to stay young and ignorant as long as the world will let me. You wouldn't want me to have to quit being known as the kissing champ just because I was old enough to know better, would you?"

We arrived at the barn before I could come up with a good answer, listening to him made me think that he seemed to be adapting to growing up faster than I did.

The last two weeks of Josh's "freedom," as he called it, flew by, and the Friday before he left they held his good-bye party at the town hall. There was food downstairs prepared by the good cooks of Sterling. Upstairs, a band that had been formed from local talent for these occasions was playing dance tunes. Almost everybody we knew in town attended the party. One of the town fathers gave a short speech and presented Josh with his watch. Most of the older folks drifted off and left the dancing to the younger group. I watched Josh in the beginning, working to put on a good face. By the time the dance was in good swing, most of the girls in town were lined up, waiting to dance with him. This and the way some of those girls held him while they danced soon had Josh really enjoying himself. Homer and I had to be home by eleven, and when Mother called us in the morning to go to work, Josh still wasn't home. When we went down for breakfast Mother said, "That was a wonderful party last night. I believe it was the best-attended one yet and Josh seemed to really enjoy it, after all." I didn't mention he probably still was, I'm not sure Mother would understand that boys will be boys as Hester did.

Josh had to leave early Monday morning so Sunday afternoon Mother prepared his favorite baked ham dinner and designated Sunday afternoon as the time for the family to say our good-byes. Everybody except Uncle Louis was there. He had been drinking since the party Friday and Mother wouldn't allow him to come to the table drunk. We all told stories on how Josh affected our lives and how much we would miss him. Francis and Hester just held him and cried. The best surprise I think for Josh was when Dad spoke. He said, "Josh, I grew up in a much more rough and tumble world than you did and sometimes it was hard for me to understand your seemingly soft ways. After having you for close to 19 years, one thing I know for sure is that you're as capable, if not more so, of handling life's situations as anyone I know." Then Dad, who had never been one to speak much or show his affection, gave Josh a big hug, saying, "Be proud of who you are, son, and stand tall for what you believe in." Then Dad left the room, going out to the barn.

The week following our good-byes to Josh was the start of school. Things were much different going to high school. We rode a bus to the Oscin High School, which left before seven in the morning. We had to walk to the center of town to catch the bus, so that meant being ready by six thirty every morning. I had to give up my morning milking but I worked afternoons in the fields to make up the time. There were kids from several of the small towns surrounding Oscin that came to that high school, making a school population of over three hundred. I thought it would be fun to be back in the same school with Karl and George and Glenn, but somehow my being a freshman made them shy away from me at school. Karl tried to explain about upper- and lowerclassmen when we were at home in Sterling, but I was too angry to listen to his alibis. I told him he hadn't been a true friend since he left grammar school. "Look how you treated me with Beverly." Joan, Jake and I formed our own group with classmates from Sterling and soon were making friends with other freshmen. The high school classes were confusing at first, with different teachers and rooms for each subject, but after adapting to this schedule it was more fun studying that way. I learned that several of the students were my cousins. I hadn't recognized them because of the lack of transportation and with Dad not the visiting kind, and there were very few family gatherings in my youth. I also found love, the kind that only a fourteen-year-old boy would understand. Three seats ahead of me in English class sat Viola Wilkins, with her beautiful long blond hair and looks that seared my very soul. Unfortunately I was paying more attention to Viola than I was to the lessons. My poor showing in class and awkward attempts to get Viola's attention made me fodder for class clown jokes and I was fast becoming an embarrassment to her as well as myself. One afternoon when I had come from the fields I met Joan for candy and our weekly walk. When we left the library and were walking to Joan's house she began talking about what it was like being in love. I told her how I felt about Viola and asked her what to do. She cried, "Caleb, I swear you are the dumbest kid in town." She started to give me one of her body hugs, then she pulled back and slapped me so hard I saw stars.

It was such, a shock, I cried out, "Joan, what the hell is wrong with you?" She ran down the road crying without an answer. I walked back to the library to get my bike, thinking about what Josh would have to say about this. Joan and I had talked about everything for years and she was the one who brought the subject of being in love up. I knew that Joan had been different with me lately, but she had never seemed angry. Figuring out girls was far beyond my capabilities. Maybe it was just this puberty thing making the girls as crazy as it does boys. At the barn that night the subject as usual was about girls and sex and how many times they had done it. None of this seemed to bother Jennie; she just called it boys' bullshit and never got involved in their conversations. As much as I heard this talk it still bothered me. I couldn't imagine girls like Joan or Viola doing the things they talked about. I often imagined holding Viola or kissing her, but so far I hadn't even gotten her to talk to me or give me a smile. I lay in bed thinking of ways I might remedy this, Josh would probably write her a poem. So I got up and went to where Josh hid his poems and after reading a dozen or so, I found one I thought appropriate. The next day in English class after being called to the board to punctuate a sentence, I slipped the poem on Viola's desk. She tried to ignore it, but the teacher didn't. She walked to Viola's desk, saying, "Well, Mr. Carney, perhaps you have produced some literature that the whole class would like to hear." She brought the poem to me and after looking at it over said, "I believe this is very good, Caleb, now read it to the class."

I was sure I was going to drop dead on the spot, my heart beat like a trip hammer and I could hardly speak. Mrs. Black said, "Well, Caleb, are you going to read that to us or maybe you would rather have Viola read it?" Oh God, I couldn't allow that to happen, so taking a couple of deep breaths I stammered out the poem.

> I cannot find any words that say,
> How my love for you possesses me this way,
> I can only say it will never leave,
> And none of it is make-believe,
> You should have no fears or show no sorrows,
> For my love will last beyond the morrows.

The kids started a mocking cheer. Mrs. Black quieted them, and if looks could kill, Viola's would have had me dead. I hid my head at my desk until class was over and rushed out at the bell. Later at lunch, Gary Wilkins, Viola's brother, came over, grabbed me by the collar and said, "Carney, I have a message for you. If you ever embarrass my sister again or even talk to her, then you are a dead man, do you understand me?"

I nodded my head and choked out a yes. Gary was the school bully and had beaten up half the boys in school, sometimes just for the hell of it. I certainly wasn't going to fight him, even for Viola. Mrs. Black asked me the next day if I had really written that poem. I told her about Josh, explaining that he was in boot camp. She said, "Caleb, I know how hard it was for you to do that reading, but you have to understand that you went from a good student to a nothing and I have to react to that somehow. It isn't a shame for a boy to be smitten by some girl, but it is a shame to allow it to destroy your work. Just remember, no girl is going to become interested in the class dummy."

Later that week I was watching a boxing match that was going on in the little room we called our gym. I had become fascinated with boxing since I had put on the gloves with my cousin and he cuffed me around at will. I guess all boys believe they can box until they meet someone who really can. When that match finished, Gary Wilkins grabbed the gloves and said, "Com'n, Carney, let's see if you can handle the gloves any better than you can your love life." The last thing I wanted to do was end up in the ring with him, but I couldn't see any way out, so trying not to look scared, I shrugged and said, "Boxing ain't my game, Gary, but I'll give it a try, just promise not to mess my pretty face." My cousin Harold stepped up and said, "Hey, Gib, those gloves were mine next, Lewis and I were going to box."

"That's O.K., Harold," Lewis said, "they can have the gloves, I don't care."

"Well, I damn well care," Harold replied, "I asked for them next and no damn bully is taking them away from me."

"Bully, am I?" Gary snorted, "Com'n, Harold, let's get at it, unless you're afraid of the big bad bully."

"Sure," said Harold, pulling on the gloves, "you're always willing to fight a little guy like me or Caleb because you know you're stronger, but I'm not afraid, especially of a blowhard like you."

Gary rushed across the ring and threw a wild right. Harold slipped under it and put a hook into Gary's stomach that knocked the wind out of him so bad he dropped both hands to his side. Harold went slap, slap, slap across his face with light mocking blows. Gary bellowed and rushed at Harold but he sidestepped and slapped him again as he was going by. When Gary came off the ropes Harold bounced around, in and out, hitting Gary at will, while he pawed air. Harold got a little careless and Gary caught him with one of his wild blows, knocking him down. Gary started kicking him. We all jumped into the ring and pulled him off. He was hollering, "Let me go, let me go."

Harold got up, slowly shook his head a couple of times, and said, "O.K., boys, leave him to me."

Harold's lip was bleeding and he favored his left leg where Gary had kicked him. Gary came to him warily, then almost in a blur of motion Harold went left, left, left, right. Gary, staggered back, Harold kept punching left, left, right, left, right, left, right. Gary sagged against the ropes, Harold kept slapping at him, saying, "Com'n, bully, where's the fight now? I'm only a little guy, ain't I the size you like? Do I need to lie down?" Gary had a bloody nose his eyes and lips were swelling. Harold kept slapping and taunting him, it was as if he didn't want to finish it. Finally one of the teachers showed up and broke it up. I helped Harold take off the gloves and clean the blood from his face. I said, "Harold, you aren't going to be able to turn your back on him now, whatever possessed you?"

"Don't worry, Caleb," he replied, "Gary won't dare sucker me. We live in the same town and he knows my brothers and I would show the whole town what he is if he's dumb enough to try anything with us. I was just tired of seeing him bullying everybody, he could of have half killed you in that ring."

That fight caused a big ado about allowing unsupervised boxing to continue. In the end, the school officials decided to prohibit all boxing on the school premises, which eliminated the fear of being challenged to box for the many of us who were untrained in the art.

In a few months the newness and fear of different school life had worn off. Freshmen were more acceptable to the upperclassmen and Viola had become one of those wonderful, unattainable things of life. As winter closed the field jobs at the farm I was assigned the task of caring for the young stock at the Coor barn in the afternoon. I had to supply their food and water, clean the stables and on good days put them out in the exercise yard. On the days they went out it took most of my after-school time to care for them and do my milking.

Josh had written often since he left. Basic training had been easier for him than he expected, though he didn't like the man-shaped targets they used in rifle and bayonet practice. He had made a good impression on his superior officers and they and the chaplain managed to get him a transfer to a medical division after he finished basic. He was due at a hospital training area to join his new unit right after basics, so he was only able to be home two days. When he arrived he looked fit and was excited about being able to serve without actually fighting. He talked about meeting men from all over the country and how much different some of their worlds were from ours. He felt that being in the service had broadened his convictions, and if he did well in his new training, he was considering becoming a doctor. We all wanted to talk with Josh alone, but it seemed that Patsy Wilson was always with him. We had some great talks at meals as a family, but not having Josh as my personal mentor now left me feeling as if I'd lost something precious. Josh's leaving reemphasized what a breach there was in our lives without him, and for days the family was downcast.

I survived the winter at school with no further calamities. When spring came the young stock were turned out to pasture. The pasture fence was in poor repair and I spent my afternoons running the fence line and making repairs. One afternoon when I was on the backside of the pasture I broke the handle on my hammer. The shortest route out was through the woods that brought me out to the road by the Stone place. Jason was there playing with Beverly's brother Alan. I hollered, "Hey, Jason, see if Alan has a hammer I could borrow."

Alan said, "Sure, Caleb, as long as you get it back soon I don't think Dad would mind. I'll go get it."

Alan and Jason went into the shed and a few moments later Jason came out and said, "Caleb, he's having a hard time finding the hammer. Come over and help us look."

Beverly came out of the house, shouting, "Alan, what are you two brats up to now?"

I tried to hide, but Jason gave me away by answering, "We're looking for a hammer for Caleb."

Seeing me, Beverly looked surprised and said, "Hi, Caleb, what are you doing up here looking for a hammer?"

I held up the broken hammer handle, saying, "I ran into a little trouble back there repairing fence, Bev, and Alan said I could borrow yours for a while."

"No problem, Caleb," she said laughingly, "I think the hammer is in the house, come on in and I'll find it for you."

The thought of going with her triggered memories and emotions that were exhilaratingly fearful, somehow I seemed compelled to go. Inside the house Beverly grabbed my hand and said, "Com'n, Caleb the hammer is upstairs, remember?" Oh, man, I thought, this was like my crazy dreams. At the top of the stairs Beverly pulled me into her room and locked the door. She held me and kissed me and we ended up rolling on the bed. Then it happened. Those stories the boys told at the barn, and the ones about the bull and the cows were all making sense. Then, lost in a trance, like a man in anger doing something he knows is wrong and can't control, I had sex. We heard the boys downstairs shouting for us. Beverly jumped out of bed, saying, "Get dressed quick, we can't let Alan catch us in here."

Downstairs Alan was holding a hammer, saying, "I found one, Caleb."

I grabbed the hammer from Alan saying, "That's great, Alan, if I hurry I can get that fence fixed before I have to go home for supper."

I needed to get out of there, before anyone saw how shaky I was, my whole insides felt like Jell-O. I walked back through the woods to the fence and set down all aquiver. Man, I was destined to go to hell for sure now. Damn that Beverly, she seemed so proud of herself telling me to come back anytime now that I was a real lover. My mind was a whirling pit of despair. It was as if I had broken some sacred trust. Words came pouring back, "It's for married people," "girls could have babies," "you can catch horrible diseases," "and they sell it at Travis's." The boys at the barn, with their "boy, I had me some last night," "you should have seen her," "boy, was she built." The fear, the confusion, the anxiety, was this the apex of puberty? *Oh Josh, why couldn't you be here?* I heard the town clock strike the hour, signaling that it was time to get moving if I was going to be at the barn at five thirty. The last thing I needed now was a hassle about being late or not showing up.

When I arrived home Homer was sitting down to eat his supper. While riding our bikes to the milking barn, Homer said, "What's with you, Caleb, did you lose your virginity or something?"

"Damnit, Homer," I exploded, "you're getting more like Larry, John and Arthur every day, maybe I should have a talk with Mother about your language."

"Whoa, Caleb, I was only jesting," said Homer, speeding ahead. "Don't

165

blow my head off, come to think of it though, Jason did say he saw you over at Stone's. What's the story?"

"There ain't no damn story, Homer," I said, riding to catch up, "and don't you start one with the boys tonight or I'll have a talk with Mother about your language and your damn kissing games too."

Homer said, "Look, Caleb, we're brothers and I can plainly see that you are upset about something. I'm not going to blab anything in the barn, I only want to help if I can."

"I'm sorry, Homer," I replied, "I know I'm a little jumpy but it's personal and I wouldn't discuss it even with Josh if he were here. I have to work this one out myself, thanks for mentioning my mood. I'd better work on that before we get to the barn." I wished I could talk about what happened like the boys at the barn but I felt more terror than conquest; besides, I sure hadn't been the conqueror in this episode even if I wasn't exactly a victim. Listening to them talk, you would think that sex was the greatest contact sport ever invented, a game that possessed their every thought. I guess that part was true, I couldn't get what had happened with Beverly out of my mind. I was extremely concerned about losing control like that with other girls. I wouldn't want to get in the kind of trouble that Bob Woods got into with Kate Curtis. *Damn this puberty thing anyway. First I have to deal with the fear of it, now I'm dealing with the trouble it causes.*

Things were normal at the barn, even if I wasn't. The bragging of their conquest and the teasing of "when are we going to hear your story, Caleb?" I spent as much time talking to Jennie as I could, testing how it would affect me. Jennie had a boyish nature, but her looks and build were all girl. I survived being close to her without losing control, despite some of the thoughts being near her created. Being with other people, even if I couldn't talk about my troubles, help to lift the doom and gloom I had felt since leaving Beverly, and after all, weren't they living proof there was life after sex?

The next day at school while we were waiting tryouts for the baseball team, I asked Harold if he had ever had sex.

He laughed and said, "I hope you aren't thinking about Viola again, Caleb. I don't think I could protect you if Gib ever heard that."

"No, Harold," I said, blushing, "it's not about her, it's all you hear from the boys that has me confused."

I was surprised that I had even brought the subject up, but I felt fairly comfortable talking to Harold and was pleased that I had, when he said, "No, Caleb, I haven't had sex, but have been awful close with a friend of mine. My mother has always been open about the subject with me and she stressed that first time sex can be very traumatic and you need to wait until your mature enough to handle it. I've found 'almost sex' trauma enough to handle right now. Why, Caleb, don't tell me you're having an affair?"

"Not an affair, Harold, more of a happening," I replied, hoping he wouldn't pry.

"Don't worry, Caleb," he said, "my brothers assure me that I will live through puberty and so will you." I was called to take my turn at bat and I guess Harold and I felt the same about that discussion because he never brought it up again.

Harold was right about living through puberty though, most of my fears were unfounded and there weren't many girls like Beverly and I sure was making it a point not to get caught alone with her.

The school year was coming to a close and the older boys were preparing to enter the service, some with great bravado and others with the quiet determination. Josh was working in a camp hospital somewhere in New York State, and he still marveled at the difference of men from other walks of life in his letters. We all felt better about Josh now that he was able to stay away from the killing. The Allies were forming joint armies for the final push to win the war. Thousands upon thousands of our boys were being shipped to Europe and Africa. What the news reports called our war production machine was in full swing. More and more women were taking jobs in the factories, replacing the men who went to war. American planes flying from England were bombing Germany daily, destroying their industries. President Roosevelt spoke on radio broadcast assuring the nation and the world that the Allied Armies of the United States, England, Canada and France would be victorious and the Axis monstrosity would be destroyed.

On the home front Beverly, Julia Sledge and Betty Hart had signed up to work for the Muldons. Larry had finally been allowed to join the Marines and was in boot camp. One thing was for sure—this wasn't going to be a typical school vacation. All indications were that my fifteenth summer was going to be a long, hot one.

Chapter 11

My fifteenth summer fully lived up to the uneasiness that I had felt. It started out with Beverly coming to work as one of the strippers at the barn. But luckily her milking skills were not adequate for the job and she was assigned to fieldwork, much to the disappointment of the boys, who had planned a special stripping initiation for her. Remembering mine, I was glad they never got the chance to initiate her. When they had tried that with Janet and Jennie, they had been threatened with their brothers and jail if they tried. Beverly probably would have thought it was great fun and would get everybody in trouble. Dad had decided to grow a bigger garden and to cut wood off our land to sell, so he bought a horse to work the garden and draw wood. Now that I was the oldest boy living at home, I was expected to do more of the work around our farm. With Golly Moses asking for more and more hours, most of my summertime was spent working. John Muldon had a 1935 Chevrolet, and many nights he and Arthur and other boys from town would drive to Oscin after finishing the milking to see movies or go cruising for girls. I finally convinced Mother that was my only chance to have any enjoyment since I didn't have time for fishing or hunting, and she allowed me to go with them occasionally. The movies were a great treat for me, because I'd only been a few times before. The older boys were acquainted with girls in the towns we visited, and when I had money enough I would invite one of them to go to a movie with me. I began to feel very grown up going out on real dates. One night John told me that there was a girl named Mamie who wanted to go to the movies with me. I wasn't dating anyone in particular, so I agreed to take her. I met Mamie for the first time at the theater, she was a pretty girl, somewhat older than me, and there was an excitement or energy about her that seemed familiar. I soon found out why. I don't recall what the movie was, because Mamie's necking became so hot and heavy that I completely embarrassed myself. Damn that John, he'd set me up with another Beverly. I became the butt of everyone's jokes all the way home and for weeks after.

Dad spent as much time as he could when we were together teaching me how to handle the horse he'd bought. All my life I'd heard the stories about what a great horseman Dad had been. Before he lost them in the house fire, he used to have ribbons and plaques that he had won at the fairs where he had competed in horse drawing contest. That was before there were tractors, when most of the logging was done with horses. I don't remember ever feeling closer to Dad than I did when we were working with that horse. I used to imagine myself a great teamster like Dad was in the stories I heard. I learned to handle the reins while cultivating the garden and hauling wood on the one horse scoot. I began to wish that all farming and woods work was still done with horses. It seemed a more relaxed way of accomplishing things. One morning Jason got up early with Homer and me. Dad had old Tom harnessed up and Jason was to ride him to the Whipple place, that was way beyond George's house over by the New Hampshire line in Richville and bring back a wagon Dad had bought. With Jason on Tom and Homer and me on our bikes, we rode through town. I was a little jealous that Jason had got to go on this important journey. That evening, Dad said, "Caleb, when you have the free time I want you to take that wagon and start hauling the manure under the barn out to the field. You probably won't be able to back the wagon all the way back in there, so just get as close as you can and shovel it out the rest of the way." It was a couple of days before I was able to find the time to hitch the horse to the wagon, but when the time came I was excited about finally getting a job that I could show my prowess as a teamster. I harnessed Tom and hitched him to the wagon, proudly driving him to the back of the barn. After quite a struggle with Tom, I finally got him to back the wagon all the way under the barn to the manure pile. I felt great pride in accomplishing something Dad said couldn't be done. After a couple of trips, Tom was having great problems trying to back up with the wagon, as the mud became deeper and deeper. I was so exhilarated about having been able to make it back there the first few trips, I wasn't aware that Tom had been hurt struggling in the mud. When I had loaded the wagon for the fourth time, I noticed that Tom could hardly pull it from the barn, and by the time I had unloaded the wagon he was hopping on three legs. I unhitched him from the wagon and led him back to the barn. I rubbed him down as much as he would let me and told Mother that Dad had better check him when he came home. When I came home from the barn that night, Dad was in with the horse. I went in and asked how he was. Dad said, "He's pretty bad off, son. What happened?"

"I really don't know for sure, Dad," I replied. "I was hauling manure and all of a sudden he became extremely lame, so I brought him back to the barn."

"I did some checking under the barn, Caleb," Dad said, frowning. "It looks like he put up quite a struggle backing up in that mud. Didn't I tell you that you wouldn't be able to back very far under there?"

"Yes, Dad, you did, but I thought you were talking about my ability and not the horse's. I only wanted to be as good a teamster as you were, Dad," I answered, suddenly feeling apprehensive.

"Well, son, I am afraid that we both made a mistake here. I should have made what I meant better understood and you should have been caring more about your horse and less about glory. I believe that Tom has thrown a stifle and if that is true his usefulness is over. We'll give it a few days before deciding what to do," Dad said, walking dispiritedly out of the barn.

The next few days Dad spent as much time as he could manage working on Tom. He made a sling to support Tom so he couldn't lie down, explaining that he probably would not be able to get up again. I helped Dad as much as I could and spent time alone with Tom trying to relieve some of his pain by sharing my feeling of culpability. The field that we had been spreading the manure on was a part of the farm that had been neglected and was growing back to woodland. We had cut the wood and burned the brush and used old Tom to haul out the stumps and doing the plowing. The second weekend after I had injured Tom, Dad borrowed the team of horses that the Muldons still used occasionally on the farm. After Dad hitched the team to a harrow, he showed me how he wanted the manure harrowed in and left me to drive the team. I felt some vindication because Dad was allowing me to handle the horses after what I had done. I drove the team riding the harrow using the *gees* and *haws* like Dad had taught me. I was just beginning to feel again the excitement of being a teamster when I saw Dad leading old Tom out into the woods. It was a pathetic sight, Tom as big as he was hopping along like a three-legged dog. I thought Dad must have seen some improvement if he was taking Tom walking and I wondered why he didn't keep Tom on the road or in the field, where it was easier for him. Dad always had his reasons, and if there was one thing I knew from all the stories I had heard, it was that he was an expert when it came to horses, so he must be doing what was right for Tom. About twenty minutes after I saw Dad and old Tom, I saw Uncle Louis leaving the house with a rifle. I was thinking, *I hope he knows Dad and old Tom are out in the woods.* But then I realized the truth—Dad had decided to end Tom's misery. Maybe ten minutes after I saw Uncle Louis enter the woods, I heard the blast of his big rifle. I began crying. Tears rolled down my cheeks and dampened my shirt. Some teamster I turned out to be, killing the first horse I drove. I don't know how long I cried, the team I was driving just kept plodding along by rote, harrowing the field. Eventually Dad came down and stopped the horses, saying, "O.K., Caleb, I think we have this harrowed enough, your mother wants you to eat and get some rest before you go to the barn tonight. You are going to have to accept what has happened to Tom and put it behind you."

I went to the house and Mother said, "Your dinner is on the table, Caleb."

"I'm sorry, Mom, I couldn't keep anything down now," I answered as I fled to my room. Throwing myself on the bed sobbing, I thought, *How does anyone put something like this behind them?* I knew that my heart had been scarred and what had happened would be seared in my mind for life. This was more pain than losing the house to fire, more fear than the fear of Gibby Wilkins, more confusion than puberty, this was the death of a horse that died because of obeying me, in my childish attempt to be a hero.

Sleep must have finally rescued me from my pain because Homer was shaking me awake, shouting, "Caleb, Caleb, wake up, it's time to eat and go do our milking."

The next few weeks I fumbled through life in a depressed haze. How I wished Josh had been there with his worldly wisdom. Since he had left I was realizing more and more how much I had depended on him. Homer and Jason had been to where Tom was lying in the woods. They said that the animals and birds were making short work of his carcass and there soon would be nothing left but a skeleton. They wanted me to go with them, but my mind already held enough horror pictures of old Tom. Mother fussed and worried about me, saying I had to buck up and face facts. I had talks with Hester about Tom and what had happened. She explained that as tough as it was for me, this too was a part of becoming mature, learning from our mistakes and moving on in life. She said that in some of the books she had read, there were people who had ruined their whole lives because of one traumatic incident in their childhood. And though I probably would never forget Tom, I needed to see it as a tragic accident caused by my immaturity as a teamster and not as a terrible thing I had done. Hester may not be Josh, but she sure was a big help in easing my mind enough so I could return to my usual way of life.

That year Mrs. Banner began closing the doors between the dance hall and the bar at the Inn, one night a week, to allow the young people in town a place to congregate and dance. Mrs. Banner supplied money for the jukebox and sold soda and candy at half price. On those nights everybody in town sang her praises.

Mother decided those dances would be good for me, and since Emma was already going she said she would show me some dance steps. Going to those dances and my occasional forays into town with John and the boys were a great help in lifting my gloom. Joan and I had not been getting together as we used to, but one night while we were dancing together at the Inn, Joan said, "Caleb, I wish we hadn't given up our weekly get-togethers."

"I know, Joan," I answered, "I miss them very much and now Josh is gone I don't have anyone but you to share with."

Joan and I met the next morning in the park after I had left Muldon's fields. I had been working in the fields every morning, after the milking, and quitting at noon or before, so I would have some time at home between milkings. Joan laid down some ground rules if we were going to continue meeting. No more hugging or kissing and no discussions about our personal love interest. Remembering how angry Joan had been last time we parted I readily agreed. I talked to Joan about Tom and how I had been feeling. She said, "Poor Caleb, why didn't you come to me sooner? You're carrying an unnecessary burden when you don't talk out a problem. What happened, Caleb, was an accident, one that could have been prevented only if you had the knowledge that you do now. You can't go on punishing yourself for not knowing. It would be wrong if you didn't feel sad, it would be wrong if you didn't admit and learn from your mistake, but it would be a terrible mistake to allow this sad incident to domineer your life. From time to time in life we all will have to face sad losses; pets, parents, family members, and we must be prepared to go on. The truth is, Caleb, that sooner or later we all lose loved ones. God's world would be an unbearable place if we all lived depressed about our losses."

We had begun walking towards Joan's house and she held my hand tightly, as I replied, "Joan, I can't tell you how much hearing your explanations of what happened with the horse means to me. Hester has been trying to help me understand and I'm not sure what Josh would have told me but I doubt it would have been more help than talking to you. I know our so-called hormones have made things different between us, but I have missed our being together."

We had almost reached Joan's house and still holding my hand she turned and faced me, saying, "Caleb, you make me angry when you talk about other girls and I hear awful stories about you going to Oscin and other towns with the boys from the barn. That makes you someone that decent girls are afraid to be seen with, sometimes I think you're so ignorant." Joan pulled me to her, kissing me quickly on both cheeks, then ran off, shouting, "See you at the dance next Tuesday night."

That night at the barn John asked if anyone was interested in chipping in and sending to get some Fourth of July fireworks. Their sale had been banned in Massachusetts, so most of us thought it was a good idea and ordered from a catalog that he had brought. A week or so later, John drove to New

Hampshire and bought the fireworks, and after work we met to divide them before going to Oscin to celebrate. Arthur and John decided to try out some of their cherry bombs before we left. They were having a grand time throwing them into the horse trough when the town constable, Albert Parks, showed up and demanded we give him all our fireworks. Arthur emptied his pockets for Constable Parks while John walked slowly back to the car. Constable Parks argued with Arthur about more fireworks, saying he guessed he would search the car. John jumped into the car and took off, leaving Arthur and me standing there by the horse trough with the constable. I didn't have any fireworks on me, the few I had been able to afford I was saving for the Fourth, and they were still in the car. By the time the constable, cussing and swearing, had reached his car, which was parked by the store, John was well out of sight. John returned about a half-hour later and told the constable he was sorry about leaving like that, but he had the runs and had to get to the barn in a hurry. The constable wasn't buying his story, but after his search of the car turned up no fireworks he allowed us to leave. Saying Muldon or no Muldon, it didn't matter to him, someday he would have John in irons, like the crook he was. We left the store, and after picking up George and Jake we left for Oscin. George was the proud possessor of a couple of cherry bombs that he said he got while on a trip to New Hampshire with his father. When we arrived in Oscin the local police pulled us over and, after having us all empty our pockets and finding George's cherry bombs, demanded the right to search the car. It seemed that the Sterling constable had called the Oscin police and arranged to have us picked up. Finding only the few bombs that George had, they let us go with the warning that they would be watching us. I began to understand about our getting the reputations that Joan had talked about. I thought if this all got back to my mother it would mean the end of my being on these trips. Jake knew a girl from the paper where he worked, who was going to be baby-sitting in Oscin that night. He said her girlfriend was going to be with her and was interested in meeting me. After finding the house where they were, we spent an enjoyable evening getting acquainted, even to the extent of some light necking. At ten thirty we left for the center of town, so the girls wouldn't get caught entertaining. It was almost midnight before we located John and the rest of the boys and headed back to Sterling. I knew I was in for it if Mother heard me come in, so I had John leave me off at the bottom of the hill so Mother wouldn't hear the car.

The next morning at the barn you would have thought that John and Arthur were some kind of big heroes, listening to their version of what had happened the night before. I was glad that John had been able to save our fireworks, but it was little wonder that the barn crew was conceived as such terrors, if these were the kind of stories that were being spread around. I'd ridden my bike to Gale's fields to help with the haying and Beverly was already there with the tractor, raking. I started cocking the hay behind the hay rake. Beverly hollered, "Hey, Caleb, I wondered when we were going to get a chance to work together. Too bad I'm not a milker like you, we could be together every day, wouldn't that have been a ball?"

"I'm sure it would have," I answered, thinking what a nightmare that would have been, especially with Homer there. "I'm only going to be here a couple of hours, Bev, and Golly Moses wants this field ready before I leave, so you'd better get raking."

Beverly laughed, saying, "Don't worry, Caleb, you know how fast I can be, we'll get it done."

Beverly raked the hay in windrows while I cocked it up for loading. When John and Arthur showed up with the truck, John shouted at Beverly, "Hey, Bev, how's our little man doing?"

"He's a cocker, John, he's a cocker," Beverly answered, laughing.

After the boys had trucked one load to the barn they came back and finished the field. Beverly said, "Hey, Caleb, how about riding back with me?"

We were about a mile from town and the last thing I wanted right then was to be alone with Beverly, so I said, "I have to hurry, Bev, it will be faster riding back with the boys."

As I was climbing on the truck I heard her laugh, saying, "Not nearly as much fun, Caleb, not nearly as much fun."

The next few weeks I was lucky—or unlucky, depending on how I was thinking or dreaming— enough not to have to work with Beverly. I'm glad all girls aren't like her or I would end up going to hell for sure. Joan and I had begun meeting regularly, most of the time we adhered to her conditions, but there were times that the devil in me wanted much more. I was always on my best behavior with Joan. Since getting back together I realized how important our meetings were to my life. Though I was careful not to mention how I felt about girls anymore, I was able to discuss personal feelings with her that I wouldn't dare with anyone else. One day when we were walking, Joan said, "Caleb, I see Karl and a couple of the other boys leave the Inn early on dance nights with girls, sometimes they come back, sometimes they don't. Where do they go?"

"Ah, come on, Joan, I dunno, but it isn't anything you or I would want to be mixed up in," I answered with my heart in my throat.

"Come on, Caleb," Joan teased, "I think you know more than you're letting on. I saw Beverly Stone trying to get you to go with them when Karl brought that Tammy to the dance last week. What goes on out there that scares one of the big bad Muldon barn boys so much?"

I knew we were getting on subjects that would ruin things, so I said, "Joan, remember your conditions, no talking about other girls. I don't want to lose what we have, so stop teasing."

When we had reached the place where Joan usually left me, she stopped and asked, "Caleb, if it had been me instead of Beverly wanting you to go that night, would you have gone?"

"Joan," I started to protest, but she just gave me a big body hug and a kiss and ran down the road.

I walked back to the center, got my bike and peddled home, wondering why it was all right for girls to make you feel like this when boys were threatened with hell or jail for acting on those feelings. Josh had told me that I would understand puberty when it happened, but I felt as if it had added questions not answers.

The next dance night, when I was dancing with Joan, Karl left with Beverly. Joan looked at me and said, "How about it, Caleb, are you going to take little Joan out into the big bad world or not?"

"Joan, oh, Joan, don't even think such things, let alone say them," I replied in a shaky voice.

"I'm serious, Caleb, I really want to go out there, want me to ask some other boy?"

"Oh God, Joan, you don't know what you're saying, please don't do anything as foolish as that," I pleaded.

"Jake looks lonely, Caleb," Joan answered, "dance over there so I can ask him"

"You can't be serious, Joan, think what you're saying."

"I know what I'm saying, Caleb, so who's it going to be?"

"O.K., O.K., Joan, I'll go outside in a few minutes, you wait a while and then join me. You don't want to be as brazen as Beverly, after all, I am one of those Muldon barn boys."

I waited outside, half hoping Joan was pulling a fast one on me, but in a few minutes she came out. I took her hand and started walking away from the center of town. I knew where Karl usually went and I didn't want to bump into him and Beverly. Joan was very quiet at first but started talking nervously when we got away from the Inn. When we reached the Larro place I walked Joan out to the back lawn. The Larros only used the place on an occasional weekend but had hired someone to keep the place up. I sat on the ground and Joan sat beside me. I put my arm around her and put my hand on her breast, she didn't talk or resist. Pulling her down on the grass, I began

176

kissing and hugging her as she rolled tight up against me. I told her, "I'm no expert, but I know you have to take your panties off." With a little help from me she got them off, and then as I started undoing my pants she jumped up and ran to the corner of the building crying. She said, "Caleb, oh God, what was I thinking, I can't, I can't, please don't hate me."

Man, hate was the farthest thing from my mind right then. I was so filled with lust that I begged her to come back.

She said, "Please don't make me, Caleb. I know this is my fault, not yours, but I can't, I just can't."

I said, "O.K., Joan, but you'll have to give me a few minutes. You stay over there away from me for a few minutes so I can pull myself together, and then we can go back."

Man, there was no doubt that the way I felt and what I wanted to do to Joan right then was going to get me a one-way ticket to hell. Maybe if I didn't lose it and got control, the Lord would forgive me. With the devil sitting on my back I prayed for strength, and slowly the fire inside me subsided. I walked over to Joan, she was still sobbing. I didn't dare to hold her, so I said, "Come on, Joan, it'll be all right. It's our secret and the world will never know. I don't expect that we will go to hell for tonight."

"I'm so sorry, Caleb, I was so stupid. I must be such a disappointment to you," she sobbed.

"Look, Joan, I think I would have been more disappointed if we had gone through with it. I wouldn't want to look upon you as another Beverly," I replied, taking her hand.

When we arrived back at the Inn, it was almost closing time, so Joan said, "Caleb, Mother thinks I'm walking home with some of the kids, why don't you walk me home so we don't have to go back in."

Joan hardly spoke on the walk home. I felt good about that, because I didn't really want to talk about what had happened. When we were close to her house, I held her for a moment and said, "Tonight never happened, Joan. I don't want this to make any difference in our relationship. I'll never speak of this again to you, or to anybody, so you go home and forget about it, and tomorrow everything will be the same."

"Caleb, I've always been afraid to tell you this, but I think I am in love with you." With that she gave me a quick kiss and ran for the house.

Walking back, I tried to make some sense out of what had happened. *Did Joan really think she had to have sex with me because she thinks she loves me? Man, I don't know about this love business. I guess you might have called my feelings for Viola love, infatuation is what the teacher called it. Whatever it was, it wasn't strong enough to survive the fear of her brother's*

177

challenge. I dunno about Joan loving me. I know that I always cared for her as a great companion, I never thought about it as love. I know I missed being with her when she was mad at me and she had evoked sexual desire even before what happened tonight. Damn, life was so much simpler before puberty, all I worried about then was hiking and fishing and that kind of fun.

A couple of weeks later, Frank Butler, who was responsible for keeping the Larro home gardens and lawns up, was getting the place spruced up for the Larros' upcoming vacation when he found a pair of panties with two red hearts and the name Joan on them. Frank, being Frank, made a big hullabaloo out of it, riding around town with the panties flying from the aerial on his truck. All kind of talk was around about who the Joan was. At the barn I was teased unmercifully about my sweet little Joan. The funny part was that I don't believe any one of them really thought it was her. I finally went to see Joan at her house, as I hadn't seen her around since the stories started, but Mrs. Walden said Joan was too ill for company and rather pointedly indicated she would prefer it if I wasn't seen with her daughter. I often thought it was funny that Joan never let me walk her all the way to her house. I guess it was that thing about me being one of the Muldon barn boys. The next night when I came home from the barn, Dad said he needed to see me out in the barn.

"Caleb," he said, "I don't know just how to ask you this, but Mr. Walden was here tonight and he has some idea that you are connected with those panties that Frank is parading around town and it has to do with you and his daughter Joan."

My first thoughts were, *My God! Joan told her parents,* and then I thought, *No, because if she had there wouldn't be any doubt.* I didn't know what to say, I hated lying to Dad, but I had made a solemn oath to Joan. I must have been standing there thinking with my mouth wide open because Dad said, "Well, Caleb, say something. Has the cat got your tongue or are you that shocked at getting caught?"

"No, no, Dad," I stammered, "Joan is one of the sweetest girls in town, I could never believe she would be involved in anything as sordid as that."

"I know you wouldn't lie to me, Caleb. I told Mr. Walden that I didn't believe you were involved and that what little I knew about his girl made me doubt that she was involved either. I bet some damn kid put those panties there for a joke on Frank. I had to talk to you about this, Caleb, I know that boys your age do get into messes like that and I worry sometimes about you working with that gang at the barn, with all the mischief they get into."

Back at the house when I went to our room, Homer said, "What's up, Caleb, I hear Mr. Walden was here to see Dad tonight, kind of unusual for him to come here, isn't it?"

I was feeling kind of bad about not being able to tell Dad the truth and really didn't want to talk about it with Homer, so I said, "Nothing, Homer, just a little man talk that Dad wanted to keep quiet."

"Yeh, I bet," Homer smirked, "I bet it was about those panties that Frank has been waving around. Isn't that Joan you're sweet on Mr. Walden's daughter? You don't have to worry though, Caleb, Arthur was telling me tonight that he was the one responsible for those panties being left there and he wasn't about to let on who the girl was."

"Damn, Homer, do you believe him?"

"Well, as far fetched as it seemed at first. He seemed real earnest, thinking it over later, yes I believed it."

The next morning at the barn, Homer hollered, "Hey, Arthur, Caleb was real interested in your little story about those panties with the little hearts on them."

"Hell, Caleb, don't believe any of his horseshit, he couldn't even get Beverly to go near him," John said, laughing.

"It's the truth," Arthur shouted, "and she was a virgin too."

"Wow, Caleb, did you hear that?" John whistled. "Arthur's on his way to jail, any virgin in this town would have to be very young, Arthur being eighteen and all could get maybe twenty, thirty years or more."

"Com'n, fellows," Jennie said, "give my brother a break, he can't be arrested for dreaming."

Arthur's story must have gotten spread around town, because a couple of days later when Golly Moses had the whole crew working to get what hay was down in before a coming storm. Mr. Walden came driving into the field. He came out of his car carrying a coiled whip. John hollered, "Hey, Arthur, look who's come for you."

Arthur screamed, "No, no, I didn't do it," and started for the woods with Mr. Walden right behind him. I guess from the sound of the screaming he got a couple of good licks in with the whip, but Arthur, being younger, was finally able to out run him.

When Mr. Walden came back to the field he was breathing heavily. He said, "I want you all to know my daughter was never involved in this filth that that damn Butler is spreading around town. We know now that the Sledge boy stole those panties off the line when he was haying at our place and caused all this uproar with his big lies. I only wish he could have been tied to a stake. I'd teach him to lie about my daughter. I would skin him with this whip. Now let this be known, if anyone of you boys ever smear my daughter's name in any way again, I'll be back with muscle enough to tie you all to a stake." Mr. Walden jumped into his car and went roaring off down the road. We didn't see Arthur again until milking time at the barn; even then, he sent his sister ahead to make sure Mr. Walden wasn't waiting for him.

Homer said, "Hey, Arthur, I heard I missed quite a race this afternoon, tell me, was the gain worth the pain?"

"Shut up, shut up, you all shut up," Arthur snarled.

Jennie said, "Let up, boys, whatever the truth is, Arthur has suffered enough. Mr. Walden came to the house and Pa beat the hell out of Arthur after he left. Between that and the whip welts, it's a wonder he even made it to work."

"It's safer than staying home," Arthur muttered as he started painfully about his milking.

On the way home Homer chattered on, wondering how anyone could be as dumb as Arthur seemed sometimes. I wasn't much in the mood for talking, knowing what I knew and not being able to talk about it was becoming a terrible burden. I knew that somehow I was going to have to get to see Joan. Lord only knew what she'd been through. We really owed Arthur a debt of gratitude, no matter why he did what he did, but he could never know. When he had showed us the whip welts and I saw his face where his father had beaten him, I wanted to cry, but I knew the real truth wouldn't help him now and it would destroy Joan.

The next morning at the barn, John said, "Caleb, did you hear the story about our great town officials? Dad talked to me about it last night, it appears that the same night we had trouble with constable Parks about the fireworks, somebody went over to Travis's and disabled all the cars that were there. Welcome Curtis, Jesse Moore and Kevin Woods' cars were all broke down in Travis's yard. They thought that they had it covered by having Frank Butler tow their cars away that night. Frank must have traded the information to some woman in town for a little amour and now that the whole town is in on it, there's hell to pay. Dad was concerned that we might have had something to do with disabling the cars, but I told him we were in Oscin and there was a police report to prove it."

"Wow! John, our town fathers caught at Travis's, what's this town coming to? First we have Joan's father with his bullwhip, and now this. Sounds like the kind of weird stories you and Arthur were talking about reading. I can hardly believe that things like this really happen," I said, moving my milk stool to the next cow.

"Caleb," John scoffed, "I worry about you always acting so innocent."

"Don't worry, John," Homer laughed, "his brothers know that Caleb lives in a different world and we watch out for him."

"Knock it off, Homer," I shouted angrily, "just because I don't go around bragging about things like you, doesn't mean I'm stupid."

"I'm sorry, Caleb," Homer replied, "I didn't mean you were stupid, it's just you always seem to be blind to what really goes on. The town fathers being at Travis's is no shock to the men of this town. But now that it is public, they're in for lots of trouble from their families and perhaps even from some of the voters, but I doubt that." Everywhere I worked that day, all the boys could talk about was the town fathers getting caught at Travis's and how they would be so much smarter if they never went there.

That night at the barn Old Golly Moses came in and said, "Boys, I don't want any of you cooking up more stories to make things worse, there is enough rumors going around without any help from the Muldon barn crew, so keep a lid on it."

After he left, Arthur said, "Damn it, what now, are we getting blamed for the town fathers' problems?"

John laughed and said, "No, Arthur, he's not blaming us. He talks to everyone in town that way, hoping to cool the trouble down." We finished milking and I was in a hurry to get home so I didn't get involved, I had a big day planned for tomorrow.

I was excited in the morning when I had high hopes of meeting Joan at the library around noon. Emma worked from time to time as a substitute librarian and when I found out she was working today I asked her to call Joan about an overdue book. Emma wasn't very interested in calling Joan at first, but I knew enough of her secrets to convince her. She was to call about a book and if Joan was confused she was to say it was the one authored by Guy Carney and she needed it around noontime. Very few people knew my middle name, but Joan had pried it out of me years ago. It had been over three weeks since I had seen Joan and I didn't want to wait until school started next week before I saw her. Everyone seemed so concerned about the Travis story, but one thing for sure, the town fathers' problems wasn't something that was going to spoil my day when there was a chance that I would get to talk to Joan.

The Muldons were cutting their silage that week, and I had agreed to work cutting corn until eleven thirty, as usual, Beverly was driving the tractor. She would jump off and help load every time the wagon was near me, saying, "Hey, Caleb, when are you going to finish fixing the fence, haven't you fixed that hammer of yours yet?"

I was glad when it came time to leave, because there was no denying the effect she was having on me. Arthur said, "Hey, Bev, don't waste your time on little Caleb, there's real men here, you know."

Beverly laughed, saying, "Real men don't have to stoop to steal little girls' panties off the line Arthur, just keep me in your dreams like the rest of your conquests."

"That story isn't true," he blubbered, "I never stole those panties."

"Oh sure," Beverly replied, still laughing, "tell us again how you got a sweet little virgin to agree to go anywhere with you, especially to a dark, deserted place like Larro's. If you wanted anyone to believe you, Joan was the last person you should have chosen."

I left with them still arguing, feeling almost as uncomfortable listening to the talk about Joan as I had been with Beverly's teasing. Maybe Homer was right about me being blind to things, I couldn't for the life of me understand how the story about Joan's panties got so far from the truth. Still the truth of that night, like the truth about my fish on Banner's wall, would never be known. *Look how that story and Arnold's wildcat story have become part of Sterling's history. The town fathers and Arthur might be spared the embarrassment of their stories becoming history though, after all, there aren't going to be any trophies hanging on a wall unless some husband ends up hanging.*

I biked home to clean up and change clothes, today of all days I wanted to make a good impression when I met Joan. Joan was at the library when I arrived, so were Mrs. Laurins and Mrs. Moore. Joan acted as if she didn't even know me when I whispered hello, so I got a book from the shelves and sat at one of the tables. Later Joan came by and dropped one of the books she was carrying. As I picked it up for her I saw a note hanging out of the book, which read, *In back of the parsonage.* I knew what she wanted, because that was one of the places we used to hide when I had first began buying her ice cream. I went to Emma and checked out the book I had been reading and left the library, taking a circuitous route to the back of the parsonage. In about ten minutes, when Joan joined me, she took my hand and said, "Caleb, I'm glad you arranged this, but I'm not going to be able to keep meeting you. You know by now how bullheaded my father is and he said he would lock me up for good if he caught me with any of those Muldon barn boys. I tried to tell him that you all weren't all like Arthur, but he won't even let me discuss it and Mother agrees with him. I felt sorry for Arthur, but I'm glad you started that story, it sure saved me."

"Joan, I didn't have anything to do with that story, it was Arthur who started bragging he was the one there with some secret girl. When your dad heard that, he must have figured the only way Arthur would ever get your panties was to steal them and he had been haying on your property that week.

Arthur is always bragging about girls, this time his lies came back to haunt him. I feel sorry and glad all the same time about what happened," I replied, putting my arm around her shoulder.

Joan leaned against me, then pulled away, saying, "Caleb, after what happened I think it's a good thing we can't be together anymore. I'm so ashamed about what you must think about me. I want to talk about why that happened."

"Look, Joan, think about what I told you that night. The best thing we can do is forget that it ever happened, the more we talk about something like that, the more apt it is to happen again. We shouldn't allow our crazy emotions to spoil what we've had for so long. You told me once you thought you loved me and that made me feel nicer than anything we might have done that night. So let's go back to that special time and forget anything that happened since." I held her by the shoulders, saying, "Joan, I want to hold you, and kiss you, and yes, I passionately wanted to do the sex thing that night, but what we have is more important. Maybe we are in love, so let's protect that."

Joan wrapped her arms around me, giving me a long, hard kiss. Then, pulling away, she said, "Caleb, I have to go, Mother said she would be checking on me, and Caleb, you're so sweet about everything. Keep finding ways we can meet, I need you in my life."

I went back to the park and got my bike and headed home. It felt good seeing Joan, but all this talk about love was real scary. My heart might belong to Joan, but my hormones sure kept Mamie and Beverly on my mind. Lord, how I missed Josh, he was the only one I ever dared to talk with about this sex thing. We hadn't heard from Josh in over a month, when he was home last time he said the scuttlebutt was that his unit was going to Africa. The news on the radio was all about invading Italy, and we wondered if Josh was involved in that. Mother was all excited when I got home, we had received a letter from Josh. Some parts had been cut out so we didn't learn much about where he was, but from the censorship we figured he must be in a war zone. He wrote how much he missed the family and that war was hell on earth. He was happy he was a medic and didn't have to shoot at anyone; he still planned to become a doctor after the war. We all had written him through his A.P.O. box number and he asked that we keep the letters coming even when we didn't get answers. He wrote a little personal note to each of us and added a postscript telling all my older sisters to assure me there was life after puberty.

The family read and reread Josh's letter, feeling the graciousness in them that was so much a part of Josh, even if we had not noticed it when he was here. All of us knew by now what a big part of our lives Josh had always been. I was proud when he told me that I was to be the big brother after he left. I knew now that wasn't to be, Homer already felt he was more worldly than I was and I'm sure that was being passed on to Jason and Francis, because they were always taking their troubles to him. Homer worked at the barn mornings without me when I was in school, and he was much more in tune with those boys than I had ever been.

School started the week after I met with Joan and at least we had a chance to talk on the bus. Of course we were careful of what we said, but at least we saw each other on a daily basis. I slipped Joan a note at school asking if we could meet on Saturday and on the bus ride home and she said she would like that. Two nights later when I came home from the barn, Mr. Walden was at the house. He and Dad were shouting so angrily at each other I thought they were going to come to blows. Mother came on the scene and said, "Now, Henry, quiet down. And you, Mr. Walden, we understand how you feel because we have daughters of our own, but you are sadly mistaken if you think our Caleb is any threat to your daughter. I don't understand how anyone as sweet as Joan can have a father who goes through her things and makes something as innocent as a note from my son into a filthy thought. If you think the Waldens are too good to be associated with the Carney family, then I advise you to turn around and leave immediately. I'm losing my temper with you, and when that happens, Henry's outburst will look mild. Now leave this yard and don't utter another word until you can apologize to us."

As Mr. Walden jumped into his car and roared out of the driveway, Mother said, "Caleb, what did you write in that note?"

"I wrote, 'Joan, can you meet me at the library at noon Saturday,' Mother," I answered.

"Now, Caleb, I don't believe that you would lie to me, but it seems impossible that Mr. Walden would be so upset over you meeting Joan. Hasn't that been going on for years?"

"That's all the note said, Mother, I promise," thinking, *Thank God I didn't write about what happened.*

Mother said, "Well, by God, the Waldens haven't heard the last of this. The bloody nerve of that man to come to my house and tell me my son isn't good enough to be with his daughter. I've heard rumors that the town fathers aren't the only ones in town who sneak up to Travis's and if I can pin down the truth of that, I'll show Mr. Mightier-than-Thou and his filthy mind a thing or two."

Uncle Louis, who had come down when all the shouting was going on, said, "Now, May, don't get yourself all upset, maybe I can have a talk with

Darren and get to the bottom of this."

"Somebody'd better do something," Dad said, "the mood Helen is in right now might make the Waldens an endangered species, and she was the one who shushed me."

Uncle Louis and Dad went out to the barn and Mother went into the kitchen, still muttering. Homer, who had been quietly taking this all in, said, "You know, Caleb, I don't know whether it's because you're so dumb that you get into these messes or you just act dumb because it gets you out of them. I don't believe there's a boy in town who can come anywhere near matching the amount of trouble you get into."

"Com'n, Homer, give me a break, it's not my fault that Mr. Walden thinks that all the boys that work at Muldon's are some kind of whore masters or something. Joan's trouble started with Arthur's dumb story about those panties, now her father thinks we're all like him." Walking to our room, I said, "You know, Homer, there are times when I wished I had never worked for the Muldons."

"Sure," Homer scoffed, "then we wouldn't have decent clothes for school, no bicycles and you would never have been able to get sweet little Joan to hide with you in the bushes if you couldn't buy her ice cream."

I whapped Homer with a pillow, saying, "Homer, don't you start making something dirty out of Joan and me. Her father is wrong, we've never done more than a little kiss good-bye."

"Keep your cool, Caleb, I didn't mean it to sound dirty. The whole town knows about you and Joan and your ice cream days, some of us younger kids used to spy on you all the time, we thought it was the greatest game. To tell you the truth though, some of us doubt the Arthur story about how Joan's panties got to Larro's and if it isn't true, then guess where the finger's pointing? I don't know about you," Homer finished, "that's enough intrigue for me tonight, I have to catch up on my homework or Mother's going to make me quit the barn."

I had homework of my own and fell asleep doing the reading for my upcoming English test. The next day on the bus, Joan was sitting with a couple of girls so there was no room for me and all day she avoided me. I was hurt, but I understood that it would be hard for her to go against her family's wishes. Later that day she slipped me a note that said, *I'm sorry, but I have to stay away from you at least for now, please understand and don't answer with a note.* I saw Joan in the hall and gave her the thumbs up sign. That was the first time I saw her smile that Friday. Late Sunday afternoon, just before Homer and I had to leave for the barn, Mr. Walden pulled into the driveway. Dad and Uncle Louis talked to him in the yard and then he came to the house and asked for Mother. Mother talked with him for a few minutes and then called for me, saying, "Caleb, Mr. Walden has something he wants to say to you."

"Caleb," Mr. Walden began, "I don't know what got into me the other day, accusing you of being a harm to my daughter Joan. I checked around town and you and your brother Josh are so well spoken of, I knew I had done you wrong and I have come here to apologize to you and your whole family. I hope that you can all forgive me."

"That's O.K., Mr. Walden," I replied, "I'm glad that you're not mad anymore. Joan and I have been best friends forever, and Mr. Walden, best friends never harm each other."

Mother said haughtily, "I hope that from now on, Mr. Walden, you will look before you leap, especially when you're defaming someone's name."

"You can rest assured, Mrs. Carney," he said, walking away. "I'll be the soul of exactitude before I shoot off my big mouth again."

Uncle Louis walked Mr. Walden to the car and they seemed to be having a rather animated conversation, but Uncle Louis had the biggest grin on his face as Mr. Walden drove out of the yard.

Monday morning when I got on the bus, Joan motioned for me to sit beside her. She said, "Caleb, did my dad come to your house?"

"He sure did, Joan. What happened? He even apologized to me personally."

"I'm really not sure what happened," Joan said smiling. "Your Uncle Louis was at the house talking to Dad Saturday for quite a while. They stayed outside, so I don't know what they talked about, but later I heard Mother and Dad arguing and it was something about my brother Kenny."

I had forgotten that Joan even had a brother, he'd been gone from town for so long, he was much older than Joan and the last I heard about him was that he was some kind of an officer in the secret services. "I don't know what your brother and my uncle have to do with all of this, Joan, but it works for us. Does this mean that we can meet without sneaking around and I'm safe from your father's black snake whip?" I asked.

"Yes, yes, Caleb," Joan replied, leaning against me lightly. "The only thing is, I had to promise Mother we would act like we had a quarrel or something and not let the truth get all around town."

At the school, I had a new English teacher and Viola was no longer in my class, which saved me some pain. Gibb, her brother, who evidently had missed a few grades, was old enough to join the Navy during the summer, so that was one less pressure I had to deal with. Jake and I had teamed up on a couple of writing projects and had some things published in the school monthly newsletter. Outside of riding with Joan every day, my cousin Harold was one of the best things about being back in school. He was much like Josh and very easy to talk to about my growing-up problems.

Things were fairly normal until the last of April. One day when I was getting off the bus, there was a state police cruiser with two cops waiting for me. They questioned me about every crime that had happened in the area for the last few years. I kept telling them I didn't know about any crimes. They would say, "Well, how about the night you were picked up in Oscin with fireworks." I didn't really understand at first why they were after me, but they showed up at the bus stop two or three days a week. Finally it dawned on me that we always ended up with questions about Travis's and the night "I was there vandalizing cars." I must have told them fifty times that I never was at Travis's. Then they would talk about a whole bunch of other crimes that they believed I must know about and then come back to Travis's problem again. About a month after they started questioning me, I received a summons to go to court, the charge was disturbing the peace. John, Arthur, George, and Jake received summons also. Jake and I were to be tried separately because we were juveniles. John and the rest of the boys hired a lawyer. Dad and Jake's parents talked about hiring one for us, but we convinced them that we wouldn't need one because we could prove where we were that night if we had to. Jake had talked to the girls we baby-sat with that night and they agreed to testify if it was really necessary. Uncle Louis had talked to a lawyer and he said the case could be reopened and witnesses brought forward if we got into any real trouble. Nobody in town could believe what was happening and blamed Constable Parks for pushing it, but he claimed his hands were tied because we were picked up in Oscin.

The day of trial finally came and we went to the courthouse in Lange. The older boys were tried first and the judge kept trying to bring up other crimes, especially Travis's. The boys' lawyer would have none of that. He said the summons was for disturbing the peace on a certain day and they couldn't be tried for anything else. The judge finally gave up and gave them thirty days probation for disturbing the peace.

Jake and I got a different judge and not having a lawyer began to look like a mistake. He went through a whole list of crimes he said he needed answers for. Jake became so upset that he started sobbing. After reading the list, the judge gruffly asked, "Well, what do you boys have to say about all of this?"

"Sir," I said, "for over a month I have been asked about those crimes. Jake and I don't know anything about any of them, believe me, if we did, the policemen who have been dogging me lately would have found out."

"Well," said the judge, "so you are two little innocents, are you? Well, answer me this, who gets up first at your house in the morning?"

"My mother, sir."

"Who starts the fire to do the cooking?"

"My mother, sir."

"Who does the cooking?"

"My mother, sir."

"Who washes your clothes?"

"My mother, sir."

"Who was up at Travis's vandalizing those cars?"

"My mother didn't do that, sir."

The judge shouted, "Then you better tell me who did or you will be spending the rest of your youth in reform school."

Jake was sobbing uncontrollably. I was scared, but Uncle Louis and Dad had said, "Just stick to the truth and you will be all right," so I said, "I'm sorry, sir, but I don't know who did it."

The judge came out from behind his desk and walked over to us, saying, "I'm going to walk out that door and talk to the other boys. If I don't hear what I need to hear before I leave and their stories don't confirm yours I will have to sentence you harshly."

Jake's sobbing became louder, Constable Parks came to me and said, "Tell him the truth, boy."

I was about to say, "I have," when Mother stood up and said, "Leave him alone, Parks, haven't you caused enough trouble?"

There was a deadly silence in the courtroom after the judge left and it was several minutes before he returned. Taking his seat, he banged his gavel and said, "The court seems to have made a grave error. I hereby dismiss all charges and release these defendants."

Jake left immediately with his mother. I suppose he was ashamed of breaking down, I would have to tell him how close I had come to joining him. That night at the barn. John said, "You know what's funny about this whole thing? I've been thinking we all know that none of us were up to Travis's that night. Isn't it funny that with all the people we know, in all this time we haven't heard who it was that did it?"

Homer said, "I thought about that too. If any of the boys we know were involved, someone would have leaked it by now. You don't suppose that it was someone in town who was mad at the town fathers or maybe even one of their wives?"

"You know," Jennie said, "Mother said something strange the other day when she was talking to Ellie Baker. She said, 'Dora and Lillian sure knew how to get even with Kevin and Welcome. I hope that they haven't brought their own houses down over their heads.' That didn't make any sense to me at the time, but put that together with what Homer's thinking and you have to wonder."

"I dunno," piped in Arthur, "I would sooner think they were whoring around to get even, quicker than I would think they were able to disable three cars without getting caught."

"I don't know about the rest of you," I chimed in, "but now that it's over and we are free of it I don't give a damn who it was that did it. I just want to finish our milking and get home. There's only three more days of school left and I want to make sure I pass my final test."

Homer and I pedaled our bikes home hardly speaking, I'm not sure what he was thinking about, but my thoughts were on my 16th summer and the hope that it would be less traumatic than my 15th.

Chapter 12

Shortly after school ended in my sixteenth summer Dad bought another horse, he told us that he only paid fifty dollars for her because she had a problem, but he was sure that it could be cured. I shall never forget the shock we felt when the horse was delivered. Besides a little hair on her scraggly mane and tail, she didn't have any hair on the rest of her body. This was the strangest-looking horse I had ever seen. The truck driver, Mother, Homer and I struggled to get her out of the truck and into the barn. The horse was frightened and disobedient and Mother wondered aloud if Dad really knew what he was doing, buying such an animal as that. When I got home from milking Dad was in the barn with the horse. When I looked in he was wiping the horse down with what looked like a greasy rag. He shouted, "Hey, Caleb, come in here, I want you to learn how to do this. I mixed up a pail of sulfur and lard, we need to wipe her down with it twice every day."

"I dunno, Dad," I answered, "she was almost more than four of us could handle getting her out of the truck. I'm not sure I'll be able to handle her by myself."

"Caleb," Dad answered, rather sharply, "you'll be seventeen the end of this year and it's time for you to take on more responsibility. It worries me that in a little over a year you could be drafted and you are still bucking leaving childhood. If we lived in a time without war that might not be so important, but as a father, I fear how you will cope when you get drafted. Josh had his problems with the world and the people in it, but he always understood the reality even when he didn't agree with it. It's time that you showed more initiative and were able to accomplish things without someone holding your hand. I hope that we are not going to have to continue going to court because you refuse to grow up and do stupid things, like following those boys at the barn when you know it is wrong."

"Sure, Dad," I replied, "look, what happened to poor Tom when I tried acting adult. It ended up with Uncle Louis having to shoot him."

"That was a hard lessen, son," Dad said, softening, "but life is like that. If we run and hide from these lessons without gaining wisdom, then that's time squandered. I learned from Tom's death that I have to be more specific when I ask you boys to do anything new. Now about this horse, she's scared because her skin is very uncomfortable and she doesn't know that she has nothing to fear from us, we have to prove that to her. The way we do that is by understanding how she feels. She was jumpy just now because I used a harsh tone of voice when I talked to you, watch the difference when I just talk to her."

Dad began talking to the horse in a soothing voice. "It's O.K., Roxie, I know it's not very comfortable to be coated with all this grease, but think how nice it will be to have hair again." I marveled at what a difference Dad was making with just the tone of his voice, for I was sure that Roxie didn't understand the words. I wondered how he had come up with the name Roxie, but with Dad you didn't ask questions when he was instructing you. He explained that we had to cover every place on her body where hair should be, all the time talking to the horse like she was some little child. Still talking soothingly, he handed me the rag and said, "Try your hand, Caleb, while I'm here to watch."

I took the cloth from him and started talking to Roxie as he had, and after looking to see why the hands had changed she stood as quietly for me as she had for Dad. Dad watched me for about ten minutes, encouraging me to keep talking to Roxie, then he said, "Now, Caleb, I want you to keep talking softly to her and then try picking up her feet, first one of her front ones and then a back leg."

I had practiced this with Tom, I was skeptical but I knew Dad would insist. Talking to her in as soothing a voice as I could manage while patting her, I picked up her leg and held it for a moment. She was skittish at first but gave me no trouble by the time I got to the back leg. Again I began feeling the pride of being able to accomplish functions from my dad's world and gratitude that this horse, that had seemed so impossible to handle this afternoon, was allowing me to feel the confidence that I had felt when we acquired Tom.

Although caring for Roxie became another chore, I began to realize how a man could become attached to horses. Summer became a haze of jobs, cutting wood at our farm to sell to help pay for Roxie and her feed. Old Golly Moses was demanding more hours as more of the boys in the area either joined the services or were drafted. Karl had joined last year and though I hadn't received a letter from him since he was in boot camp, his sister said in his macho way he was still enjoying life in the service. Jake and I managed to get together despite our working different jobs. Jake really was enjoying working at the paper and even had a couple of his articles published. One article was about the war and I was surprised how much of his pacifist attitude he had lost. I guess what we heard on the radio and newsreel reports that we saw at the movies changed his mind about whether we should have been involved before. That and the fact American forces had been caught sleeping by the Japanese. Josh's letters were few and far between and any mention of where he was or what he was doing was cut out. We still assumed that he must be in the war zone, somewhere in the Pacific, from the markings on his envelopes. The only address we had when we wrote was an A.P.O. number for an address but he said he received most of his mail and asked that we keep the letters coming. What little he wrote about the war that got through the censors indicated that war really sickened him, and though he had thought that some people in Sterling were cruel, man's inhumanity to man in war was beyond his wildest nightmare. He wrote that he was receiving lots of mail from Patsy Wilson and other friends and that it was the letters from home, especially Patsy's, that kept him reminded that there was another world and just maybe God wasn't dead. Mother mailed a letter every week and each of us added a little to it or slipped in a note of our own. I always wanted to write and ask for advice on how to handle this sex thing now that I was so full of it but didn't because I was afraid Mother edited our letters. Mostly we wrote about things that were happening and told him how much we missed him.

I had heard that Beverly was going to take a job in Lange at the shoe factory. They had received an order for army boots and were desperate for workers. I was happy about that because I wasn't sure I could keep putting off her crazy advances or even if I had wanted to. One morning after milking, I was sent to the Rook barn to move the hay to the front of the loft so when they came to pick it up, the tractor wouldn't be tied up too long. I hated working in the hayloft, where the chaff clung to your sweat and itched like crazy. I moved all the hay to the front of the loft, then went to the well in back of the barn and drew a bucket of water to wash it off. The chaff was imbedded in the belt line of my pants so I took them off to clean them. There weren't any houses near the barn so I wasn't worried when I heard the tractor. I was old enough not to be afraid of being seen in my underpants by the boys. I washed the chaff off my body and was slapping myself dry when who should appear from the barn but Beverly. She shouted, "Hey, Caleb, Old Golly Moses said you would be here to help me, but I didn't think you would be that anxious."

I thought I was going to faint, but not wanting to seem childish, I said, "Be with you in a minute, Bev, just let me get my pants on."

"Don't bother, Caleb," she said, laughing. "I've been trying to get them off you again ever since the day you broke your hammer, remember?"

"Remember, oh I remember, Bev. It's been a cross between my sweetest dreams and my worst nightmares every since," I said, pulling on my pants.

"Com'n, Caleb, let's get the hay loaded I have to get the tractor back to the field."

I hurried to the barn with fear and excitement cruising my every nerve end. Beverly was already in the loft, pitching hay onto the wagon. When I joined her in the loft she grabbed me and started kissing, the next thing I knew we were rolling in the hay having sex. Afterwards, she jumped up and said, "Com'n, Caleb, we have to rush and get this hay loaded, you don't want the boys to get suspicious, do you?"

This time I couldn't run off, so I grabbed my fork and joined her pitching hay, saying, "Damn it, Bev, do you have to entice me into having sex every time we're alone?"

"You know what, Caleb, I saw how excited you were getting standing there without your pants on when you saw me come around the barn and I don't remember hearing you yelling no. I'll tell you what though," she said laughingly, "now that I'm sure you're not a virgin anymore, it won't happen again unless you ask me."

We finished loading the hay and I rode back with her to the milk barn. On the way she told me that this was her last week working for the Muldons, she talked about Karl and his letters and how she missed him. She acted as if nothing had happened. I couldn't understand how she could seem so unaffected by something that I was afraid I was paving my road to hell with. After I helped her unhitch the hay wagon, she gave me a little squeeze. Kissing my cheek, she said, "Caleb, you are a wonder of our times, but don't worry, the devil isn't going to get you for having sex with me, and Joan will never know if you aren't dumb enough to tell her."

Still trying to act more macho than I felt, I said, "I'm hip with all that, Bev. It's just I don't want to end up feeling about girls like the rest of the boys at the barn, it seems so dirty when they talk about it."

Beverly had started to leave with the tractor. She stopped, and quieting the motor, she said, "Caleb, you're too much like Josh for you to ever be like them. Look how long you have worked with them and you're still a sweetheart. If I had done it with one of those boys, and I never would, they would be chomping at the bit to brag about it. No, Caleb, you don't have to worry about being like them. You're more in danger of having a girl be your ruin than being led astray by those bums."

Bev sat on the tractor looking kind of mournful. For a moment I thought she would cry, then with a roar she took off. I was off until the evening milking so I slouched against the hay wagon trying to piece the morning together when I remembered that Joan had said she would be at the library this morning. Man, as much as I loved my time with Joan, it didn't seem right to meet with her today. I jumped on my bike and hoped I could get through the center of town without seeing her. I was just going by the horse trough, when Joan yelled, "Caleb! I'm over here in the park." I joined her on the park bench and she said, "Well, Caleb, I thought you weren't going to make it. The librarian said, she saw you and that Beverly Stone go by with a load of hay."

"Yeah! Old Golly Moses sent me up to the Rook barn this morning to clean up last years hay so the new crop wouldn't bury it. Beverly came with the tractor to pick it up after I got it ready."

"I don't like to think of you being in a hay mow with her," Joan snapped. "I hear her asking you to go for a walk on dance nights, and I know what happens out there, remember."

"Joan, look, you know I have never been on one of those walks except for that once with you. I tell you something else, Miss Uppity, you were the one who insisted we go that time. Now this isn't the first time you have brought up other girls and this sex thing when I thought we had agreed not to discuss things like that. I don't believe that any of you dumb girls realize what you put boys through sometimes." I could see by Joan's face that I had said enough. She sat quietly for a minute while her face grew redder and redder.

Suddenly she jumped to her feet and started pounding on my shoulders with her fist, saying, "So that's it. I'm just another dumb girl, at least I'm not dumb enough to have sex just to please you. Well, Caleb, let me relieve you of the burden of this dumb girl, you go running back to your Beverly. I never want to see you again." Slapping me side of the head, she turned and ran out of the park crying.

Homer, who had evidently been standing by the park fence for a while, said, "What the hell did you do, Caleb, pinch Miss Prissy where you weren't supposed to? What you trying to do, get her old man running after you with his whip again?"

"No, Homer, I didn't lay a hand on her," I answered, "she's upset because I was working alone with Beverly this morning at the Rook barn. How was I supposed to know that Old Golly Moses was going to send Beverly there with the tractor, even if I had I doubt I could have changed his mind even if I wanted to."

"What did you tell, Joan," Homer said, laughing, "that you were up there rolling around with Beverly in the hay? I hear the boys all bragging about what they would do if they had the chance that you had this morning."

195

"I didn't tell her anything, Homer," I answered angrily. "Her imagination just got the best of her and she thought I was like the rest of that barn bunch, when the truth is that most of their stories are just B.S. that they make up."

"Don't be so hard on the barn boys, Caleb," Homer said, smiling. "Remember, it's just a boys-will-be-boys thing, and when you work as close to the gutter as we do, it gets a little gross sometimes."

I didn't want to get into any discussions with Homer where I would have to lie about what happened at the Rook barn, so I ran to my bike and pedaled madly towards home. I guess Homer had other plans, because he didn't follow me. At the bottom of the hill to the house, I pulled my bike into the woods and sat under a big pine tree pondering the day. The guilt and fear of what had happened with Beverly tugged at the excitement and pleasure that I had experienced when it happened. Part of my mind knew I was going to hell. What was it that Josh and Hester said, it was like the fruit in the Garden of Eden, a temptation of the devil. Maybe if I had continued going to church I would have been stronger, most of the family went regularly. Mother insisted when I first started milking that I would have to continue, but the first Sunday I went straight from the barn, it was suggested that I could be excused if I couldn't get home in time to change and wash up. What was so upsetting to me, why I couldn't be like most of the other boys, they considered it a wonderful thing to have sex. Sex was a challenge to be pursued with vigor and excitement, with each conquest a new mark on their shield of manhood. I even heard Uncle Louis bragging about his conquests a couple of times when he was in his cups. It was an unacknowledged fact in our house that he still went to the Travis house often. I had to leave, I couldn't spend any more time galling over my life, I had promised Dad I would start skidding out the logs we had left in the woods when we cut our cordwood. We needed to sell them before the worms got at them.

That night at the barn, John said, "How was it when you got Beverly alone at the Rook barn? You must have some pull with Uncle Joe to get a chance like that. He sure as hell wouldn't send me."

"Com'n, Caleb, talk to us," Arthur chimed in, "boy, if I got that chance I'd still be up there rolling in the hay with her."

"Hell, boys, you think that's something, guess where I saw him before noon? He was in the park wrestling with Joan, though I'm not sure he won that battle," Homer said, laughing. "How's that grab you? He's with his second woman faster than you two can make up those stories you're always telling."

"The hell he was," Arthur shouted. "Beverly told us all about how her little virgin, as she called him, he acted like a perfect gentleman."

"Damnit, Arthur," John said, "can't you ever keep your dumb mouth shut? We could have teased Caleb for ever if we could have got him bragging about this morning first."

"You boys are so stupid, all you talk about is sex, sex, sex. Did it ever cross your mind why none of the girls in town want to be seen with any of you except Homer or Caleb? You know," Janet finished as she headed towards the milk house, "I get asked how I can stand working here. I tell them it's a job I can do well and a place where I get to study stupid men." With that she slammed out of the barn.

Arthur and John started damning Janet while Homer just laughed. I was angry with Homer at first when he started talking about Joan and me but realized his changing the subject had saved me from an embarrassing situation. I was shocked at what Beverly had said but remembered what she had said about Joan never finding out unless I told. With all the mixed emotions Beverly had caused in me, this was the first time I felt respect. I said, "Com'n, boys, give Janet a little slack, I think sometimes we forget that we have a girl working with us. You all know that she hears us all say things we would never say in a mixed crowd outside of this barn, let's try to show her a little respect from now on."

"What do you think, Arthur?" John guffawed. "Shall we be respectful? Do we know how? Maybe Caleb can teach us how. I know he can teach us virginese, and then if we are in the hay mow with Beverly, we'll know what to do."

"Nuts to you, John," Arthur replied, "I wouldn't need any coaching from Caleb, if I get a chance like he had."

"Com'n, Caleb," Homer said, laughing, "let's finish up and get out of here before their jealousy gives them epileptic fits." I wanted to thank Homer for being there for me at the barn as we rode home that night, but he didn't seem to want to talk, so we rode silently home.

Time seemed to be passing so much faster my sixteenth summer than it had the other summers. Days sped by, hurrying from one job to the next, trying to keep Old Golly Moses and Dad satisfied with all they asked me to do. We still went to Oscin occasionally to pick up girls and see a movie, but the excitement must have been wearing off, because I fell asleep one night on a girl's shoulder. George must have been having a busy summer too, because every plan we made to go fishing fell through. One day Homer and I biked to George's secret fishing spot. The fishing was good, but it didn't seem as exciting as before, though Homer sure got excited about all the fish we were catching. I felt bad about coming without George, it was like breaking a pact, but from the signs on the banks I could see the secret was out and we weren't the only ones who had been fishing there. It was wishful thinking that these signs might have been left by George and his dad. I had heard that his dad had accepted his plight much better in the last few years and was over his depression. I will always remember what a different George I saw the first day he took me there and revealed how painful it was that his father would no longer come to what he considered their sacred place. Homer had sworn a blood oath that he would never tell anyone where we caught our fish and I believe he never did, though he went there a few times without me, he wouldn't even take Jason.

It had been nearly three weeks since Joan had blown up at me in the park and I hadn't seen her anywhere since then. On the day the library was open I made sure I was finished early, thinking I might catch Joan in the park or at the library. I didn't see her in the park so I went to the library. The librarian said she had been in early and appeared to be in a hurry to get home. I took that to mean she was avoiding me and remorsefully biked away. When I arrived home, Mr. Banner's Packard was in the yard and he and Mother were sitting at the kitchen table. Mother looked as though she had seen a ghost. Her face was white and tears were rolling down her face. Mr. Banner was saying, "Now, now, Mrs. Carney, let's look on the positive side, he's still alive and they expressed great hope for his recovery."

I rushed to Mother's side, crying out, "Who got hurt Mother, what happened?"

Mother held me while great sobs wracked her body and said, "Caleb, Josh was in a terrible explosion. He-he needs me." With that she broke down so badly she wasn't able to talk.

"Caleb," Mr. Banner said, "Josh gave them my telephone number because you don't have a phone. You're the big boy of the house, let me tell you what they said while your mother composes herself. Josh sustained a minor wound during the fighting. He was still mobile, but not capable of being in the battlefield. They have been sending some of our more seriously wounded boys home on the cargo ships that bring them supplies. Because Josh would still be able to care for them, he was sent back on one of the ships as their medic. They left the battle area in a convoy with a destroyer escort. About halfway home a submarine got by the destroyers and torpedoed two of the ships, one of them was Josh's. The ship was not sunk immediately, but there were terrible explosions on board and one was where the sickbay was. Josh wasn't hurt in the explosions but was badly burnt trying to save his men from sickbay. He went back again and again bringing them out. Those who lived, including Josh, were transferred to another ship before that one sank, but between his wound and the fire and some damage done while he was being transferred, Josh is in bad shape. When the convoy was close to our shores it broke up and the ships went to different ports, the ship that Josh was on docked in Boston and he's in a hospital there." Mother had gone to her room completely distraught. I had never seen her lose control before and it scared me. Mr. Banner said, "Look, Caleb, I'm going to have to trust you to handle this with the rest of the family. I'll send one of the ladies over to be with your mother. Tell your dad that I'll be able to drive them to Boston tomorrow if he wants me to, or perhaps he can just take the Packard himself if he doesn't trust his car. I have to leave now, Caleb, but I'll have someone here in less than a half hour, can you handle it until then?"

As frightening as the news and Mother's wailing was to me, I still felt pride that Mr. Banner was treating me like an adult, so I answered, "Yes, Mr. Banner, you do what you have to do, I will hold the fort until help arrives." Luckily all the younger kids were at a church bible school that afternoon and wouldn't be home until later. I went and knocked on Mother's door, and with great gasping breaths, she said, "Just leave me be for a while, Caleb. I need to exorcise this pain before the rest of the children get home."

Josh's leaving had caused a massive void in my life, no more leaning post, no safe harbor to salve my fears. Life without Josh when he left was so debilitating, I had locked Josh and my life with him behind a wall in my mind. I knew I couldn't let him out now, all battered and burned like he was, or I would collapse worse than Mother. Mother quieted and soon came out of her room and washed the tears from her face. I sat there traumatized, trying to keep my walls intact. Mother came and sat down across from me. She said, "I'm sorry, Caleb. I've lived with these fears ever since Josh left, and when Mr. Banner started telling me what happened, they just exploded. I wish you didn't have to see me like that, but I needed to get it out of my system before I could be there for Josh and the rest of the family. I pray that God spares him. Josh has always been such a good boy."

"I'm sure God will, Mother," I answered, choking back a sob. "I don't believe that he could have made it this far if he wasn't going to live."

Ellie Baker came through the door and gave Mother a hug, saying, "what can I do to help, Helen?"

Mother said, "It would be nice if someone went to the church and got the rest of the children home so they won't hear about this on the street."

"Good idea," Ellie answered, looking relieved that there was something she could be actively doing. "If you're sure you two are O.K., I can do that."

Mother was worried how to inform the family, Hester and Emma were working in Oscin; Homer was working at Muldon's in the fields; and Jason, Francis and Nellie were at the church. Dad always got home after Homer and

I left for the evening milking, so it was going to be some time before all the family was informed. "Caleb," Mother asked, "do you think it would be better not to talk about this until everyone is home?"

"I don't think that will work, Mother. If Mr. Banner mentions this at the Inn then I'm afraid Dad or one of the kids will hear about it before they get home, that would make it awkward for everyone, I think we should tell each one as they come in."

Ellie came in with Jason, Francis and Nellie, and you could see by Nellie's tear-stained face and the boys' shocked look that they already knew. Ellie said, "I tried to keep it from them, Helen, but some men coming from the Inn hollered and asked Jason how bad Josh got hurt, so I told them what I knew and brought them straight home."

Nellie ran to Mother and threw herself against Mother's breast, sobbing. Mother said, "Now we must all be as brave as we know Josh will be. Even though the news is bad, he could have gone down with the ship. We should be thankful he didn't. Now, Jason, you and Francis fill the wood boxes and take care of your chores. Nellie, you start peeling the potatoes and vegetables for supper, and Caleb, you go see to Roxie."

We no longer greased Roxie down with the lard and sulfur. Her hair had all grown back and she looked like a normal horse. I realized Mother had decided it was best if we kept busy, so I brushed Roxie down and cleaned her stable while struggling to keep the walls of my mind locked. I was leaving the barn when Homer came tearing in on his bike, calling, "Caleb, what is this I heard about Josh?"

I told him what Mr. Banner had told us and how he had offered to take Mom and Dad to see Josh tomorrow. Homer said, "Caleb, let's see if we can go too."

"I don't believe that's going to be possible right at first, Homer," I replied, trying to ignore the tears welling up in his eyes. "I think we'll have to wait until Mother and Dad check out where he is and find out how many visitors he can have." Homer went in the house gave Mother a hug and rushed to our room. I knew he would be crying and wanted to join him but felt if I ever was going to be the big brother Josh had said I needed to be, the time was now. I stayed in the barn for a while talking to Roxie and then went to help Jason, who was having some trouble bringing our cow in from the pasture. Horses seemed to understand and sympathize when you were upset, but cows were more apt to react by being upset themselves.

Homer and I talked about having to find someone to replace us at the barn, but Mother said, "No, Caleb, I think it would be better for us all if we stayed as close to our normal routine as possible." Homer and I had to leave for the barns before Hester, Emma or Dad were home, so we wouldn't be there when they heard the news. I wanted to stay home until Dad got home. Mother was always soothing, but Dad was our strength when things got tough. Still, I realized it was important to Mother that we all kept to our usual routine. There was a quiet sadness at the barn that night. After telling us how sorry they were, everyone seemed to be keeping their own quiet counsel. We all knew that men were being maimed and killed in war, and though Sterling had already lost one of its boys, this was the closest it had hit to our group. I knew that although the barn boys used to tease me about Josh, they all had a great respect for him, like all who knew Josh.

When Homer and I returned home from milking, Hester was sitting with Mother. Emma was in her room sobbing and Dad was in the barn talking to Roxie. After talking to Mother and Hester I went to the barn, Dad looked old and worn standing in the stable, absentmindedly brushing Roxie. He was telling her, "Josh is going to make it, if God let me grow hair on a bald horse, I'm sure he will let me keep my oldest son." As much as I wanted to talk to him, I decided it was better he was left undisturbed, so I went back to the house.

Mother said, "Caleb, please go up and see if Emma can be consoled."

I went to the girls' room and Emma threw her arms around me and sobbed, "How can this be, Caleb? Why Josh of all the boys in the world, why Josh?"

"Oh, Emma," I said, fighting not to break down, "I don't know why, but I do know that Josh wouldn't want us wishing it was someone else."

"I didn't mean that, Caleb, I only meant why did it happen to someone as good as Josh? Everyone I knew envied us because he was our brother, he always seemed so virtuous."

"I know it's true, that Josh is someone special, Emma," I said, moving to the edge of her bed and sitting down, "that's all the more reason to believe that he's going to be all right. Do you remember when the bull dragged George Phelps and how bad he was broken up? Look at him today. With the exception of a few scars he looks as healthy as any of us. We'll have to pray Josh makes out that well."

"Oh, Caleb, that's what we have to do, pray with me," she said, as she kneeled beside the bed.

I joined her beside the bed, and we prayed that Josh would heal well and be able to come home without a handicap. Emma thought we should end with a real prayer. The only prayer that I knew was the Our Father one, so we ended our praying with that. The praying seemed to make Emma feel so much better that we went to the kitchen and joined Mother, Hester and

Homer. Mother said, "Your father has made arrangements with Mr. Banner to go to Boston tomorrow. Emma, I want you to stay home and care for the young ones, I believe it's best that the rest of you continue with what you are supposed to be doing. Hester, you can explain to the company why Emma is not in and help Emma with the household chores tomorrow evening, if we're not back, Caleb and Homer can take care of the animals when they're not working at the milk barn."

I left, heading towards the barn, hoping I might get a chance to talk with Dad, but he was over by the woodshed talking with someone sitting on the steps. It was Uncle Louis and he was very drunk. Dad called, "Caleb, help me get him up to his room before your mother sees him or she'll want to be kicking him out again." While we were helping Uncle Louis up the back stairs he kept reciting,

If only the earth would vomit the bones,
Of all of history's dead warriors
Upon life's pleasured shore
Perhaps the sight would add real meaning
To the words, we will war no more.

Uncle Louis still carried the terror from the trench warfare when he fought in France during World War I, but the only time it showed was when he was in his cups. He kept insisting that Dad have a drink with him. Dad said, "Sure, Louis, just as soon as we get you to your room." After we had him in bed, Dad took a long drink from his bottle and stuck it under his mattress. I had never seen Dad drink before and it troubled me the way he seemed to relish it. By the time we had returned to the kitchen Mother said it was time we all went to bed, that tomorrow was going to be a long day.

Homer and I went to our room. I wanted to discuss the day's events, but Homer had retreated into one of his quiet spells and didn't want to talk. I must have fallen asleep fairly quickly, because it was only around midnight when I woke screaming from a dream where Josh was running in and out of a big fire carrying people. I was yelling, "Josh! don't go back, don't go back." Homer had shaken me awake and Mother was standing by my bed, saying, "It's O.K., Caleb, it's just a bad dream."

Mother went back to her room and Homer said, "Damn, Caleb, aren't things bad enough without you scaring the wits out of us all?"

The next morning, Mr. Banner was at the house early, before Homer and I had left for the milk barn. He thought it would take about four hours before they got to Boston and found the hospital. When I got to the barn, Jennie was waiting for me outside. She gave me a little kiss on the cheek and a hug and said, "Caleb, give that to Josh for me when you see him."

Old Golly Moses came to the barn and said, "Caleb, tell your dad if there is anything the Muldons can do for him or the family just ask. If you or Homer get a chance to go see Josh, you go ahead, we will manage the milking without you for a short time."

Waiting for information about Josh's condition made this a long day and everybody was inquiring about Josh, destroying our efforts to pretend that the world was the same as it was before yesterday. It was late that evening before Mr. Banner's Packard pulled into the yard. All seven of us were sitting in the kitchen, waiting for news of Josh. Emma jumped to the window and said, "Look, Mother is smiling and joking with Mr. Banner, that's a good sign." We knew Dad would be angry if we all rushed out there, so Hester went out alone to greet them.

When they came in the door, Nellie started crying, "Josh, Josh, Mummy, where is Josh, why didn't you bring him home?"

Mother picked Nellie up, saying, "Josh is going to be all right, Nellie, he just has to stay where he is, so the doctors can fix him. Now all of you listen, Josh has some bad burns and a couple of broken bones and a minor bullet wound, but he's off the critical list and should be out of the hospital in a few weeks. The doctors say there will be some minor scarring but he should be as good as new in a year."

There were cheers of joy as all of us released the pent-up fear we had been harboring since we heard about Josh. Dad said, "It's sad that we won't be able to be near him very often because of the time and expense of going to Boston, but we can make sure he gets letters and cards."

Hester, laughing, said, "Don't worry about, Dad, most everyone I have talked to has already asked for his address, especially the girls in town. Caleb tells me that Jennie Sledge even wants to send him a kiss and a hug."

"Yeah, Dad," Emma chimed in, "Patsy Wilson asked if letters to his old address would still get to him. I told her I thought they would, but if he had a different address I would get it to her. Wait until she finds out that the address is in Boston. She has it so bad for Josh she will probably walk there." The good news about Josh eased the turmoil in my mind, and the next few weeks seemed to fly by. Joan had come to see me when she heard about Josh and we were meeting regularly again. It was great to have someone whom I could talk freely with, except of course about girls. Joan hadn't been back to dance night since the trouble about her panties. I tried to convince her that she should, but she said she was too ashamed although no one ever said anything about us leaving the dance that night. Mother and Dad had been going to see Josh almost every weekend and things seemed to be going well. After about three weeks, Hester and Patsy Wilson somehow had convinced Frank Butler to drive them to see Josh. Homer and I tried to go with them, but Mother said they wouldn't allow that many to visit. Dad was against them going with Frank, but Mother thought it would be all right and that it would do Josh good to see some of the younger folks. When Hester came home that night she had been crying and looked awful.

Dad and I were coming from the barn and saw her when she got out of Frank's car, Dad said, "Did you have trouble with that damn Butler?"

"No, no! Dad," Hester sobbed, "it isn't Frank, it is Josh, he looked so sick and I don't think he even knew us."

"I don't understand," Dad said, putting his arm around her. "He was always weak, but he seemed to be getting stronger each time we saw him. He knew us even the first time and always asked about the family and about what was happening in town."

Mother came out, asking, "What's wrong out here? Hester, are you hurt?"

"No, Helen, she's not hurt," Dad answered. "She's upset about Josh. She says Josh is so bad he didn't even know her or Patsy, that doesn't fit with what we've been seeing."

"Did you talk to the doctor, Hester?" Mother asked.

"I tried to, Mother, but all I could get was a nurse, his doctor wasn't available. The nurse told me that Josh had developed a fever the day before and the doctor was treating him for it and studying why. She felt he would be better in a couple of days. Oh, Mother! He looked so sick and pale, Patsy was in hysterics all the way home, saying she wished she had never gone to see him."

Mother said, "Com'n, Henry, we're going to the Inn and calling the hospital. I need to know what's happening."

When Mother came back, she told us the only information she could get was that Josh was doing as well as could be expected and that the doctor might be available to talk to tomorrow. That night I heard her and Dad talking. She was all fired up to go right to Boston in the morning. Dad said, "Helen, we owe Mr. Banner more than we are probably ever going to be able to pay him now. We'll call the doctor tomorrow and decide after we talk to him what to do." Hearing the depression in Mother and Dad's voices re-ignited my fears and nightmares. After a fitful night where Homer had shaken me awake a half dozen times to tell me I was dreaming, I awoke to a house of gloom. Dad was already leaving for work and Mother looked like she had cried all night. As we left for the barn Homer gave Mother a big hug and said, "We have to think positive, Mother, Caleb and I will come home after the milking to go with you to make the call."

Later at the Inn, after several calls, Mother was able to speak to the doctor who was tending to Josh. He said they were puzzled by Josh's setback and were testing several possibilities and if she would leave a number he would personally call when they discovered the cause. He thought it would be unproductive to visit Josh then, but to wait for his call. Mother seemed somewhat reassured after talking to the doctor and that produced relief throughout the family.

A couple of days later, late in the evening, Mr. Banner's Packard drove in the yard. Sensing this was word about Josh, Mother went out to meet him while we all silently prayed the news was good. Mr. Banner spoke to Mother briefly and they came to the kitchen. Mother said, "Caleb, get your father."

When I returned with Dad, Mr. Banner said, "Henry, you might not want the children here."

The youngest had already gone to bed, only Hester, Emma, Homer and I were present. Dad said, "Whatever it is, Leslie, they will have to know sometime, so I believe they'd better stay."

Mr. Banner seemed very hesitant as he spoke, "The doctor called and they know what Josh's problem is. They believe that the smoke from the fire poisoned his lungs. Remember, Josh kept running back into a burning sick bay to get his men out. They found out that two of those men have expired with the same symptoms that Josh is showing. They think something in the smoke poisoned their lungs and they're trying to find a medicine that is effective against the poison for Josh."

Mother started sobbing, and Dad said, "Ill get off work tomorrow and we'll go right down, Helen."

Mr. Banner said, "I'm sorry, Henry, but the doctor recommended that you come right away. I am prepared to drive you now, if that's what you decide."

"There is no decision to make," Mother sobbed, "give us a minute to change our clothes."

After they left, we sat in sober silence until Emma broke down and started crying. Hester, with tears openly running down her face, held her, trying to be comforting. After Hester and Emma went to their room, I sat at the table with my head in my arms, fighting desperately to maintain the barriers that I had built in my mind when Josh left. With a painful exclamation Homer broke the silence, "Life without Josh, God! Caleb, what are we going to do?"

At first I couldn't answer, my mind seemed to explode with his words, a thought that couldn't be accepted. When Josh left, he had said, "Now you have to be big brother." *I knew I couldn't, I didn't have his way, his words, I only have this great fear of life. Oh God, why Josh? Take me instead. I never think nice like Josh and I have already paved the road to hell with Beverly.* Thinking about God brought back the memory of Karl and me, at the springhouse, saying out loud prayers to God for George, when he was broken up so badly by the bull, and how George had made it. I said, "Homer, let's ask God to help Josh, Karl and I asked Him to help George when he got hurt and it worked." Homer and I sat at the table, asking God to save Josh and saying the Our Fathers out loud. Jason, who had been woken by Emma's crying, came downstairs and without talking sat at the table. Hester and Emma, hearing us pray, came and joined in. I'm not sure how long the five of us sat holding hands, each in his own way asking God out loud to help us, but it did help me sleep that night.

The next day Homer and I rushed home from the morning milking to be there when Mother and Dad came home. About noon Mr. Banner's Packard drove in the yard. As we watched from the house, Dad got out of the car looking old and broken. As he headed for the barn, Mr. Banner helped Mother to the house. Mother could hardly walk and great sobs shook her body. The direful scene said it all. Without hearing the words we knew Josh was gone. As great cries of painful grief echoed throughout the house, Mr. Banner came in and settled Mother into a chair before leaving, saying, "I'll get someone to come over and help, Caleb."

The next few days were a painful blur as neighbors were in and out bringing food and trying to comfort the family. Dad went to work every day but seemed not to be able to deal with the family about Josh. He retreated to the barn at every opportunity. Mother, with Ellie's help, was regaining her composure. Homer and I kept up our milking duties, and for once there was no teasing or joking. I would find myself milking with tears running down my face, and Jennie or one of the boys would offer to finish up for me. I would refuse and recite a couple of lines, from one of Josh's poems.

At those times that life's terrors come on awful strong,
we must assure ourselves that life goes on, life goes on.

I recalled Uncle Louis and his recitation of the earth vomiting bones, I wondered if that might have been Josh's. Funny how words that once seemed meaningless could become so prophetically true now. Harry was in the service now, but Eunice came home a few days for the funeral. Sitting in chapel staring at Josh's cold corpse lying there, my mind kept screaming over and over. Where the hell is that great God now, where is He now? If Josh wasn't saved, as good as he was, where was the meaning in all their teachings? When we returned from the cemetery the kitchen was loaded with food and drink and there were people everywhere. I was constantly being held or patted on the back, with people telling me how great Josh was and how he was in heaven now. What did they know, them and their God? How could there be a heaven without God? Even if there was a God, He had forsaken the Carney family. Maybe because of what I had done. I couldn't stand listening anymore, so I ran to the woods and stayed there until almost everybody had left. Homer said, "I'm glad you came in, Caleb, Mother is worried and was just sending me to look for you."

Mother said, "Caleb, Caleb, are you all right? I was getting worried, no one seemed to know where you were."

"I'm O.K., Mother, I just needed to be alone for a while," I said, giving her a hug.

"You know, Caleb," Mother said, still holding me, "school starts Monday and I'm going to need you to help me get things back to normal. As terrible as losing Josh is, we must remember that he wouldn't want any of us to ruin our lives because of losing him."

I knew Mother had to believe this, so I agreed with her, but I thought that life could never be normal, normal was having Josh, and he was gone. God had forsaken him, how could I even think normal, with this big why screaming in my head?

Monday morning came and Mother busied herself getting everyone ready for school. Emma had graduated last year and was keeping her job in Oscin. This was Homer's first year in high school and Mother was telling him not to worry, I would show him the ropes. I staggered through the last few days before school started, completely numb to the world, but the normalcy was more than my heart could stand. My mind cried out, *Josh is dead. Doesn't the world know it, and how can things just be the same?* I gave Mother a hug and left with Homer to walk to the bus. Partway there, I said, "Homer, I just can't do it. I can't go on like nothing has happened, I'm not going to school."

Homer stopped, looked at me for a moment and said, "I understand, Caleb. We all have been waiting for your grief to implode. Tell me what you're going to do and I'll cover for you if I can."

"I really don't know, Homer, I think I just need to be alone and work this out myself, everything people say to me seems to make it more painful and I get so angry with them."

Homer said, "I really understand, Caleb, you do your thing. I'll go ahead to school and don't worry about it being my first day, you know I'll make out. Besides, the challenge will keep my mind off what happened."

Homer went along to the bus stop. Watching him walk away, I thought how he was more like Josh than I was. I took a back trail and hiked up Mt.

Fay, hoping to regain from her my strength and belief in life, for it was one of the places that Josh loved and wrote about.

Her name in legend, is from a little girl,
Who died there, in her mother's arms,
While a captive of the Indians,
Returning from a raid on the farms,
There are those who say it isn't true,
This legend of how her name came to be,
Still, no matter how others have named her,
Mt. Fay is my mountain to me.

When Josh had read this to me, he said, "Caleb, do you know that this is really our mountain? That no matter where we go or what happens in our lives we will be able to return to Mt. Fay, if not in body, at least in our minds to share its strength and beauty?" I hiked to the ledges above the cave where Karl and I had hidden from Bob Woods. I hoped Josh had been right, I sorely needed strength and there was no beauty anywhere in my present world. I wandered the mountain all day searching for a balm for my pain, salving my hunger with a few late-fall berries and the mountain's sweet spring water. I heard the town clock strike two. Knowing the school bus would be back soon, I decided it would be better if I showed up at the same time as Homer, so I hiked back down the mountain. I met Homer halfway home and asked, "How was your first day, Homer?"

He answered excitedly, "Man, it was a blast, Caleb, there are sure are a lot of pretty girls in that school. Some of the boys from Sterling asked me if I was going to kiss all of them too, I told them I sure would try." He must have seen the hurt in my eyes, because he stopped and said, "I'm sorry, Caleb."

I wanted to tell him it was O.K. but I couldn't, so I said, "What are you going to say about my not going, Homer?"

"I dunno, Caleb, I hope it doesn't come up. No one in our house knows except you and me, maybe I won't have to lie to anyone. Nobody at school seemed surprised you weren't there, nobody asked except Harold and I told him you just needed some time to yourself, he seemed to understand and sent his best."

I went with Homer that night to do the milking; though the Muldons had found replacements for us in the mornings we still had the evening shift. The boys treated us with quiet respect, and when we were done milking, Jennie went to the park with me. She had sat and quietly held me and after a time, she said, "Caleb, you need someone to share your pain with and for the love of Josh I will always be here for you." After holding me a while longer she kissed me softly on the cheek and left. Josh and Jennie, I wondered. Most of the boys steered clear of the Sledge girls, at least in the open. Though Jennie had always seemed less coarse than Janet, unless one of the boys pushed her too far. Then again, I knew that Josh would have befriended anyone who he thought needed a friend. The next morning I told Homer I wasn't ready yet to face school and hurried back to the mountain. Again I wandered the mountain, searching for a reason to go on living. As I sat in a grove of great pine, I realized that this was the place we had watched Bob undressing Katie Curtis and I understood now why Karl had grown so excited and almost got us caught. It was strange how the mountain stirred all these memories. I must have dozed off because I thought I was back in a darkened tent, too scared to sleep, like the first night Karl and I stayed here overnight. Then I experienced other nights, when we had become braver and started exploring the woods after dark. I recalled the first night that I'd stayed at the mountain with Jake and how I felt like I was the big hero when he got scared. I relived the after-school hikes we used to do every year and remembered George vowing that he would never be doing that again, the year he graduated from grammar school. I must have dozed off, when I woke to the sighing of the wind in the treetops, it sounded like a familiar song or verse, and while listening intently I thought I could hear Josh's voice. "We must assure ourselves that life goes on, life goes on...."

I shouted out, "Josh! Josh!"

The wind whispered back, "Let him free, let him free."

I jumped to my feet and ran, ran like we had run from Bob, blindly looking for escape. When I came to the ledges I threw myself down and cried, cried with great heaving sobs that seemed surely to tear my body apart. I don't know how long I blubbered, but hearing the clock strike one, I realized I had to pull myself together before Homer's bus came. I went to the spring and washed the tears from my face in the little brook that ran from it. My thoughts kept tearing at my heart as the echoing breezes seemed to call, "Let him free, let him free," as I slowly wound my way down the mountain. When I met Homer, Joan was with him, he said, "I hope you don't mind, Caleb, but she insisted on coming."

"Oh, Caleb," Joan cried out, "don't be angry, I just had to see you. Homer told me you needed to work some things out. Please let me help you, we've been close for so long I'm sure I can."

I hadn't seen Joan since the funeral, I was scared that with her I would break down completely and make a fool of myself. Thinking I had done that alone on the mountain, I said, "That's O.K., Homer, I was planning on seeing Joan anyway."

"I'm so glad, Caleb. I've worried so much about you and was looking forward to school starting so we could be together," Joan said, giving me a big hug.

Homer said, "I'll run along and leave you two lovebirds alone. I'll tell Mother you're with Joan, Caleb, so she doesn't worry."

Joan and I walked into the woods. We found a nice spot to sit, and she held my hand and asked if I wanted to talk about Josh. I started to say no, but then I told her about being on the mountain, the memories, the voices and how I had broken down. She held me close and kept kissing me and saying, "Caleb, my poor Caleb." I don't know how long we sat like that but the kissing and Joan's breast pressed against me started arousing me.

I pushed Joan away, saying, "Joan, we have to stop or we are going to get into trouble."

She said, "I know, Caleb, but if it will help you, let's."

"Oh God, Joan! I can't, I can't, I've spent two days on his mountain searching for an answer and I can't let it be this."

Joan took my hand and said, "Com'n, Caleb let's go. I'm glad we didn't, but you know I love you and I wanted to if it would help."

I walked Joan back to her house. She clung to me when I kissed her good-bye, saying, "Please don't lose me in your grief, Caleb, try to remember, I love you."

I walked home with my mind coursing between *how could I desire sex at a time like this* and *why did I say no*. Now there was Joan with her "I love you." *Joan is so dear to me, but love, how do I deal with love when puberty alone is driving me crazy, they both seem so connected. Oh Josh! You told me someday I would understand, but I don't, Josh, how can I, who can I go to now that you're gone?* I arrived home still distraught, tears still rolling down my face. Mother held me, saying, "That's good, Caleb, that you are finally letting it come out."

That night I dreamed Josh and I were walking on the mountain. It was like he was going far away and he was trying to prepare me. He said, "Caleb, you have to set me free. I won't always be here and I will feel like I crippled you if your life becomes troubled. I want to go worry-free, knowing you are strong enough to handle life without me." Then he recited one of his poems.

Do not cry for me,
If God has called me from this earth,
For where I go is a far superior place,

210

If you must shed a tear let it be,
That my leaving
For a time leaves a hollow space.

Suddenly we were at the chapel, Josh a corpse in his casket, whispering, "Please, let me free, let me free." I woke screaming, with Homer shaking me with Mother standing by the bed. Mother held me, saying, "Caleb, if anyone could be closer to a child than a Mother it must have been you to Josh. Life has to go on, Caleb, as much as it hurts. I believe that if Josh was able, he would tell you himself."

"Oh, Mother," I sobbed, "he's trying to tell me, on the mountain and just now in my dream he asked me to set him free, but Mother, it's so hard."

Mother held me tighter, while Homer said, "You have to listen to him, Caleb. You said you were looking for an answer, maybe this is it. Losing Josh is so painful for us all, but remember the night when we all sat and prayed for him? Part of what we asked was that God's will be done. I asked God that night that if it was His will to take Josh, for Him to make me strong. I feel now that Josh is with people who are full of the goodness he always sought for, and if we will let him, he will be happy."

With tears in her eyes, Mother hugged and kissed us both as she left. Before going back to sleep I thanked Homer, thinking again he was more of a big brother than me. I dreamed again of Josh, this time I was on the mountain and Josh was above in a cloud with many smiling people. Josh shouted, "Good-bye, Caleb, be happy for me."

I returned to school the next day. Riding on the bus with Joan every day was tentatively comforting, but I still spent the next few months feeling like I was an observer, instead of a participant in life. Harold was very understanding and defensive when anyone remarked about my melancholy behavior. He had two brothers that were missing in action. One was in the islands fighting the Japs, the other had been in Europe. He said the family had little hope for the one in the islands being alive, but the one in Europe had his name mentioned on a Nazi prisoner of war list broadcast by a Canadian radio station. Jake got me to collaborate on a paper about the war, with my pain about Josh and Jake's passion against all war, we wrote an article that won great acclaim throughout the school and was published in all the local papers. Jake's insistence that I should write more and more about my pain, and Harold's stoicism about his brothers, along with my good-bye dreams with Josh, slowly drew me back to life. As spring arrived with new existence budding all around me, life, with the exceptions of an occasional relapse, returned to the normalcy that I was so sure could never be.

Joan and I met occasionally outside of school; consciously or not, she seemed to make sure we were never alone anymore. When I ran into Beverly she would act real ladylike but always managed to whisper, "I'm still waiting, Caleb," before she left me. Jennie Sledge had been real friendly since Josh died and we sat in the park many nights, talking after we finished the milking. One night when we were there, she said, "Caleb, if I come to dance night will you dance with me?"

I was a little taken aback at the question but thought, *What the hell, Joan doesn't go anymore and it isn't like we would be dating, she only wanted to know if I would dance with her.* "Why, Jennie," I exclaimed, "of course I would dance with you. I've stepped on the toes of nearly every other girl in town, I'd be proud to add you to my collection. I don't remember ever seeing you there or I'm sure we would have danced."

"I only went one night, Janet wouldn't go with me and I was alone and nobody ever asked me to dance, so I didn't go again."

I put my arm around her and said, "Well, you come next time and I'll dance with you till our blisters get too much."

Jennie turned in my arms and said, "Caleb, I want to kiss you."

"What the hell, Jennie," I answered, "I ain't no Homer, but I don't know of any reason to stop you."

Jennie pressed her body against mine, kissing me so long and passionately that I didn't know what was going to happen first, embarrass myself again or suffocate. Suddenly, Jennie jumped back, saying, "See you tomorrow, Caleb," and left.

A couple of days later Joan asked me if I could get next Tuesday night off. It was her birthday and her mother had asked me to come for supper. I told her I would try. I talked about it at the barn, wondering who I could get to take my place. Jennie said that Arny would be able to fill in for me. Later at the park, she said, "Caleb, do you realize that is dance night."

"Oh damn, Jennie, I never gave it a thought," I replied, wondering how to handle this. "I could tell Joan I couldn't get the time off."

"No, Caleb, I've waited this long to go dancing, one more week isn't going to hurt, but thanks for thinking of me," she said, giving me a hug and a kiss.

Jennie's kisses were really affecting me. I never thought of her sexually before, but lately some of my thoughts about her had been wickedly entrancing.

I went to Joan's house the night of her birthday. This was the first time ever that I had been invited there. Her dad answered the door, saying, "Hello, Caleb, welcome to our house," and shouted, "Joan, young Carney is here."

Mrs. Walden wasn't near as pleasant, and all through the dinner I felt like I was just there so she could subtly show Joan I was some kind of lowlife trash. I think I made it through the dinner without making too big of a fool of myself. After dinner came the cake and ice cream and then the presents. My God, I had forgotten about getting one, so I lied and said I had ordered something at Kay's Jewelers in Oscin and hadn't been able to get there to pick it up. It wasn't a complete lie, I had seen a pretty heart-shaped locket in Kay's window once and thought how nice it would be to give it to a girl. After ooh-ing and ah-ing over Joan's presents and how expensive they were, her mother started in with the twenty-question routine. How did I like working at the barn? Didn't the smell bother me? Was I ever able to get it out of my clothes? Did I think I would always be a farm boy? Then the subject turned to the war and how awful it was. Did I think about joining like other boys before I finished school? Then came the clincher, wasn't it too bad that wars always take the good boys like Josh, when some of the trash around didn't even go to war? The evening had worn on me and at the mention of Josh I could feel tears welling in my eyes and the plague of depression settling back in.

Joan said, "That's all, Mom, Caleb has to go home to finish his school work." Relieved, I hurried out, despite her mother's protest Joan walked with me back towards the common. We stopped at the schoolyard and sat in the swings. There was so much pent up inside me that I couldn't speak. Joan came over and held me, saying, "I'm sorry, Caleb, I didn't know Mother could be so vicious. Don't take it so personal, you have older sisters, you know how parents can be when boys start coming around."

Not personal? Not personal? I wanted to scream that an evening with her mother had ended up making me feel lower than the shit in the gutters in the cow barn. I gave Joan a squeeze and a soft kiss and ran off. I could hear her shouting, "Caleb, Caleb, don't leave this way." As angry as I was, I didn't want to hurt her, but I kept running and running.

Though I seemed to be able to go on with my work at Muldon's and at school, life felt obscured in a heavy dark cloud. I didn't sit with Joan on the school bus anymore and though the hurt in her eyes bothered me, how could she help? Who could understand that Josh had been the anchor that had kept me from floating away on my sea of unworthiness and fear that barred me from adulthood? How could I tell anyone about the relief I had felt after my episodes with the ghost of Josh on the mountain or of his release in my dreams? Nothing mattered anymore. The plague was back upon me worse than ever. Who would understand that the walls to my heart and mind had been breached like they were a child's sand castles at the beach before a wave? Who could explain why one night at the Waldens' made the world such a heavy burden on my shoulders?

Jennie reminded me that I had promised to dance with her and Homer kept prodding me with, "For goodness' sake, Caleb, go with her, do something. Your gloom is getting contagious." So despite my misgivings I found myself at the dance. Jennie was a wonderful dancer. She even managed to keep me from stepping on her toes most of the time. I had envisioned having to dance with Jennie all night, but as the night wore on she was so popular she was telling the boys, "No, this one's Caleb's," so I could dance with her. While we were dancing, she said, "Caleb, some of the boys are asking to walk me home, may I please tell them I'm with you."

"Why, Jennie," I replied as we were dancing a slow dance, "I would be proud to escort you home, aren't you flattered with all their offers?"

"To hell with them, Caleb," she laughed, "they're just thinking with their pricks, they're not choate like you."

"Whoa, Jenny," I said, shocked, "watch the language, we aren't at the barn now. Do I dare ask what being choate is?"

Jennie laughed again, saying, "Why, Caleb, I didn't think a barn boy could be shocked. I saw this word choate in a book I was reading and had to go to the library to look it up. It means whole, or not lacking, and I thought at the time how this strange word fit Josh and you."

The mention of Josh lowered the cloud that had been lifted slightly by the evening, and I told Jennie I would prefer not to talk about him. Jennie whirled her way through the last dances brushing against other boys as she danced, flirting unashamedly. The other girls in the room stared at her murderously and I was sure the gossip tomorrow would be all about Jennie and Caleb Carney, when I walked out with her. When we left the dance, Jennie said, "Why so quiet, Caleb? Let's go sit in the park and talk." By the time we got to the park benches I was feeling low and not wanting to talk. I said, "I'm sorry, Jennie, I think I'd better go."

"No, no," she said, "Caleb, because of you I had a wonderful night, I want to help you, let me help you. Talk to me, Caleb."

I don't know how it happened, but like a bursting dam spewing water I sobbed out all my pain. My fear of puberty, my sinning by having sex, the loss of Josh and my anchor, the ghost on the mountain, Josh's good-bye dream and how my night at the Waldens' had torn down my walls and left me feeling lower than the gutters at the barn. Jennie held me tighter, saying, "Caleb, Caleb, my poor Caleb, let it out, share your feelings, allow me to help you stomp them out." She kissed my lips, my neck and my ears, all the time pressing tighter. The pressure of her breast was arousing me, when she noticed, she said, "Com'n, Caleb, let's go in back of the library."

I thought, *What the hell, why not, school will soon be out, my childhood sure is past, my reputation is mud anyhow and I will soon be in my seventeenth summer, standing on the threshold of manhood, inadequate as ever. So what's to lose?*

Chapter 13

My seventeenth summer started without the excitement of summer vacations of former years. I was lost in the fog and fear that surrounded me. The joys that used to permeate my very soul this time of year with exciting dreams had died in the reality of what was my real life. Mrs. Walden had certainly showed me that holding hands with Joan didn't put me in her class of people. I could still hear her asking if the smell comes off, it was plain it never would for the likes of her. Now that I was supposedly big brother, it was painful how inadequately I was equipped for the task. Homer was better at it than I was. Then there was the war, with Josh and boys like him being ripped from their family and friends to die in some strange land or hospital. Harold and I had talked often about how we would be drafted as soon as we graduated. Harold, like most of the boys, kept a gung-ho approach to serving, while I, in my cloud of despair, couldn't see any glory of becoming cannon fodder and ending up like Josh. Just before the end of school we received the news that Germany had been conquered. There was much speculation about what that would mean about being drafted. There was still Japan, and scuttlebutt had it that our forces would suffer over a million casualties in taking their main island alone, and there was more islands to conquer before we attacked their mainland. It looked as if the draft would be in effect for some time yet. Though I never had admitted it to anyone but Jennie, I was deathly afraid of how I would shape up as a soldier. With the despair I felt with my family and friends around trying to support me, I just knew I would be doomed out there in the big world alone.

My seventeenth summer was also the summer that my working world changed immensely. Dad, who had been trying to get a raise in pay at work ever since we had bought the farm, had quit his job in anger and gone back to driving horses for another logger. I believe that losing Josh had much to do with the change in Dad's disposition. The first few months after losing Josh, Dad spent much of his time at home in the barn, and he didn't seem to welcome company. Mother told us we all had to be patient with each other because everyone had to grieve in their own way. When Dad finally did rejoin the family, he approached life more aggressively, quitting his job, then being unhappy with his new position, and he contracted a lumber job himself. He bought another horse to team with Roxie and a flatbed rubber-tired wagon that had been built from some old Essex car axles. Shortly after, our new horse Molly showed up, Dad asked me to join him while he trained Roxie and Molly to work as a team. He showed me how to harness them as a team and hitch them to the wagon, allowing me to do most of the driving. There was a time I would have found some happiness and pride in working with Dad as a teamster, but as hard as I tried, I didn't seem to be able to drag my head from the dark clouds that pervaded every move. Dad explained about the job and the responsibility and challenge of going into business for himself, saying, "Caleb, it's time you left your job at Muldon's and started doing a man's work. I want you to come work with me sticking lumber. I'll be able to pay you as well, if not better, and it will give me the summer to get the business situated."

At the time, I didn't much care what I did, so I said, "O.K., Dad, I'll tell the Muldons tomorrow. When will we be starting?"

"It looks like the mill will be ready the first of next week," Dad answered. "Caleb, try to leave on good terms with the Muldons, you might want to work for them when you go back to school."

The next morning when I told Joe Muldon I would have to be leaving, he said, "Golly Moses, Caleb, how's a man supposed to run a farm with all the boys either going off to war or finding better jobs?"

"I'm really sorry, Mr. Muldon," I answered. "I remember how good you were to me when I first came here and how you gave me a chance even when you thought I was too small to do the job."

Golly Moses laughed and said, "I remember, boy, none of us thought you stood a chance, but over the years you have proved your worth. We are going to miss you. Now, you remember if you need work again, you come see me."

"Thank you, Mr. Muldon," I replied. "I was hoping I might come back sometime. I'll be able to finish out the week and if you need a milker in a pinch I'll try to help you out."

That night after the milking, Jennie and I walked to the park. She said, "I'm going to miss you, Caleb."

"What the hell, Jennie, I'll still be around. It's not like I'm going away to war yet," I answered as I gave her a hug.

"No, Caleb, I've been thinking about us," she said, pushing away from me. "We've started something that has no place to go and we have to stop it now before it becomes too domineering for us to stop."

"Jennie," I cried, "don't tell me you're going to abandon me too?"

"No, I'll always be here for you as best I can, but the sex has to stop, Caleb." She held my hand and said, "Look at me, Caleb, when we got involved it was at a very emotional time. No matter what you say now, someday you're going to walk away. I don't want you to have to deal with that guilt and I don't want that pain."

"Jennie," I started, "I wouldn't ever."

"Stop it, Caleb, stop right there," Jennie hissed. "I told you I've given this a lot of thought. Now we're either friends on my terms or I'm walking away right now and we can be enemies." I sat there holding her hand, absorbing what she had said, knowing there was some truth in it. I had never really pictured her as a girlfriend, just a great friend and sex partner.

Softly, I said, "Jennie, I don't want to lose your friendship, but it will be hard being with you without thinking."

"I know," she said, cutting me off again. "No more kissing and hugging, and we will just have to avoid being alone too much, that should make it easier for you."

"Well," I said, "since this is our last night as lovers, how about once more for old times' sake?"

Jennie stood up smiling and slapped me lightly across the face, saying, "Damn all you boys," then walked out of the park.

The next few days working at the farm and during the milking, everyone was teasing me about finally being man enough to get a real job and how I would find out what real work was trying to keep up with my old man.

Saturday was my last day at Muldon's and all week they had been needling me about a going-away party. As we were finishing up the milking most of Muldon's younger workers started showing up at the barn. Leonard Cross, who was home on leave, showed up; Jennie was already there; her sister Janet and Beverly Stone came as well, even though she wasn't working for the Muldons anymore. We had a grand party and everyone had a good laugh about all they had put me through, the stripping, the snipe hunt, the home brew. John brought kielbasa, Arthur brought cheese and they had hidden beer in the watering trough. Leonard brought a bottle of vodka. I don't know how long we partied. Homer had already left, I was beginning to feel the effects of the booze and decided I had better leave.

John said, "What the hell, Caleb? We go through all this effort to have a party for you and you're bugging out on us?"

"I'm awful sorry, John," I lied, "but I thought you were joking about a party and I made other plans for later tonight and I have to go."

"Oh, Caleb," Beverly teased, "do you really have to go? I thought tonight was the night you wanted to ask me something."

219

"Oh damn," I stammered, thinking maybe I would stay. I had thought often about my encounters with Beverly and not unpleasantly. She did say I would have to ask.

Jennie came over and took me by the arm, saying, "Com'n, Caleb, or you're going to be late."

The boys started hooting and hollering, "So it's true about you two, is it? What the hell, stay with this party, maybe you'll learn something."

Janet came over and took my other arm and said, "Let's go, Caleb, before this party gets any dirtier."

John started shouting, "Well, I'll be damned, who would have guessed, both Sledge girls on the same night, our little Caleb will surely be a man before morning."

Janet said, "John, you shut your filthy trap. If I ever hear you said a bad thing about my sister or me, I'll fix you so you wish you had never been able to talk."

We walked away from the barn with them singing, "The boy has gone and left the farm, a girl swinging from each arm, we hope he gets his plowing done, before he wilts in the noonday sun."

Janet walked us to the park and said, "I'm going back and get Beverly out of there. She keeps pouring that vodka down and lord knows what will happen."

Jennie and I started for the park benches, when she said, "Whoa, Caleb, we have to quit that stuff, remember?"

"Ah, com'n, Jennie," I pleaded, "after all, this is my last night."

Jennie held my face in both her hands and kissed me softly, saying, "I'm sorry, Caleb, but we had our last night, as far as sex goes, and that is final." Still holding my face in her hands, she kissed me again. I sat in the park alone thinking about the mess my life was in, trying to fathom what it was about the girls in my life. I wished it could all go back to being simple, like when Joan and I used to sneak off eating ice cream, with the ice cream being the important thing.

I heard Janet and Beverly coming, Beverly sounded a little high, and my first thoughts were, *All she's waiting for is for me to ask.* Then I recalled Jennie's soft good-bye and the seeming sadness of it, and of Joan crying out for me that night at the swings. I began thinking that maybe I was becoming the bum Mrs. Walden made me out to be. This was too disparaging, so I left for home before they saw me.

The next morning Dad woke me early. I was a little groggy from the night before, but Dad's excitement over his new venture made him oblivious to it. Dad had been working at the mill site the last few days building a shanty barn for the horses. I was to drive the team to Roymond, New Hampshire. It would be about a fifteen-mile trip, so I had to leave early. We had gone over the route several times so I was familiar on how to stay on the unpaved roads as much as possible. Mother had packed me a lunch, Dad had instructed me how to feed the horses with their feed bags and made sure I had a pail so I could water the team at any of the several streams I would cross. I had asked Dad if it was all right for Jake to come with me, he said that would be fine as long as we treated the horses well. When I arrived at the center of town where I was supposed to meet Jake, Karl and Beverly were waiting there. I had only seen Karl once since he had gone into the service. The last I had heard, he was in a hospital somewhere on the West Coast and had lost an arm fighting on one of the islands in the Pacific.

Beverly said, "Caleb, Karl came home late last night. He only has a couple of days, he was hoping to get a chance to talk to you before he went back. I knew you and Jake were going to be here this morning, so we came down."

I hadn't thought much about Karl lately. We seemed to have grown apart from the time he started high school. I didn't know what to say and I could hardly take my eyes off from the funny-looking artificial left hand.

Just then Jake showed up, saying, "Karl, good to see you, man. I heard you had quite a time of it over there."

"That's a fact, Jake, one that I hope you and Caleb never have to go through," Karl said, shaking Jake's hand.

I felt awkward, but I climbed down off the wagon and gave Karl a little hug, saying, "It's good to have you back, Karl."

While Karl and I talked, Beverly was bending Jake's ear at the back of the wagon. Jake said, "Caleb, I got a call from the paper, so I'm not going to be able to go with you. I already had a lunch made up, I brought it along in case you wanted it."

Beverly said, "Karl, why don't you take Jake's place? That way you two will have all day to talk."

"I would like that very much, Beverly," Karl said, smiling, "but it's up to Caleb, not us."

As confused as I was about what was happening, I could see that Karl truly wanted to go, so I said, "It'll be like old times, Karl, just you and me, on one of our crazy trips."

"Man, you can't know how often I wished I was back doing that," Karl said as he followed me onto the wagon.

I saw the glistening of tears in Karl's eyes and was thinking, *Now what have I let myself in for?* Jake said, "Hey, Karl, take my lunch, you're going to need it before you get back. There aren't any restaurants out there in the woods where Caleb is taking you."

As we drove off, Karl said, "Caleb, I heard about Josh. I know what a loss that is to you. I'm here if you want to talk about it."

"No, Karl," I answered, rather sharply, "that's something I'd rather not talk about."

The first couple of miles we talked about the horses, why we had them and how it was probably a good thing for me as well as for my father that he had started his own business. Karl was quiet for a while, then he said, "Caleb, I know we aren't little boys anymore, but I have often thought about all the things we've done together, I often wondered how you perceived those days."

"You know, Karl, I was just thinking about that when school let out this year. How work, the war and the draft have taken the joy out of the last days of school. I remember the excitement when we used to plan and dream of the days of summer," I answered, wondering if I was giving up too much of myself to this new Karl with the funny hand.

As we began talking about the things we used to do, it was like opening the door of childhood and walking back in. We relived the wonders of every moment, my fish at Banner's, George getting mangled by the bull, our trip up the river with Karl's uncle. Even after feeding and watering the horses we still went on and on. Bob Woods and Kate Curtis, and how we both felt our hearts were beating so loud that Bob would hear them when we hid in the cave. We admitted how scared we had been the first night we had camped out on the mountain. I almost told how I had caught that big fish, but I thought I'd better save that for later years.

We had been so excited with reliving our youth that we hardly realized how much of the day had passed or how far we had come, when Karl said, "Caleb, how much longer will it be before we get there?"

"I figure about an hour, Karl, give or take ten minutes," I said, checking my watch. "It doesn't seem possible that the day went this fast. We're just about where Dad figured we should be at this time."

"Caleb," Karl said, "I need to tell you something. I wasn't sure I would ever be able to talk about this, but being with you today has made it possible. When I was wounded, Caleb, I lay in the battlefield a long time before they were able to get me out. The fighting was fierce and many men died in that battle, because we couldn't establish a beachhead to evacuate the wounded from. A corpsman had come and bandaged me up and gave me plasma, but he was killed when he started to leave me to help someone else, I just lay beside him drifting in and out of consciousness. I don't remember them taking me to the ship or much of anything else until I came to at the hospital. When I became fully aware of what had happened to me, I didn't want to live. My hand was gone, I had horrible scars on my back and side, and for a while they were unsure if I was going to be able to walk again. There was this woman that kept coming in to talk to me, she reminded me of an older version of your Joan. She would talk to me about everything, even my ending it all. One day while we were talking she told me that even in the most miserable life there are memories that make life worth keeping, if only on the chance that you could again feel that joy. That night, instead of lying there wallowing in my pain and miseries, I started thinking about my life, and I realized that what had happened could consume me or just become a part of my life. I searched my memory for the good times. Suddenly I was back in Sterling with you on the mountain, in school with our friends, out with Beverly, but so often the memories were about being with you as a child on one of our crazy adventures. This was strong medicine, Caleb, soon I was up walking, and though I can't say I'm happy about my arm, I have accepted it. Last night when I first arrived in Sterling I began to worry that I had dreamed too much into my life here. Beverly sat with me most of the night listening to my fears. She knew about your trip today and I think she set this whole thing up by talking Jake out of going. I know we can't go back, Caleb, but talking to you today, I know our lives here are more than just good memories, they are a foundation we can build on to give our life meaning. I hope I haven't leaned on you too much about our times, Caleb, but I probably wouldn't be able to talk to anyone else like this."

"Hell, Karl, I live as much for those days as anyone. My trouble since losing Josh is believing that there will ever be that kind of joy in life again," I said, wondering if I was saying the wrong thing. "I know I haven't lived through the hell that you have, Karl, but I know about the dark clouds of despair, they follow me everywhere."

"Beverly told me that you were still having a bad time, Caleb, and that is understandable. Maybe we will be good for each other again. If nothing else, we have secrets that belong to only us and it can be a good thing to share them sometimes," Karl said, patting me on the shoulder with his artificial hand.

We were arriving at the mill site, and I really wanted to respond to Karl's overtures in some significant way before we met Dad. Despite the fact that revisiting our childhood memories had been heartening, it had not entirely lifted the dark cloud that engulfed me. So I said, "Karl, meeting you and talking about old times is good medicine. I hope we will always keep the comradeship that we developed in our youth. I always believed that we had lost that when you went on to high school, now I know we didn't. Still, after losing Josh, facing the draft and now a new job, summers aren't the same, and I'm not sure I will ever be able to enjoy life that way that again. Still, listening to you today and hearing that you found our life here something to cleave to was exciting, so don't let my despair dampen your thoughts."

Karl was quiet for a moment, then he said, "Caleb, I'm only going to be here a few days. I have to go back for therapy and training for my arm. Write me and remember today. If war has taught me anything, it is to save room in life for dreams."

When we pulled into the mill site there was a small city of shanties set up across the road and another one at the edge of the woods beyond Dad's shanty barn. Dad was there to meet us and said, "Well, you boys made good time and the horses still look rested. I guess there's a chance to make you a teamster yet, Caleb." He noticed Karl's arm as he swung off the wagon and said, "Hey, you're not Jake."

"No, Dad," I said, "Jake had to go into work and Karl asked to come in his place, you remember Karl, Dad, Karl Hart, he was wounded in the island and is home for a short visit."

Dad shook his hand, rather stiffly, and then turning abruptly, started explaining the mechanics of using the shanty barn, showing me where to hang the harnesses and how to place the grain and hay to protect it from the weather.

After listening to all of Dad's instructions, I said, "Gee, Dad, is this how it was, back when you and Mother first were married? I often heard Mother talk about living in a shantytown, was it like this?"

"Very much like this, Caleb. This is a real throw-back, most woodsmen in the old days lived like this, moving their shanties from job to job. Mr. Jocklin, who we're contracted with, owns the mill and likes to do things the old way."

"This is kind of exciting, Mr. Carney," Karl said, "riding all day behind a team of horses, then seeing an actual shantytown. Caleb and I have heard about this, but I didn't ever think we would ever get to see it, except in the history books."

Dad kind of warmed up to Karl then, saying, "It's exciting for me too, Karl. I know this isn't progress, but it's like being young again. See that big shanty barn over there, that's where they will stable the horses that are going to do the logging. Those are the kind of teams I drove when I was younger, they're not here yet, but they'll be bigger than this team."

Karl and I walked down to the mill setting and checked it out. I had watched a mill run before, but this would be the first time I ever worked at one. I started feeling the excitement of it. Karl said, "Did you see your dad's face when you introduced me, Caleb? We were warned that when we met someone who had lost a child to the war that at first they would resent that we got back and not their son."

"I noticed he was a little cool, Karl," I said, as I skipped a pine bug across a little pool in a brook by the site. "Do you really think he thought that? He seemed better later."

"Yes, I'm afraid I do, Caleb," Karl said, joining me in skipping bugs to the fish. "He shook it off right away, I suppose there will be those who won't though."

We were having a grand time skipping bugs and watching the fish rise when we heard Dad calling. We talked about coming back here and fishing someday. We helped Dad finish currying the horses, fed and watered them and rode back to Sterling in the back of Dad's truck.

When we dropped Karl off in town, I asked, "Can we get together tomorrow night, Karl?"

"No, Caleb, I have to be at a family get-together all day tomorrow and I will be leaving early the next morning." Karl hugged me like he didn't want to ever let go, saying, "Don't forget, Caleb, remember, write to me. I'll mail you my new address as soon as I know it. Today was wonderful, Caleb, so wonderful."

I got in the cab with Dad feeling kind of funny about Karl's long hug, when Dad said, "That boy sure shows real strength, handling losing his arm so bravely."

"You know, Dad, that's it," I said as the day's meaning started to penetrate, "that's what Karl has been trying to say all day. The arm is minor, considering what he almost lost. Not so much that he could have died, but that he could have survived only to live a meaningless life. He was so full of the joys of our youth today, and so sure life had more joys to offer. It was as if he has seen some great enlightenment that lifted him beyond the pain of losing his arm."

"War really is hell, Caleb," Dad answered, "throwing young boys into terrors like that either forces them to grow up fast or destroys them. It looks like your Karl is going to make it. Your Uncle Louis is an example of one who never quite conquered his terrors from the fighting in France during the First World War, that's why we have so much trouble with his drinking."

I spent a fitful night. When I did sleep I dreamed that Karl was lying in a foxhole with Josh working over him. Somehow I was there, Josh told me to take care of Karl, and as he was leaving, he was shot down in a hail of gunfire. I woke with Homer shaking me, saying, "Caleb, Caleb it's only a dream, stop screaming."

Mother came in and asked if I was all right. Homer said, "It's O.K., Mom, Caleb just had a bad dream."

The next time I woke it was Dad who was shaking me, saying, "Com'n, Caleb, we have to go to work early so the horses have time to eat before they start to work."

This wasn't something I had planned on, the mill started at 7:30 a.m. and Dad wanted to be with the horses before six, that meant we had to be out of the house a little after 5 a.m. every morning. The first day at work it was hurry up and wait. They had to keep making adjustments to the mill and the logging teams weren't very well prepared and had a lot of equipment breakdowns. Dad worked to show me how to handle the lumber with the most speed and least effort. I wondered at the necessity of having to be so precise, but with Dad, you did it his way. He insisted that we always had two rows of bedding lain, this was the foundation of each pile of lumber, built with the waste lumber and slabs.

I felt real confident the first few days at the mill, but as the week wore on and production increased more and more, I couldn't believe how hard the job had become. We were always behind; as fast as we emptied the lumber pit it was refilled, and if the mill crew took a break most of the time we had to keep working to catch up. When we were caught up, we had to lay bedding. I was glad that Dad insisted the horses have an hour for lunch or we probably would never stop. Even then, we sometimes had to lay bedding or work on the wagon or harnesses. My years on the farm had never prepared me for this. I know if I had been working for anyone else but my father, I would have quit the first week. For the first month of that summer there was little to my life except crawling out of bed at 4:30 a.m., sweating out the long day and coming home to eat and fall back into bed by seven thirty or eight each night. Gradually I grew stronger and my stamina increased. Instead of each day being just a challenge to get through, the challenge was trying to become faster and more adept at the work. The mill began producing between sixteen and eighteen thousand board feet of lumber for us to stack every day. Dad and I became the talk of the mill site. I heard Mr. Jocklin telling a man visiting the site he had never seen the likes of Henry Carney and his boy in all the years he had been in business.

Now that I had toughened to the work at the mill, I went to the barn some evenings to talk with the boys and find out what night they planned on going to Oscin. The boys teased me about the new muscle that I had developed. Jennie seemed real pleased to see me the first time I went, but she still stuck to her just-friends attitude when we stopped to talk in the park. One night when I was in town, Beverly flagged me down and we sat in the park and talked about Karl. I had written a couple of times since he went back, Beverly seemed anxious to hear what had happened the day he rode with me on the wagon. I told her as much as I thought Karl would want me to without mentioning the depth of meaning that the day had taken on for both of us. She said, "Caleb, I didn't know for sure how it would work out that day, but seeing you seemed so important to Karl. I conned Jake into letting him ride with you, I hope you weren't angry."

I had often dreamed about Beverly and how she had practically raped me those two times. So putting my arm around her, I said, "Beverly, you know that you've scared me a couple of times, but I've never been mad at you."

As I tried to caress her breast she pulled away from me, saying, "No, Caleb, please stop."

"What the hell, Bev," I said, taking my arm back, "you're the one who said I'd have to ask, well, I'm asking."

"No, Caleb, you're too late," she said, putting her hand on my shoulder. "No more fooling around for me, Karl and I have an agreement and I know you would never hurt him."

I guess I should have seen that in Karl's letters, he mentioned Beverly a lot and he had written that many of us do things when we are young that we are better off forgetting. "I'll be damned, Bev," I answered, "he never let on. This spoils all the dreams I had of getting even with you for stealing my virginity."

Beverly laughed, saying, "I'm sorry, Caleb, letting you get even sure sounds like fun. I'd better get the hell out of here before we both forget about Karl."

"Not to worry, Bev," I stammered, "Karl and I are blood brothers. We cut our thumbs and mingled our blood years ago." Beverly still insisted on leaving and I was glad, because more than anything right then, I wanted to forget Karl and their understanding.

The next morning Dad teased me when we got to work about being out all night chasing girls, because he had to wake me up again when we got there. I was making a little extra money by feeding the logging teams in the mornings. Their owner, Mr. Leclat, didn't like getting there so early and Dad had suggested that he hire me to feed his teams. Dad hated seeing horses get mistreated, and before I started feeding them, many mornings the Leclat horses had been put to work without having time enough to eat. The shanty on the edge of the woods, by the barn, belonged to a French Indian named Edgar. He was one of the choppers who cut the logs. Many mornings he would come over and help us with the horses. He took care of the horses on the weekends when we weren't there. Dad had taken a liking to him from the beginning, because he was so good with the teams. Edgar became a true friend. He talked about his life and the prejudices he had learned to live with. Some of his stories made me angry, and I asked how he could accept such crudeness.

He said, "Caleb, the word you have to remember here is accept. I could spend the rest of my life fighting to change other men to no avail, or I could see their fault for what it was—their problem, not mine. We must all remember if we want to make everything right in the world, we have to start by making ourselves right, for most men, that's a lifetime occupation. I had to learn to accept the world for what it is, instead of raging at it for what I want it to be."

I teased Edgar, saying, "Is this Indian philosophy class two or four?"

"No, Caleb," Edgar said quietly, "it's just some hard-earned lessons of life, that I voluntarily share, trying to help others avoid the pain of learning them the hard way. Speaking of pain, Caleb, I always felt that you were carrying a burden that was too heavy for you. I thought at first it was just the hardship of your new job, but even though I've seen some growth since we met, I still sense a kind of fear or bitterness in you."

I'm not sure why, but I started telling Edgar everything. Over the next few days I talked about my fear of life without Josh, the draft, Joan, Mrs. Walden, I even talked about Beverly and Jennie. I told him about Karl and his fixation on our youthful escapades, and how I found it both comforting and troubling. Outside of encouraging me to go on, Edgar hardly spoke.

After Edgar had spent days listening to me pour out my soul, he said, "Caleb, who are you?"

"What do you mean?" I answered, taken unaware. "I'm Caleb Carney, Henry Carney's son."

"Caleb, is it," Edgar said, "that's just a name given to the flesh that you are, but what is that flesh? Are you just a pile of barn manure because someone says so, an abject slagheap because you can't be Josh, unfit for manhood because you fear war? I could tell you what I think, Caleb, but that's not important. It's what you think that counts. Think, Caleb, how many times has someone called you a son-of-a-bitch? Did that turn your mother into a dog? Wouldn't your God have made you more like Josh if that was what He wanted? I have read the biography of some of the world's greatest men and they all dealt with fears of some kind, and fear of war was one of the most prominent. You know, Caleb, you could learn from your friend Karl. There is gospel in what he did. In time of great pain and despair he looked for a rescuing grace and grasped on to the most joyful moments of his short life, his boyhood's treasured moments. He is sure to have more joyful memories throughout his life, because he has made room for them by learning to master his horrors and relish his joys. One thing life has taught me is that we are a product of what we believe and do, not of what other people think."

Many nights I fell asleep mulling over my talks with Edgar. It was helpful having someone to talk things out with. With Edgar it was different than talking with Josh. Edgar forced me to think things out for myself, while Josh had thought for me. One night riding home after work, Dad said, "You and Edgar hit it off pretty good, Caleb. I could be jealous of course, but Edgar is a good man and you seem so much happier lately. Mother asked what was happening with you, she noticed the difference and was real pleased that you had found someone who you could talk to. I know that it was hard on you at first being the only young boy on the job, but I have been proud of the way you worked out. I'm going to miss you when school starts."

We had talked about my quitting school and working with Dad, but Mother was strictly against that. Quitting school would have made me eligible for the draft as soon as I turned eighteen in November, instead of after I graduated. Even though I had grown less fearful of life I still wasn't interesting in hurrying my induction.

For a short while during the last school session, in English class, we had been blessed with a teacher who seemed to make written words come alive. He was only with us for a couple of months when he disappeared from town. Rumor had it he was much too interested in boys and had quietly been run out of town. None of the school children that I knew had any problems with him, though some insisted they knew from the beginning he was queer. That he was different was plain enough, there weren't many men who acted out readings the way he did. One of the things he emphasized was if you wanted to write, then you should read the writings of Irving, Poe and Hawthorne to study how they developed and focused their characterizations. Jake had been after me to continue writing and had suggested that I should do a paper on my blue period, now that I had it mostly conquered. While thinking about doing that, I remembered what Mr. Blassard had said and was on my way into the library one Saturday to look up some things by those authors, when I met Joan. My first instinct had been to brush past her, but remembering my talks with Edgar and seeing her questioning look, I said, "Hi, Joan, I was just going in to look for some stories by, Poe, Irving or Hawthorne. Do you have time to help me find them?"

"I'm sorry, Caleb," she said softly, "but Mother is waiting to take me into Oscin, we just have to pick up some papers for a college I'm interested in. I should be back in time to help you this afternoon, if you can wait."

"No hurry, Joan, Dad told me to take the day off, even from my farm chores. I haven't anything planned until tonight, when I'm going to Oscin with the barn boys," I said, wishing I hadn't mentioned the barn boys. "How about I walk a ways with you, Joan? We haven't talked in a long time."

"I think I would like that, Caleb. Have you gotten over being angry with me?" she asked.

"It wasn't that I was angry with you, Joan," I replied, searching for words to explain. "I let myself be so hurt that I hid behind a fence of despondency, lashing out at life. I know now how much I needed what we had before, but in my distress, I drove you away."

"Oh, Caleb," Joan said, putting her arm around my waist, "I never went very far. I've been waiting for you to call, praying it would come before you completely disappeared in that dark cloud of yours."

Walking, holding her hand, I wondered if it was that easy. Edgar had said we can't always go back, but we can always build on what we left behind. Remembering that, I said, "Joan, I would be real pleased if we could be together again."

Joan kissed me passionately, and as she pushed me away, she said, "I'll be at the library this afternoon, Caleb," and hurried to her house.

I walked back to the center of town, marveling at what had happened. Beneath the hurt and embarrassment that I felt about Mrs. Walden, I had always desperately wished that I could separate that from my feelings for Joan. I often longed for the days when we shared so much of our lives, without the feeling that I was somehow inferior to her and her family. When I reached the center, Jake was coming out of the library. He shouted, "Guess what, Caleb, I talked the editor into doing an article on Sterling for the newspaper and he suggested I try writing it, want to help?"

"I dunno, Jake," I answered, "I won't have much time for research, but when you have a draft I would like to see it, maybe I can help then."

Jake and I sat in the park and talked. Jake was as worried as I was about being drafted. He said, "From what I've been hearing at the newspaper, Caleb, the Allies are talking about bombing the Japanese into submission instead of invading mainland Japan."

"I sure hope they find some way to end the war without invading," I said, feeling the old fear of combat well up. "After losing Josh and talking to Karl, the glory of going to war sure is losing credence with me."

"You know how I feel about war, Caleb," Jake said with an incredulous look. "Karl actually talked to you about what happened? They wanted to do a piece about him in the paper, but he refused to be interviewed. Did he tell you how he lost his arm?"

"Karl and I spent a whole day together, remember, Jake?" I started, excited about what I knew.

Then I remembered Karl saying, *I wouldn't be able to tell anybody else except you, Caleb.* I said, "Most of our talking was about all the things we used to do and how thinking about them helped him while he was in the hospital."

"Well, I guess we'll have to wait awhile to hear Karl's story, by then it won't be news," Jake said, as he started to leave. "You know what though, Caleb, maybe my article could use something like 'wounded soldier's thoughts about his youthful exploits in Sterling sustain him through harrowing hospital ordeal,' see you around, Caleb."

After Jake left, I walked over to the barn. The cows were out to pasture and the only one there was Jennie, she was sterilizing the milkers in the milk room. I was standing there daydreaming about my times there, looking back thinking how some history can be good, when she spotted me.

"Hey, Caleb," she called, "what you doing, slumming?"

"No, Jennie," I laughed, "I've been busy, but with summer winding down and school starting soon, I thought I'd wander around town looking up old friends."

"Well, I don't like the old part, Caleb," Jennie said, smiling, "but I hope I'm still a friend, com'n in and talk to me, while I finish up here."

Jennie and I talked about my years at the barn, enjoyably laughing about some of the escapades, careful not to mention our times of amour. She told me she had kept track of how I was doing through Homer. He had told them I was finally conquering my depression with the help of some Indian. I laughed, saying, "You know what they say, Jennie, time heals all wounds, though I have to admit Edgar is a great counselor. It is helpful to see your problems through someone else's eyes sometimes. I do feel better now and that's why I am out visiting today."

"Speaking of visits, Caleb," Jennie asked, "wasn't that Joan I saw you talking with at the library earlier?"

"Oh, thanks, Jennie," I said, getting up to leave, "I'm supposed to meet her there now to do some research."

As I reached for the door Jennie put her arm on my shoulder, saying, "Good luck with the research, Caleb, and be careful not to tie your heart to a stone that's too heavy."

I left slightly addled, Jennie not only had a way of tugging at my libido, as Edgar called it; now she was stirring my mind, how could I tie my heart to a stone? Joan was just coming through the park when I got to the library.

231

The Joan in most of my thoughts was the little girl I bought ice cream for while the Joan coming across the park was a beautiful young lady. She met me at the door, saying, "Now, what writers are we looking for?"

"Irving, Poe and Hawthorne," I replied, hoping she hadn't read my thoughts. Entering the library, I worried I was making mistake. Joan had been a close part of my youth. I always enjoyed being with her, except when she talked about being in love, which frightened me. It electrified me as I watched Joan locating those authors, her grace and charm obliterated how bad her mother had made me feel the night she invited me to dinner. Besides, Edgar had tutored that what others think isn't what makes you, it's what you think about yourself that counts. Talking to Jennie and meeting with Joan had triggered a lot of emotional thoughts, some that I knew were not to be trusted. I couldn't really imagine Edgar being in this kind of a situation.

Checking out the books, we walked through the park. Joan said, "Caleb, I have to be back home, we can talk on the way. I hear you and Jennie cut quite a rug for a few weeks at youth night at the Inn, do you go anymore?"

"I haven't been this summer, Joan," I answered, wondering how much she had heard. "Morning comes early with my new job and I don't go out many weeknights." This got Joan talking about her work for the summer, and before we knew it, we were almost at her house. I stopped where we always had. I felt strangely fearful, the kind of fear that says, *Get away, run.* So I said, "Joan, I hope I see you around again, and thanks for helping me."

Joan holding both my hands faced me, saying, "Caleb, don't I even get a kiss?" I pulled her to me, kissing her on the lips, then turned to go. Joan took a few steps and then said, "Caleb, will you take me to the dance this week?"

Some part of me wanted to say no, but instead I said, "O.K, Joan, I might be a little tired but I'll meet you there."

"Caleb, can't you pick me up at the house like a real date?" Joan asked.

"No, Joan, I'm not prepared to do that, see you Tuesday night," I shouted, walking away. Considering how flustered I felt, it surprised me how much I relished the idea of being with Joan again. When we arrived in Oscin that night, Jake and I went to a movie. I wasn't in any mood to join the boys going cruising for girls, Jennie and Joan had exhausted my infatuations enough for one day.

The next day Jake came riding into our yard, shouting, "Caleb, Caleb, have you heard? We dropped a bomb on Japan that destroyed a whole city. I got a call from one of the boys at the newspaper. He said it was an atomic bomb and thousands were killed. The Allies are calling on Japan to surrender or there will be more bombs. This is great, Caleb, it might mean we won't be drafted if the war ends."

"Are you sure, Jake?" I asked, afraid that this was just another rumor.

Everybody was running out of the house to see why Jake was so excited. "What's going on?" Emma shouted.

"It's the truth, Caleb," Jake said as he was catching his breath. "It came in on the wire and they're printing the headlines now."

"What's the truth Jake?" Mother asked, coming through the door.

"It's great news, Mrs. Carney," Jake said, repeating what he told me about the bombing.

"That is great news, Jake," Mother said over all the cheering, "I pray they do surrender before thousands more are killed."

It took the bombing of another Japanese city before their leaders saw the futility of resisting further. There were great celebrations throughout the world, but as the stories and pictures of the devastation and death that had been caused by only two bombs became available, trepidation developed over what our labors had wrought.

One writer wrote, "Even as men saluted the greatest and most pyrrhic of victories, in all the gratitude and good spirits they could muster, they recognized that the discovery which had done the most to end the worst of wars might also, quite conceivably, end all wars if only man could learn to control its use."

Jake was very much into this type of philosophy and often brought these kinds of writings to my attention. It reminded me of Jake's pacifist leanings when the war began. As for me, the end of the war lifted the terror of having to prove myself on a battlefield, though the uncertainty of what the outcome of that would have been, will probably forever haunt me.

There was great joy and celebrations about the war's end, everywhere, at work, at play, no matter where you went. Mrs. Banner even had a big party for us at the Tuesday night dance, with free food and soda. Joan was late in showing up, and when she came in, I was dancing with Beverly. Beverly spotted her by the door and waltzed me over and said, "Here, Joan, I have been protecting him for you."

Joan protested, saying, "It is O.K., Bev, finish your dance."

Beverly laughed, walking away, said, "No, Joan, you dance with him, my feet are sore enough."

The dance that night was wonderful. Mrs. Banner supplied the coins for the jukebox, we were allowed to play any of the songs we liked, she even kept the dance hall open an hour longer than usual. I danced a couple of dances with Jennie, not the close dances or the bump and grind of previous dances, but it was still fun dancing with her. She came with some boy named Ricky from out of town, and even though we were just friends, it bothered me. Joan didn't dance with other boys at first, but by the end of the night she was dancing with other boys every time I danced with Beverly or Jennie. When I was walking home with Joan, she said, "Caleb, are you in love with Jennie?"

"I dunno about love, Joan," I said. "I like Jennie a lot, she was there for me during a real hard time, we have become good friends. I like a lot of people, I just don't know about this love stuff."

"How about me?" Joan asked. "Do you love me or am I just a friend?"

"Joan, it's hard for me," I said, holding her a little closer. "You know how close we have been over the years. It's harder now, there's this puberty thing, the way your mother hates me, and love scares me. Is what I felt about Josh love, is how I feel about the rest of my family love, am I going to hurt as much if I lose them as I did losing Josh? Do you think the way I feel about girls now is love? If it is, then I'm in love with at least half the opposite sex that I know. You know I care for you, Joan. I missed being with you, I wished things could have stayed the way they were. We both know that's not possible now. I feel closer to you, Joan, than any girl I have ever known, even my sisters, but it's dangerous when boys and girls of our age become too serious. So let's stay the closest of friends while traveling towards adulthood together. My friend Edgar says that this time in our life is full of growing pains and we will look back on them someday with pleasure and laugh about our fears."

Joan was quiet most of the rest of the way to her house, except for insisting that I walk her to the door. I figured because we would not be able to linger there long, that she must be angry with me. At the door she embraced me for the longest moment. Still holding me, she said, "Caleb, what you said makes sense. There's a saying that the longest journey starts with the first step. I feel like this is ours."

I laughed, saying, "Joan, how can that be? We have been walking together for years!"

"I feel like we were only children then, Caleb," she said, hugging and kissing me. "Good night, Caleb, I had a good time tonight. I'm glad we're back together."

As she turned to go in I saw her mother peeking out a window. Joan saw her too and she came back and kissed me so long I thought I was going to lose my breath. Then, without talking, she turned and went into the house.

The last couple of weeks of my seventeenth summer became much more enjoyable than the beginning. I was seeing Joan again, even picking her up at her house when we attended the dances. Though I was curious about what her mother said that night, I didn't want to ask. One day when I was walking her home from the library she told me, "Mother and I had a big argument about my being with you. Father finally stepped in and told Mother that she was being foolish, that at our age all that was important was that you treated me like a lady. You know, Caleb, I was so mad I almost told them how much of a gentleman you were the night we almost had sex."

"Good thing you didn't, Joan," I said, startled. "You would have been locked in a closet and my dad would have probably tied me to a post for your father to use his whip on."

We were laughing about that as we reached Joan's house. Joan's mother was working at a wall in her flower garden, she was trying to move a fairly large rock. She said, "I hope you two are not laughing at me?"

"No, Mother," Joan replied, "we were just laughing at something that happened at the dance. Com'n, Caleb, let's give her a hand."

After Joan and I easily moved the rock to where Mrs. Walden wanted it, she said, "Well, Caleb, since this is your last year in high school, what are your plans for college?"

"Mother," Joan exclaimed.

"That's O.K., Joan," I answered, cooler than I felt, "Jake and I have been talking about finding a school in journalism that we can afford. The people at the newspaper have done a lot of research on different schools for us, and we're going over them with the teachers at school this year."

"Caleb," Joan said, "how come you never told me?"

"Well," I said, "it was the kind of a dream that you don't really believe, so you don't want to talk about it. Lately we've been encouraged by the people Jake works with, now it seems as though it might be possible."

Joan gave me a big hug, while her mother went into the house, saying, "Journalism, well, I never."

I gave Joan a little kiss and told her I had to get back to help Dad get some hay in. When I got back to the house, Mother called me into the kitchen, she said, "Caleb, how would you feel about sharing that back bedroom we've been restoring for you? We got a letter from Clem Baker this morning, and he wanted to know if we could board him when he gets out of the service. He received a Dear John letter from Ellie a few months ago and doesn't want to go back to the house they shared. Dad is going to ask him to work in your place. He might not be here before school starts, but Edgar's crew have cut enough logs ahead to allow him to work with Dad until Clem gets out."

I had been looking forward to having my own room, but I realized that helping Clem, whom I had always liked, would also help Mother and Dad. So I said, "That's O.K., Mom. It's a big L-shaped room, I'm sure I'll be comfortable there with Clem." I was surprised about Ellie, nobody had ever said anything about her leaving Clem, the last time she was here with Mother they were having a heated argument. I hadn't seen her at the house since. When I went to the field to help Dad with the haying he told me he was pleased about Clem. Thinking this would be a good time, I told Dad about wanting to go to college.

He said, "I hope we can do it, Caleb, Mother and I will help all we can. You have the money that Mother has been banking for you since you went to work for the Muldons."

I had forgotten all about my savings, I hadn't touched them since we bought the farm and wasn't even sure of how much they was. When I told Jake about my savings the first day of school at the bus stop, he said, "That's great, Caleb. I have an uncle on my mother's side offering to help anyone in the family with college expenses if their marks are good enough. Mother sent him a copy of my report cards and he wrote saying he would be glad to help me, asking for more information and a letter from my teachers at the end of this year. Mother said it wouldn't be enough to pay all my tuition, but enough to make it appear possible for me to go."

"Can you believe it, Jake?" I asked excitedly. "Who would have believed that a dream Old Hanna put in our head is actually becoming possible?"

The possibilities that Jake and I were going to college dominated most of my conversation with Joan as we rode to school on the bus. Joan said, "Mother wants me to go to an all-girls college. I'm not fighting it yet, Caleb, but I want to go where you go."

I hadn't thought about Joan going to college. Most families didn't have money to send girls, but rumor had it that there was money on her mother's side of the family and that's why she looked down on some of us. Harold was there when we arrived at school, it was good to see him, I had only seen Harold once all summer. He said, "Isn't the news great, Caleb? It looks like we won't have to go into the service if we don't want to. My brother who fought in Europe was found in one of the German prison camps and will be home after a short visit in a hospital. The one in the Marines is still listed as missing in action and the government isn't expressing much hope. We can only pray."

I found that school, which had been such a drag last year after we lost Josh, was much more stimulating with college an actual possibility. Jake had talked it up with all the teachers, and Mr. Ghoul, who was teaching English that year, advised me that I should write more if I was really interested in journalism. Jake already had many articles he had written working for the paper. Not all of them were published, but they gave Mr. Ghoul a chance to help Jake with what he called his weak points. Jake disliked some of the teacher's ideas and talked with the paper's editor about them. The editor said that while he didn't always agree with Mr. Ghoul, he did think having him for a teacher was beneficial to Jake. Jake's article about Sterling had been published on the front page of the newspaper, so he used it for an assignment in school. Although Jake had received great huzzahs from everyone in town, Mr. Ghoul found much to criticize. It made me think twice about using the story I had written about my dark period, as Jake called it. Jake wanted me to pass it in, but I thought it was too personal. The reason I had written it was to help me understand myself. Mr. Ghoul kept insisting I needed more length and depth to my writing, so when he gave an assignment to write about strong emotions, such as fear, anger or love, I passed it in. The next day in class, Mr. Ghoul said, "There were some very inspiring papers written for your last assignment, some of them are very personal so I will not mention names, but I want to read you a passage that shows what I was looking for in this lesson." He read, "I found myself posed there, among the tear-stained faces in the chapel, heeding the wailing, while silently staring at my brother in his coffin, with my mind screaming, *Where is that miraculous God now, where is that great God?*"

After class, Jake said, "You know, Caleb, I knew you had written something special, it is so cognitive of our time that the complete story should be published.

"Sure, Jake," I answered ruefully, "I'm going to let my inner feelings get spread all over the place. I had no intention of using that story, but between filling in at the barn and seeing Joan I didn't get the story I was writing finished. I knew Mr. Ghoul wasn't going to give me the kind of a mark that would help me get into college if I didn't write a long paper, so I used it."

A few days later Mr. Ghoul handed back my paper. He had marked it excellent and included a note that said the world should see this. When Jake saw the note, he said, "Caleb, let me show the story to my newspaper editor. It can be printed anonymously if that's what you want."

Mr. Ghoul's note stirred me, so I decide to let Jake take the story to show his editor, telling him, "If word gets out that I wrote this, Jake, I'll never forgive you."

"Don't worry, Caleb," he said excitedly, "I won't even tell the editors who wrote it."

A couple of days later, Jake said, "Caleb, the editor is crazy about your story but he won't publish it without a release. He will print it anonymously but he wants signed permission in his file before he uses it. He says good pieces like that are plagiarized all the time and he needs to be protected."

The article, headlined "Youthful Lament of Our Times," was in

Saturday's paper, and Mother and Homer recognized my writing, but they were understanding about the anonymity. It was well received and by Monday it was the main topic on the bus ride to school. Some were saying that they thought Mr. Ghoul had read from that in class once. When he was asked, he said he had not read the paper, so he couldn't comment on it.

Though on occasion I was remorseful when I thought about Josh, school and the excitement of going to college isolated me from my darkness and made the next several months fly by. Many of the boys who went straight from school into the service came back to visit after they were discharged and gave talks at assembly. Some of what we heard was a lot of bull, but Karl and others like him came across with a sincerity that expounded on the horrors of wars, not just the glory of victory.

One morning at the bus stop Jake showed up all excited, saying, "Caleb, I received a phone call at my house yesterday. It was a call from a lawyer's office to confirm an appointment with their office for Saturday. I told them they had the wrong person they assured me they didn't. They asked me if I could meet with them at 11:00 a.m. Saturday, they wouldn't tell me why except to say it was something pleasant."

Everybody on the bus was all abuzz about what was going to happen to Jake, by the time we arrived at school the stories ranged from a great inheritance to being tapped by the F.B.I. to becoming a spy. When I reached home that afternoon Mother handed me an official-looking envelope, saying, "We've been waiting anxiously to see what this is about, Caleb."

The letter was from Attorney Welsh's office in Oscin requesting me and a parent or guardian to meet with him at 11:00 a.m. Saturday. Mother appeared upset, so I told her, "Don't worry Mother, Jake Wilson is going too. He received a call from them yesterday and they told him it was something pleasant."

I think my family's imagination on what this might mean exceeded that of the kids on the bus. Homer had me inheriting a great farm so he could run it for me; Jason hoped I would get a great touring car for him to ride in; the girls wanted a beauty parlor when I got rich; Francis and Nellie wanted a saddle horse.

Dad said, "Now, children, don't allow your imaginations run away with you, whatever it is, Mother and I hope it is something that brightens Caleb's life. Caleb, we haven't heard from you, what do you want?"

"What I want, Dad," I replied, laughing, "is for it to be Saturday so I'll know what this is about, maybe then the butterflies will leave my stomach."

Saturday finally arrived. Mother and I rode to Oscin with Jake and his father. At Attorney Welsh's address we were ushered into his office. It was impressive, big leather chairs, a bookcase full of books that took up one whole wall and a massive mahogany desk. After introductions, Mr. Welsh said, "I suppose you boys have been on pins and needles all week waiting for today."

"Not just the boys, Mr. Welsh," Mr. Wilson said, smiling, "their parents are concerned also."

"Well, let's get to it then," Mr. Welsh replied, "I have been appointed administrator of the will of one Hanna Cullings. She has bequeathed something special to Caleb Carney and Jake Wilson with certain conditions, and my job is to see that her requests are carried out. She arranged an investment years ago to help finance advanced education for both of you. The stipulations are that you must attend college and maintain above average grades and contribute financially yourself. Any money left is to be divided equally between you when you obtain four-year degrees. The will allows you six years from the time you graduate from high school to accomplish this, minus any time you might spend in the service. Failure of one or both of you to adhere to these stipulations and your share will be donated to a fund whose name I am not at liberty to indulge unless you forfeit. I know that there will be many questions, I will answer any that you have today and we will set up another appointment to go over this again, when you're ready."

My mind was so full I hardly dared speak. Old Hanna, who would have dreamed such a thing as this? I was always grateful for the time she spent with Jake and me and our writing, but I never imagined her coming back into our lives this way. Jake grabbed my arm, saying, "Caleb, this takes all the ifs and buts out of going to college. Now we know for sure we can, this is wonderful, wonderful."

Mr. Welsh said, "I can see why she picked you two. I often wonder why someone is chosen in these situations, it is heartening to see it so well deserved. I will list what you have to do legally under this will, and then we will have to go before a judge to have it court approved. Then we can meet and you can always call me for any needed clarification. That will be better in case there is something the judge doesn't allow. Essentially it will be copies of your college acceptance, the end of semester marks and things of that nature."

Driving home from Oscin, Mother, Jake and Mr. Wilson talked elatedly about all the possibilities this opened for us. I felt strangely agitated about what this meant. Though my wanting to go to college had been real, I never really felt it would be possible. Now that college was a fact, leaving Sterling and going into a new world was almost as frightening as being drafted. No family, I thought, no Joan or Jennie to seek solace from, just little Caleb out in the big world all by myself. Jake shook me from my reverie by cuffing me on the shoulder, saying, "Gee, Caleb, you're kind of quiet for a guy who just had his dream come true."

"I'm as thrilled as you are, Jake," I answered, pushing him back. "I was just thinking how much our lives will change, leaving Sterling and all our friends."

"Caleb, I know we see some things differently," Jake said earnestly, "I always planned to go to college, even if it meant I had to sweep out bars and wash dishes to pay for it. Now we can go without struggling to pay for it, with more time to study and explore other ways of life. This is better than good, Caleb, this is great."

Mother put her arm on my shoulder, saying, "Caleb always ponders the whole picture when it is anything new, Jake. I'm sure he feels as fortunate as you about Hanna remembering him in such a meaningful way."

"Believe me, all of you," I said, grinning, "I'm delighted that I was chosen by Old Hanna for such an honor, I was just overwhelmed by thoughts of all the changes this is going to make in my life." When we reached Sterling, I asked Mother if it was O.K. if I stayed in town.

Mother said, "Of course, Caleb, you will want to tell your friends the good news."

Jake couldn't stay with me because he had to work that afternoon. When I arrived in the center of town, Jennie was coming from the cow barn where she had been spreading ensilage in the silo. I called to her, saying, "Jennie, I have great news, do you have a minute?"

"Sure, Caleb," she replied, "as long as you don't mind that I smell like vinegar."

I laughed, saying, "It's all right, Jennie, I'm used to barn girls' perfume."

I told her what had happened at the lawyer's office. She said, "Caleb, I'm so glad for you. As lost as you sometimes seem to be, I know that you only need the right chance to blossom. When you come home will you date me once, so I can say I dated a college boy?"

I laughed and said, "I will surely look forward to that, Jennie. I hope dreaming about it doesn't disturb my studies."

"Only as friends, Caleb," Jennie said, leaving, "only as friends."

When I went to the Waldens to talk to Joan, her mother was in the garden. She said, "How are your college plans coming, Caleb? Have you raised enough money?"

"I have funds for four years, Mrs. Walden," I said as Joan was coming out the door, "I just came from Attorney Welsh's office in Oscin and it's all arranged."

"Well, I'll be damned," Mrs. Walden exploded, "I thought your going to college was just a pipe dream."

"Mother," Joan shouted, "Caleb and I are going for a walk, maybe you can be a little more gracious when we get back."

Joan's mother stood in her garden with her face almost as red as a beet. Joan and I walked out of the yard. Joan said, "Caleb, you'd better not have been conning Mother or we're both dead." I told Joan about Old Hanna's will, she was quiet for some time, then said, "This probably means we will be far apart next year."

"I don't know where I will be going yet, Joan," I said, giving her a hug. "Maybe we could end up at the same college."

"Not if my mother can help it," Joan said ruefully. "She has been saying that when I went away to college I would forget all about you. I heard her tell Dad that she couldn't imagine you ever being college material. Dad said, 'I guess you didn't read the Youthful Lament that was in the paper, rumor has it Caleb wrote it.' Caleb, is that true, if you wrote it, how come I didn't know?"

"No one was supposed to know, Joan," I said, still wishing I hadn't let Jake talk me into letting it be published. "Please don't tell anyone."

We walked to the park and there to my surprise was Reilly Muldon, I hadn't seen him since he left for the service. He shouted, "Hey, little stripper, come on over, let me see if you have grown any yet."

It was good to see Reilly, we talked of old times, laughing about my snipe hunt and the time all the boys got sick on my dad's home brew. We recalled all the times he had protected me when I first started working at the barn. He said, "It was great to see you, Caleb, I only have a few days and I'm trying to see all the old crew before I go back, it looks like it will be some time before I'm mustered out, my outfit's going to Japan."

After Reilly left, Joan said, "Well, that was an education. What else went on at that barn?"

"Oh, com'n, Joan," I said rather sharply, "it was all in fun, a kind of an initiation into the barn mentality, as your mother would say."

"Forgive me, Caleb," Joan pleaded, "I'm just upset thinking about us being separated next year, not with Reilly."

"That's O.K., Joan," I answered, "I know what you mean. I'm troubled about leaving here too."

I was supposed to be working at the barn that night and we planned to go to Oscin after work. I walked Joan home around 3:00 p.m., I kissed her good-bye and headed home, to change clothes. I was anxious to get to work so I could tell the barn crew about Hanna, hoping Reilly would be there.

That night at the barn was like old times, the boys teased me about being Old Hanna's pet and asking what a stripper would do in college. Jennie got into the act by, saying, "I suppose when you become one of those fancy college dudes, you won't want to associate with your old pals from here."

"Com'n, fellas," I laughed, "this barn and all who have worked here have been a large part of my life. How can you think I would forget, or snub any of you?"

Reilly said, "You know what, Caleb? You're going to find out there are much bigger things in the life out there than this barn, I did."

"Case in point then, Reilly," I answered, "your being here tonight shows that you remembered the barn and us."

"Truth is, people," Reilly said softly, "remembering what we have here got me through many frightening and lonely times. Speaking of the truth, Caleb, I know that everyone here is proud that one of our group is going to college, and I expect some are even a little jealous."

They were all smiling and nodding their heads, when John said, "Besides that, Caleb it gives us an excuse to have another going-away party."

When I left the barn that night the whole gang was all cheering, "Party, party, party." The next day when Dad went to do some repairs on his wagon, I went too, so I could tell Edgar about my good fortune. He was very interested and supportive, saying, "Caleb, most of us have opportunities in life that we fail to recognize at the time, this could be the opportunity of your life, so you had better make the most of it. It is O.K. to carry your life in Sterling with you in your heart, but not on your back or cluttering your mind. Keep your mind open for all the newness there is out there for you to experience."

When Jake and I returned to school, the teachers were all very interested in our choice of colleges, but after several discussions it dawned on us that each was advocating their own alma mater. Except for Mr. Ghoul, he gave us a list of schools that had good journalistic curriculums and advised us how to write for more information. I received a letter from Eunice. She wrote that Harry had won a big building contract and would have a job for me this summer if I wanted to move to Oklahoma. She also enclosed literature on colleges that were in that area, suggesting that if I chose one of them, I could still be near family. The last few weeks of school were a whirlwind of activity. Dad thought that going to work for Harry would give me an opportunity to learn a trade I could fall back on. Though he never said anything, I could feel that Dad didn't think much of writing as a way to earn a living. Jake said he always dreamed of going West and thought Oklahoma was a great idea. One of the colleges Jake was intrigued with was called

Oklahoma Panhandle State University, but after investigating we found it was an agriculture college. So we finally settled on Oklahoma State University, whose curriculum was more suited for us want-to-be writers. I tried to talk Jake into going out with me during the summer, but he and his family thought that staying with the paper would be more beneficial. Harold had already spent the last two summers in apprenticeship in plumbing with his uncle, so I couldn't interest him.

School closed Wednesday. Mother made all the travel arrangements and I was to be on a train in Oscin on Saturday. I planned to work at the barn until Thursday night, though I told Golly Moses I didn't want to work during the day. Homer and the girls, except Nellie, worked during the day. Jason, Francis and I went fishing at George's secret place. It wasn't secret after all these years and the fishing wasn't near as good, but we had a good time. Later Nellie and I went for a hike in the woods, it seemed impossible she was almost eleven years old. Nellie seemed to have Josh's sixth sense of things. She asked me, "Caleb, how scared are you?"

"Whoa, Nellie," I exclaimed, "just like that, not 'are you scared?' but 'how scared are you?'"

"Don't be mad, Caleb, I was just thinking how I would feel."

I couldn't be mad at Nellie, she was right. All of this seemed to be happening with hardly any conscious thought on my part and much too fast to govern. So I said, "More than I would want anyone to know, Nellie, so this has to be our secret."

"Cross my heart and hope to die, if I heard it said, I'll say they lie," Nellie said, giving me a hug. "Seriously, Caleb, many times I feel things about people that I would never tell, especially in the family. I know it's kind of weird, so I never tell anyone."

"Josh was a lot like that, Nellie," I said, just before we reached the house. "Don't feel weird about it, just use it for people's good, the way Josh always did."

At the barn that night when we finished the milking, the gang had arranged a party. Leonard Cross, who was home on leave waiting to be mustered out of the Army, came, so did Janet and Beverly. The girls brought some Polish horse collars and cheese. There was beer in the watering trough and Leonard brought some booze. Homer, who was always smarter about these things than I was, left after eating some kielbasa without touching the drinks. Janet wished me well and left shortly after warning Jennie not to drink more than one. The boys kept telling me I had to learn how to hold my liquor if I was going to be a college boy. After a couple of beers and a pull on Leonard's bottle, I could feel the alcohol starting to have an effect. Jennie must have seen this, for she came over and said, "Say good-bye to the gang, Caleb. It's getting late and we have to go, you haven't said a proper good-bye to me yet."

That got the boys started with their "What about us? How come it's always Caleb?"

Beverly, who had been quiet tonight, said, "I'm coming too, Caleb. I don't want you to leave remembering me here." I said good-bye to each one of them personally and was walking away with the girls. They started singing, "The boy has gone and left the farm, holding a girl under each arm, we hope he gets his plowing done, before he wilts in the noonday sun."

We walked to the park, arm in arm, the three of us. I wasn't happy about leaving, but being between these two girls seemed like a better party. We had only been in the park a few moments when Homer showed up, saying, "I'm glad to see you away from the barn, Caleb. I worried you would get drunk and spoil everything for Mother and the family tomorrow night."

"We rescued him from those big bad boys, Homer," Jennie said, laughing.

"I'm thankful for that," Homer replied, "now I'm wondering if he needs rescuing from you too, Jennie."

"The truth is, Homer," Jennie said, "I was just going to say good-bye to him." Turning, she gave me a long hug and kiss. Releasing me, she walked away, saying, "Write to your friend Jennie, Caleb."

Homer, who was standing there looking dumbstruck, finally said, "I guess you don't need me, Caleb," and left.

Beverly, who was still sitting quietly on the bench, said, "Caleb, will you hold me?"

Satiated with the desire that Jennie had created, I sat and held Beverly. She said, "Caleb, did you know that Karl has fallen in love with one of his nurses?"

I knew that the last time Karl was home he told me he was infatuated with a nurse and was sick wondering how she felt. I told him to just ask her, it was better than torturing himself. Beverly said, "Yesterday, I received a reverse Dear John letter from Karl, telling me about his love for her."

I held Beverly tighter saying, "There is more than one fish in the sea, Bev, and you will have plenty of men to pick from after all the boys get home."

I don't know how long we sat holding each other, but when it became too much for me I gave her a little kiss. As I was pulling away, she said, "Don't leave, Caleb, tonight is the night for you to get even with me, let's find a place."

The next morning I slept until 9:00 a.m. Mother was in the kitchen. She said, "Must have been some party last night. You didn't do anything foolish, did you, Caleb?"

"No, Mother, I was just out saying good-bye to my friends and they wouldn't let me go," I lied, feeling evil. Francis and Nellie came in and saved me from answering more questions. Mother fixed my breakfast and asked, "What do you have planned for today, Caleb?"

"I'm supposed to meet Joan at the library at 11:00. We're going to hike on the mountain if it's O.K., Mother?" I said.

"You and Joan have a good day," Mother answered, "I'll pack a picnic basket, just be home by 4:30 this afternoon, I want you to spend your last night with the family."

"O.K., Mother, but if Joan is free may I invite her?" I asked

"Oh, Joan's family now, Caleb?" Mother queried, laughing. "I think it would be nice if she joined us."

I met Joan at the park. We hiked more than halfway to the top without talking. I was glad for the silence. I had whiled away so much of my youth meandering these trails that it was as if I came to say good-bye to an old friend. Finally Joan broke the silence, asking, "Penny for your thoughts, Caleb."

"I was just thinking about the times I've hiked and camped here, with Karl and Jake, my brothers and sisters, and how great it was as a child to have a mountain for a backyard."

"You know, Caleb, I was always jealous of you and your mountain and all the time you spent up here with your friends," Joan said, giving me a little slap. "That's for never inviting me into your world."

"Joan," I said, acting surprised, "you have always been a part of my life even as a little kid, before I started buying you ice cream. I even had eyes for you then."

"What happened since then? Those were such magical times for me, Caleb, can we ever have that again?" Joan asked as I steered her to a spot where we could look down the backside of the mountain.

"I don't believe that anything can ever be exactly like that again, Joan, because we have changed. You know, puberty and all that," I said, opening our picnic lunch. "Edgar told me that if I spent all my time trying to recreate the past, I was wasting now and destroying the future. I think today is a good example of what he meant, we have today, Joan, who knows when I'll be coming back."

"It's not the when of your coming back that worries me, Caleb," she said, pouting, "it is whether or not you will be coming back to me. Mother is elated that you're going so far away. She says you'll forget all about me when you see some of those college girls."

"What about you, Joan," I asked, "you will be one of those college girls soon. Will you be coming home to me? It would be neat if you and I and Jake all went to Oklahoma State University."

"Fat chance," she replied indignantly, "you know Mother would never let that happen."

"Com'n, Joan, let's drop this deep stuff and enjoy the day. Do you want to climb to the top or go to the ledges?" I asked.

"I would like to just stay here for a while, it is so quiet and peaceful," Joan said, giving me a little kiss.

We sat holding each other for hours, talking over the old days and of our trepidations about leaving Sterling. The kisses and close body contact started filling my mind with thoughts of amour, so I jumped up, saying, "Joan, time's running out and I would like to climb to the top before we have to leave. You ready yet?"

Joan jumped up laughing, and said, "I guess that is a good alternative, Caleb."

We climbed swiftly to the top, the strenuous climb cooling our ardor. On reaching the top we raced up the fire tower steps, at the last landing Joan held me so tight I could feel her heart beating wildly. She said, "Caleb, promise me that it will always be like this with us, crazy and free."

"It will, it will," I answered. "welcome, Joan, welcome to my mountain, now you never need be jealous again."

"Thank you, Caleb, for having me and thank you for sharing my life," she said as we started down. "Your Edgar was right, what a shame it would have been if we had wasted today on yesterday. Let's race down the mountain."

After resting awhile at the foot of the tower, we raced down the mountainside, crazy and free, running until we collapsed in the field at the last gate, both gasping for breath. I asked her about coming to the house for dinner. She said, "Caleb, don't misunderstand this, but I want our day to end with this. Your mountain and you have given me a day that I don't want to chance marring. Even if fate prevents us from ever doing this again, today will rank high among my greatest memories."

I walked Joan home and even though it was daylight, she kissed me passionately. As I released her, I said, "Joan, if I ever loved any girl it has to be you." She gave me another quick hug and rushed into the house.

Walking away from Joan's, I wondered if her fears had merit and this might really be good-bye. John Muldon and Arthur Sledge came by with Muldon's truck and stopped to tease me about leaving with the girls the night before, asking if I had another party going for tonight.

I laughed and said, "Not the kind that you fellas would enjoy. Tonight is family night, Mother's orders, no two-girl night for me."

Arthur said, "We're going to miss your naïve little act with the girls, Caleb. Maybe now after you're gone we will have a chance."

John said, "He's just jealous, Caleb, you know Arthur. All kidding aside, Caleb, it is going to seem strange not having you around after all these years. Hop in, we'll give you a ride to your house." I climbed in the truck. "I don't suppose that you will ever return to the barn once you've earned big money in construction and have a college education," John continued. "I hope you don't forget to visit old friends if you ever return."

"I'll return, John, there isn't any doubt about that," I said as I started getting out of the truck at our yard. "I don't understand why some people think this is so final."

"Think about it, Caleb, how many people do you know who were away from Sterling very long that came back here again to live? You watch, I bet most of the boys that went in the service won't come back here to stay. Think about it, Caleb, you'll see why." John said as he backed out of the driveway.

The housed smelled of roast pork with garlic, Mother was cooking my favorite meal. She had made sure that everyone was there. To my surprise Uncle Louis asked if we should say grace, we normally only did that on special holiday meals. Mother said, "Then let's all hold hands."

Emma said, "If only Eunice and Josh could be here."

Mother said, "If we have them in our hearts and minds they will be. I'm sure Josh is always with us, let's pray."

The meal was fit for a holiday. Mother had made several pies, one of them my favorite, chocolate. We spent the better part of the evening at the table gorging ourselves. All my family was so happy for me I couldn't let on how terrified I really was about leaving. There were hugs and kisses from my brothers and sisters, a talk with Mother and Dad. Mother about my character, Dad on the responsibility of being on my own. Uncle Louis slipped me forty dollars, saying, "This is traveling expenses, Caleb. I'm so glad it's college instead of the draft."

After saying my final goodnights we went to bed. Homer said, "Pretty scary, huh, Caleb, leaving the nest and all."

I was going to try lying at first but figured I wouldn't fool Homer, so I said, "Does it show that much, Homer?"

He said, "Not really, Caleb, it's just that I know you better than the rest. Working at the barn and seeing you under different situations than at home. You know, Caleb you are a lucky guy, this is your chance to escape this town and make something of yourself. Don't be afraid, dream a little."

Damn, I thought, *even Homer, doesn't anyone love Sterling? Not wanting* to entrust my feelings, I said, "I guess I just have the normal jitters facing something new. Good night, Homer."

The next morning I said my final good-byes to my brothers and sisters, and then Mother and Dad drove me to the railroad station. Much to my surprise, Edgar was there. He said, "I had a chance to be here, Caleb. I'm so glad, for I have something for you. Here, so you won't forget." He handed me a silver medallion with a braided leather necklace. The medallion had a picture of a team of horses carved on it with a young teamster at the reins, with the word 'Caleb' underneath. I felt like hugging him, but he held his hand up in a kind of Indian peace sign and said, "Embrace the future, Caleb, with your mind wide open," and then he walked away.

Dad said, "You have a good friend there, Caleb. He asked me last week from where and when you were leaving. I wonder how he got here."

Mother said, "Three minutes to train time."

Dad gave me a big bear hug, saying, "I'm going to miss you, son."

Mother held me silently until the last minute. I gave what I hoped was a cheerful good-bye, turning so they wouldn't see my tears.

Then I was alone, holding back the tears of fear and doubt, going to where I had never been, sitting in the strangeness of a train, listening to the blast of its whistle as it dragged me apprehensively into my future.

The End

Printed in the United States
68835LVS00003B/253-348

9 781413 735512